TELL ME
LIES

BOOKS BY ED JAMES

ED JAMES
TELL ME
LIES

bookouture

2/2020
Jh

Published by Bookouture in 2020

An imprint of Storyfire Ltd.
Carmelite House
50 Victoria Embankment
London EC4Y 0DZ

www.bookouture.com

ISBN: 978-1-83888-164-1
eBook ISBN: 978-1-83888-163-4

To Susi Holliday, for a character name,
and for a pair of ears when I needed to talk.

CHAPTER ONE

Tuesday, October 2, 2018

Faraj

The wooden bench pressed into Faraj's legs as he reached into his locker. He sifted through his bag, right to the bottom, and touched something hard. His soccer shoes, smelling dark and musky, though the leather was freshly polished, just like his daddy told him—black polish covered the three white stripes to mask the logo. Daddy would be proud of him, proud of the hour he'd spent on the back stoop, brushing and brushing until they shone in the fading light.

The usual chatter filled the locker room, excitement at getting out on the grass, nervousness at who'd be last pick. Then silence, like Coach had entered. But he hadn't.

The acrid tang of body spray hit Faraj's nose, inflaming it already. He stifled a sneeze as he looked around, eyes stinging, blinking away tears.

Hayden stood across from him. Blue eyes, blond hair swept low, just above his eyebrows. Topless, just wearing tighty-whities. He sprayed again across his pale skin. *Before* practice, like always.

Who is he trying to smell nice for? Coach?

Hayden stepped closer to Faraj, brandishing the can like a weapon. "Got anything to say?" He jabbed a finger into Faraj's chest. It hurt. "Towelhead." That hurt worse.

But Faraj still didn't look up.

Never look up if they'll see the fear in your eyes. That's what his daddy told him. *Only look up when they'll see the righteous fury they can't hope to deal with.*

"Hey, Towelhead." Hayden prodded Faraj's shoulder now. Then again, harder. "I'm talking to you, Towelhead."

Faraj felt it now, the rage building inside him, boiling at the pit of his stomach, burning through his veins into his arms and legs. Now he looked up, fists clenched. "What did you say, mama's boy?" His voice sounded shrill and childish, quiet and distant. *Hardly a threat, hardly the righteous fury they can't hope to deal with.*

Hayden laughed. "I heard about your daddy, Towelhead. Heard he left you and your mama. That right, Towelhead?"

Faraj stood up as tall as he could get, but he still had to look up at Hayden. But he had rage on his side. "Shut up!"

"Your daddy ran away, Towelhead. Who's the mama's boy now, huh?" Hayden pushed him.

Faraj stumbled backward, his shoulder hitting the locker, his knees bumping the bench. He tried to stay standing, to show no fear, just rage and fury, but he fell down, his ass cracking off the wood.

Weak. Pathetic. A victim.

The other kids sat watching in silence. Nobody trying to help, nobody looking away.

Hayden stood over him, his fist pulled back like he was going to punch. Instead, he reached down and grabbed Faraj's soccer shoes from the floor. "Aw, did your daddy get you these before he left you, huh, Towelhead?"

"Give me them back." Faraj reached for them.

But Hayden threw them to a buddy, then pushed Faraj again.

His head bumped off the locker. The pain was almost as bad as the hatred broiling in his stomach.

Hayden caught one shoe and put his hand in, holding it like a club. "These smell older than you, Towelhead. Your mama can't afford new ones?"

"Go, Hayden!" His accomplices joined in the laughter as they tossed the soccer shoes around. "You the man, Hayden!"

The rest of the class sat round, watching.

"You not going to speak, Towelhead?" Hayden grabbed Faraj's chin with his free hand and jerked his head up to look in his eyes. "It's no fun if you don't say anything."

"Stop!" Jacob charged across the locker room toward Hayden, his muddy-brown hair in a bowl cut dancing around, ruddy cheeks redder than ever. He slapped Hayden's bare back, a sharp sting that shut up the crowd. "Stop!"

Hayden took his time turning around to look at Jacob, the practiced menace he'd seen in the movies. He looked him up and down, then laughed again, face screwed up, head tilted. "Get outta here, Fatboy." He brushed off Jacob with a flick of the wrist.

"I said, stop!" Jacob pressed his forehead into Hayden's and held it there. He was fat, that's true, but he was taller than Hayden and much heavier. And he had power on his side, maybe even rage and hatred. "Faraj is my *friend*."

"Friend, huh?" Hayden made kissy-kissy faces. "Get a room." He made to walk off, but Jacob put a meaty hand on his shoulder. Hayden looked down at it. "What do you think you're doing, Fatboy?"

"This." Jacob stepped forward and locked his right leg around Hayden's, then nudged his chest. Hayden toppled backward, landing on the tiles with a sickening crunch. You could hear the gasp around the room as Jacob flipped Hayden over, pushing his face into the floor. He knelt on Hayden's back and grabbed at his chin, pulling his neck back, like they were on WWE. "Submit!"

Hayden shook his head as much as he could. "Never." His voice was a thin croak, sounded even weaker than Faraj's.

None of Hayden's helpers were getting involved.

Faraj walked toward them, ready to stop them if they attacked his friend.

Jacob yanked at Hayden's chin again. "I said, submit!"

The door clattered off the wall. "What's going on?" Coach Smith stood in the doorway, hands on hips, eyes wide. His gray hoodie done up over his belly, at least two layers of white tees underneath. A whistle hung around his neck, but he hadn't used it once in all the time of coaching them. Took him a few seconds of mouth breathing before he stormed into the locker room. "*Jacob?*" Even he looked shocked. He wrenched Jacob off Hayden. "I thought you were better than this, Jacob."

Jacob slouched over to his locker space and the kids on either side shifted to give him space. Space meant respect. In those few seconds, Jacob had climbed a few rungs up the ladder. He glanced over at Faraj, a smile flashing across his lips, then looked away, muttering something to himself.

Coach helped Hayden to his feet. "You okay, son?"

Hayden limped over to his locker, rubbing the back of his head. His friends had shuffled around, narrowing the space. He picked up his body spray and gave a blast before tugging his soccer jersey over his head. "He attacked me!" The way Hayden spoke, it was like he couldn't work out which of those words surprised him most. That someone had attacked him? Or that the someone was Jacob?

"He was protecting me." Faraj couldn't look at Coach. The rage and fury had turned to shame and embarrassment. "Hayden called me Towelhead."

"Hayden Johnson…" Coach shook his head, jowls wobbling. "Son, I don't want that sort of language in my locker room, do you hear me?"

"But Coach, he—"

"I don't give a damn, Johnson." Coach swung around the room. "The rest of you, get your asses out on that practice pitch this minute. Two laps, you hear?"

"Yes, sir!" They couldn't get out of there fast enough, even to two laps of the soccer pitch.

Coach watched them go, his eyes narrow.

Faraj put his feet into the shoes. They felt too tight. Got worse as he tied the laces. He chanced a look at Jacob and caught a sly smile from his friend.

I don't care what punishment we get, I have a friend now.

"Johnson, I'm disappointed with you." Coach stuffed his hands in his three-quarter-length track pants. "This isn't how a team captain behaves, okay?"

Hayden pulled his soccer shorts up to his knees. "I don't want no Muslims on *my* team. I just want Americans."

"That's it." Coach pointed at the door. "My office, *now!*"

Hayden stared at him, open-mouthed.

"You heard me, right?"

"I heard you." Hayden tugged up his shorts. "Soccer's dumb, anyway." He stomped out of the room and slammed the door behind him.

Coach sat next to Faraj. "Hey, son. What that boy said to you, nobody should hear that. Okay? *Nobody.*"

Faraj wedged a finger down the side of his soccer shoe. Pins and needles already. Definitely too tight.

"Son, where I grew up, they don't like black dudes like me there." Coach didn't look black, but then he didn't look white either. Like Faraj, he was stuck in the middle. "I'll make sure he's disciplined for what he said, you hear?"

Faraj nodded slowly. "I hear you." He caught Jacob's smile again.

Something thumped outside the room.

Coach looked at the door.

Footsteps rattled out in the hallway, heavy and lots of them.

"Boys, stay here." Coach walked over to the door and peeked out into the corridor. Then he stepped back, hands up.

A soldier stepped into the locker room, his face hidden by a mask, pointing a rifle at Coach's chest. Two others flanked him. "Faraj al-Yasin?"

Without taking his eyes off the rifle, Coach pointed into the corner.

The two other soldiers marched over and hauled Faraj clean off his feet.

Sweat trickled down his back. His guts churned. *What are they going to do to me?*

The first soldier pulled his mask to the side to show a hairy mouth, his tongue like a snake's. "S-son." Sounded like he was covering a stutter, like Ashlyn in Faraj's class. "We need to speak to your father. Where is he?"

The soldiers gripped his arms tight. Faraj looked around the room for help, for answers, for anything. Jacob sat there, open-mouthed, panting like a dog. Coach wasn't any help, still holding his hands up, staring at the gun.

Faraj looked at the soldier. "I don't know where he is."

"Sure about that, *son*?" The soldier's tongue ran over his lips like the Joker in that Batman film Faraj wasn't supposed to have seen, but which still woke him up at night. "We can do this the hard way, son, or the easy way. Choice is yours."

"I don't know where he is!" Faraj tried to wriggle but they held him tight. He locked eyes with Coach, pleading for him to help.

And he did, finally. Coach clenched his jaw. "I thought the military exercise was later?"

"Well, it's happening right now, mister. I'd advise you to stay out of this." He pointed the gun at Faraj. "Now, where is your father?"

Faraj couldn't speak. He just shook his head, like it could get rid of them.

"So you *really* want to do this the hard way? Okay." The soldier didn't give him another choice, just set off toward the door. "Come on."

Jacob lurched forward, roaring as he slammed into the soldier's leg, like a linebacker spearing a quarterback.

Almost.

Jacob only knocked the soldier off balance, not clean over. The other two soldiers let go of Faraj and grabbed Jacob. They pulled him away, but couldn't lift him off his feet.

"Stop!" Jacob kicked and screamed, breathing heavily, gasping for breath. "No!"

Coach stood there, eyes bulging, hands higher than ever.

The first soldier, the one with the stutter, took Faraj by the arm and pulled a hood over his head. Faraj felt a sting in his neck and his legs stopped working. Jacob's shouts stopped as everything went black.

And that's the last thing Faraj saw.

CHAPTER TWO

A year later

Saturday, November 30, 2019

Mason

I shuffle out of the Starbucks and take the table nearest the edge. It's got a good-enough view of the mall's lower level, but also across to Pottery Barn Kids. They're still inside. A couple minutes until I need to move, so I scrape back the chair and sit. The semi-automatic clunks off the plastic seat.

The two women at the next table don't notice the sound. Instead, they put their wallets away, like I'm going to steal them. One of them wears lavender perfume so thick I can taste it.

So I wait, sipping bitter coffee through the lid, getting milky foam stuck in my beard. Just a regular guy having coffee at a Starbucks.

Tuna fish hits my nose. One of the Golden Girls nibbles at a toasted sandwich, her birdlike movements catching in my peripheral vision. But she's looking at me.

Never leave an impression.

Shouldn't have bought the coffee, shouldn't have sat down. But I need to blend in while I scope out my targets. So I shift three tables down, putting a plastic plant between me and the Golden Girls. Shoppers have left pennies in the plant's soil, confusing a Starbucks in a suburban mall for an ancient burial ground.

The view from this new table sucks—a walkway obscures the mall's ground floor, and I'm too far from the Pottery Barn to see clearly. I can still make out the line inside, though, almost reaching the door. No sign of anyone leaving yet.

Mall cop at ten o'clock, downstairs. Cuffs, flashlight, and nightstick swaying from his belt. Wants people to know he's a big shot. Maybe he was, back in the day. Some kick-ass detective until he busted his knee. Or he's just full of himself and wants to pretend. He's taking it slow, thumbs in his belt loops, nodding at passing shoppers, their bags bouncing off him. He disappears under the walkway and I lose him. And you can't control what you can't see.

The Pottery Barn door opens and the noise level swells. Kids scream, inane music blares, and parents try to talk above the racket. Two fathers in full preppy uniform are out first. Sweaters over polo shirts, 501s, Nike sneakers. Probably Microsoft or Amazon drones spending quality weekend time with their families. Four sons dressed the same, all preschool but acting the same, heading to the same jobs in twenty years. Assuming there still are jobs then.

A big man walks out the front door, holding hands with two small boys. His sweatpants are ripped almost to the point he shouldn't wear them. But he does. Bet his wife's happy with him.

Next, a group of soccer moms, perfect hair like their daughters, all beaming at the coffee mugs they've just painted.

And then she walks out, strutting like she owns the whole mall. Megan Holliday, homecoming queen fifteen years later. Aviators push her blonde hair up and back, more elegant than a headband but completely unnecessary on a Seattle Saturday morning, and inside to boot. Red lipstick. Blue-striped blouse and black leggings, a thousand-dollar bag dangling from her shoulder. Boy does she look harassed, like everyone's out to ruin her day, especially her kids, a pair of polecats fighting each other around the stroller she's pushing, even though her kids are too old to need it.

Avery is a clone of her mother: matching blouse and leggings, but with jet-black hair instead of blonde. She walks away from her brother, carrying herself like she's at a beauty pageant, wide smiles and drama in every precise movement.

Brandon has his mother's hair, worn long to match his baby grunge gear, ripped jeans and plaid shirt, though his sandals kind of ruin the look.

She's four, he's three. All ages are difficult, but those are pretty much the worst.

Megan talks to them, but I couldn't hear her even if I was next to them. Brandon hops in the stroller, rocking like he's on a bronco, and Megan pushes him toward the elevator. Avery stomps alongside, slapping away her mother's outstretched hand, her face twisted with petulance.

I give them ten seconds while I finish my coffee, then I pull on my shades and tug my hood up over my head, pull the baseball cap low. As I pass, I stuff the coffee cup deep in the garbage can—never leave a trace—and shadow their footsteps on the opposite side of the mall, sucking in cinnamon smells from the donut kiosk, avoiding the line of mall walkers powering toward me, a centipede of velour and white hair.

On the opposite walkway, Megan's pleading with Avery, both of them frowning. She keeps checking her reflection in the store windows, not even pretending to listen to Avery's complaints now. Heard it all before, so many times. She parks the stroller by the elevator and hits the call button. Then she crouches, making sweet promises to her daughter, offering the world for a minute's silence.

Avery buys it too, her pout becoming a grin just like that. Ice cream, maybe.

Megan navigates them into the elevator, and I quicken my pace over the walkway.

The door starts to slide shut, but I catch it with my foot. "Thanks."

Megan's head tilts to the side as she examines me sidling into the small space, mama bear guarding her cubs. Her shoulder bag lies between her feet, Avery hiding behind her legs.

I reach down to rub my knee, and groan. "An old war wound."

Megan gives me a curt nod and hits the button again.

The doors close this time, then the elevator rumbles, grinding like a streetcar as it takes us down to the parking lot.

I lean against the bar, the metal cold through my hoodie, though I don't grip it. Never touch anything. The camera points at Megan, not at me, but it wouldn't get anything useful even if it did. No detail I couldn't change.

"Mommy, Brandon's had the stroller for *so long*." Avery's broken her promise already. "It's *my* turn!"

Megan smiles at me, embarrassed. "You're too old for that, sweetie."

"But I want—"

"We're getting ice cream on the way home, honey. Okay?"

Got it in one.

Avery kicks a foot on the floor. "Okay." Doesn't look like it.

But ice cream is a complication. Could go either way. Meaning I need to act now.

Megan rolls her eyes at me, shame flickering in them. Maybe anger, maybe despair.

"Heard that so many times myself." I give her a warm smile. "Got a boy of my own. Older, but I've still got the scars."

Megan rolls her eyes at her kids. "It never stops."

"Oh, it does. And then you miss it and you'd do anything to get it back."

"I'll take your word for it." Megan grabs Avery's hand as the elevator crunches to a halt. "Now, don't you let go, okay? And what do we do?"

"Look both ways!"

"Attagirl."

I'm already out into the garage, tasting the stale gasoline as I place my forearm over the door, guiding them out like a concierge, all gentlemanly.

"Why, thank you." Megan trundles the stroller out, clutching Avery's hand tight. Brandon's already asleep.

I tip my imaginary cap at her and sidle off in the opposite direction. Pretend I'm getting into a sedan, but I'm just crouching, watching Megan and her brood through the glass of ten parked cars.

Avery's complaints are getting louder, not believing she'll get the ice cream, demanding she gets in the stroller.

Megan's minivan lurks over in the shadows, boxed in on both sides by a pair of SUVs. A light flickers above.

I wait, watching her put the children in back, fastening them into booster seats, buckling them in and checking. Once, twice, three times. She slams Brandon's door and the noise echoes around.

Now it's just us down here. Me and them.

I set off, keeping low and sticking to the walls, where the light's faintest, can't even hear my footsteps—she has no chance. Past an SUV and I'm behind her. Waiting, so close that her prickly perfume hits my nostrils. Fresh and organic, like rose petals.

I reach into my pocket for the syringe.

Megan opens her door, but the elevator clunks open again.

Footsteps come from behind, loud and fast. "Ma'am?" The mall cop is hurrying across the garage, holding something above his head. "Is this your bag, ma'am?"

Megan's hand shoots up to her shoulder. "Dammit." Then she's all business, flashing her smile at the mall cop. "Thank you, sir. That's so kind of you."

"You left it in the elevator." He adjusts his security hat and stands there, thumbs back in his belt. Just a regular guy doing his job. "All part of the job, ma'am."

Megan gets in the minivan and the engine spits as the door clicks. She reverses out of the space, the mall cop watching her, whistling an old Elvis number over the drone.

I missed my shot.

And it was way too risky here. Too many moving parts, too much out of my control.

But time is running out. No time for this shit, no time to wait.

And it hits me. *"We're getting ice cream on the way home, honey. Okay?"* There's a gelato store on the route back to their McMansion. And I know every permutation of the route back.

Time for Plan B.

Second time around the block and it's clear. Rain teeming down, thundering off my roof, slicking the windshield as the wipers struggle with the biblical flood that Seattle contends with every day. I pull up and sit there, letting the gears click around in my head. Real sweet neighborhood, a realtor's dream. Lights on at this time, glowing in the gloomy downpour. Porches, wooden boards painted gray, bigger front yards than you'd expect, but old enough to have mature shrubs, young enough that the trees don't need serious trimming yet. Three-car garages, with all the cars out on Saturday morning errands—swim club, shopping, birthdays, soccer practice.

I swallow hard, the pain digging deep into my gut.

This is it. This time. No mall cops to stop me. Should've stuck to this plan, should never have even considered the mall. What was I thinking?

I grab my backpack and get out into the rain, taking care to shut the door quietly. Checking out each window for signs of movement. Listening hard to the thundering rain, tasting the Pacific in each drop.

Nothing. Nobody. Good to go.

I march over to the house, acting like I own the place, crunch up the long drive past a shiny VW sedan, the only car in the street. I knock on the door and dump the bag at my feet.

Nothing inside. No lights, no sounds, no smells.

I step back and scan the street again. Neighbors on both sides, trees rustling behind, the wind licking them hard, knocking droplets of rain off. The Victorian opposite looks empty—no lights, no plumes of heating outlet—so I hide behind the shrub at the side of the house, the eaves shielding me from the rain.

The perfect spot to wait, eyes closed, focusing on the sounds. Rain pattering the ground, but I can tune it out. Distant traffic, then the roar of planes landing at SeaTac. Then kids playing soccer, girlish squeals and parental shouts. I swallow hard, biting down on a memory.

An engine approaches, heavy, diesel. I glance around the bush.

A pickup rolls on down the road.

I let out a breath. Didn't even know I was holding it.

Where are they?

Ice cream means picking up a cone, the kids licking the gelato as they watch a Disney movie on the back of the car seats, hypnotizing them into a light sleep.

Doesn't it?

Maybe they were eating in, Avery and Brandon digging spoons deep into giant dishes, while Megan sips an espresso, wishing she could have a smoke or a cocktail.

I should've tracked their journey, kept my eyes on the target instead of surveilling the acquisition site.

I could still drive over there, watch them and—

No. Wait here. Stay the course. This is a good plan. It will work. One way or another, they will be here. It's still safe.

Another engine rumbles. I don't even look, because I know the sound. Slowing, the drive belt whirring as the minivan turns into the driveway, where it stops. The mailbox clatters and the din of a kids' movie bleeds out of the minivan.

I check the gun, cold through my gloves. Just in case. The syringe is where it's at, though. For now. I uncap it, locking it between my fingers, my thumb touching the plunger, my heart thudding in my ear.

Then the music dies and the car rumbles again, inching toward me. It stops again and the engine dies this time, the suspension sighing as it deflates. The driver door opens. One heel clicks down, then the other. The door shuts again.

And I'm off, grabbing my left hand around Megan's mouth, my right hand stabbing the syringe into her neck. Keys tinkle as they hit the pebbles. I don't give her a chance to look around to see who's doing it. That's not what this is about.

Inside, the kids stare at the TV screens mounted on the back of the front seats, dialogue droning through the glass, dulled music swelling.

Megan's head rolls to the side and she's a dead weight.

I snap off the syringe and stick it back in my pocket, then walk Megan over to the porch, much harder than it should be. I sit her down, resting her head against the door, and place the typed note on her lap, out of the rain's reach. They'll never trace it back to me.

Part one done, but I can't stop, not even for a second.

I jog over to the minivan, checking my pocket for the two remaining syringes, then snatch up Megan's keys and my bag in one fluid movement. I get in the driver side and stow my backpack in the passenger footwell.

"Where's Mommy?" Brandon breaks off from Disney long enough to look at me, his little pink face still showing traces of chocolate around his mouth. I can barely hear him over the movie.

My free hand opens another syringe. "She'll be here soon."

*

My wrist aches with each twist of the screwdriver, the final tightening sending a flare of pain up my arm. I yank up my sleeve and check the damage. A tiny imprint of Avery's teeth, my skin broken in a few places. I roll my sleeve down and step back to inspect my work. Even I couldn't tell the plates didn't belong to the car. That'll do. I put Megan's plates back in the bag and scan the parking lot again. Still empty, just a boarded-up Burger King sleeping across the cracked asphalt, the realty signs offering a steep discount nobody's taking.

The freeway moans downhill, hidden by a row of condos stalled mid-construction. The nearest intersection is empty.

Nobody's watching me. Nobody's listening.

I get back in the minivan. Behind, this morning's *Seattle Times* rests between the sleeping kids, their chests rising almost in time with each other. I reach into the backpack pocket for the burner cell phone and snap a photo. I send it to the cell's only contact along with a message:

Big Al's truck stop off I90. Be there by noon or they die.

CHAPTER THREE

Holliday

Senator Christopher Holliday held his iPhone to his ear, listening to the ringing tone as downtown Seattle rumbled past through the tinted glass. The street was quiet, just a young couple pushing a stroller through the rain. He reached the voicemail, the first few words of Megan's warm welcome message. He hung up and put his cell in his jacket pocket, trying not to worry.

She must still be out with the kids, hitting the mall. Hitting the credit card, filling our home with yet more bags of designer clothes the kids'll grow out of in seconds.

The limousine slowed to a halt, so smooth he barely noticed it. The Henry M. Jackson Federal Building loomed out of the rain above them, thirty-plus floors of concrete, glass, bureaucracy, and waste. In the distance, the sun burned over Elliott Bay, bright light flaring as a rainbow battled the usual Seattle downpour.

Crowds lined First and Second Avenue, filling the block between Marion and Madison, soaking but angry and loud. Banners read N30+20—the twentieth anniversary of the WTO protests that wrecked half the city. Hordes of old hippies and woke hipsters protesting globalization and government intrusion into their lives, the world eroding their liberty, stealing their freedom. And who said city folks didn't care? Their instincts should be tempered by money and education, the pursuit of progress, but here they are, disgusted by the world their parents had shaped.

Who arranges a congressional hearing on a Saturday morning when there's a humongous protest raging?

Oh, I know exactly who.

The limo caught the tail end of the protest as it moved on, keeping a respectful distance like a hearse at a funeral, then came to a halt right outside the main entrance. Holliday's Secret Service goons got out first, earpieces in, shades on, black suits bulging over barely concealed handguns. Before Holliday was out of the door, an umbrella covered his head, the rain patting off it. He stood up tall, puffing out his chest as he buttoned his suit jacket.

Always walk like you're the president. The camera crews might be here for the protest, but they'll take me home with them.

A red streetcar rumbled nearby, shaking rain off the cables. Bells tolled on the Bainbridge ferry as it slipped off through the Puget Sound, but trees obscured the view down to the shoreline.

Outside the Federal Building, the soaked Stars and Stripes still looked like it was flying in the breeze, even though it was dead still for once.

Holliday saluted the flag as he passed.

"Sir, if you'll follow me." Agent Lewandowski gestured up the steps. A walking stereotype cast in muscle and hard jaw. Ex-this, ex-that, top of his class here, Medal of Honor there, even rumors of being ex-CIA. And here he was, guarding a boy from the wilds of rural Washington, a town still full of redneck loggers no matter how much Seattle spread like a tumor. Lewandowski marched off up the damp steps, scanning in every direction.

Holliday fell into his slipstream, another two agents following, then entered the foyer. Ornate brick arches hung over curved wooden desks, three stations spaced out across the expanse, smiling faces guarding the new museum. Spotlights shone from the ceiling, much lower than you'd expect. A line formed by the elevator, waiting for the next car up.

Photographers gathered at the far end, their flashes hammering the crowd of people entering the conference hall.

Holliday primed his million-dollar smile for them. Just enough teeth to warm their hearts, not enough to dazzle. Creased forehead, a mix of congeniality and experience, like he really knew *you*, but like he also knew how to get stuff done.

"Chris!" A hand parted the wave of a security detail twice as big as Holliday's. Richard Olson. Tall, rower's shoulders, contractor's gut, billionaire's suit open at the neck. His thick beard was peppered with gray, matching the white at his temples, adding distinction to the dyed-black look. He barged through his guards to meet Holliday, then gripped his hand tight, clapping his back as they shook. "Can you believe they spent three million bucks on this shithole?" His gaze swept around the foyer, mischief twinkling in his blue eyes. "Nice to see my tax dollars being spent so wisely."

"You barely pay any tax, Richard." Holliday got his hand back, stuffing it in his pants pocket. "While I completely agree, you should take it up with the governor next time you tee off."

"That's a good one. Like Duvall would listen to a shmuck like me."

Holliday held Olson's gaze for a few seconds, struggling to keep up the smile.

"Let's walk and talk." Olson started off at a slow pace over to the conference hall, footsteps clicking on the marble, both of their security details following at a respectful distance. "You should've stopped this, Chris."

"Not in my wheelhouse, Richard. You should take that up with Delgado. Make sure you get value for money from your donations."

Olson flashed a wide grin, but his eyes were full of menace. "You know that punk is going after me? After all the money I've given his campaigns?"

"Richard." Holliday gave him *that* look. "So long as your hands are clean, you'll be safe."

"Pathologically clean."

"There's nothing I can do, okay? Just let this show play out. Let him have his moment, then you'll be golden."

Olson looked him up and down, then clapped his arm. "See you on the other side." He set off with his entourage toward the scrimmage line of press.

The other side of what, though?

Holliday leaned in to Lewandowski. "I've got it from here. You can go."

"Sir, I can't—"

"Yes, you can and you will." Holliday tried to make eye contact through the shades. "You were to protect me from threats. They've moved on. I'll get a cab back. You enjoy the rest of your weekend, you hear?"

"Sir." Lewandowski wasn't going to protest. *No idea if he has a wife and kids, no idea if he even has a goldfish.* "Thanks, sir." He pointed at his colleagues then set off across the foyer.

Holliday walked over to the hall, slapping the smile back on for the cameras, pointing and waving at journalists, like they were important enough to warrant it.

Katie Chan from *CNN* evaded his gaze. *No questions for me, no pressing scandals she needs a US senator's opinion on. A good sign.*

Holliday passed through the doors and scanned for his seat. The hall took up half the ground floor, reaching up through the next two. Oak paneling, white-marble floor, the state and union flags on either side of a stage, set up like a court. Could be anywhere, in any major city.

Olson was right. Three million bucks for this?

Congressman Xander J. Delgado stood on the stage, his wiry frame facing away from the crowd. His arms waved as he talked, microphone muted, to a panel of five of his peers, three men and two women. Then he took in the audience again. Dark hair, perfect teeth. Navy suit, white shirt, red tie, like the Stars and Stripes outside had got up and started walking around. Delgado could just as easily be Davis, Duffy, or Dublowski. Just so happened that the Spanish daddy's name was the one to survive through history. One of those city boys whose only Latino attribute was the name that attracted the Hispanic votes in his ward. He kept shifting his focus back to the audience, locking on to targets like in the many military stories he bored people with on the campaign trail. Listen to him and he singlehandedly took down al-Qaeda.

Holliday took his seat near the side of the stage. No streamers this time, no champagne corks popping, no big-money donors pressing the flesh to take their pound, no ten minutes of rapturous applause. Not like last time. Or the next.

Delgado spotted him, giving a curt nod and wave. He looked around his audience. To him, this wasn't a congressional hearing, it was a campaign rally, the Delgado story turning another page.

What's next on his march to the presidency? Governor? Senator? Keep your hands off my seat.

Delgado tapped the microphone and waited for the hush to settle. "Ladies and gentlemen, thank you for your time and your presence here, especially on a weekend day. Unfortunately, myself and my colleagues here have business in that other Washington, the District of Columbia, through the week." He got up and paced the stage, like some tech CEO giving a TED Talk, or some snake-oil salesman hawking his own brand of motivational advice. "This hearing has been convened to look into Operation Opal Lance and…"

Holliday's cell buzzed in his jacket pocket, feeling like a second heartbeat. *Megan and her perfect timing…* He checked the display—unknown caller. *This is my private cell, must be some telemarketer asking for campaign funds or a charitable donation.* He killed the call and put the phone away.

But it buzzed again. Just once, a long thrum. A text. *Probably a voicemail. Nothing to worry about.* But dark thoughts flooded his brain.

Megan in a car wreck, begging for a stranger's cell to call her husband, their kids dying on the back seat.

He fished it out and checked the display. Almost dropped it. Not a voicemail. But a photo. Brandon and Avery… in Megan's minivan, asleep, that morning's Times propped up between them. And no sign of their mother.

Underneath was a text. He read the words but couldn't believe what they said.

CHAPTER FOUR

Carter

Carter parked in his usual space at the usual time for a Saturday morning and killed the engine. The wipers stopped scraping the rain clear, the downpour quickly flooding the windshield and blocking out the downtown Seattle street. He craned his neck round.

Kirsty sat in her booster chair on the back seat, wavy mid-brown hair hidden under her favorite red beret, her black-and-white hooped dress bunched up by the seatbelt. She stuffed all of her fingers into her mouth, picking away at her teeth. "It hurts real bad."

That was the last thing Carter needed today. "You need me to take you to the dentist, pumpkin?"

Kirsty inverted her hands, making her fingers into a twitching monster's mouth. "Raaaargh!"

"Oh no!" Carter put his hand to his chest and let his mouth hang open. "It's Cthulhu girl!"

She tugged against her seatbelt, making worse monster sounds. "RAAAARRGHHH!" Her voice was deep and filled with eldritch fury.

"Help!" Carter let his belt go and eased out of the seat. He slipped out of the driver's side into the thick rain, then rounded the black Suburban to open the back passenger door. He leaned in, making his own monster face at Kirsty. "Daddy monster is going to bite *you!*" He used his monster-tendril fingers to tickle her until she squealed. "RAAARGH!"

"Stop it, Daddy!" Kirsty wriggled in her chair, laughing hard.

Carter bent forward, the rain lashing his jacket, and clicked the lock to liberate his daughter from her seat. He raised up her hood and picked her up, hugging her tight, then set her down on the sidewalk. "You going to be okay today, pumpkin?"

"I'll be *fine.*" Secondhand YouTube sass, partially hidden by her raincoat. "When will you pick me up?"

Carter shut her door. "I just got to do a few things today, then we'll go wherever you want, okay?"

"Okay, Daddy." Kirsty huffed on her backpack and brushed hair out of her eyes. "I want to walk the last part to Chrissie's on my own."

"We've talked about this."

A tiny shrug. "Mommy said I can."

Carter didn't quite believe it, but he didn't want to cramp her instincts. He looked down the road, just over half a block to the daycare's door. Instinct kicked in—thirteen front doors, eighteen pedestrians shivering in the rain, that parked Camry over there, the exhaust pipe pluming in the downpour, the taillights glowing across the sprawling puddles. "Okay, but I'll be watching you all the way."

"Thank you, Daddy." Kirsty made another monster face with her fingers then hugged him. One last look and she walked off.

Carter watched her go, each footstep making his heart crawl up his throat toward his mouth. His little girl, still so young but determined to make her own way in the world. Another footstep and she swiveled around to see him, waving her gloved hand back at him, her cute smile hidden by her hood. He gave her a wave of his own, his hair now soaked through. Then she set off again, her head bobbing in time to some tune he couldn't hear. Almost at the steps up to the door to Chrissie's walk-up now.

The lights in the car across the road turned off, the idling engine dying in time. The driver's door opened and an elderly man got out, his back slightly hunched.

Instinct kicked in and Carter ran off, splashing through the puddles, each step matching one of the man's as he powered over the road toward Kirsty. Gray hair, trimmed beard, gold-framed glasses, a big body but wasting away with age. He beat Carter to Kirsty by seconds. "Hey, princess."

Kirsty stopped to look up, her little face twisted into confusion.

Carter swept between them and grabbed the man's left wrist, hiding his movements from his daughter as he disabled him, pressing his thumb into hard bone and getting a satisfying yelp. He smiled at Kirsty. "You go inside now, pumpkin. Say hi to Chrissie for me, okay?"

"Okay, Daddy." She didn't seem to notice what was going on, skipping up the steps and singing a little doo-doo-doo tune. She pressed the button, the door opened, and she slipped inside the daycare.

Carter swung around, tightened his grip on the left wrist, and twisted the right hard. Subtle, so nobody would notice. "Get away from her."

"Can't I speak to my granddaughter?" Bill Carter looked at his son, his shriveled-up face twisted, his filthy eyes glaring through rain-spattered glasses. "You've got a nerve, thinking you can—"

"*Bill.*" Carter felt the heat rising in his neck as he nodded back toward the Camry. "Get out of here."

"Or what?"

Carter pressed his right thumb harder. "Just go."

Bill took one hard look at his son, wincing through the pain but clearly trying to hide it. Anyone watching would see two men in a heated discussion, but Carter knew what was going on behind those eyes. The calculations, the mental gears clicking and grinding. "Max, I just want to see my granddaughter."

"And I don't want you to see her. Ever. Are we clear?"

Bill sighed, then gave a reluctant nod. "And I need your help, son."

"Here was me thinking you 'just wanted to see your grand-daughter'." Carter snorted. "Now, get out of here before I call the cops."

"Max, son, I'm—"

"I'm serious, Bill. If you don't leave us alone, the cops are going to get involved. And you don't want that, do you?"

Bill took one last look at him, then wriggled free from the loosening grip. He walked across the road through the driving rain, head bowed, rubbing his wrists, and got in his Camry. The lights clicked and the engine plumed again, then he shot off into the traffic, hauling his seatbelt on as he gave one furious look at his son.

Carter let out his breath and stepped up the steps. Through the door, Chrissie the supervisor was helping Kirsty out of her coat. She looked fine, hadn't noticed anything. Carter left them to it, and set off back to his car, putting his phone to his ear. "Hey, Em, it's Max."

Office noise swirled around Emma. "What happened?"

"Nothing." Carter took another look back down the street, scanning for any rogue Toyotas doubling back around. "I was just dropping Kirsty off when Bill tried to speak to her."

A tight gasp hissed down the line. "Is she okay?"

"She's fine. He—" Carter got into his car and sat behind the wheel, rainwater dripping off his coat onto the upholstery. "I think he got the message this time."

"That's the fifth time you've thought that."

"You're right." He sighed. "What do we do?"

His cell connected with the car, and her voice came out of the speakers, too quiet. "Do I need to come over there?"

"No, I'll email Chrissie and make sure Kirsty's only picked up by you or me."

"Fine." Emma didn't sound like it. "So, what now?"

"Into the office. Paperwork, paperwork, and more paperwork." Carter took another look at the daycare. "Wish I was doing something with Kirsty. Wish I wasn't like my father."

"Hey, hey, hey. Stop that. You're nothing like him, Max. Okay?"

"Yeah, maybe."

"No maybes, Max. You're nothing like him."

The dashboard display lit up. Incoming call from Karen Nguyen.

"Em, the boss is calling. Probably wondering where I am. Better take this."

"Okay. Call me when you pick her up this afternoon, okay?"

"Sure. Love you." He switched calls, trying to get himself into the right frame of mind. "Hey, Karen. What's up?"

"Just had a report of a child abduction, Special Agent." Nguyen's robotic voice almost froze up the air in the car. "I'm texting you the address, but it's just around the corner from your current location. Need you there ASAP."

Carter stepped out of the Suburban into the maelstrom, only the hum of human activity now that the rain was giving them a temporary reprieve, just leaving that ozone taste in the air. What would normally be a quiet residential street was filled with black SUVs just like his. Local SPD cops knocked on doors. Shouts came from the trees behind, accompanied by the occasional bark. A huddle of federal agents in identical suits looked over at Carter.

The eye of the storm was a wood-sided house, tall and wide. Two story, mid-gray paint. Three-door garage on the left. No tall trees next to any windows. A platoon of uniformed officers filled the front yard. Big enough for kids to play in, even had a tire hanging from a sturdy oak. Big enough that the neighbors were far enough away. Pay a lot for that space, especially around here.

A four-door Volkswagen sat on the pebble driveway, basking in the sudden sunlight. A high sheen, like a dog's coat, looked after by a father who takes great pride in his car, or who can pay for someone else to take that pride for him.

That dad being one of Washington's two US senators.

No media yet, but just wait for the Amber Alert to kick in and then watch them head over here from the protests.

A loud engine roar announced the mobile command center's arrival, a monster-sized Winnebago with more communications equipment than a TV broadcast truck outside CenturyLink Field for a Seahawks game.

Agent Elisha Thompson got out of her Suburban and looked around. Tall, sharp cheekbones, her red hair in a ponytail. Black suit, flat heels, with her lilac blouse the only softening touch. Her dark-brown eyes did the same trained dance as Carter's, soaking in the vicinity, sucking in every detail and processing it, turning raw data into rich information. Cross-referencing, looking for the gaps and discrepancies. But finding none, just like him. She joined Carter by his car. "You want me to lead?"

"Next time." Carter walked toward the house. "A senator's missing kids means we could be dealing with just about anything here."

A uniformed police officer stood with a pair of panicking women, his bulk contrasting with their slender frames. Soccer-mom types, expensive blouses, plain black leggings that probably had an equally expensive label inside.

One of them broke off and pointed a finger at the beat cop, her blonde hair flying around. "Get your hands off of me!"

Carter recognized her immediately—Megan Holliday, the face of so many campaign photos with her husband and their young kids. He got between them and gave a reassuring smile. "Mrs. Holliday, can I have a word?"

She looked him up and down, her sneer as wide as her friend's frown was deep. "Who are you?"

Carter raised his eyebrows at Elisha. She took Megan's dark-haired friend to the side, knowing to get the story straight. Details changed over time, things got lost. Those items could be key.

He focused on Megan, trying to make eye contact, but she looked everywhere but at him. "Special Agent Max Carter, FBI. I head up the Seattle Field Office's Child Abduction Rapid Deployment Team. Can I call you Megan?"

He knew to use her name, and to keep using it. Gain trust, then maintain it. Never lose it.

Her gaze darted over and locked on to him, then the badge he was still holding out. That seemed to work, seemed to be the currency she needed. She looked at him, forehead creased, lips pursed. "Call me whatever you like, so long as you find my kids."

"Megan, we're going to do what we can to—"

"What you *can*?" She crunched across the pebbles and smacked her left fist into his chest.

He let it sit there, let her get her anger out of her system, bleed it like a hissing radiator. Then keep it empty and let her focus on the story, on the facts, on the truth.

"Do you *know* who my husband is?"

"I do." Carter held her gaze. "Where is the senator?"

Megan inhaled deeply, then a wave of calm washed over her. "Not here."

Carter tried to reframe the narrative. Missing kids meant one thing. Add in a missing husband, and it could mean anything.

When that father was a senator, it changed everything.

A pending divorce, hidden from the press.

Or something more sinister. Carter couldn't wrap his head around the senator abducting his own kids, though. He had way too much profile around here. "Is there anything I should know about your marriage, Megan?"

"Nothing. He's just not here."

"Is he in DC?"

"He's home for the weekend, but working. That congressional hearing?"

"Right." Carter had seen something in the *Times* about it, relegated to page six, the N30+20 protests taking center stage. "Megan, we've issued an Amber Alert." He waved around the neighborhood. "Every iPhone and a good chunk of Android phones in the state will get the warning. I've got thirty highly trained FBI agents from across the state here. There are twenty police officers searching this street alone." He pointed behind her house. "Another twenty in the woods there, with four trained K-9 units. More on their way too. Megan, the most important thing you can do right now is take me through everything. Brandon's three and Avery's four, right?"

Her anger was still there, flashes of it burning in her glare. She blinked it away, the rage replaced by moisture. "Right."

"Okay. Take me through whatever you can remember."

"I was driving. We'd just been to the mall and we stopped at that gelato place on the way home. The kids were acting up." She stared at him, daring him to contradict or even agree with her. "You know how it is, right?"

"Megan, I know how hard this is for you."

"Okay." Sighing, she frowned over at the mailbox, the sort you'd see outside any house in Middle America. "I pulled up and picked up the mail. The kids were watching *Frozen* on their car screens, that song going on and on and on." Her hand went to her neck, rubbing slowly. She pointed at the curbside. "I drove up there, collected the mail, then into the driveway. I got out of the minivan and felt a prick in my neck." She waved at the front porch. "Next thing I know, I woke up with a note on my lap." She passed him a sheet of paper.

He snapped on nitrile gloves and took it from her. Plain, letter-sized, folded and torn near the top. Black text in a thick font, filling the page in landscape:

DO **NOT** CALL THE POLICE

Carter stuffed it into an evidence bag and thought it through. Someone warning her. Meant it was more likely an abduction than parental. But still nowhere near conclusive.

"You did the right thing calling us, Megan. We're going to do everything we can to find your children."

Megan looked like she was struggling to hold it together. Shivering, rubbing her arms. Worry and fright in her eyes, that she'd cost her kids their lives by making a phone call. "Do you think the monster who—" Her hand shot to her mouth. "The monster—" She swallowed down her rage. "Could they know I called 911?"

"It's doubtful, Megan. Police radios are encrypted these days. People can't monitor them." Carter waited for her nod. "Have you received any other notes like this?"

"None." She bit her lip. "No. I mean, Chris might have, but he'd tell me, wouldn't he?"

Carter couldn't answer. He filed the concern away for later. "Megan, our first step is to validate that your children aren't hiding."

"You don't believe me?"

"Megan." Carter held up a hand. "It's not that I don't believe you, it's just that kids are kids. Got one myself. And you'd be amazed how many apparent disappearances are just kids hiding somewhere. It's way more common than you'd think."

"I've searched the house for them. Searched the back yard. There's no sign of them. Someone put me to sleep and *took my kids*."

Carter knew not to press her, not to force her to clam up. "Have you had any strange phone calls? Any emails not caught by your spam filter? Any messages on Facebook or Twitter?"

"Nothing. I've been through my phone since the cops showed up. There's nothing. Just that note."

"What about over the last few days?"

She thought about it, carefully. "No, no. Nothing." She frowned again. "I mean, my husband, because of who we are, he gets threats, but it's always about him. Never me, and never the kids."

"Okay." Carter held up his hands, wide, trying to bring her back to somewhere near calm. "Have you contacted your husband?"

Her fingers were like claws, digging into her arms. "He didn't answer."

Carter couldn't shake the feeling that the senator might be deliberately avoiding her calls. He tried piecing together the window of opportunity in his head, slotting all the facts into place. "Let me get this straight, you called 911 at 10:57." A glance at his watch. It was 11:43 now. "When was the last time you checked a clock?"

"Ten fifteen we were at the gelato shop. That was the last time I checked the dashboard." She nodded, but it looked like she was trying to convince herself, more than an absolute certainty. "No." She snorted, nostrils flaring. "Ten twenty-five. Definitely. Yes. I saw the time when I checked the mail." She was nodding now. She believed it, it was now a memory, a fact. "I checked the house before I called 911."

"Okay, and how long did you search the house for? Five minutes? Ten?"

"Less than five. It's all open-plan, nowhere for them to hide. Kind of by design. I went through the bedrooms. Ours, Brandon's, Avery's and the guest room. There are three big cupboards upstairs. And I checked the attic."

"Is there a basement?"

"Chris wants to dig one out, but we haven't done it yet."

Carter nodded at the half-open garage doors, eight legs visible inside. "And in there?"

"I checked too. Chris keeps it tidy. The cabinets are all still locked."

Carter suspected that the four officers were wasting their time. Then again, standard process was to start at the center of the locus, clear it, then move outward. He hoped it was all just a mistake, that Megan suffered some undiagnosed allergy and nobody had abducted her kids. "You said you tried to contact your husband?"

"He didn't answer. I tried again. Beth heard me." Megan waved at her friend talking to Elisha, rubbing a hand over her forehead. Clearly shopped at the same places as Megan, went to the same salon, just her hair got a red dye rather than blonde. She was taller with softer features and a few extra pounds. "Beth helped me search for the kids after I called it in."

"Okay, Megan. Here's what I'm going to do. We'll get you to give a detailed statement to one of my agents. Think of anyone who could've taken them, list them, and we'll speak to them all. Meanwhile, the team will be looking for your children."

She nodded, slowly. Then frowned. "Will you find them?"

"Like I said, I'll do my best. Megan, has your husband ever disappeared like this before?"

"I mean, most of the week he's in DC, so it's not like he's here all the time."

"But before that?"

"No, never. He'd always call me to tell me what he's up to."

A US senator going off the reservation the same day his kids were abducted? It'd take a lot to persuade Carter that they weren't connected.

"I promise you that we'll do everything we can to find your children."

CHAPTER FIVE

Mason

I slow the minivan to a crawl and let the Range Rover pass. Olive green, looks real vintage to me. Not the sort the feds would drive, but you never know. You just never know.

I pull up and wait. The neighborhood is a lot less salubrious than the Hollidays', that's for sure. Low-rise apartment blocks mixing with bungalows, surrounded by patches of bare earth instead of landscaped lawns, chain-link fences reining them in instead of stone walls. Someone built the houses in a hurry and the people who moved in left them like that—there's never enough time to fix up your place when you're working three jobs just to put food on the table.

But the Range Rover is back. Either it's lost or it's taking another pass at me.

The feds can't be onto me already. Can they? The dash clock reads 11:40, not even forty minutes since… Since I took them.

So I follow it around the block, turning right, then right again past a row of new condos, walled off from the rest of the neighborhood. The Range Rover pulls up on the left at the far end and I slow as I weave past. A dark-haired man punches the steering wheel as he shouts at a blonde woman. She gets out, slamming the door and strutting off. Real tall too, her unnecessary heels making her strut like a bird. In my rearview, the man punches the wheel again, both fists this time, then again, harder and harder. He pulls off with another shout through the window and passes me.

Okay, so they're more likely to be investigated by the feds. And if they're deep cover, they're very good.

Child abduction means black SUVs homing in on a target, lights flashing, sirens blaring. Not a busted old Range Rover. It's still okay, I'm still in the clear.

Another right and I'm back at the freeway intersection, but I take the turn again and pass the house, one last time. It's clear. No other cars following, no tails. Nobody watching from their front stoop, nobody peering through windows.

I pull up and get out, taking my time as I walk up the path to the door, checking every single step of the way. Still nobody watching me, so I press the bell.

The front door snaps open and Layla looks out, arms crossed over her chest. Dark rings under her eyes, hair hanging either side of her narrow face. Her skin tone could be Latino, Arabic, even African-American. She looks around. "Were you followed?"

"I *know* I wasn't. Switched the plates and drove back roads all the way here." I wave my hands around to the new condos, to that scene of domestic *whatever*. "Did a loop back there and nobody followed. We're cool."

She doesn't look reassured. Twitchy, nervous. And I can't blame her. "Show me them."

I lead back to the minivan, scanning around again, looking for anyone, anything, any sign someone's watching us. Still nothing, but my heart's thudding, adrenalin pumping. I open the back door.

Brandon and Avery are both still asleep on the back seat, still tucked up in their car seats.

Layla gasps, covering her mouth with a hand. When she pulls her fingers away, a coy smile crawls over her lips. Then it's her turn to look around. "Let's get them inside."

*

Layla opens the door to the bedroom. The walls are covered in posters—European soccer players in reds and blues screaming with joy, sliding on their knees. And Marvel, obviously—Spider-Man, Captain America, Iron Man, movie versions and their comic-book equivalents.

I carry Avery over and rest her on the bed by the window. It smells stale, dust piling up on the wooden frame. The girl's still out of it, but she's breathing. "That dose will be good for hours."

"You're sure?"

"I gave them a stronger dose than their mother, one that'll last."

Layla rests Brandon next to his sister and sticks her head to his chest. "This is just— I don't know." She shakes her head at me. "What have we become?"

"It's okay." I crouch in front of the bed and watch their angelic faces, their chests rising and falling. Like they're asleep, and we've just brought them home from somewhere, and it's all normal, and we're a happy family and—

"Oh no." Layla grabs my hand, making my wrist burn again. "You're bleeding!"

Layla wraps another layer of bandage over the wound. The disinfectant still stings, but it dulls with each second. "Like this?"

Sitting on the toilet, I flex my hand around and it feels tight enough. "That's perfect."

"You're *sure* this is enough?"

"A field dressing is all I need. Trust me, this'll do."

"You're the expert." Layla tapes up the bandage and perches back on the edge of the tub. She tucks her hair behind her ears, the gold rings catching the harsh overhead light. "We should've taken the mother."

This again?

I fight to hide my frustration, but it's not easy, coming out in a harsh sigh. "Two reasons we didn't take her, remember? First, it's easier for me to explain two sleeping kids in back. A sleeping mommy who doesn't respond to jostling? A lot less so. And a sleeping senator's wife? No way."

The logic seems to penetrate her skull a bit, but she's still clenching her fists.

"Second, assuming she ignores the note and calls 911, the chaos of the search will play to our advantage. Megan Holliday has no idea who we are. They'll be looking at the senator's college girlfriends, bitter campaign donors, or any number of Twitter or Facebook asshats. Not us. We don't exist in their world."

She stares hard at the floor for a few long seconds, the crease in her forehead deepening. "Look, I get it. I really do. It's just... I worry that we're turning into *them*."

"It's eating away at me too. Constantly. But we have to be strong. We have to stay the course. What we're doing. This? It's the most important thing in our lives."

With an almighty sigh, she gets up to put the bandages and disinfectant back in the medicine cabinet above the toilet. She brushes against my arm as she rests back on the tub.

She's not putting her full self into this. Seen this so many times, when shit gets real... That's when you see who really means it.

I grab her hands and make her look at me. "We're in execution now, okay? Our perfect plan is turning into a flawed reality. What's important is improvisation and constant vigilance. For this to work, we've got to put what's left of our hearts and souls into it."

She breaks off from me and gets up, starts pacing around the bathroom. "Are you saying I'm not putting everything into this?"

I worry she'll break, worry she's not strong enough. I sit back on the toilet and fold my arms. "Reassure me."

She fishes her iPhone out of her pocket, frowning deeper as she hands it to me.

Only one notification—an Amber Alert, some text alongside a photo of Brandon and Avery. The children sleeping in the room next to us. The kids I abducted from outside their home.

I hand the cell back. "Well. Megan's awake and didn't heed my advice."

"Some mothers might, but her?" Layla raises her eyebrows. "She thinks the country works for her." She sits back on the edge of the tub. "So what do we do now?"

"The plan doesn't change. We anticipated this might happen. We're just waiting for the next move now. Okay?"

She digs the heels of her palms into her eye sockets, then covers her mouth with her fingers.

I try to make eye contact with her. "If we stick to the plan, if we keep one step ahead of them, then we'll get what we want. What we need."

She looks at me, looks more sure now. I've been honest with her and she appreciates that. "Okay."

I get up and tiptoe through to the bedroom. They're still there, still sleeping. Avery and Brandon. So small and so fragile. So easy for them to die at that age. Or so you think.

Layla runs a hand over my arm, brushing it up and down. "You're right. We've got this covered. Sorry I'm freaking out a bit, it's just hard."

"I know that. Remember, this is what we planned for, what we expected might happen."

"I know that, it's just…"

All I can do is shrug. "Megan calling it in won't make things any harder for us. This is still perfectly doable, okay?"

She nods again. Even smiles. "Okay."

A rumble in my pocket, then that sound, like a dentist's drill. My burner phone is ringing.

CHAPTER SIX

Carter

Carter walked away with Elisha as another agent took over managing Megan. "Talk to me."

Elisha flipped out her notebook and ran a finger down the page. "No previous history at the house or with the family. Just a teenage DUI on the mother back in Aberdeen."

"Nirvana country."

"Like I'm old enough to know that about them." Elisha put her notebook away. "Nothing's jumping out at me, Max."

"Well, the fact this involves a senator's kids should leap out, screaming at you."

"Come on…"

"And the fact said senator isn't here and has been avoiding his wife's calls."

"You think he's involved?"

Carter shrugged, keeping his options open on the matter. "What did the friend have to say?"

"Lives over there." Elisha pointed at a large Victorian almost exactly opposite the Holliday's home. "She heard Megan screaming and shouting at the 911 operator, out here on the street. Said she was frantic, screaming in the pouring rain. She rushed out and helped her search for the kids a second time."

"That checks out, I guess." Carter tried piecing it together. "Here's what I've got." He swept his hand back at the road. "She pulls into the driveway, opens the mailbox, then drives up to the house. Doesn't park in any of their three garages. Gets out and someone grabs her. Injects her with... something." He did the math in his head. "Someone knocked Megan out and took her kids. She was out for twenty-six minutes. Any number of drugs could've done that, any dose."

"Huge amount of risk doing that. You need to know exactly what you're doing, otherwise you can kill them. Fast acting, though, so—"

"We'll get a blood toxicology, Elisha. It'll confirm which drug. But it'll take time. And it won't find her children."

"Max, we should—"

"Right now, it does not matter what drug they used, okay? We'll waste time if we look into it." Carter waited for her to catch up. She nodded, grudging, but she was with him now. "When Megan woke up, she lost twenty-six minutes and two children, but gained a warning note. She checks the house and there's no sign of the kids. But she's smart and she ignores the warning, calls it in and here we are."

Over by the house, Megan wasn't talking to her agent, just standing there, one hand clutching her elbow, teeth biting her lips.

Something gnawed at Carter. "Why take the kids but leave the mother?"

"Kids are easier to control." Elisha stared over at the house, her eyes narrowing. "Meaning the abductor is likely alone. Could be female or a diminutive man."

"Or they're not interested in her."

"Right. And they could be buying time. Whoever did this knew she'd either heed the warning and wait, but more likely she'd ignore it. Assuming that, they know we'll get a hundred different leads from Megan, so he knows that none of them lead to him."

Carter nodded slowly, starting to get into the abductor's mind. "Whoever did it, they must know her Saturday routine. But they surprised her with a blitz attack, knocking her out with a syringe of something." He did another scan of the street. One of those newer neighborhoods that herded everyone in, but kept the houses from looking in on each other. Made it easier to hide in plain sight, especially in the Seattle rain. "This whole operation was executed professionally. Not sure they planned it out meticulously. Maybe they followed her, maybe they knew her every movement, maybe they just lay in wait ready to strike. Our highest priority is working out how they took away two kids without being seen."

"That neighbor didn't see or hear anything until Megan was shouting at the 911 operator." Elisha looked around the street at SPD cops and Carter's agents. "Doesn't look like anyone's gotten anything yet." She pointed at the woods behind the house, bright flashlights tearing through the deluge. "That look like the logical way to take two kids to you? Carrying two children through undergrowth? Way too risky."

"There's always risk, Elisha, but it's how they minimize it. Kidnapping a senator's kids is about as high risk as it gets, so there's got to be a big payoff." The gleaming car caught his eye. Passat, 2017 plates. Turbo Diesel. He stepped closer and peered inside the sedan.

"What is it, Max?"

Only one child's seat in the back, the interior otherwise immaculate.

"I got out of the minivan and felt a prick in my neck."

"This isn't Megan's car." Carter raced over to the house, stopping his agent mid-sentence. "Megan, you said you were driving a minivan?"

"Chrysler Pacifica. My husband buys American."

Carter took another glance at the German sedan. Then snapped out of correcting her. And he saw it, clear as day.

You wouldn't move the kids in daylight, hiking through a wooded area.

No, you'd separate them from their mother, take her out, then drive off in her car. Probably knock them out too.

Meant they were organized, focused, disciplined. Not an opportunist, but someone hunting them like game. Someone who'd maybe been stalking them for days.

While the statistics leaned toward someone who knew the family, and heavily toward someone in the family, Elisha's insight meant this was something else entirely.

Elisha was already walking away, already speaking into her cell, the evidence bag flapping in the breeze. "Tyler, I need you at the command center ASAP."

Carter focused on Megan. "You said your husband didn't answer when you called him?"

"That's right."

"What time was this?"

Megan stared at her smartphone, a slimline Samsung model with a cracked screen. "He called me! I didn't see it. I was with Beth and that agent and—"

Carter snatched the phone off her, just about able to read the call log through the spiderweb of cracks. Chris called at 11:02, while she was speaking to the first attending officer. "Was his car here this morning?"

"He was getting picked up by a car at ten." Megan was frantic, mouth hanging open, tired eyes flicking around. "What if they've got Chris too?"

She was right. If her husband was going to take the kids, he wouldn't inject her when she got back from the mall. He'd take them out for the day, but not return.

Unless he wanted to cover his tracks.

Stop.

Carter knew that was way out in outlier territory, with no supporting evidence. Yet. Stick to the facts—this is a planned abduction, most likely not a family one, at least not directly. "Megan, I need you to call your husband for me."

"Okay." She took the cell and tapped the screen, then put it to her ear, biting at her rose-red lips. "Come on, come on, come— Chris!" She stared at Carter, wide-eyed. "Have you got the kids?" Then she frowned, listening. "No. No! Someone's taken them! Someone's got our kids!"

Carter snatched the phone out of her grasp. "Mr. Holliday, this is Special Agent Max Carter of the FBI."

Megan clawed the air as she reached for the phone and her husband's voice.

"What's going on?" Senator Christopher Holliday. The People's Senator. His voice was polished and professional, years of public speaking and training.

"Someone has abducted your children, sir. I need you—"

"What can I do?" Sounded like he was in a car. "Do you need me to speak to someone? Call in favors?"

"I need you to return home immediately, sir."

Holliday paused. "I'm on my way."

CHAPTER SEVEN

Holliday

Holliday put his phone away and stared out of the window at the passing freeway, thick with trucks and muscular pickups. He checked his watch again—still nine minutes to get there.

Rushing off to the middle of nowhere in a broken-down cab? Lying to a federal agent? Am I doing the right thing here?

Do I even have a choice?

I could go cap in hand to Special Agent Max Carter, but I have so many skeletons in my closet that they speak to me at night.

I really don't need the FBI breathing down my neck unless it's the only hope I've got.

Hugo the cab driver frowned, his old eyes creasing in the rearview. Guy was a long way from Cuba but hadn't lost his accent. Or attitude. The taxi was as old as he looked, rattling along the 190, passed by just about anything. "Sure I don't know you, boss?"

"You're mistaken." Holliday leaned forward in the back of the cab. Stank of stale cigars and broken leather. "I've just got one of those faces."

"Must be that, boss. Here we go." Hugo turned off the freeway into an empty parking lot, not even a broken-down truck.

Holliday craned his neck around and caught the sign: BIG AL'S TRUCK STOP. FULL SERVICE FOR YOU AND YOUR PRIDE & JOY! The lights were out and a couple of letters had fallen off, replaced with coarse graffiti.

They cruised over damp bitumen, cracked with grass growing in clumps, nature taking back what was once its own. In the middle were a bar, a burger joint, and a tiny store, all shuttered.

Holliday tried to open the door, but it was locked.

"Twenty bucks, boss." Hugo grinned at him through the rearview. "Business is business."

Holliday got out his billfold, a tiny brass clip holding hundreds of dollars. Made him look like a pimp, but you never knew when you needed untraceable hard currency. Besides, it was invisible in suit pants, and image always mattered. "I need you to wait for me."

"Okay, boss, but you're gonna have to put some greenbacks in my hand first, know what I'm saying?"

"I know full well." Holliday tore off a fifty and held it up, keeping a grip as Hugo tried to grab it away. "You'll stay, right?"

"Boss, do I look like a man who'll drive away and leave you?"

"No, you don't. But who does?" Holliday snatched the bill back and tore it in half.

"Boss, that trick from the movies—"

"—works. You need the other half for that to be worth anything. So wait." Holliday handed over one half, seeing greed overtaking frustration in the cabbie's eyes. He got out of the cab. The rain had faded to a fine mist, but he had to step around deep puddles as he made his way over to the truck stop. He tried to calm his breathing as he peered inside the building, through a window that had slipped its board, the glass long gone. An empty room, with a serving hatch at the far end. Typical truck-stop posters: naked women, oil company ads, Sports Illustrated calendars. Another look around. All that he could see was a phone booth, the only thing lit up in the gloom.

Holliday got out his iPhone. Five minutes since he'd spoken to that FBI agent, still four minutes until the deadline.

Do I call him? Tell him I'm being blackmailed?

But what if whoever sent the message turns up here and I'm gone?

Holliday dialed the number that sent the text.

"We're sorry, but this number is disconnected."

He clenched his jaw, hard enough to grind his teeth together. Fear crawled up his spine.

His iPhone flashed up a notification. An Amber Alert, a photo of Brandon and Avery cuddling together. Megan took it that weekend out at the lake. He touched the screen, rubbing a finger over Brandon's face, stroking Avery's hair.

The clock hit twelve.

Holliday took another look around, sniffing back the tears. The sound of Cuban horns blared out of the taxi.

The clock's ticking and there's no sign of anyone. Just a truck stop. Nothing around but a phone booth.

Wait a sec…

Holliday jogged over to the phone booth, splashing through oily puddles, and pulled the door open. Water sprayed over his thick coat. Inside, a basic flip-phone sat where the coin-operated telephone used to be. He reached for the cell but dropped it. Losing it. He crouched down to pick it up, taking a deep breath as he flipped it open. A piece of card floated out. He caught it before it hit the damp ground: CALL THE NUMBER.

Holliday pressed the power button and the phone lit up to the wake screen. He hit the green button and the call history showed up. Just one number there, a cell with a Seattle area code. He selected the number and hit dial, then waited for it to connect.

"Hello, Senator." A man's voice. Deep, local, though maybe not a city boy or not for the whole of his life. Either way, Holliday didn't recognize him. Sounded like he was inside somewhere, but not enough reverb for a bathroom. "I started to wonder if—"

"Where are my kids?" Holliday swung around, scanning the truck stop again. Just Hugo in his yellow cab, surrounded by his horns and cigar smoke.

"This isn't how you should start this exchange, Senator."

"Where are they?"

"They're safe."

Even though it could be a lie, Holliday felt a surge of relief. "So let me speak to them."

"Not going to happen."

Holliday felt a thrum in his pocket. His iPhone telling him he had a message. *Megan? That FBI agent?* He tightened his grip on the burner. "How do I—"

"Check that message, Senator. I'll wait."

Holliday swallowed hard as he held out his iPhone, the dumb phone still pressed against his ear, his breath coming softly, like he did this every day. A text, from an unknown number, a different one this time. Seattle code again. He tapped the notification and the iPhone unlocked.

Avery and Brandon lay sleeping on a bed, surrounded by soccer posters, Iron Man looking over them like he was protecting them.

His heart fluttered. "How do I—"

"It's a video. Watch it. You can see that they're breathing."

Avery's chest rose and Holliday let out a shrill gasp.

"It's why I sent that rather than a photo. It's proof."

"How do I know this is live?"

A hand waved in front of them on the screen. "See?"

"Touch Avery."

A bandaged hand reached toward his daughter to stroke her cheek. She jerked, but stayed asleep.

Holliday collapsed back against the phone booth's metal wall, all that stopped him from falling over. He couldn't take his eyes off the screen, their small chests pumping in and out. "What do you want?"

"I'm nobody, Senator. You don't know me. I'm not what's important here. You are—and what you can get me."

"You want money, is that it?"

"I don't want your money."

"I can pay. Whatever you need. Just let them go."

"And where did that money come from, Senator?"

A shiver ran up Holliday's spine. "Please, don't bring them into this."

"Whatever this is." He paused. Sounded like he licked his lips. *What does he know about me?* "Now, have you spoken to the cops or the FBI?"

"I—" Holliday killed the video playing and pocketed his iPhone. "No. I haven't."

"I can tell when you're lying, Senator. Bad things will happen if you lie to me."

"I'm not. They—" Holliday swallowed hard, felt like his throat had tightened up to nothing. "I spoke to Megan. She called 911. She put me on with an FBI agent. He told me to come home."

"And yet here you are. Good boy."

Here.

Is he watching me? Gloating?

Holliday dashed out of the phone booth and looked around again, drawing another blank. "Where are you?"

"The question is what are you hiding, Senator? Your kids are missing, you speak to the FBI, and yet you come here to meet me. What have you done that makes you more scared of them than me?"

"Because I'll do whatever it takes to get my kids back."

"That's better, Senator. Much better." Silence as Holliday walked away from the phone booth toward the cab, Hugo drumming at the steering wheel. "Here's how it's going to work. We'll meet up and I'll return Brandon as a sign of good faith, okay?"

"What about Avery?"

"I'll keep her until you've helped me. Quid pro quo."

"How do you know I can help you?"

"A little bird told me you can, Senator. And if you screw me around and the feds show up, your boy will die in front of your eyes. You'll never even hear of Avery again."

Holliday sucked a deep breath through his nostrils, snarling like a rabid wolf. "You—"

"Senator, you know the stakes here. And I'm not just talking about your kids. Now, there's a parking lot two blocks due east from where you are. Be there in twenty. And leave your own cell phone behind here."

"Listen to me." Holliday kept his cell in his jacket pocket. "Meet me at my home or this whole thing is off."

"I'm not stupid, Senator. The clock's ticking." Click. The call was over.

Holliday walked back to the cab, checking his watch. It was 12:05. *I have to be there by 12:25. There's no time to even think. And what did he mean about 'not just my kids'? Megan? Or does he know something else?*

He opened the taxi door and got in, trying to burn the time into his memory.

"You *sure* I don't know you from somewhere, Boss?"

Holliday locked eyes with Hugo through the rearview again. His mouth was dry.

I know where he will be. I can report it to the FBI.

But he'll only have Brandon. Save my boy, but take a chance on my daughter's safety.

I've got to do this, alone.

Holliday passed him the other half of the split fifty and sat back. "Here. Now there's a parking lot a couple of blocks east of here."

CHAPTER EIGHT

Carter

Carter checked his watch again—12:17. One hour fifty-one minutes since the abduction. He took in the scene again. No more progress on the door-to-doors, and the dog searches sounded farther and farther away, and that felt like more and more of a lost cause. He focused on Elisha. "What's your assessment?"

"Megan's leads seem like long shots." Elisha stared into space, her mind devoted to enriching the scant data they had into information. "And I don't think the husband's taken them."

Carter took another look at the VW, gleaming in the noon rain. "But there's still no sign of the good senator. Until he's here and we can grill him, he's staying in the picture."

Elisha clenched her jaw, teeth clamping together, the skin pulsing, forehead creasing. "Everything points to an abduction. The kids are too young for runaways. They wouldn't get far, and they'd usually freak out when we search anywhere near their hiding place." She nodded slowly, building on her theme. "Factor in Megan being attacked, and it doesn't look like a false report." She smiled, grudgingly. "Which means you're right. Given that the father was uncontactable at the time of abduction, we shouldn't rule out parental kidnapping."

Carter walked over to the car and peered inside again. Immaculate, like it'd just driven off the lot. A half-empty bottle of Evian sat up front, the only sign anyone had ever been inside it.

Elisha joined him. "Taking his own kids in broad daylight seems all kinds of wrong to me. Many reasons why someone would kidnap a senator's children. Politics is a murky world and it's only getting worse." She folded her arms. "Could they have taken the kids to change his vote in an upcoming bill in the Senate?"

"It's a possibility." Carter got out his laptop again and rested it on his right arm. "Senatorial blackmail was the first thing that came to mind, so I checked his schedule. If they wanted to influence him, it'd be something current. But it's a Saturday and Holliday's in his home state all week for that congressional investigation."

"Is he involved?"

"Not directly, no." Carter snapped the laptop shut. "We really need to speak to him." He spotted Megan Holliday in the crowd, talking to one of his agents, combing her hand through her hair. Frantic with worry, but keeping it together, just barely. "Can you ping his cell, see where he's got to?"

"Already on it." She set off toward the mobile command center.

Carter followed. "Trouble is, I can't find any logic suggesting that Megan is the reason they've been taken."

"And if we find the motive, we'll find the children?"

"Right." He opened the door and stepped inside.

The command center's interior wasn't as grand as the exterior. Six rows of beige tables, four agents sitting at each, combing through the scant evidence they had, searching for what they didn't know. The place stank of bleach, like a crime scene that had been scrubbed down, mixing with coffee aroma and cinnamon vape sticks.

Elisha stopped by the first table and crouched next to the agent staring into his laptop. "Tyler, did you send that note to the lab?"

"On its way now." Agent Tyler Peterson pulled off his head-phones, revealing the half-ear that sucker-punched Carter's gut every time he saw it. The rest of him still had the look of a kid fresh out of college, even though he'd spent four years in dusty hellholes on the other side of the world. Losing half an ear to an

IED hadn't affected him, probably made him appreciate not losing the rest of his body. "Fast tracking it now. Should be back within the hour." Even sitting down, he towered over Elisha. He glanced over at Carter and gave a nod. "Sir." Then back at his laptop, typing away. "I've just got access to street surveillance footage from outside." He waved around the agents sitting next to him. "We're sharing the workload across the team."

"Good work." Carter joined Elisha in a crouch. "What have you got?"

Tyler tapped his screen. "This is from the Victorian across the road. It feeds into the Seattle public network, so we're lucky." He clicked the mouse and sat back, letting Carter see without having to crouch.

A grayscale image of the street filled his display, pointing right at the Holliday home. The time stamp read 10:20. Before the attack. The houses were so big that the feed only caught a couple of them. A man walked up the Holliday's drive, head bowed. He stopped at the end of the drive and glanced around, his identity further hidden by a baseball cap and a hooded top. A dark shadow or a thick beard covered his face. He stepped around the bush by the front door and waited, becoming part of the scenery, just some pixels. Barely breathing. Meant a low heart rate, even in a high-stress situation like this. Meant the guy was physically fit, athletic. Added some information to the file marked military.

Minutes later, Megan's minivan pulled up by the mailbox and she reached into it. Both kids were visible in the back, looking like they were watching some TV. Megan edged the car forward, stopping at the top of the driveway before getting out, her face full of rage and irritation and joy and fear, all the everyday emotions of a stay-at-home mom.

Then the man shot into action, jabbing something into her neck. She crumpled into his arms and he walked her over to the house.

"Tyler, wind it back." Elisha was standing now, frowning at the screen. "When he injects her."

"Sure." Tyler replayed the footage, freezing on the frame where the attack happened. "She's out of it almost immediately. We can narrow down on what he—"

"Agent Peterson." Carter's tone made Tyler look around. Their colleagues were listening in, but not looking over. "We've confirmed Megan's story up to this point. Keep going."

Tyler hit play again and footage wound on, back to him walking Megan over to the house and placing the note on her lap. She slumped back against the door, like she was napping. The attacker walked over to get in the car, grabbing a bag on his way.

Carter leaned forward, but he couldn't see what happened inside the van. Twelve seconds, according to the clock, then Megan's car drove off. The two children were still in back.

"So it's one hundred percent an abduction." Carter leaned over and touched the car on the screen. "Peterson, track this vehicle, okay?"

"Sir." Tyler was off, winding through the footage to get the best view, then tapping his laptop keyboard, entering details into search windows.

Elisha stood up tall, resting on the back of Tyler's chair. Didn't seem to annoy him the way it would Carter. "We still can't rule out the husband."

"Not yet, no." Carter walked over to the door and looked out onto the street. Megan Holliday made eye contact with him, her mouth hanging open like he might have news for her. He gave a tense shake of the head and scanned the area again.

"What is it?" Elisha was next to him. "You got something?"

Carter pointed at the house. "That footage starts with our guy entering the shot, okay? Comes in from the right."

"You mean, how did he get here?"

"Right. He drove off in Megan's minivan, but…" Carter looked around again. The street was filled with cars, mostly standard black

FBI Suburbans, but the residents' cars were mostly high-end and German. "How did he get here? Also, if it went wrong, someone operating in this way would have a contingency. He'd want a quick getaway."

Elisha pointed behind the house. "Through the woods?"

"Not with the kids, but maybe if this went south." From up on the command center's step, Carter could see into the small field and the thick woods beyond it, probably the only trees in Washington state not turned into lumber. Flashlights shone through the drizzle. "Get someone searching the vicinity for another car, okay?"

"Okay." Elisha didn't look sure, but she set off, a loyal soldier.

Carter focused on Tyler, working away. He looked around, then leaned in close. "Get the federal wiretaps set up on Holliday's phone. All cell phones, his residence here and in DC. Congressional abduction protocols apply here, so we don't need a warrant. Get everything you can. And dig into Senator Holliday. Anything you can find on him."

"Okay…" Tyler almost rolled his eyes. "I'll do my best."

"Peterson, I know being cooped up in this van can feel like a yawnfest, but I've been here, I've done this job. Maybe not with the same tech you've got access to now, but I've been here. Feels like you're wasting your time, but you're going to be my MVP here, okay?"

"Sir."

"I need you come to me first, okay? I'm taking point here, so whatever you find, you come to me. Even if SAC Nguyen asks you directly, even if she's standing here, you come to me."

"Will do, sir."

Carter pulled up the chair next to him and stared at the footage. "Now, we really need to get a location on that minivan."

"I need access to the local surveillance network, which they're refusing to grant."

"Huh." Carter grabbed the laptop and put a finger to his lips. "You didn't see me do this, okay?"

*

"Where is it?" Elisha was behind the SUV's wheel, hurtling across pockmarked concrete through a derelict parking lot. "I can't see anything."

Carter sat next to her, his right hand clutching the handle above the door. His laptop was open, resting on his knees, showing the tactical map of the area. Only one way in or out. "Pull up." He waited for her to stop, then got out and scanned the area.

The parking lot was a few hundred yards square, the front edge running along the freeway. A thick hedge blocked any view and most of the sound. Could still smell the diesel mixing with the fresh ozone from the wet pavement. A tall chain-link fence lined the other two sides of the parking lot, facing some recently built condos, none of them directly overlooking the parking lot. An old Burger King sat back, boarded up and dead. No security guard, no surveillance camera. No point in either. The whole place looked ready for development, for yet more condos. A ten-foot brick wall towered behind the Burger King. According to the map, a housing project was on the other side. Didn't look like any way through.

"Our guy found this place, knew it was perfect." Carter couldn't shake the nagging doubt that they'd never find the kids. "We're here because Agent Peterson tracked Megan Holliday's minivan across multiple cameras. But, there's no surveillance *here*." He waved a hand at the BK. "It's off-grid. And only one way in or out. Maybe our guy could scale the fences or the wall at the back, but carrying two kids? No way."

"Either way, the Pacifica isn't here." Elisha was on his side of the SUV, arms folded. "He triggered the freeway's surveillance camera when he came in, but left without a trace. The minivan's not here, meaning he swapped plates."

"It's one explanation. Can you trace the plates for me? Follow the minivan, see where it goes next?"

"Gimme a sec." Elisha got out her cell and jogged back to her side of the Suburban.

Carter leaned back against the car, trying to keep his breathing slow and his thoughts under control. He failed at both. What did it mean?

This was all executed according to a plan, probably carried out with no snafus so far. That or the guy had contingencies for all problems, certainly all the big ones, like Megan calling it in against his direct advice. The guy was organized and meticulous, which they already knew.

So why target the Hollidays?

Both from Aberdeen in rural Washington, the old lumber country hugging the Pacific coast. Same graduating class at school. Megan was a cheerleader and homecoming queen, then worked a beauty counter in her hometown's only mall. Christopher, on the other hand, was the quarterback to her cheerleader. Sports scholarship to Washington State, full tuition, though his family were rich enough. Majored in Politics. Enlisted when he graduated, served in the Marines. Then worked for one of the Big Four management consultancies in Seattle. A chance meeting at a high school reunion rekindled the old flame. Marriage, kids. Then Christopher ran for Senate. Fresh faced, one of those rare beasts who appealed to both Democrat and Republican voters. Small government, but big on social care. Christian. Married to a homemaker. Perfect.

Was there anything in that?

On the surface, like Elisha said, there was an incredibly low probability that Megan was the target. Unless it was some ex-boyfriend, but she hadn't mentioned any, and in this situation, she would have. Even so, it was unlikely they'd go to such lengths or be so organized with such a basic motive.

Meaning Senator Holliday was the likely reason their kids were taken. Could have been campaign donations, murky lobbyists, jealousy, hatred of government, terrorism. Anything.

Precision planning. Precision execution. Meaning they really needed to speak to Holliday.

A shiver ran up Carter's spine. Where was Holliday?

Elisha reappeared, her face set hard. "Tyler's found the car. He tracked it leaving five minutes later with out-of-state plates on." She grimaced. "Lost it turning off the I405. There's another dead spot there. And he didn't pick it up again."

"So either our suspect changed the plates a second time or he dumped it?"

"Tyler's going to check both. Thing is, there's a disused truck stop near the turning. Perfect spot for a meeting."

Carter got out his cell and called Tyler, switching to speaker. "Peterson, is Senator Holliday back there yet?"

"Hang on." Sounded like Tyler was walking. A door opened, then the din of a hundred cops and civilians talking, the odd dog barking, rain drumming off a metal roof. "Sorry, sir, he still hasn't turned up."

"Are you still tracing his cell?"

"Sir. He was in motion, last I checked." Sounded like Tyler was back inside. "Just running it now." Then the clattering of a mechanical keyboard. "Okay. Got it. He's at… a parking lot?"

"Get units over there now!"

Carter locked eyes with Elisha, her expression mirroring his suspicion.

CHAPTER NINE

Mason

I pull up at the edge of the parking lot, taking a space close enough to the woods that if this goes south, I can—

It won't go south. This will work.

Keep focused on the here and now, on the plan. And it'll all stay on course.

I look around and Brandon's still out of it. Still breathing, however slowly. Still alive.

The place isn't empty, but I'm far enough away from the nearest car. And besides, they all look empty.

I check the clock on the dash—Holliday still has time, but how long can I wait? I gave him twenty, but I'm not going to keep him to that. He'll get the benefit of the doubt, I just hope he doesn't realize. What's at stake here will always haul me back to generosity. The biggest risk here is that it'll become a weakness, an opportunity for Holliday to gain the upper hand somewhere down the line, to get his kids back without us gaining what we need.

Another scan of the cars and Holliday's definitely not in any of them.

Wait a sec.

A man leans back in a sedan, facing me, looking around, his face a mixture of pleasure and fear. The faint trace of a bobbing head at his groin.

Oh no…

I've picked a hook-up site to meet Holliday.

A bright-yellow taxi cuts through the gray morning, trundling over the parking lot and pulling up not far from the prostitute and her john.

Here it comes. I give him Brandon, he puts him in the cab, the cab takes the kid to safety and we drive off, Avery all the leverage I need.

I roll my window down and listen in.

Some Hispanic music plays, Buena Vista Social Club. "This the place, boss?" The driver is almost definitely Cuban.

The back door opens and Holliday steps out into the deluge. He's tall and has that quarterback look, the guy in charge, the one calling all the shots, making the plays. High cheekbones and a cleft chin. You can see his military training in the way he surveils the parking lot, just like I do. Mapping the vicinity in his head, spotting threats, cataloguing opportunities. You never lose that training, it never loses its hold over you. He leans down and hands some money to the driver. "Thanks." He steps away and the cab heads back to the exit to the roaring freeway beyond. It sits there, signaling right for a few seconds, then it trundles off.

Leaving Holliday on his own.

I focus on Holliday, the rain battering his coat, my heartbeat racing. The cab goes out of the equation, Brandon's rescue having to come from some other source.

He assesses the area again, squinting at the john in his Ford. A spark of ignition and the car drives off in the cab's slipstream, the woman's head appearing halfway over. Part of me wonders if they'll go elsewhere to finish, or if they're done for the day. If he's paying or if it's a romantic thing. Either way, they're unlikely to come forward as witnesses to anything.

Time to get this whole thing in gear. I give him a flash of the headlights.

He doesn't seem to notice, just stands there. Maybe going through the same shit in his head as I am, processing the same logic or similar. This is like having an affair, each step taking you closer to a line you shouldn't cross. But you don't stop, you keep going and, once you're over that line, you're locked in. Freewheeling, out of control and the stakes are higher than ever.

Another flash and he twitches. He takes a step forward then stops, his fists tightening.

Come to papa.

He speeds up, his stride lengthening. He's crossed the line now. Better to get over it before—

Shit.

A cop car pulls up alongside me. Didn't spot its approach, distracted by Holliday's bullshit.

The Amber Alert means they've got people out combing the area. Nobody's come anywhere near the minivan since I took them. Since I crossed the line myself.

The cop gets out of the squad car into the hissing rain.

I check I've got a round chambered and stuff the gun in my pocket, ready for action if needed.

The cop comes over and knocks on the window.

I let my seatbelt go as I reach over to roll down the passenger side. "Can I help, officer?"

He leans in. "Good morning, sir." Canadian accent. Grizzled features, but nothing behind the eyes, like he's lost all the fire that made him sign up in the first place. He's just a guy doing a job he doesn't care about any more. He holds up a photo of Brandon and Avery. "Wondering if you've seen these two, sir?"

Play it cool. Stay calm. Ignore the thudding in your chest. It's just you and him. You've got this.

I take my time checking the snapshot, frowning for his benefit, trying to look like I'm doing a thorough job. I hand it back, making sure my grip's steady. "Sorry, officer."

"Sure?"

"Sure. They're the senator's kids, right? I got an Amber Alert on my phone. Sickening."

The cop nods in agreement, but takes too long looking around the car. He frowns, meaning he sees Brandon in back. The boy's facing away, asleep, but even so…

"That's my son. Jacob. We had a long drive up from his mother's in Frisco."

"Frisco. Huh." Cop can't take his eyes off Brandon. "Where you headed?"

"Vancouver. You a fellow Canuck too, eh?"

He looks back at me, something stirring in his eyes. I'm winning him over. "Born and bred, sir. You from Van City?"

I give him a slow nod. "Just pulled off the road to get a break, you know? My GPS said there's supposed to be a burger joint here, but I sure as shit can't see one."

"I know. Believe me." The cop takes another look at the kid, then steps back. "Okay, sir. Going to need to see title and registration."

Shit.

I'm in Megan's minivan with fake plates, so of course I can't show him anything even vaguely legal. What do I do? Think fast…

"Buddy, wondering if you could cut me a break here. My ex took this car when she left us, you know how it is? We drove down to pick it up from the bi— From her new place in Frisco."

"It's her car?"

"*Our* car." I flash a smile. "In her name, though. She took it when she left me and Jake. I mean, what kind of woman leaves her kid, right?" Play to his institutional sexism. "Then I get a call from her, saying how she wants to swap this for her Honda. Can you believe it?" Keep asking him questions, keep involving him in the lie.

But he's having none of it. "I need you to step out of the car, sir."

I open the door and put my foot down in a puddle. "We don't need to do this."

"Come on, sir."

I have no choice here, certainly not sitting here. He's a big guy. Six two, maybe, but only about one eighty. I can take him down. Wait till he's cuffing me, then overpower him. So I get out and follow him over to the radio car.

He speaks into the car radio, but I can't make out what he's saying.

No sign of Holliday, now. Shit.

The woodland behind the parking lot is maybe forty yards away, probably less. The whole reason for choosing this place. I can make it if I dart between the cars. Four seconds, maybe five, then I'll be in a woodland, hidden by tall bushes and trees.

I won't have Brandon, though.

But we'll still have Avery. We'll still have leverage.

"Okay." The cop stands up and puffs out his chest. "Sir, I'm going to need to—" His voice is cut off by wailing sirens. He spins around to check.

A quick glance and I'm in deep, deep shit.

Flashing lights on black Suburbans. The FBI.

The cop waves at the approaching vehicles.

I smash him in the gut with an elbow, then crack his head against the radio car's roof. Still time to get away, so I run for the minivan.

"Stop!" Another glance and the cop is lying on his side, reaching into his pocket for something.

I keep going. Not far now, focus on the target and how to get there.

"Stop!" A gunshot, high in the air above our heads. A warning. The next shot will be in my legs or my back. "Stop!"

I'm already diving for it, as the air slices apart above my ear, a gunshot lashing past. I hit the ground inches from the minivan, then scrabble forward, spider-style.

There's a bullet hole in the rear glass.

A scream erupts from inside.

CHAPTER TEN

Holliday

The second gunshot echoed around the parking lot. In amongst the white noise, glass smashed.

Holliday dared to look up from behind the sedan, that old adrenalin surge spiking in his veins.

Flashing blue-and-red lights of the black Suburbans rumbling over the parking lot, sirens wailing.

Closer, a cop car sat next to the car that flashed him. Next to it, a patrol cop dropping a pistol in a puddle, his eyes wide, mouth hanging open.

Holliday ducked back and caught movement off to his right, a man sprinting between scattered parked cars, heading toward the woods.

The son of a bitch who dove away from the bullet. The man who summoned me here. The man who has my kids.

The man cleared the parking lot and was soon lost in trees and undergrowth.

Then a scream tore out behind him, high-pitched and childlike.

No.

No.

No, no, no!

The cop stood by his car, close to hyperventilating. Holliday knew that stance, knew the expression on his face. A bullet shot in anger, the intent not met by the resulting action.

Another scream. Came from somewhere between them. A car, the rear windshield smashed and splintering.

Megan's Pacifica!

Holliday pushed away from the sedan and shot across the pavement toward the minivan. The crumpled rear windshield fell into the trunk.

The cop leaned against a radio car, muttering to himself, staring at his gun lying on the ground like it was Satan. He didn't seem to notice Holliday.

A bullet hole punctured the side door, just below the passenger window.

Another scream, louder, ringing in Holliday's ears now. He stepped toward the car, toward the screams. Felt like he weighed seventy tons, each step like he was underwater, strapped down with weights. He reached for the door, his throat thick.

Behind him, tires squealed and feet pounded toward him. Someone grabbed him, pulled him away. "Sir." A man's voice. "I need you to—"

Without even looking at him, Holliday pushed him away. The pressure on his arms released, and he tore at the car door, his shaking fingers fumbling at the handle, but it opened.

Brandon lay in his car seat, his cream-and-navy plaid shirt dyed red.

Mechanical training took over and Holliday kicked into action, jabbing the release button and pulling the corpse away from the car seat, the gray fabric already taking on the color of Brandon's blood. He tore at the boy's shirt, snapping the buttons until he was at his undershirt, lifting it over his dead son's head like it was bath time, like everything was okay and it was all fine and—

A tiny entry hole puckered the right side of Brandon's chest, surrounded by a bloody spiderweb. He touched his son's cheek with his left hand, the fingers of his right probing the gunshot wound.

CHAPTER ELEVEN

Carter

Carter's breath came thick and slow as he picked himself up off the ground. His whole right side was damp from the puddle he'd landed in. Holliday had decked him in one shot.

The senator stood by the car, cradling his son in his arms, his face emotionless. Guy was huge, no two ways about it, still had that military look about him. He looked a lot younger than the age on his profile, despite his graying hair.

The boy's torso was a mess of blood and bone.

Felt like everything twitched in Carter's body as his brain connected the dead body to Kirsty. The muscles in his arms felt like jelly.

He had to snap himself into focus. This is a murder now. Preserve all the evidence. He assessed the scene, trying to keep everything inside him in check.

No sign of any killers or abductors, just Holliday, cradling his dead son, and a cop leaning against a radio car, muttering to himself. A firearm lay in front of him in an oily puddle.

Carter tried to play it back. Someone ran toward the minivan. Had the cop shot?

In the here and now, a scream curdled his blood. Brandon. Alive.

Carter's gut lurched, hope breaking free of the despair.

Holliday's mouth hung open, shock written all over his face.

Carter snapped into action, pressing a finger to the boy's blood-soaked neck. There, a pulse. And the kid was still breathing.

Holliday laid his son on the minivan's hood and leaned in to his chest, squinting as he inspected the wounds.

Carter could only watch as the senator worked. Something in Holliday's file tugged at his brain—Holliday was a trained field medic in his service days, sure looked like he knew what he was doing.

He took in the scene again, reassessing everything. The car was Megan's Pacifica, but the Oregon plates didn't match. At least that part of the story checked out.

Then back to his memories. The cop had waved as they approached in their wave of black SUVs, clearly had his gun drawn.

On Holliday? Why?

And what was Holliday doing here?

Sirens snapped Carter back. An ambulance pulled up next to them, the flashing lights reflected in the puddles. An EMT jumped down with a splash and dashed straight over to Holliday. He got a shove for his trouble. The senator wasn't letting anyone else get at his son.

Carter gripped Holliday's arms tight and eased him away. "Sir, you need to let the professionals do their jobs." He gestured at the EMT, eyes wide, forehead creased, begging for trust.

Holliday stepped aside with a nod as the second paramedic joined them. But his hands twitched, like he couldn't just stand around as they tried to keep his son alive.

Another scream cut out into the morning air.

The EMT cradled Brandon and carried him toward the ambulance, his partner following.

Holliday stood there, his jaw clenching and unclenching. He got a smartphone out of his pocket and focused on it. Then cocked his head to the side. "He murdered my kid!" He marched over to the beat cop, his shouts lost in the rain. He pushed the officer, pinning him against the car, his right hand wrapped around the cop's throat, his left hand pulled back, ready to strike.

Carter darted over, grabbed Holliday's arm, yanking it behind his back, his other arm wrapping around his neck. "Let him go!"

Holliday swung around, fire burning behind his eyes, then he went slack.

The cop got up, rubbing at his throat as he scrambled away.

Carter kept them separated by an arm's reach. "Senator, I need you to stay calm, okay?"

Holliday looked dazed, but compliant, his flash of rage long gone.

Carter let go of him.

Holliday jerked forward, wrapping his fingers around the cop's throat again.

Carter tried to repeat the grab, but Holliday was wise to it, swapping submission for an elbow to the gut. Carter recoiled, pain flaring up from his stomach, yanking his breath out of his lungs. He stepped back and kicked low, his heel cracking off Holliday's shin, then pushed a fist into his chest. The big man tumbled backward, twisting as he landed on the car's hood.

Carter grabbed his wrist and flipped him so he was face down, then snapped his other arm behind his back, the position for cuffing. "You've got a choice here, Senator. Keep fighting, and you'll end up in jail. Stop, and I'll let you go."

Holliday made the wise choice. He went prone on the car's hood.

"Are you going to play nice?"

Holliday nodded.

"Okay, we're going for a walk." Carter pulled him up to standing and checked him over. Seemed to be compliant now. Finally. He led him away, back toward his Suburban and the ambulances, their lights still flashing. He tried to make eye contact with the senator. "Take me through what happened here."

"He shot my son. That cop." Holliday was looking everywhere but at Carter. He seemed to settle on the beat cop, standing with Elisha, just shaking his head, staring at the ground. "He shot my son!"

"You saw it?"

Holliday nodded, all the answer he was prepared to give.

"Why are you here, Senator?"

Holliday looked Carter up and down. "Who are you?"

"Special Agent Max Carter." He got out his badge. "We spoke on the phone. You were supposed to—"

"You're the guy who didn't do his job and let some whacko kidnap my children?"

Carter decided it was grief talking and gave him the benefit of the doubt. "Sir, I understand what you're going through."

"Do you? Someone's kidnapped your kids, huh?"

"I've—"

"You know *nothing.*" Holliday waved at the ambulance. "My son is *dying* in that van because that asshole cop fired wild." His jaw clenched, his Adam's apple bobbing up and down. A deep breath and he looked right at Carter. Then he collapsed back against the SUV, looking like he might go down.

"I can't even begin to think what you're going through here, sir."

"Why did you stop me?" Holliday glared at Carter. "He shot my boy! I saw it with my own eyes." He looked over at the Pacifica, at the cop and Elisha. "Someone ran away, the cop fired a warning shot, up in the sky. Then he aimed for him. The guy dove out of the way and— You see how high the shot was?" He held his hand level with the SUV's door handle. "He should've been trying to take the guy down, aim for center mass. Aim for the legs, but that asshole was going for a headshot like he was playing a video game. Going for the kill."

Carter took another look at the Pacifica and tried to replay the path of the bullet. The back glass was shattered, but there was a small bullet hole in the passenger door. He traced it all the way back to the long puddle by the radio car. "Was he lying down?"

"Guy decked him. Must've been distracted or something."

Made sense, given the bullet's trajectory. "And you've no idea who he was shooting at?"

Holliday scowled, like he was being questioned by an insect, someone so far beneath him. "Excuse me?"

"The reason I'm here, Senator, is that we tracked your cell phone to two nearby towers." Carter pointed at a distant building, then a block of condos. "It let us triangulate your location to here. Problem is, I asked you to return home. You said you were heading home."

Holliday stood up tall, letting a slow breath out of his lungs.

"Can you explain why you're at a parking lot and not at home with your wife?"

Holliday took a long look at Carter, face screwed up. Then he collapsed against the SUV, tears mixing with the rain on his face.

Crocodile tears. Precise timing. The guy was hiding something, just what exactly? Not that Carter didn't have a few ideas.

"Right now I need to find your daughter. Do you know where she is?"

"You really think I'm involved in this?" Holliday dug his palms into his eye sockets. "He shot my boy, and this is how you treat me?"

An EMT dropped out of the back of the ambulance and took a long look at Holliday. "Sir, you can ride with your son in back."

Holliday looked up, his gray eyes gleaming. "Okay." He set off, brushing at his cheeks, and stopped by the back of the ambulance and locked his gaze on Carter, the gaze of a pleading politician. "Find my daughter. Please."

"Believe me, I'll find who's behind this." Carter left a long pause. "I'll see you at the hospital."

A fresh scream came from inside the van. Holliday flinched then disappeared inside.

And they were gone, reversing with a high-pitched squeal, then powering over to the freeway, the siren wailing.

Carter took a deep breath. Couldn't get the boy's screams out of his head.

Holliday knew more than he was admitting to. But what? Was he really involved in the abduction? Or was someone targeting him?

A phalanx of fresh SUVs headed toward him, the middle two swerving to avoid the ambulance.

Time to get the search started. Find this man, find Avery.

Hopefully alive.

Carter turned back to the vicinity of the shooting. Elisha was already running the crime scene, her efficiency kicking in. A pair of uniformed cops cordoned off the area, enclosing the patrol car and the Pacifica. A forensics team suited up beside the minivan. The rain started washing away the trail of blood.

The K-9 unit's handler was in the back of the Pacifica, letting his Labrador get a hold of any scents from Brandon or the abductor. They set off toward the woods, his dog straining at the leash, already picking up a trail. "Come on, Dora, let's get him." They hit the line of trees, beyond which flashlights glinted deeper in, some calls sounding even farther away.

Carter doubted it would yield anything. Thirty agents and some dogs weren't going to find a physically fit guy with that much of a head start. The helicopter stood a better chance, but the rain was going to hamper it.

He tried to overlay Holliday's take on events. He said the cop shot once in the air, then aimed low as a man ran away. Brandon's abductor, running back to the minivan. Probably saw Carter's team approaching and panicked, figuring he could get away before they turned up.

But Holliday was the ultimate mystery. What was he hiding? And what kind of man ignored a direct request from the FBI agent investigating his children's abduction?

And why was he here?

Meeting the man who ran away from the cop was an assumption, but a good one. Finding that man was the key to learning what happened here, but more importantly to finding Avery Holliday.

So Holliday couldn't be trusted.

His cell rang out. Bill. Wanting to apologize? Or was it just more of his nonsense. He let it ring out and tried to focus on the here and now.

Elisha was over by their Suburban, standing with the cop who'd shot Brandon. White-faced, deep in shock, muttering to himself, staring into the puddles, their oily surfaces dotted with raindrops. *J. Calhoun*, according to his badge. His navy radio car was standard Seattle Police. He took a halting breath, no doubt replaying the incident again in his head. Over and over and over again. Still muttering, telling himself there was more he could have done, that he could have caught the guy and saved the boy's life. Or he could've let him go and saved the boy's life.

Carter walked over to join them.

Calhoun looked up at Carter, his thick skull protruding over bushy eyebrows. Mid-forties. Cauliflower ears, like he'd done a lot of Greco-Roman wrestling. Gut like he'd done a lot of drinking—beer, and not the light kind either. His eyes flickered as he tried to focus.

Carter held out his badge. "I'm leading the investigation into Brandon and Avery's abduction."

Calhoun stared into space. "Is the kid dead?"

Carter gave a reassuring smile, masking a grimace before it formed. "He's on his way to the hospital as we speak." He plotted the likely route in his head, taking the toll bridge over Lake

Washington back toward downtown Seattle, and came up with about twenty minutes. Hopefully long enough to keep Brandon alive before he hit the ER. "Your quick thinking rescued the boy from his abductor. Thanks to you, we have him now."

"What?" Calhoun frowned, lips pinched tight. "I *shot* a *kid*."

"Accidentally, right?" Carter waited for a nod. "That child was kidnapped from outside his home and, thanks to you, he's back in our care." He paused, waiting for some reaction. There, a flicker of hope in Calhoun's eyes. "Now, I need to find Avery, his sister. The best chance I've got is for you to tell us exactly what happened here, and I need the truth. Okay?"

"Okay." Calhoun's nod was slow and measured. "I pulled up, saw a guy in a car, asked what he was doing here. This is a bit of a hook-up place for hookers and their johns."

Carter played that through—taking a child to a place like this could mean sex trafficking. So why just bring Brandon? And why meet Holliday here? Two kids, separated, meant one was used as leverage. That was off the table. For now.

Calhoun cleared his throat. "But he had a kid with him. A boy, I think. Didn't get a good look but, you know, I don't want to be the guy who ignored it and that SOB gets away, you know? So I asked for title and registration. The guy didn't have any, so I get him out, took him over to the patrol car and radioed it in." He patted the SUV. "Right then, you appeared in the distance and… Aw man, I got distracted."

"It's okay. I just need to know what happened."

"The guy hit me, right in the guts, and I went down. He ran for it. I warned him and shot in the air to show I meant it, but the guy didn't stop." Calhoun gave a shrug. "So I shot again, aiming for his center mass, you know, trying to take him down. Guy was already diving, so I missed and…" He shut his eyes and swallowed hard. "I hit the minivan. I heard the boy scream." His voice was shrill and thin. Poor guy was going to be in therapy for months, if not years.

Carter stood there with him. Didn't look the sort to appreciate a hug, so he tapped him on the arm. "I've worn those shoes." He flashed back to his own dark past, to a similar shooting in hotter conditions. No less horrific, no less bloody. "It's not easy but, with the right counseling, you will accept that this wasn't your fault and you will get over it. Always remember that you tried to take down the guy who abducted those kids. You need to cling to that. Nobody will blame you. And I mean nobody."

"Senator Holliday did."

"He's grieving. He's angry."

Seemed to settle him down a bit. "But I didn't stop that SOB. He got away."

Carter took another look at the trees, searching for any hope. And seeing none. He gave Calhoun the truth in the form of a nod. "Officer, the man you shot at was probably the kidnapper or an accomplice. He still has Brandon's sister. Avery. You've got her photo. So I need to know everything about him. Any detail at all—maybe seems tiny just now, but it might help. Okay?"

"Okay." Calhoun huffed in a deep breath. "Guy was white, really pale skinned. Maybe thirty-five, forty? Said he was Canadian, heading home to Vancouver from San Francisco with his son. Spun me some line about his wife taking the Pacifica and wanting to swap it for a Honda." He sniffed. "But I tell you one thing, he wasn't a Canuck."

"You're Canadian, right?"

"Right. Married a Seattle girl and moved here twenty years back. Believe me, I know a fellow Maple Leaf when I see one."

"You get a look at his face?"

"Red hair, longish." Calhoun held his hands below his jawline. "Grunge length, you know? Long enough to mosh, short enough to tie up to look tidy in most professions. All the benefits of a mullet without the obvious downsides." He frowned. "Guy's skin was marked, though, like he had bad acne as a kid."

"What about his eyes?"

"Mid-blue, but kinda bloodshot. Didn't notice anything about his nose, cheeks, ears. His mouth was small, you know, like that actor? Cusack, or something? The guy smiled but his lips were still tiny. Oh, yeah, I mean, he had a beard, same red as his hair."

"Tattoos?"

"Not that I saw. Wait a sec… I saw a tattoo. When we were fighting." Calhoun rolled up his left sleeve and brushed his forearm. "Looked like Semper Fi, you know?"

Another token tossed on the pile marked ex-military. "You think he was a marine?"

"That type, yeah." Calhoun sucked in another breath, scratching at his chin. "When I got him out of the car, he was couple inches taller than me, a few pounds heavier. Lean, though. Really lean, but *built*. I know that's a contradiction, but—"

"No, I get it. What else was he wearing?"

"Maroon hoodie, long sleeved. Don't remember a logo. And faded jeans, stonewashed."

"Okay." Carter swung around and caught Elisha's attention with a raised eyebrow. "Get a facial analyst here *now*."

"Sir."

"Thanks." Carter took one last look at Calhoun then walked off, pulling out his cell phone. "I better break the news to the boss."

CHAPTER TWELVE

Mason

My feet pound across the ground, thick with pine needles, mud squelching underneath each stride. Uphill now, my breathing harder. My foot slides back, but I catch myself on a tree and pull up, taking a few steps to the side to get leverage on the wild grass. Then I set off again, into a clearing, my breath steadying, my heart rate climbing as I cut between the trees, back through the mud.

Shit.

Mud means footprints. Even though the rain here is constant, it's never enough to wash prints away. So I stop and think, soaking in my environment, looking for options.

Back down at the distant parking lot, red and blue lights flash through the rain. Seven SUVs parked in formation toward the... toward where it happened. Nearer, a dog barks. They're on to me.

My time advantage is slipping. They'll be on me soon enough. And I can't lead them straight to Layla's door and to Avery.

What's the play here?

Keep moving for a start.

No. Get rid of the burner first. Their presence shows they can trace me. They're onto me. Somehow.

Got to be Holliday.

Don't know. Can't know, but shit. It's likely. Jackass.

I pull the SIM from under the battery and snap it, then bury it deep in the mud. I rub the cell clear of prints and toss it far away.

Okay, so now what?

I check behind me. Flashlights and shouts from inside the woods now.

Where do I go?

Doesn't matter, just go.

I walk off slowly, stepping on the inside of my shoes so I don't leave a full print. And soon, through the thick foliage, I see a row of houses, the first signs of Seattle. A row of trees leads me over, the ground lined with rotting leaves.

Okay. A plan. A destination.

I keep my slow-step shuffle until the first tree, then I break into a run, using the carpet of leaves to cover my tracks. When I stop to look back, *I* can't even see the way I came. Only the best military tracker could follow me, and they're all abroad. Domestic FBI agents don't stand a chance.

So I set off again at pace and bound up the tall wooden fence, using my momentum to climb, then reach for the top, catching hold with my fingers. My wrist screams out as I haul myself up. For once, I'm thankful that I never let my pull-up regime slip.

The fence is sturdy enough that I can stop and check back the way I came. Shouts from down below, crisscrossing the path I've taken. Hopefully muddying my smell. A dog barks. Shit. They're close, way faster than I expected.

Keep moving. I slide down the side of the fence and stop dead.

A small child sits in a chair by a pair of French doors, a TV playing some cartoon behind him, the music bleeding out through the glass.

And the disgust hits me. Brandon and Avery were doing the same thing when I dragged them into my world. A pair of innocents, watching Disney noise. And Brandon got shot because of what I wanted, what I tell myself I need.

His scream will follow me to the grave.

Brandon's dead and I've turned into a monster. I've become *them*, like Layla feared we would.

Snap out of it!

The kid hasn't seen me, he's still stuck in the TV's attention field. He rubs his nose with a tissue. Got a cold.

Keep focused on the mission.

I step across the patio slabs through the rain and duck down the side of the house, emerging into an older neighborhood. An old Honda Civic rusts in the driveway, the rain snaking over the windshield. Perfect.

But don't get carried away, don't rush and ruin everything. I lean out and take a look.

The street's quiet, nobody around, no houses directly overlooking.

I try the Honda's door and it opens. Another look around, no sign of the kid's mother or father watching the car. So I get in and sit on the driver's side, muscle memory taking over as I pull out wires and get the ignition sparking in seconds.

I take the intersection and pull in to a stop two blocks from Layla's house. I can see it, halfway down the long stretch. I check in all the mirrors for signs I'm being followed. Can't see any of the seven candidate cars for tailing I'd identified on the way over—three Toyotas, two Fords, a Nissan, and a black Saab.

I keep telling myself—this isn't an anti-drugs sting, the FBI will be all guns blazing, sirens wailing, and lights flashing, like back at the parking lot. SUVs from all directions, swooping in to catch me. SWAT teams. Helicopters.

Not a woman pushing a stroller. Not an old dude in a beat-up Chevy.

So I wipe the few spots I've touched and get out of the car, don't even lock it. The neighborhood's not so bad that it'll be stolen within the hour, but it's not far off.

I take it slowly over to Layla's house, trying to avoid looking over my shoulder, trying to avoid looking like a criminal on the run. Using car sideview mirrors to check behind me. Still don't think I'm being followed. One last chance to check as I wait to cross the road, going through the list of possible tails. None of them approaching, none of them parked nearby. I'm in the clear.

So I jog over the road to her home, stopping to let an almost-silent Prius past. Still freaks me out how quiet they are. Bastard almost hit me.

I knock on the door and wait. Try to avoid looking behind me but I fail, my head jerking around. Nobody's watching me. Not that I can ever be a hundred percent sure.

Feels like I'm waiting forever, stuck with the knowledge of what my actions have done to a small boy.

It'll be all over the news. She would know. She should have gone. Leaving me alone, but still keeping Avery as leverage. Means I should run and hide, put this behind me.

Meaning I've failed.

The curtains twitch on the room facing the road, and I catch a glimpse of Layla's eye. Seconds later, the apartment door opens and I slip inside.

Layla takes a long look at me. She knows. She turns around and leaves me in the hallway. Avery's still sleeping in the bedroom.

I lean against the wall. "That cop saw me. My face will be everywhere."

"Come on." Layla grabs my arms and leads me through her apartment. Backpacks ready to go, but she hasn't gone yet, instead letting me explain myself. In the back room, the TV is playing, cable news blaring out, loud enough to wake a sleeping child, just not a drugged one. She mutes it and jabs a finger at the screen. Doesn't even look at me. "You *shot* Brandon, didn't you?"

I swallow hard, staying standing. "He's dead?"

She still doesn't look at me. "Did you kill Brandon?"

"I swear I didn't." I perch on the edge of her sofa and run a hand through my hair. The screen's moved on to some Seahawks sports news, but I'm tracking the news ticker for updates. Nothing on Brandon's condition. Then I catch myself tugging at my beard and stop. "A cop stopped me."

Layla finally focuses on me, her face twisted full of hatred, disgust, shame, revulsion. "Did you shoot him?"

"The cop did. I took him out, then ran for it. He fired a shot in the air, warning me, so I dove and he shot again. Missed me, but… he got the kid." Saying it out loud like that, none of it seems real. Just a story now, not events leading to a boy's death. Might as well have shot him myself. "I don't know if he's dead or not, but I swear, Layla, I didn't shoot him."

She looks hard at me for a few seconds then holds out a hand. "Gun."

I reach into my hoodie pocket and the lump of metal's still there. I hold it out, but she snatches it from my grip.

She pulls the magazine free and checks it. Then the chamber. A sigh, then she rests the gun on the chair's arm.

"So you believe me?"

"For now." She gives me another look, but this time it's full of fear and worry. "What are we going to do?"

"We've got a choice here, Layla. I could take Avery. Drive her somewhere, call the FBI. I could call Holliday. We can disappear like we planned."

"But then what would we do?" She looks at me with raised eyebrows. "We'd have no answers, just those questions still burning away at both of us. And you've committed a federal crime. People will hunt you until the day you die."

I smile at her. "Which might not be too long coming."

"This isn't funny." She slaps me, hard. My cheek stings. "All this, for nothing other than a boy's death?"

"No, I agree. But…"

"What?"

"Layla, you're not involved." I follow it up with a shrug, my face still on fire. "Nobody's seen you. Your DNA isn't on any evidence. You're nobody to them. But I am. No matter how careful I was, my DNA will be all over that car. It's just a matter of time before they process it and match it to my military record. Then they'll find me. It'll take days, maybe, but they'll find me. Layla, I can take Avery and return her. Stop any blowback on you. Stop this before it gets any worse."

She looks like she's considering it. "Was Holliday there?"

"I think so."

"We need better than 'I think so'. Was he there or not?"

"I flashed the lights at someone who looked a lot like him, and he started walking up to the car. Right height and build. But the cop stopped me and I didn't see him again."

"So he hid?"

"Must've."

She thinks it through for a few seconds, staring at the TV. "Either way, he'll know what's at stake now."

"What do you mean?"

"If Holliday was there, then he saw what happens when he doesn't go along with our plan. And if he wasn't, then his son got shot. Either way, it means he'll fear us."

"Fear *me*. You're not *doing* this. You can still get out."

Layla's glare shoots over at me. "If we stop now, we won't have any answers and a boy will be dead for no reason."

I glance over at the door, not far from where Avery's sleeping. "Is this worth the cost?"

"I'd *die* for this information." She picks up the gun and carries it over to me, wiping it with a sleeve before putting it in my hands. "I can't stop until this is over. If this is already over, if they're onto us and it's just a matter of time before they burst through that door, then I'd rather be dead and not have to suffer anymore."

She means it too. Every single word.

"It all comes back to that information. We have no lives to get on with, no 'the way things were'. All we can do is kill the pain for short bursts of time, mute the noise in our heads when we fail to sleep at night."

And I agree with her. I'd rather die than suffer the pain for another night. Whatever happens, this ends today.

I let out a sigh. "That cop will give them a description of me from the parking lot."

Layla walks over to a drawer and gets something out. She drops a pair of clippers in my lap, the dangling plug hitting off my ankle bone. "There's a razor and shave gel in the medicine cabinet." She tugs at my hair. "I suggest you take it all off, right down to the skin."

I stand up and look her deep in the eyes. "Are you still in?"

"One hundred percent." Every movement multiplies her words, her nodding, her stern smile that turns to a grimace. And I see it in her eyes. She wants this as much as I do. Maybe even more.

"Okay." I take the clippers through to the bathroom and plug them in.

Then I notice a burner phone sitting on the side of the bathtub. I pick it up and dial a number from memory.

CHAPTER THIRTEEN

Then

Faraj

Faraj woke up, breathing hard, blood pumping hard in his veins. No rage, no fury, just sheer terror.

Pitch black. He couldn't see anything.

An oily smell.

Eerie silence.

He tried to move his hands and feet, but he couldn't. Sharp pain bit into his wrists and ankles. Something metallic clanked, sounding way louder than it should.

He twisted his head, but something dug into his neck. He shifted his left elbow and it hit something hard—cold metal.

His stomach rumbled with hunger, his lips dry. Something covered his mouth, and all he could do was whimper, dampened by bitter-tasting leather.

I'm trapped.

I'm going to die here!

The fury burned in his gut. Not righteous anger, but dark, dark fear.

Calm down. Center yourself.

That's what Daddy said.

Use the anger, don't let it use you.

He tried swallowing, but there was no moisture in his mouth.

Start over. Think it through.

What do you know?

How did you get here?

And it came back.

Hayden's body spray. Jacob fighting him. Coach Smith stopping them. And those soldiers bursting in. Coach doing nothing. Jacob trying to protect me.

And…

The soldiers grabbed Jacob as they took me.

Is he here?

Is that what happened? Did Jacob save me?

"Jacob?"

Barely a sound. Nobody to hear it either.

Faraj lashed out with his elbow again and the metal clanged. He tried to speak but he couldn't make any sound.

I've been buried alive like in that film Jacob found in his daddy's closet. I'm going to die alone.

"Jacob?"

Something cracked, and bright lights burnt at his eyes.

"Wakey, wakey." A man stood on the left, his pale skin bleached even further by the bright light. All Faraj could make out was his lips moving. Nasty lips, bitter, sneering. "You had enough yet, s—son?"

The soldier with the stutter!

Faraj looked around, his eyes adjusting. He was on his back, looking up. The man was in a room, dark behind the bright light. He could make out the shape of the box he was in—a metal coffin.

They're going to bury me!

Another man leaned into the hatch and put a bottle of water to Faraj's lips. He started pouring and didn't seem to care that most of it splashed over his chin and body, soaking the soccer shirt.

Faraj put all his effort into speaking. "Where am I?" Still sounded like a mouse whispering, but his lips were less dry. "Is Jacob here?"

"Just tell us where your father is, son."

Why do they want to speak to my daddy?

Give them nothing. Silence is the best way. Means you keep all the cards.

"Son, you want to go back in this box? Or you want a burger and fries?"

Faraj couldn't keep his breathing under control. *I have to do this…* "He left us! I don't—"

"Cut the crap, you little cocksucker." A hand reached into the box and grabbed Faraj's throat. "We know you've been speaking to him. How do you contact him?"

"I don't know where he is!"

"That wasn't the—" The man stopped. His nasty lips pushed together. "Okay. But you *do* know how to get in touch, don't you?"

"No!"

"That's how you're playing it, then." He leaned over and grabbed Faraj's throat, hard, fire burning his neck. "We're not playing, son. We will kill you if you don't answer our questions."

Warm liquid trickled down Faraj's leg.

"For the last time, son, how do you contact your father?"

"Where's my mom?"

"*Son.* You're not going to see her until you start talking to us. Okay?"

"Please! I want my mom!"

"I'm going to lower this coffin lid again. Maybe then you'll want to talk, huh?" The man leaned over and grabbed a handle.

"Wait!"

"So you do know?"

Faraj lay back, eyes closed. "Signal."

"Signal? The app, right?"

"Right. It's on Mom's phone. I send Daddy a message and he calls me. Told me how to delete the messages when we're done."

The man stood there, frowning. "Signal, huh. You need a cell number for that, right?"

Faraj stayed silent.

"Son, what's your father's number?"

Daddy told me to keep it secret, even from Mom. I can't tell him.

"Son, you want to see your mom again, you better start talking to me."

I don't have a choice. They'll kill me if I don't give them it!

And if I do? Will they really let me see Mom?

"Son, I've got some Ben & Jerry's in the next room. You like a bowl of that, huh? I'll even give you the whole pint."

"Two oh two. Five five five. Oh one oh two."

The soldier looked over at someone else.

"It checks out. That's a Seattle area code."

"So he's still in the country?"

"Doesn't work like that. You can go to Syria and still use a US cell number."

Faraj leaned back and let the clamps caress his neck. "Are you going to let me see my mom?"

CHAPTER FOURTEEN

Now

Holliday

The Seattle Children's Hospital. The place where hope dies.

The burner cell started throbbing in Holliday's pocket. He looked around and, for once, nobody was watching him. He dumped the cell in the trash and started pacing around the hospital waiting room, decorated like a spaceship, all white glass and chrome. Designer tables and leather chairs.

He could hear other struggling families in adjacent rooms, lost in their own bubbles of grief. Bright daylight coursed through the tall windows, a double rainbow intersecting the view across Laurelhurst and over Lake Washington. Some days that'd seem like an omen. He collapsed into a leather couch, eyes shut.

Then his iPhone throbbed in his jacket pocket.

That's how the feds traced us. He told me to ditch it, but I had to be the hero.

When the feds pitched up, they made the cop flinch. Made him shoot at that madman. Hit Brandon. If I hadn't lured the feds there, this would've been different.

"Chris?"

Holliday looked up at the voice. Megan. "They—"

"I know." She was standing in the doorway, hand on hip, face unreadable. She fixed a glare at a male FBI agent in a cheap suit.

Looked like half his ear was missing. "I need a word with my husband." She held the agent's gaze until he nodded and walked off. Then she came over and perched on the sofa next to him. "What happened?"

Holliday hesitated, trying to decide what the truth would do to her. Would she be on my side? Would she hate me for trying to save Brandon's life? Would she tell the FBI?

"Mr. Holliday?" The doctor appeared, wearing green scrubs. Spiky dark hair a few shades too dark to not be dyed. A long, long face, accentuated by a soul patch tucked under his bottom lip. "I'm Dr. Alex Benedict, one of the ER surgeons here." He sat on the Chesterfield opposite and smiled at Megan. "I assume you're—"

"Megan Holliday." She held out a hand, like Holliday had seen so many times before. Coquettish, like she could make any man eat out of that hand. "When can I see my son?"

"Well." Benedict dragged his top teeth over his soul patch, the beard hair rasping. "Brandon's being prepped for surgery now and, based on my initial triage, he'll be *at least* six hours, maybe more."

Megan closed her eyes and exhaled slowly. "Are you going to save him?"

"I'm not the sort of doctor to promise recovery." Benedict repeated the teeth scratching. "My initial assessment is the bullet passed through his chest, which is potentially good news. Given he's still alive that means it's missed all vital organs. We've stabilized him, but…" He rubbed his stubble. "The bad news is there's a lot of internal bleeding. Probably the—" He stopped himself. "Look. I won't promise that I will save your son, but I will promise to try everything in my power. Okay?"

"I'm hearing that a lot." Megan folded her arms and let out a deep sigh. "So I can't see him?"

"Like I said, he's being prepped for surgery." Benedict checked the clock above their heads. "And I need to get going. Ask at the nurse's reception for hourly updates, okay?" He hurried off across the foyer.

"*Reception*." Megan watched him go, then her head slumped forward. "Like this is a *hotel*."

"They charge enough."

She swung around to glare at him. "We're going to spend every last penny saving his life. Okay?"

"That's not in any doubt."

Megan leaned over and let him hold her. "I just want to see our son."

"I know, but…" Holliday blinked back the image of his son lying in the car seat, blood trickling out of his chest. Could still hear the scream. Could still feel the weight of his body as he carried him over to the car hood. Then trying to… failing to… He gasped. "Trust me, you don't want to see him. It's—"

"*No*." Megan lurched to her feet, her mouth twisted into that rictus of rage and hatred he'd seen too many times, her perfect features distorted. How someone so beautiful can turn so ugly so quickly… "This is my grief, not yours."

"Meg, I'm just—"

"Stop being a control freak!" Her shout rattled around the room. "You always have to try and make me into someone I'm not. Let me be *angry*. *My* kids have been kidnapped and someone shot *my* son!"

Holliday couldn't look at her. He slumped back in the chair and ran a hand down his face.

"What's going on in there?" She pinched his chin and tilted his face up so he couldn't do anything but look at her. "I woke up and someone had taken my babies. I tried calling you." Her lip quivered. "But you didn't answer."

The iPhone vibrated in Holliday's pocket again. He looked up at Megan, standing over him, still holding his chin. *Decision time—own up or try to play this guy at his own game.*

"Why didn't you answer the phone?"

Holliday glanced away, focusing on the still life on the wall by the door. A half-eaten pear next to a bowl of oranges. His cell stopped vibrating. "I didn't have my car and I'd sent the security away so—"

"I need you to snap out of whatever is going on inside your head. You're always the same, always pushing yourself to the limit, running on empty all the time, so when something happens there's nothing left in the tank. Someone *kidnapped* our children. Brandon is *dying* in the ER. And they've still got Avery."

"I know that, Meg. They're my kids too."

"What's going on?" She clenched her jaw. "Are you *lying* to me?"

"I swear I'm not. My car's at home because I got Secret Service to escort me in because of the protest. But I didn't need them. Said I'd get a cab home. Then I spoke to you and… I had to hail a cab. It all took time."

"*Chris.*" Megan took a long look at him, a frown twitching on her forehead. "Why were you there?"

"What?"

"The FBI agent said you were at this parking lot when… when Brandon got shot."

Holliday stared hard at her, right into her eyes. Kept his breathing level. "Meg, listen to me. Our son was shot. And I swear I don't know why." He got to his feet and smoothed down his pants. "I need to go to the bathroom."

"You're just going to leave me here?"

"I'll be back soon, okay?" Holliday pecked Megan on the forehead and walked off.

Holliday entered the bathroom and listened hard. Just the dripping faucets and a toilet tank filling in one of the stalls. He kicked the first door and it opened. Empty. Same with the second and third.

He entered the last stall and locked the door behind him, sitting and listening to the white noise of the water filling.

He held the iPhone in his hands. A missed call from a Seattle cell number, different from the one he'd called, different from the one that'd called him.

I can still go to the feds and tell them what happened. Show them this call record.

The phone rang again and Holliday hit answer without thinking.

"Hello, Senator. I told you to ditch your phone."

Holliday leaned forward, pressing his forehead against the door. "Listen to me. My son is dying because of you."

"You know I didn't shoot him, Senator. Don't you? You were there, you watched the whole thing. You know the cop shot him. He panicked when the feds arrived. And you know the feds were there because they traced your cell. This is all on you. Listen to me. I'm in charge here. Okay? If I say something, you do it. Otherwise…"

Holliday didn't have anything to say. Just clutched the phone tight.

"You know I mean business now. And you know I've still got Avery."

"What do you want?"

"You've got a choice to make. But it's not a coin toss. The odds aren't equal. Choose wrong and the feds will never find me or your daughter's body."

Holliday's mouth went dry. *Son of a bitch can't mean it.* "You won't kill her."

"Don't test me. You've seen what happens when I'm not in control of the situation." He paused, a few seconds. Holliday focused on the sound of the dripping faucets. "If you help me, I'll let your daughter go. But the factor that might tip the balance in that favor is that you were there when Brandon was shot. How do you explain that to the feds?"

Megan was already asking me. The FBI agent was going to ask. And I don't know how to explain it.

"So, Senator. You've seen what happens when I don't control the situation. Anything could happen the next time. And the next time it'll be to Avery."

He's right. There's no way I can toss the coin and hope.

"Time's up, Senator. What's it going to be? Trust the feds or work with me? Only one way your daughter lives."

Helping this asshole… But what if I go along with it, get him to the point where I can snare him and rescue Avery?

Calm rushed up from Holliday's feet, right up to his brain.

"What's it going to be?"

Someone stepped into the bathroom, the faintest sound, barely a click. But the door mechanism squeaked. Definitely someone out there.

Holliday killed the call without giving an answer.

"Senator?" A knock on the stall door. "It's Special Agent Carter. It's time we spoke."

CHAPTER FIFTEEN

Carter

Carter walked along the hospital corridor, felt like he was strolling through a high-end country club or a five-star hotel. He stopped outside the family room and listened. Silent inside. He opened the door and peered in.

Megan Holliday sat on one of a pair of duck-egg-blue sofas, head in her hands. He knew the feeling, angry and powerless in the face of severe grief.

No sign of her husband.

Carter cleared his throat and made her look up.

She sat back and ran a hand across her face, tears smudging her makeup. "They won't let me see my son."

Carter took the Chesterfield opposite. "I understand how hard this is for you, but you need to trust the professionals."

"I have no faith in experts."

"It's pretty common these days."

"Why are you talking to me instead of finding this *animal*? Do you think I'm involved?"

Carter leaned forward on the sofa. "We still don't know why your children were taken, Megan. How does your husband seem to you?"

"You mean about why was he at that parking lot?" She waited for his nod. "I asked him, but he went to the bathroom."

"Is he being evasive?"

"My husband's always evasive. Doesn't mean he's lying. But…"
She sighed, shaking her head.

Holliday's son was in the ER, fighting for his life. And he was
there when Brandon was shot. Why?

The Henry M. Jackson Federal Building to their home up
near Harrison Ridge was, what, fifteen minutes, maybe twenty
with traffic. Okay, so his car was at home, but he would've hailed
a cab or an Uber.

Instead, Holliday ended up in a parking lot in Bellevue, across
the lake from his home.

Definitely something going on here.

Carter got up with a nod. "I'll be back in a few, okay?"

Carter stopped outside the bathroom. Play it cool, let him slip
up. He eased the door open and stepped inside, keeping it quiet,
listening hard. Two of the four faucets dripped into the sinks.
Heavy breathing in stall four. Someone muttering, whether to
themselves or a hushed phone call, he couldn't tell. He padded
over and caught the shine of Holliday's shoes under the stall door.
"Senator?" He thumped the door. "It's Special Agent Carter. It's
time we spoke."

"Just a second." The toilet flushed and the door opened. Too
quickly, like he hadn't been doing anything in there other than
hiding. Holliday stood in the doorway, eyeing up Carter. Then he
sloped off to the sink and washed his hands, slowly and methodi-
cally like he was the one scrubbing up for his son's operation.
"Have you found her?"

"Not yet, sir. But I heard you talking in there."

Holliday started drying his hands with one of the clean towels
piled up behind the sinks. Not paper here, just finest Egyptian
cotton. "I talk to myself when I get stressed."

Carter leaned against the bathroom door. "That so?"

"You don't think my son getting shot might be stressful?"

"I get it, Senator, believe me I do. And you have my deepest condolences. Trouble is, I've been wondering something. Why—"

"I haven't got the time for this." Holliday's hands were in his pants pockets. "I don't know if you've noticed, but my son—"

"I've noticed. Your son was shot. I was there just after it happened. Stopped you attacking a police officer. Well, you got a good few blows in, but he's not going to press charges."

"I should think so."

"What's digging away at me is that you were there too." Carter held his gaze. "Been running through this in my head, and I can't figure it out." He got out his service smartphone and went into the maps app. "See, you were here." He pointed near Elliot Bay and all the famous Seattle landmarks. "Downtown." He traced a route northeast along East Madison, then he cut up. "This is your home here. Very nice neighborhood, near the lake, but close enough to downtown." He kept his eyes on Holliday, looking for any reaction. Nothing. He spread his fingers on the screen and zoomed out, then tapped on a location across the lake. "Trouble is, your son was shot over here. West Bellevue."

"Cut the Columbo act."

"I told you to come home, Senator. Instead, you went across the lake. Why?"

"The taxi driver didn't hear my instructions properly. I was too grief-stricken to notice."

"That so?"

"The driver was Cuban, I think. Some Latino immigrant. Don't get a lot in this state, thankfully."

Carter bristled at the casual racism. "I could believe that story, but the trouble is you happened to be at the exact spot where your son was shot."

"Listen, you little worm." Holliday towered over Carter, trying to use his bulk to intimidate. "My son is in the ER!" He jabbed a finger at the door. "They're operating on him *right now*, and you're—"

"Why were you in a parking lot in West Bellevue, Senator?"

"I—" Holliday stepped back, his rage dissipating slightly. "I was—"

"You were meeting the kidnapper, weren't you?"

Holliday leaned back against the sinks and shut his eyes. Didn't have any defense. Just played the same card as back at the parking lot. More crocodile tears.

"What did the kidnapper want from you, Senator?"

Holliday muttered, "You don't understand."

"Try me."

Holliday just shook his head. A guilty man, defeated. Owning up to his actions and their tragic cost.

"Senator, when your wife woke up, she tried calling you. You didn't answer. Why?"

"I was in a congressional hearing. You can't have cell phones going off in there."

"Don't lie to me. You were meeting the kidnapper."

Holliday just clenched his fists.

"Tell me why I shouldn't slap cuffs on you right now?"

Holliday surged forward, stopping just short of Carter. "I know the director of the FBI!"

Carter laughed in his face. "By all means, try and cover your complicity by putting my head on the block, Senator. It's not going to find your daughter, is it?"

Holliday stepped back into a combat stance, his old military training kicking in.

Carter laughed at him. "Senator, quit the macho bullshit. What did the kidnapper want from you in exchange for your children?"

Holliday was rocking back on his heels, like he was a snake coiled up and ready to strike.

"You need to talk to me. Tell the truth. Are you being blackmailed?"

Holliday lashed out, his giant fist pounding toward Carter's head. He stepped aside, caught the blow, and used Holliday's momentum to push him over, the larger man cracking on the bathroom floor.

Holliday lay there, breathing slow, shaking his head. "My daughter's... My daughter's..." His nostrils flared. "How can you understand?"

"I've got a daughter." Carter kept him on the ground. "Her name is Kirsty. She's the same age as Avery. I'd do anything for her."

"Right. But nothing's ever happened to her, has it?"

"Doesn't mean anything. Doesn't mean you get away with opening up to blackmail."

"I'll have your badge."

Carter applied more pressure. "Let me tell you a story. Instead of this job, I could've done anything else. I could've moved elsewhere and become SAC of some other field office. Boulder, Memphis, Austin. I've had offers. Could've worked in Quantico. But I didn't. I *chose* this, chose finding missing children in Seattle. My objective is finding every single child that goes missing in this city or this state. I need to find them and reunite them with their families. And every time I don't do that, it kills me. What you're going through with Brandon? The next time I sleep, all I'll think about is how I could've stopped it happening."

"But you're just doing a job. This is my *child*. Her—"

"Don't fool yourself, Senator. You're the one who could've stopped it. You could've told me you were being blackmailed, could've stopped your son getting shot."

Holliday tried to lash out with his elbow, but Carter had him.

His cell rang. He got it out with his free hand—Special Agent in Charge Karen Nguyen. Never good news.

"Are you going to answer that?"

"Depends on whether you're going to behave yourself."

"Let me up."

Carter released his grip and stepped away, eyes locked with Holliday as he stood up and dusted himself off. "Ma'am, I'm—"

"Need you to come to the family room now, Max." And she was gone.

Carter sighed as he put his phone away. "One last chance, Senator—what did he want from you in exchange for Brandon?"

Holliday pushed past Carter, heading out into the corridor.

Carter followed him out, keeping an eye on his movements.

Nguyen stood at the end of the hallway, her forehead creased as she offered kind words to Megan Holliday. Local police brass stood around, dark-navy Seattle PD uniforms weighing heavy on their shoulders.

Megan ignored them, focusing her frosty smile on her husband as he approached.

Nguyen walked over to Carter. Short, dark-haired, skin heavily lined around her eyes, the toll that years of service took. "I need a summary, Max. Now."

Holliday sloped back into the family room and sat on a sofa, wrapping an arm around his wife. She nudged herself away.

"We need to be wary of him. I believe he's met the kidnapper. He might still be in touch with him."

"That's a strong accusation, Max." Nguyen followed Carter's gaze, her eyes widening. "He's a US senator, for crying out loud."

Carter settled his focus back on her, raising his eyebrows. "That doesn't mean he's above the law."

CHAPTER SIXTEEN

Mason

Sitting on the edge of the tub, all I can do is stare at the piece of shit burner.

Holliday hung up on me. Actually hung up on me. Guy has balls, that's for sure.

And keeping his cell when we met. What was he thinking?

How do I play this now? Wait for him to call back? Or do I call him back?

Shit, this wasn't in the script. We hadn't planned for this. Abduct his kids and he's our drone, ready and willing to do what we need. Drones don't hang up on you.

A glance at my smartwatch tells me my heart rate's at one-ten. My resting is fifty-two. I need to keep it cool.

I pocket the cell and look around the small bathroom, trying to give myself some space and time to calm down.

"You look like someone who's kidnapped some children." Layla is standing in the doorway. "Put these on." She holds out some fresh clothes. A frat-boy polo shirt, salmon pink with a lime sash. A pair of chocolate chinos, like it's still the nineties.

But she's right, again. I need to change my appearance before I do anything. Whatever else happens, a kid got shot because I kidnapped him. They'll have a description out there of me. Just cutting my hair and beard isn't going to be enough. I need to become someone else.

I take off the hoodie and the plain tee in one go.

She looks me up and down as I let my jeans fall to the floor. They're covered in mud, splash marks all the way up both legs. My socks are soaked through. "Holliday came to meet you. He was there when his son was shot. He's implicated in this now. He'll comply. We still go through with this, as if there had been no distractions."

"Layla, Brandon getting shot isn't a *distraction*."

She rolls her eyes at me. "Call Holliday and set up another meet."

"Sure you shouldn't be doing the outdoors stuff?"

"You know that's your skillset. And Holliday knows you now. He'll freak out if someone else contacts him." She grabs the clippers and plugs them in above the sink. "And stop overthinking things. Our plan is still good. Have a little faith." She sets the clippers running and attacks my hair, the vibration drilling through my skull. A big tuft of orange falls into the sink.

I lock eyes with Layla in the mirror. "You're right."

Another long tuft drops to the floor, another patch of pale stubble revealed. "What were you swearing at earlier?"

"I wasn't swearing."

"I heard you."

The call. Didn't even notice myself swearing out loud. I squat to fish the burner out of the pants pocket and toss it to her. "I called Holliday. He hung up."

"What are you playing at?" She flips it open and snaps out the battery, then flushes the SIM down the toilet. "They can trace us, you idiot! Trace us here!"

"I saw it and thought—"

"Stop!" She jabs a finger in my sternum. "We're in this together. You *do not* make decisions on your own. Am I clear?"

I'm standing there in my jockey shorts, cold and wet. But she's right. She's always right. "Okay, I screwed up. No more maverick bullshit, okay? I'll run everything by you."

"Good." She hands me the pants, and I slip them on. I zip up the fly and start slipping my belt through the loops. I slip on the polo. She tugs at my collar, making it stand up like a frat boy's. "You need to get a new burner. And stop being so stupid."

The rain is back, softer than earlier. I walk past the beat-up old car for the third time and stop. A '98 Chevy Malibu, the gold paint job hiding the rust. Just about roadworthy, but super anonymous. Bought as a pair from a junkyard for cash, spared from death row. I could see in his eyes that it was touch and go deciding whether the three hundred bucks in cash was better value than chucking them both in a compactor. Saving the effort and hassle swayed him in the end, I guess.

Nobody's watching me, so I unlock it and slump low behind the wheel. Another look, mindful of SUVs swooping in, but also of just about everything else. Thirty seconds of nothing, just worrying about that stupid-ass phone call I made.

And about the matching gray Malibu, parked up near the Holliday home. The car I drove from the mall but left there. Only a matter of time before that FBI agent's goons find it and start checking the history. The paperwork's still in the wind, so neither car will trace to me or Layla without going to that junkyard and negotiating with a guy who doesn't want to negotiate. And all they'll find is an address that doesn't exist.

The front curtain in Layla's place twitches, just like the nerve in my wrist.

It's all planned out. Even the problems. We can still do this. We can still get answers.

One last look, and it's clear. I twist the key in the ignition.

*

I scan down the store's small selection of burner phones, 2002's models still on sale to drug dealers and kidnappers. And the powers that be don't do anything to stop it. Gotta love the free market.

I take the cheapest clamshell up to the counter and hand it to the guy. An old dude, wearing a Seahawks cap, old enough to have suffered the long years before that first Super Bowl. Doesn't even look at me as he scans the barcode, just waves a shaking hand in the vague direction of the TV set next to the register. "You see this, son?"

A composite photo of my face fills it.

And I panic, adrenaline starting to fizz like aspirin. The old bastard's trolling me. Saw me pull up, already called the cops.

But I realize it's my old face. Long hair, thick beard. Pretty good likeness too. That cop had it down pat. I run a hand over the stubble on my head, checking I didn't dream shaving it off. Coarse and sharp. Can't stop playing with it.

The TV cuts to a photo of Brandon and Avery, artfully zooming in on the boy's smiling face.

"Sickening, huh? Some *vermin* shot a kid. A senator's son too. Time was, people had respect for this country."

The news switches to an Asian woman in downtown Seattle, talking to camera. "Some minor controversy this morning at the congressional hearing taking place in Seattle, looking into the military exercise known as 'Operation Opal Lance.' Richard Olson, CEO of GrayBox Industries, was dismissed after pleading the fifth."

Then it cuts to inside the building, and Olson is sitting in front of an array of politicians. Rubbing his hands, grinning, smug.

I get a cold sweat from seeing the filthy degenerate. The psychopathic piece of shit doesn't care. Can't care. But I bet he sleeps like a baby, every single night.

After what I've done, I'll never sleep again. I haven't since what happened, but I know I'll never be able to shut my eyes again. The things I've done, though—I used to think nothing could ever be worth that, but now I know different.

"These rich dudes think they can get away with what they want." The dude in the cap taps the burner packet and holds out a hand. "Twenty bucks, son."

*

I get back in the Malibu and open the Wendy's box, tearing at the wrapper and biting into the burger, barely tasting it. It's just fuel. I power up my smartphone and take a second mouthful, chewing slower this time. The burner is on the passenger seat, waiting. On the smartphone, I fire up Signal and the app goes through all the usual checks and says I'm secure.

I tap on Bob Smith and our chat appears, the history long since deleted, but there's one unread message:

So?

Sent just now. I type a reply:

You've seen the news?

I saw.
Collateral damage or mission over?

You tell me.

We're still in play.
Unless you think otherwise?

I'm still going. We're still going.

Good
Did you have to kill Brandon?

It wasn't me.
A cop did it by accident.

Proof?

He stopped me.
Minor SNAFU.
I ran, he shot.
I got away clean.
We still have Avery.
What now?

He's silent, not even the icon showing him typing. I force down another bite of burger, getting most of the pickle.

What now?

I keep telling you.
Holliday is the key.
He will yield.
Be patient.
Keep the faith.

Keep the faith? Keep the FAITH? We need more than Bon Jovi songs to get through this.

Asshat clown.

I finish the burger in one angry bite, mayo and ketchup smearing my lips. I pick up the burner and make the call.

CHAPTER SEVENTEEN

Holliday

Holliday sat on the sofa in the family room, facing the hallway outside. The leather was cold against his legs.

Megan slipped out again, maybe to spill all to an FBI agent. But she knew nothing.

He glanced out into the corridor to watch her. Carter, the lead FBI agent, kept glancing at him, but he was sidelined by a stern-looking woman. *Probably his boss, enforcing the chain of command. Now they had an injured child, and they were complicit in the shooting it was ass-covering time.*

Senior police officers stood next to them, trying to look useful, black ties done up to the chin. Holliday didn't recognize any of them, certainly not the chief, and nobody from the mayor's or governor's offices. Yet. They'd be here soon enough, shaking his hand, patting his back, making promises of vengeance. And it would all come at a price—they'd look for payback the next time cuts loomed.

Carter looked over at him again, his expression darkening.

Holliday felt his iPhone thrum in his pocket again.

Less stuck between a rock and a hard place, more between an FBI agent and a madman who has your daughter. And who knows what the agent will find if he starts digging?

There was an accessible restroom down the hall from Carter, a wide oak door with a handrail. The phone gave another buzz, so Holliday got up and walked over, his heart thudding as he kept his pace even. He grabbed the handle and tried the door. It opened. He pulled it wide.

"Senator?" Carter was frowning at him. "You okay?"

"Sorry, I must've eaten something that disagrees with me. That or the stress." Holliday walked inside the room, yanked the door shut behind him, and twisted the lock. Tried it twice to make sure that fed couldn't sneak in. He sat on the toilet and got out the phone, still ringing on mute.

A puff came from the air freshening unit above him, and pretty soon he could smell the sweet perfume.

He answered the call, his hand shaking.

"Never hang up on me, Senator. Am I clear?" The guy sounded pissed.

"You don't know what—"

"Shut up. I know you want your daughter to stay alive, so I'll assume there's an innocent explanation."

"The FBI agent. He's… He's onto me."

"So, just like me, he sees smoke and starts looking for the fire, huh?"

"Tell me what you want."

"First, I need your undivided attention. I seem to have that. Second, I need your assistance. Something only you can do. Do I have your word?"

Holliday swallowed through the silence. "Is Avery still alive?"

"She's fine as long as you do what I say. No deviation, no improvisation. Am I clear?"

Holliday leaned forward, nibbling at his thumbnail. "Okay, but I won't be able to get away from the hospital for a few hours. At least."

"Your son's shooting, I get it." Sounded like he was smiling. "I sympathize, Senator. Believe me, I do. This wasn't my fault. It wasn't yours either. *You* didn't call the feds." He left a long pause. "Did you?"

"Of course I didn't."

"Then your conscience is clear, Senator. Unless you didn't ditch your cell when I told you."

"You son of a bitch!" Holliday regretted it as soon as he said it.

Another long pause. "Here's what's going to happen. We're going to meet. I'll text you the location. And you know what'll happen to Avery if you bring the feds. And I don't like waiting. Thirty minutes or she's dead." And he was gone.

Holliday held out his phone, staring into space. The stale bathroom smells were twisting his already broken guts. The air freshener could only mask so much.

The phone vibrated again, a long buzz. A text appeared on the screen, a pair of long numbers. Coordinates.

Holliday frowned. *Is he ex-military? Is that what this is about?* He plugged the numbers into Google Maps on his iPhone. It pulled up a strip mall a couple of blocks from the hospital, centering over a Starbucks open until ten, rated 4.3 out of 5.

Not far from here, but my face is all over the news. I need transport. Can I risk taking another cab?

Holliday looked at himself in the mirror and didn't like what he saw. Sweat dotted his brow, exhaustion lined his eyes. He took slow, deep breaths and used a towel to dry his forehead. Then he splashed cold water on his face. Didn't do anything, no sharp shock, no flood of adrenalin.

When we met, he flashed his lights at me, but I didn't see him. If I meet him, then I'll at least see who he is. It's got to be someone I know.

One final breath and Holliday opened the door a crack.

Carter was in the family room, sitting with his superior. Megan was opposite, sitting next to a female agent.

Holliday left the bathroom and walked the other way, acting like he owned the place.

*

As the elevator descended, Holliday gripped the rail behind him, taking deep breaths as he thought it all through. The elevator ground to a halt, rocking slightly as it settled, *and* the doors slid apart, revealing a face Holliday didn't expect to see.

Wyatt Duvall, his tanned forehead creasing as he frowned. Then a wide smile spread over those perfect teeth. "Senator?"

"Wyatt." Holliday thrust out a hand, slapping Duvall on the back as he shook it, like they'd done so many times. "What are you doing here?"

"I saw the news about your kids." Duvall went back to frowning. "You trying to tell me you don't want the state governor in your corner? Help you whip those useless FBI idiots into shape?"

"Right. I appreciate it."

"C'mere." Duvall grabbed him in a hug, tight and close. "You got this, Chris. You hear me?"

Holliday broke off and stepped away.

Duvall wrapped his arms around his Armani suit. "Anything I can do to help?"

"The FBI are running the show." Holliday swallowed hard, sucking down the bitter taste of making a decision. "Megan's upstairs."

A frown twitched on Duvall's forehead. "You going somewhere?"

"Need some fresh air."

"No reporters out there yet, Chris." Duvall patted him on the arm and gave a tight smile. "Who've the feds sent?"

"Nguyen, I think?"

"She's admin. Who's lead? Carter?"

"Right."

"Ignore what I said. They're good people, Chris. They'll find your girl."

Holliday felt his bottom lip go. "I don't know to do, Wyatt."
Head upstairs. Tell the FBI. Give them the whole truth.

"Stay strong, Chris. For Megan. For yourself. And for your kids."

"That's good advice, Wyatt. I appreciate it." Holliday patted Duvall's arm with a smile. "I'll see you up there in a few."

"You want company?"

"I need to be alone."

"Sure. I get that." Duvall nodded like he understood everything Holliday was going through. "See you up there." And he stepped into the lift.

Holliday set off through the foyer, keeping his head low as he passed two agents talking on their cell phones. Didn't recognize either of them. He pushed the revolving door and stepped out into the cold air. He dumped his iPhone in the trash and walked off.

CHAPTER EIGHTEEN

Carter

Carter sat down on the sofa. "The description the cop gave is out there. Should've been all over the news half an hour ago."

SAC Karen Nguyen didn't look very hopeful, her shoulders slumping. She clung to the settee's arms like it was a life raft. "You think we'll get anything from it, Max?"

Carter thought it through, but couldn't find anything to help with her buoyancy. "Probably not. We're dealing with an organized individual or individuals. One step ahead of us so far. Maybe he got lucky at that parking lot, but..." He felt the sofa tighten underneath him. "Holliday was there when Brandon got shot. It's possible he's involved in this. Might be—"

"Careful what you're saying, Max." Nguyen arched her eyebrow, her pupils shifting to the corridor. Outside, the chief of police was grilling his direct reports, their voices low in that way that meant jobs were on the line. "Him and Holliday go back a long way."

"So I should just back off because of some old boys' club?"

"Get over it." She inched closer, her instinct for gossip overcoming her political machinations. "You seriously think Holliday kidnapped his own children?"

"I've been doing this a long time. So have you. Nothing should surprise you." Carter decided to play her at her own game, so he leaned in, all conspiratorial. "But I think blackmail is the likely explanation. Only one kid in the car. Doesn't that seem like they're holding Avery back, letting him wonder when the other shoe will drop?"

Nguyen blew air up her face. "Okay, so what do you propose we do?"

"I want to stick him in a room, grill him, find—"

"*Max.*" She punched the sofa's arm, struggling to keep her voice low. "His son's in the ER. How will that look?"

"Brandon was probably shot because of Holliday's actions."

Nguyen laughed, emotionless and empty. "You're a cold fish, Max, you really are."

Carter thought it took one to know one. "Karen, I'm trying to do an impossible job to the best of my abilities. His son's fighting for his life, sure, but his daughter's still out there, and her life is in the hands of these people."

Nguyen got up and paced around the room, exhaling slowly. "Okay." Looked like she'd bitten into a lemon. "Interview him. But I want to be present."

"Thank you, Karen. That's all I asked."

"But if you step over the line, that's it. Am I clear?"

"Crystal clear." Carter walked back out into the corridor.

Duvall, the state governor, was chatting to the SPD chief, wearing full uniform, more chains than a medieval mayor, more badges than a four-star general. They gave Carter the once-over, then went back to their chicanery.

Carter's cell rang. He took it out and scanned the screen. Speaking of can't be trusted… Against his better judgement, he answered the call. "Bill, this isn't a good time."

"It's always a bad time with you, you sniveling little shit." And he was drunk. His voice always reverted to that London drawl when he was loaded, like he was traveling back through time to before all that happened. "You never want to help your old man! Never let me even see my lovely litt—"

"Never call again, Bill."

"Oh yeah? You and whose—"

"I'll block your number."

"You wouldn't dare."

"If you try and speak to Kirsty again, then I'm calling the cops. Do I need to remind you of the protection order?"

That cut through the noise. Sounded like Bill took a drink, the ice clinking in his highball glass. "Son, I need your help."

Again. Always the same story with him, always trying to leverage Carter's better side. And it was always the same, just Bill wanting to control things, like he always did.

"Goodbye." Carter stabbed the End Call button. He pressed the little "i" icon next to the call record and it took him to the contact for Bill Carter, his location pinned to a few miles down the freeway in Redmond. Carter rolled the screen down to the bottom, and his finger hovered over "Block this Caller". He pressed it and got a warning message. He didn't read it and hit "Block Contact". He locked the cell and put it away, sucking in a deep breath to re-center himself.

Elisha was still sitting with Megan, both sipping from cardboard cups, locked in silence.

No sign of Holliday.

Elisha clocked Carter. She patted Megan's arm and left her, meeting Carter with a nod. "What's up?"

"Where's Holliday?"

Elisha frowned. "I saw him go to the bathroom."

"That was earlier." Then it hit Carter—he'd gone to the accessible restroom. With a sigh, he walked over to the door, as calmly as he could given the eyes on him, and tried it. Locked.

Wrong. Holliday was in there, after all. Just Carter's brain seeing conspiracies everywhere he looked.

He knocked and spoke at the door: "Senator, I need a word when you're done."

The door rattled open. An elderly man leaned on a cane, scowling. Big guy, but he'd lost a lot of weight. Wearing a plaid shirt, but a lumberjack rather than a grunger.

"Sorry, sir. I thought Senator Holliday was in there."

"That prick? Haven't seen my son-in-law since I got here. Should be helping my daughter, if you ask me."

Carter pulled out his cell phone and started dialing.

Carter raced out the front door into the ambulance bays and the parking lot. The Children's Hospital was more like a high-end Marriott, but with EMERGENCY in huge red letters above both doors. Farther away, it was all trees and grass, bisected by a busy highway.

Carter looked both ways. No sign of Holliday.

Elisha was clutching her cell to her head. Her eyes widened, then she opened her laptop. "Max, Holliday left the hospital twenty minutes ago."

Carter shut his eyes. "Where has he gone?"

"Tyler's pulling the surveillance footage." Elisha swiveled her laptop around.

The screen showed where they were, the gray revolving doors rattling as Holliday sloped through, head low, passing a crying mother hauling two children toward the hospital. The video ran at quadruple speed and Holliday jerked over to the road.

The screen changed to a long tree-lined avenue. At the right, a red sign hung above a low building, WELLS FARGO in yellow. Holliday made for it, skipping behind a Ford Ranger as he crossed the road. A yellow cab sat in the bank's parking lot, the engine idling. Holliday flagged it down, getting a flash of lights. He got in and it rolled off. The video stayed on that frozen image, cars whizzing past.

Carter grabbed Elisha's cell. "Peterson, can you follow the cab?"

"I'll try, sir." Tyler's voice rattled out of the speaker, sibilant and warped. "I'm pulling out all the stops just to get that footage."

Carter walked over to the street. He could see the Wells Fargo from here, the sign glowing through the rain. "Holliday is meeting the kidnapper, isn't he?"

Elisha joined him, folding her laptop shut, her cell clamped between ear and shoulder. "Blackmail? Why him? What can he get them? What on earth could justify kidnapping both of his kids?"

Carter didn't have an answer for her. "Tyler, can you get a trace on Holliday's cell? Also, start going through his cell records." He paused, long enough to clock the anger in Elisha's eyes. He spoke in an undertone: "Are you blaming yourself?"

"Don't you? We were here with him, and he just walked out."

"This isn't on you, Elisha. It happened on my watch."

"Even so." Sighing, she passed her laptop to Carter.

"Got it." Tyler hissed down the line. "Calls and texts. iPhone XS, by the looks of it. Oh, here we go. Network ping says he's right by the entrance?"

Carter raced over, scanning every face, but Holliday wasn't there. Two male patients sucked on cigarettes. Three schoolkids skipped through the front door.

Then a groan as his realization hit.

He darted over to the trash. Sitting on top, a white-and-silver iPhone. He tugged on some gloves and fished it out. "We'll never unlock this thing."

Elisha bagged it for him. "Not never, just not in the timeframe we need."

Carter held up her phone. "Tyler, you still there? He's trashed it."

"Right, sir. Okay, I've got something. Fifteen minutes after the abduction, Holliday got a text and a photo message from a burner phone." Frantic clacking of a keyboard clattered out of the speaker. "I'm sending it to Elisha's screen."

She grabbed her laptop back and pulled up the photo. Brandon and Avery sleeping in a minivan, this morning's Seattle times sitting between them.

"There's a text, says 'Big Al's truck stop off I90. Be there by noon or they die.'"

Carter checked it, and it was just where he thought it was. Google Maps said it was permanently closed. Not too far from the parking lot in Bellevue where Brandon was shot. But whatever happened, receiving texts from his children's abductor proved that Holliday was being blackmailed. "Peterson, do whatever you can to get me his current location, okay?"

Back upstairs, Megan Holliday was at the nurses' station, eyes closed. "I just want to know how my son is doing."

"Dr. Benedict is still in surgery, ma'am." The nurse gave a hollow smile. "I'll come and find you as soon as I hear anything, I promise."

Megan looked like she was going to press it further, but she trained her glare on Carter, her rage simmering away behind her eyes. "Have you found Avery?"

He gave a slight shake of the head. "I need to ask you a few questions."

"Now?" She clenched her jaw. "Can't you ask my husband?"

"That's kind of the issue." Carter beckoned her away from the station, leading her toward their family room.

Megan stayed standing, arms crossed. "What's going on?"

Carter nudged the door shut behind him. "Just after the abduction, your husband received this message." He showed her the laptop screen and the photo. "We also believe he intended to meet the kidnapper around the time of the shooting."

Megan slumped on the couch, eyes shut. "Idiot."

"You didn't know?"

"My husband always has secrets." Megan opened her eyes again, the full force of the fury back. "It's the nature of being a politician. You always need angles on people. Chris is always playing games, trying to leverage any slight advantage on his opponents and enemies."

"I believe your husband is being blackmailed. Has he talked to you about it?"

"You think I'm involved?" She snarled out a laugh. "Of course I'm not. But trusting you got my son shot. I should never have called 911 in the first place. I should've just sat it out. Brandon would still be okay."

"Mrs. Holliday, that wasn't—"

"I know." Megan held up a hand. "Let me be upset, will you?" She let out a deep breath. "Believe me, Chris never mentioned this to me. I would've come to you if he had."

"Can you think of anywhere your husband could go?"

Megan sat there, rubbing her forehead for a few seconds. "I can't think of anywhere here." She ran her tongue over her lips. "Washington DC is his playground, not Washington state. I know of a hundred restaurants, bars, and private members' clubs he'd go to in DC. But nothing here."

Carter's phone rang. Tyler Peterson's cell number.

Carter smiled at Megan. "I need to take this." He slipped her a business card. "Give me a call if you need anything, day or night. Okay?"

She took it without a second look, without a word.

Carter walked out into the corridor and took the call. "What's up?"

"Sir, I'm going through Holliday's records." Sounded like Tyler was somewhere he shouldn't be, somewhere he wouldn't be overheard. But he heard him double. Tyler was in the corridor, waving at Carter, cradling his phone. They both killed their calls, and Tyler walked over. "This isn't exactly aboveboard. I had to pull a few favors with a buddy."

"The ends justify the means, Peterson. What have you got?"

"Holliday got a call from a burner thirty minutes ago."

Carter checked his watch. That explained when Holliday was in the accessible bathroom. "Give me the number."

"What?"

"I'm going to speak to this guy. Try to reason with him." He got Tyler to type it on his cell. "Need you to run a trace on that number, okay?"

"Sir." Tyler hunched down, back against the wall, laptop resting on his knees. "Just a second."

Carter waited for a nod.

Tyler looked up and gave it.

Carter hit dial and put the cell to his ear, listened to it ringing and ringing.

It was answered. Quiet at the other end, like the guy was inside. Slow breathing, steady and unemotional. No words, though.

"I know you're there." Carter kept his focus on Tyler, laser-like precision. "And I know you've got Avery."

No response, but his breathing was slightly faster. Meaning Carter was getting to him. So some response, some reaction.

"If you return her, I promise I'll make sure it's okay."

Faster breathing, then a snort through the nose. Dulled car sounds, meaning he was out somewhere. Possibly a mall, possibly just a street.

"I know you didn't kill Brandon."

"Kill?"

Got you. American accent. Seattle, at a push, based on one word.

"It wasn't you. It was an accident. Give me Avery, and we can do a deal. You'll walk free."

Much faster breathing now. He didn't think he'd crossed a line, but now he knows he has. A dead child on his conscience, even though Brandon was still fighting for his life.

"Listen to me, my priority is Avery's safety. You give me that, and I'll give you whatever you need." Carter paused, letting the words sink in. "What do you want?"

"I didn't kill him." Click, and he was gone.

Carter ended the call and stared hard at Tyler. "Well?"

He twisted his lips together. "I've got a general location for him. Two cell sites we can triangulate."

"That's not great, but it's a start."

"Sorry, sir." The laptop pinged, and Tyler frowned at the screen. "But I've just got a trace on the taxi Holliday got in." He looked up. "It's heading toward the cell locations."

CHAPTER NINETEEN

Holliday

Holliday got in the back of the cab and slumped in the seat, watching the mall parking lot drift by. Heavy lunchtime traffic, office drones out with their families on the weekend, liberated for two days. *Lunchtime? Is that all?* He kept looking behind for anyone following.

The cab driver kept looking in the rearview, focusing on Holliday like he couldn't place him. Big black dude with patchy hair, clumps of gray, chunks of baldness. "You got to be there at a specific time, sir?"

"Don't worry about it."

"Some kind of meeting?"

"That's right."

The driver signaled left and waited for a bus to pass. "Man, I wish I had to meet people instead of taking them from place to place."

Holliday gave a noncommittal grunt. He reached into his jacket pocket and took out the plastic packaging. That clear stuff that was almost welded shut, that you needed scissors to open. He got a way in near the cut-out for hanging the product, soon slicing the plastic at the back right down to the bottom, a curved cut, but good enough to get the knife out. Walmart's finest, sharp and small, but deep enough to kill with. He dropped the packaging onto the floor and kicked it under the driver's seat. He grasped the knife upside down, hiding the blade in his sleeve.

"Here we go." The driver cruised over to yet another mall, smaller than the one they'd just left. "Anywhere in particular, sir?"

Holliday looked around and spotted the Starbucks. "Here's good, thanks." He handed the guy a twenty with his left hand, keeping the knife in his right. "Keep the change."

The driver gave a heartfelt nod as he folded the crisp note. "Thank you, sir."

Holliday got out into the drizzle and marched over to the Starbucks. Every single eye was trained on him, or so it felt. *Right out in the open here, the one place where everybody knew his face.* He stood in the doorway and looked inside the coffee shop, the metal warm in his hand now.

Nobody he recognized, just thirty or so unfriendly faces all glaring at him, hating him for what he had let happen to his son. Wondering why he was out and about. Wondering why they voted for a loser who couldn't save his own son's life, and who cowered while some cop shot his boy, who wasn't even in the hospital with him. Who let them take his daughter too.

Holliday turned back to the parking lot, but a tight grip on his shoulder stopped him.

"Come on, Senator." That voice. Sounded deeper in person. "Let's walk."

Holliday didn't look around. His mouth was dry. He tightened his grip on the knife.

Stab him now, take him down, gut him and get him to say where Avery is.

An arm reached out, a long tattoo running up the arm, a gloved hand pointing over to the parking lot. "See the Malibu?"

Holliday scanned the nearby cars. An old beat-up Chevy, burnt orange or nicotine yellow. Fifteen yards away. "I see it."

"Get in the driver's side. Keys are in the ignition."

Holliday started walking, but his legs were like jelly. He stopped by the car to grab the hood for support. Almost dropped the knife.

"Come on, Senator." Anger in the voice. Standing right behind Holliday.

No gun at my back now, just the threat of my daughter's life.

He slowly turned around, then flicked the knife in his hand and lashed out with the blade.

Didn't even get a look at the guy's face. He blocked the wild slash, cracking Holliday's hand against the car door. The knife clattered and rolled under the car. The hair at the back of Holliday's head burned, and his head slammed against the glass.

Holliday stumbled to his knees, tiny stars prickling his vision. A boot to the side, and he fell flat.

"Don't even think about doing that again." The door opened and Holliday was pulled up to standing, then shoved in the driver's seat. He sat there, struggling to breathe. Smelled like cheap burgers and twenty years of cigarettes. The keys rattled in the ignition as he shifted his leg over.

The passenger door opened and a man got in, closing it behind him. Nice and quiet. His features were too small for his face. Acne scars covered his cheeks. Dressed smart, a salmon-pink polo underneath a gray jacket. Shaved head, and the skin on his cleft chin was smooth, but the guy had the kind of red stubble that even a shave couldn't fully remove. The sort of face you'd remember.

And Holliday didn't.

I thought I'd see some freak from a town hall who kept ranting about his guns and the federal government and forming militias.

But it's some random I've never seen.

"That was very stupid, Senator. Don't think about attacking me again, okay? Have you ditched your cell?"

"It's in the trash at the hospital. You can frisk me if you like."

So he did. Sitting down. His hands chopping Holliday's legs and arms and back.

"What's going on here? What do you want from me?"

"I want you to drive."

"What. Do. You. Want?"

"I've told you, Senator. I need your help. If you don't want to help me, well that's your choice. You'll never see your kid again, and the feds will start digging into why you've run away from your dying son to hook up with me."

Holliday felt a raw ache deep in his gut. "What do I call you?"

"What do you want to call me, Senator?"

"Dead?"

"Cute. If you want to call me something, call me Mason."

"Is that your name?"

"It's good enough." Mason tapped the dashboard with a revolver. "Drive."

"No."

Mason laughed. "You saw what I can do to you. You think you've got a say in this?"

"You really going to shoot me in a busy parking lot?"

"Don't doubt I will." Mason pressed the gun to Holliday's side. "I'll shoot you and your daughter will die. You won't even know that she's dead, but you'll die here knowing there's nothing you can do to save her."

I can't do this, I can't do this, I can't do this, I can't do this.

Holliday pushed his teeth together until it hurt. Then chanced another look at the madman. Still didn't recognize him. "You'd honestly kill a young girl?"

"Don't test us."

Us?

Of course he's not acting alone. Someone else had Avery when he tried to drop off Brandon. Meaning an accomplice who still has her.

"What was the plan?" Holliday tried to clear his throat, but it was too dry. "You had Brandon in the car. Were you going to take him with us?"

"No, Senator. I was going to drop him outside a police precinct. Or put him in a cab. You'd know he was safe."

"Show me that Avery's okay."

Mason sighed. "Okay." He got out a smartphone, then tapped some buttons. Within seconds, the screen was filled with a shot of Avery lying on a bed.

Holliday gasped.

Mason spoke into the phone, "Wave."

A light-brown hand appeared in front of Avery. *Hard to fake, especially in real time.*

Mason put the smartphone away. "So, Senator, what's it to be?"

Holliday focused on him. "Before we do anything, I want to know what this is all about."

Mason thought it through for a few seconds. "Just drive."

"No!"

Mason looked pissed, slamming his head back into the headrest. *He expects the FBI to show up at any point.* "Chris, you don't want to mess with me. If you're a good boy, then your daughter lives. But if you cross me, she dies. It's that simple."

Holliday gave him a long hard look, but it didn't make any difference. "How do I know you'll let Avery go?"

"You have my word. What happened to your boy was tragic and I wish I could change it, but I can't. But I've got your daughter and if you want to see her again, you'll play nice." Mason pulled the gun away from Holliday's side. "Now, are you going to play nice?"

CHAPTER TWENTY

Carter

Carter gripped tight as the SUV hurtled through the thick traffic. The sun beat down, a brief window in the deluge. He hugged his service laptop to his knees and followed a security feed on the screen. "Peterson, I can't see him!"

"He was there, sir." Tyler's voice boomed in Carter's earpiece. "Outside the Starbucks."

"Got it."

On the laptop screen, Holliday stood outside, looking inside the coffee shop.

Carter braced himself as Elisha took a fast corner into the strip mall parking lot. When he looked back at the screen, he'd lost Holliday. One second he was there, and then he wasn't.

Forget it, focus on the here and now.

Elisha pulled up and Carter hopped out, leaving his laptop on the seat.

The SWAT team swooped into position, securing the Starbucks and the parking lot. Patrons stood around, open-mouthed.

Carter scanned their faces. No sign of Holliday. No sign of the kidnapper either. He raced over to the store and looked in. Place was quiet, none of the customers a match for either. He stomped back outside and scanned the parking lot. "Peterson, speak to me."

"Sir, I've—" Tyler gasped. "He got in a Chevrolet Malibu."

"Which space?"

"Right where you're standing, sir."

Carter looked over at a surveillance camera. He looked around the parking lot, but there was no sign of any Malibus. "They're gone?"

"Drove off like a minute before you got there."

Meaning they'd been sitting there for ten minutes.

What were they talking about?

And where were they now?

CHAPTER TWENTY-ONE

Mason

Another check of the sideview mirror, and we're still not being followed.

I look over at Holliday and try to figure out the calculations going on behind his eyes as he drives. He's agreed to come with me, knowing what's at stake, but shit, I can't trust the guy. Turn my back on him for a second, and it'll be my life against Avery's.

We're speeding down a long diagonal cut into Seattle's grid system, trees and cars lining the slowly climbing road, covering the sort of condo block you'd see anywhere across this great nation. On the right, a basement Chinese laundry takes in a fresh van-load. Then past a Shell on the left and through another intersection, the stop lights green.

Holliday looks at me, briefly locking eyes, not paying attention to the road. I hope he's not like that when he's shouting at Megan for some bullshit reason, and he's got his kids in back. "Where are we going?"

I settle down in the seat, still hiding, as Holliday eases the Malibu around a corner. "You tell me."

He looks over at me again, his jaw set. "We're heading downtown. That where you want me to go?"

"Well done, Senator, you know your city."

Holliday looks back at the road, frowning. "Just tell me where you want me to go."

I suck in a breath, the pain resurfacing from the deep as I watch the traffic, lost to the hurt swelling in my chest. "Take us to the Federal Building."

Holliday tightens his grip on the wheel. "I was there this morning. You could've—" He shuts his eyes as he accelerates, up and over the brow of the road. "The protests, right?"

"Correct."

"You picked today because of them?" He whizzes downhill past a deli. "The FBI will mostly be co-opted to that, meaning you've got a clearer run?"

"You're good, Senator. Right now, they're fighting their way over to the Washington Convention Center. It's over a mile away."

He thinks it through, long and hard, then blows air up his face as we pass a low-grade bar, almost in downtown. "Okay." He takes a right, and we head down another long street.

Down the slope, the Federal Building sits a couple of blocks away, one of many skyscrapers springing up out of the ground. The streets are empty, just the trail of garbage a protest leaves behind, no matter how right-on the protestors are. You can see the Sound from here, Bainbridge Island over the water, the ferry trundling back.

Holliday pulls up by a bus shelter and kills the engine, blowing air up his face again. "I can get us in there. What do you want when we're inside?"

I sit there for a few seconds, thinking it all through. Then I realize there's nothing else to gain from holding back. "I need some information about Operation Opal Lance. About the exercise at Tang Elementary."

Holliday's gripping the steering wheel. "You kidnapped my kids for *this*? It's got nothing to do with me! My boy is *dying* because you want some information on a military operation?"

"You know I didn't want that to happen, right? It wasn't in the plan."

"But you want information in exchange for my kids' lives?"

"And you know what'll happen to Avery if I don't get it." I look around. "I don't need to explain what Opal Lance was to you of all people."

"Are you going to sell information to the Russians or the Chinese?"

"No, Senator. Guess again."

"Because if my son is dying because of some spy-versus-spy spook bullshit..." He gasps. "Are you working for Olson? Rooting around for GrayBox, trying to get juice on what Delgado has on them? Is that it? If you are, I'll kill you both with my bare hands."

"You think I'm working for that piece of shit?" I can only laugh. But Holliday shuts up. Maybe he can see in my eyes that I mean it. "I hate the guy, Senator. Get real."

"Why do you think I can help?"

"Because you're involved in the congressional investigation, aren't you?"

"I'm not." Holliday swallows hard. "This is nothing to do with me!"

"Don't lie to me, Senator. You fought for that exercise. Put a bill through the Senate."

"I was just trying to secure my state!" Holliday sits there, trying to figure out his options.

"Chris, it's simple—you either help me, or I kill Avery. That's it."

Holliday tries to swallow, but his throat is tight. "Look, whatever you want to know, I can't get you it. You need to speak to Xander Delgado, not me. Why didn't you just ask him?"

"Don't you think we've tried? Do you think people like you listen to people like me unless I hold a gun to your head? You listen to donors and lobbyists and your corrupt peers, cooking up deals. But if you can't afford to donate or pay a lobbyist, bad luck. Democracy's not for you. Right?"

"My son is in the ER because of this bullshit?"

"Chris, deal with it. Get me information on what happened, and Avery walks free. So do you." I grab his wrist and press my thumb into the bone right in the middle, making him yelp like a dog. "Listen to me. You need to believe in yourself. Have a little faith." I let go of the wrist. "Now what's it going to be?"

Like I'm giving him a choice.

Holliday points at the handgun. "You can't take that inside."

"Good point." I lick my lips as I stow it away in the glovebox. "I've still got my cell phone. Any shit from you and my friends will kill Avery. Then I'll kill you."

"Believe me, I know." Holliday gives me a slow nod as he opens the driver door like a good boy. "What do you want to find out?"

"There was an exercise in Seattle on October second, last year. At Tang Elementary. I need to know exactly what happened there."

CHAPTER TWENTY-TWO

Then

Faraj

How do I get out of here?

Faraj was covered in sweat, matting his hair, soaking into his thin jumpsuit. Still in darkness, still locked in place. It'd been days. Maybe even weeks. He'd lost count.

Then he heard something. A dull thud. His cage cracked open, bright light blinding him again. He tried opening his eyes, but they stung, a deep throb all over his eyes. He blinked it away and took in the room. A different place than before.

They've moved me and I didn't even notice.

A face appeared in front of him. The other soldier, the one that didn't stutter. "You're awake, then?" He opened the door wide and grabbed Faraj's harness, pulling him out like he was leading a dog on its leash. "Come on, son." He took him over to a table with two chairs. A brown paper bag sat on top, crumpled but full of something. Smelled like fries. "You like a burger?"

"My mom says I—"

"Halal, right?" The soldier snarled, baring yellowing teeth at him. "Relax, kid. This is halal meat. Only kind I can get here." He sat Faraj down on a chair, then secured his harness in place. "Dig in."

Faraj had just enough energy to tear at the bag. A pink-and-white wrapper covered a brown bun, the darker meat covered in cheese and ketchup, a pickle sticking out like a tongue. He bit into it all and chewed slowly. *Can't remember the last time I ate.* "How long—"

"Two weeks, kid." The soldier sat across from him, leaning back, arms folded. "Almost to the second."

Faraj took another hungry bite, swallowing it down without chewing. He felt it stick in his throat but took another, chewing this time.

"Your daddy's dead."

Faraj stopped chewing. The burger dropped onto the table, spilling some lettuce onto the shiny wood.

"You've got to understand, your father was a bad man. He did a lot of bad things and he needed to be punished for that. Do you understand?"

Faraj shut his eyes, hard, until they hurt because he was squeezing them together. "Can I go home now?"

"To your mom?"

Faraj gave the slightest nod. *This man is a bully. Daddy told me to not give them the satisfaction of seeing my pain.* "I just want to see her. I won't tell anyone."

"See, I could do that." The soldier reached over to the bag and took a fry from the yellow container, then ate it in two goes. "But my problem is that you represent a problem, Faraj. People like you, sons of martyrs, they have a habit of trying to kill us. We're the good guys, but you think we're the villains."

"You killed my dad! And you're keeping me here!"

"See?" Another couple of fries, chewed together. "You think I'm a bad guy."

"I won't tell anyone."

"And I just take your word for it?"

"I swear!"

"And I wish I believed you, kid, really I do. Wish I could." He took a handful of fries but kept them in his hand, like Wolverine's claws in the X-Men, one between each finger. "But I've got two choices here." He ate the first fry. "One, I let you go." Then the second fry. "Two, I keep you here forever. Son of a known terrorist, a war criminal who murdered two American GIs. Easy." Then he frowned before eating the final fry. "Shit, there is a third option."

Faraj was struggling to control his breathing. Sweat trickled down his back again, a fresh wave of it. "What is it?"

"I kill you right now." The soldier looked around the room, smiling. "Makes it a whole lot cleaner for me."

Faraj stood up as much as the harness would let him.

"You don't look too well, kid." Another handful of fries, a worse grin. "Maybe I've already killed you? Maybe there was poison in that burger? Maybe we just sit here and wait for you to die?"

Faraj lashed out, the harness clanking as he swung his arms.

But the soldier caught his hand and squeezed. "Relax, kid. I'm messing with you. I know exactly what's going to happen to you." Another smile. "Now, eat your burger."

CHAPTER TWENTY-THREE

Now

Carter

Carter walked through the Starbucks, through the wall of customers speaking to agents. "Peterson, I need you to follow that Chevy ASAP."

"I'm on it, sir. It's taking time." And Tyler was gone.

The SWAT were already standing down, their number joined by some Seattle Field Office agents.

Carter walked over to the Starbucks. Looked inside, just like Holliday had moments before.

Elisha was talking to an elderly man in a checked shirt wearing a red MAGA baseball cap. "Thank you, sir." She left the man with a suited agent and headed Carter off by the cash register. "That guy saw Holliday here. Says he voted for him, shook his hand at a rally. You get the drill. Wondered what the senator was doing in this part of town. He spotted someone go up to him, looked like he stuck a gun in his back."

"So he thinks Holliday was abducted?"

"Sounds like it. Tallies with what Tyler got from the surveillance footage. He snuck around the back, making sure he wasn't spotted."

Carter wanted to punch something. "We almost had them."

"One step ahead of us, huh?"

Carter set off toward the SUV. "We're getting close, though. And we now know for sure that Holliday's in contact with the kidnapper. I just want to know why, Elisha. Holliday's only been a senator a couple years. He doesn't have any power, not yet anyway. He's a junior member of a committee. Only reason he'd work with the man who'd abducted his kids is he's either in on it, or he's being blackmailed."

"If what that guy back there says is true, then it's looking like abduction."

"But he slipped out of the hospital to meet this guy. Why?"

Carter's cell blasted out. He answered it on speaker. "Go ahead."

Tyler, announcing his presence with a moan. "Sir, Holliday's just swiped into the Federal Building downtown."

What was Holliday up to?

CHAPTER TWENTY-FOUR

Mason

Holliday leads me through the building's foyer. Very grand. The kinda place the good senator is most at home.

And Layla's choice of clothing is perfect for it, my preppy look matching a few guys standing around. A sign points to the congressional investigation in the main auditorium. Place is empty, though. A busted flush from that news story.

He walks toward the security guard, swinging his ID badge. "You know that me using my ID is dangerous, right? They'll be searching for me." He stops in the middle of the floor, clenching his jaw. "The *FBI* are looking for me."

"Which means you've got to make sure we get our answers quickly, Senator."

Holliday gave him the side eye. "Of course, you're trapped in here. I could let them catch you, let them interrogate you."

"If this goes south, Avery dies. Besides, I know you want to avoid the feds, Senator. What dirty, dark secrets are you hiding? You know if any of this gets out it'll end your career, don't you?"

He knows.

Holliday wipes some sweat from his forehead and walks over to the guard's post, casually, like this is normal and he isn't being threatened.

The guard looks up, so obese the only thing he's catching is type 2 diabetes. "Senator."

Holliday hands his badge over, and the guard checks it. Then he hands it back and looks at me. "Need to see some ID, sir."

Holliday coughs. "John Mason is, uh, my new assistant."

The guard gives me a once-over, taking so long that I think he's on to me, mentally altering the composite photo the cops issued, subtracting hair and beard to get what I look like now. He reaches down for something, and I've got my cell phone in my hand, ready to call Layla and tell her to get out of there, let her decide whether to kill Avery or not. I figure I can get out front before any of the guards catch me. They're not the FBI, they're not the cops.

But he slides a clipboard over the marble. "Sign here, sir."

My breathing slows as Holliday starts filling it in. I even get a nice little badge:

MR. JOHN MASON, PERSONAL ASSISTANT

Holliday swipes his ID through an office door and the lights flicker on. A big windowless room, piles of boxes on either side. That stale smell of old paper. "This is where the investigation is happening. Much cheaper in Seattle than DC." He goes over to a desk in the middle and pulls out a three-ring binder. "What was the date?"

"October second."

He flicks through the pages, slowly.

Is he playing me? Buying time before the guards appear? Even if they're all donut-munchers, I'm still stuck inside this building. Ten swipes of his ID to get this deep into the building. Be at least half of that to get out.

I should've stayed outside, waiting for him, trusting him on a long leash. But I can't trust him. Even though I've got his daughter's life hanging over his head, he's the kind of dog who's liable to turn at any moment.

I need to get out of here, and fast.

But we need that information.

"If I don't check in by the hour—" I raise my cell, high enough that he can see it. "Then Avery dies. Okay?"

Holliday looks over at the clock, and his eyes bulge. "I can't work that fast! I don't know what I'm looking for!"

"If you get somewhere, then I'll call in and extend the time. Just don't think you can stall me and let the FBI save her. Okay?"

He shakes his head as he starts shuffling through the file again. Guy has a sweat problem. It's dripping on the floor, soaking into the carpet. He tears at the binder. "I can't—"

Something behind us clicks. The card reader switches from red to green. The door opens.

"Chris?" Xander J. Delgado stands there, the congressman leading the investigation, his thin fingers wrapped around a paper coffee cup, his platinum wedding band catching the light. I voted for this guy. Looks like his suit's wearing him, hanging off his runner's frame. "Chris, what are you doing here?"

And this is what heading south looks like.

Holliday drops the binder. "I need something."

"And you didn't think to ask?" Delgado frowns at him. "Isn't your kid in the hospital?"

"You know me, Xander. I can't focus on that. I need to distract myself, and my new assistant here isn't cutting it."

I scan the room, looking for options. The boxes might work as a weapon, if they were heavy enough, but it's too slow, too far away. There's a mail system by the window, with a brass letter opener lying on the "In" tray.

Bingo.

I take a step toward it.

Delgado shuffles over to Holliday. Still hasn't looked at me. And to think I voted for him. "Dude, Megan needs you right now."

"Megan *never* needs me." Holliday's head hangs low like he actually means it.

Delgado takes a sip of coffee and looks at me for the first time, then back at Holliday. "Oh?"

"She's not coping with this very well. Pushing me away, trying to deal with it on her own, like she does with everything. I can't sit around in a hospital, so I've come here."

"Doing what?"

Holliday huffs out a sigh. "I lost Mandy. She's working for that schmuck Duvall."

"Tough break."

"And then Duvall calls me, says he needs something like yesterday. And you know what he's like about stacking up favors like he's playing Texas hold 'em?" Holliday waves over at me. "I'd ask John here, but he's new and…"

Delgado tilts his head at me. "This your new boy Friday?" He holds out a hand to me. "Xander Delgado."

I shake it. Guy's got a tight grip. "John Mason. A pleasure, sir. I voted for you."

"Then the pleasure's all mine." Delgado took a slug of coffee, grimacing like it was fine whiskey. "So what's Duvall looking for?"

"He, ah, asked John some questions." Holliday picked up the binder again. "John called me up and I thought so what, you know? Something about an exercise in Seattle on October second, last year, at some school."

"Tang Elementary."

Delgado looks at me, his eyes narrowing, but he doesn't say anything.

Holliday holds up the binder. "Thing is, I can't find anything on it. Any chance you could—"

"This isn't your investigation, Chris." Delgado sets his coffee down. "You can't just bring people in here."

"He's on the level." Holliday wipes a hand across his brow. He's thinking on his feet, improvising, but he's good at it. Covering lies with lies, building a house of cards that's all glued together, one that'll stand strong. "John's good people. After Duvall hired Mandy, I needed a new assistant, and he's helping with some work here in my home state. You know there's always blowback on senators from an investigation of this size."

Delgado doesn't seem to relax, instead finishing his coffee and crumpling the cup. "Chris, I should call Duvall right now, get him in here."

"Be my guest."

Delgado takes another long look at me, tilting his head to the side. "What explicitly was Duvall asking for?"

I give him a smile. "He said a woman has been calling up his office, asking him to investigate the exercise at Tang Elementary on that date. Kept talking about GrayBox."

"Seriously?" Delgado's nostrils flare wide. "Chris, I sent you a summary of our work to date last Tuesday. I told you that we raided a ton of stuff from GrayBox." He looks at me, eyes narrow. "Next thing I know, you're turning up with this douchebag?" He trains his glare back on Holliday. "Chris, is he working for GrayBox?"

"What? Of course not." Holliday tosses the binder on the desk. "He's on the level, Xander. I picked him personally. Vetted by two private detectives. He's just here to help me with admin."

I take a couple of steps closer to Holliday, and crucially toward the letter opener.

Delgado doesn't seem to notice me as he settles back against a wall of boxes. He folds his arms then shrugs. "Chris, you're a piece of work, you know that?"

"Just help me and we'll be out of your hair."

"Fine." Delgado picks up a box and thumps it down on the desk. "The problem is, whatever Duvall's looking for, it all checks out. Far as I can tell, GrayBox ran an exercise at that school on that date, under the cover of Operation Opal Lance." He tore the lid off the box. "Hence me asking Richard Olson at the congressional hearing this morning."

I hold his gaze, the first time he'll let me since I shook his hand. "What did he say?"

"That was the only question that douchebag answered, other than his name and occupation." Delgado laughs. "Olson said he can't comment on the grounds of commercial confidentiality."

"That's bullshit."

"Quite the expert, huh?" Delgado picks up the binder and flicks through, then takes a file out of the box and blows the dust off. "There was an exercise at the school on that date. GrayBox operatives supported US Army soldiers to evacuate the school. Supposed to be preparation for the event of an invasion." He reaches in and gets out some more files, tossing them onto the desk. "These are witness statements from businesses and residences near the school. Ten people saw soldiers enter the main building. Minutes later, they started bringing the kids out, all organized. Then they start involving our witnesses, closing their stores and securing them too."

I realize I haven't been breathing. "What about the sports hall?"

Delgado sneers at me. "What do you know about that?"

"Did anyone go in there?"

"Chris, what is he talking about?"

Holliday gives him a shrug. "It's what Duvall is looking for."

Delgado shakes his head again. "That douchebag should've come to me."

"It's not how he likes to run things, you know that." Holliday gives him a broad smile, impressive given the stress he's going through. "But the way you're talking about it, it's like something happened and you know what."

"It's probably nothing, but we've got two witnesses who saw three soldiers running across the football field, said they entered the sports building." Delgado licks his finger and eases it through the file. "Strangest thing, though—they later recanted their testimony." He sifts through a box and gets out a page. "These weren't US military operatives, Chris." He held up a wad of black-and-white photos, circling the armbands on some masked soldiers in combat fatigues. "They were GrayBox."

Holy shit.

My fingers are actually tingling.

All along, I'd focused on the hunt, the mystery, and ignored the emotion, dulled it down until I couldn't feel any more. I never stopped to think what knowing I was on to something would feel like.

We're on the right track. Our first answer.

"Have you got—"

A siren blares out, accompanied by a robotic voice: "This is a security announcement. The building is on lockdown. Please stay where you are and remain calm until further notice."

I snatch up the letter opener and grab Delgado, pointing the blade at his throat. "Get us out of here. Now."

CHAPTER TWENTY-FIVE

Holliday

"Keep ahead of me, Senator. Hands where I can see them." Mason still had a knife on Delgado, sticking into his suit jacket as they walked close together. "That's a good boy."

Treating me like a dog.

Holliday walked slowly, adrenalin pumping, carrying a box file, full of the evidence they needed. *That* Mason *needed. Whatever his name actually was. He* stopped by a locked door, still no decision made either way.

Delgado swiped through a reader, then glanced at Holliday as he put his ID away, sheer terror in his eyes. *Holliday had brought him into this world, and he couldn't process it. He had no skin in the game he's been forced to play by this lunatic.*

Join the club.

Mason gestured for Holliday to open the door. "Come on."

Holliday stayed standing. "Don't you need to check in?" His mouth was drier than in the Iraqi desert. "You need to tell your accomplice that it's okay… so they don't kill Avery."

Mason smiled at him. "I texted them. It's all good."

Holliday stepped into the dark garage, full of oil smells. The silent alarm was on, lights flashing, their footsteps echoing.

"My car." Delgado pointed at a silver Lexus parked against the far wall.

"Okay, Xander. Here's what's going to happen." Mason pressed the knife back against Delgado's throat. The madman's face was blank, like he was a robot going through steps of his programming. *He's not getting any pleasure or satisfaction out of our misery. Maybe he is telling the truth.* "You're going to give your keys to the senator here. Then you're going to get in the passenger side and we're going to drive off. If we don't get out of here, then I'm going to slice your throat open. Using a letter opener will be excruciating, but be under no illusions that it won't do the job. Are we good?"

Delgado just nodded as he held out his keys, the Lexus logo catching the flashing lights.

"Chris, I know you're cool with this." Mason tossed over the keys.

Holliday caught them. *Not that I've got any choice.* He pressed the unlock button and the lights flashed. He stowed the box file on the floor behind the driver's seat then got in front.

The passenger door opened, and Delgado sat next to Holliday. "What on earth is going on, Chris?"

Before Holliday could answer, the back door opened and Mason's face appeared in the rearview, eyes darting around, surveilling the space. "Drive."

Holliday thumbed the ignition and stuck it in reverse. He arced around, the engine whirring, then slid it into drive and took it slowly, but not suspiciously so.

Mason switched the blade to Holliday's throat. "You know where you're going, Senator?"

"Been here a few times. It's just up and out." Holliday swallowed, feeling the cold metal touch his skin. "There'll be a guard. At least one."

"I'll deal with him if and when."

Holliday turned onto the up ramp, a spiral curving left.

Delgado looked over at him. "Sure this isn't for your friend Richard's benefit?"

In the rearview, Mason's eyes focused hard on Holliday. "You know Richard Olson?"

"He's a campaign donor." Holliday's voice sounded fake, thin and high-pitched, like even he didn't believe it. "My campaign manager handled it all. I have no idea how much he's given." He cleared the ramp and navigated the car down a lane, bare concrete on both sides. Ahead, the security barrier was down.

"Play it cool." Mason took the blade away from Holliday's throat and sat back, out of sight of the rearview. "You know the cost."

Holliday stopped by the barrier and rolled down his window.

The guard was tall, and built too. H. LINSKEY was stitched on his pocket. "Sir, the building's on lockdown. Orders from the Federal Bureau of Investigation." He snarled, like he'd just been forced to swear. "Can't let anyone out."

Think fast.

"I need to get to the hospital. My son's been shot."

Linskey frowned at them. "These are orders from the FBI, sir, I can't just—"

"Didn't you *hear* me? My son's been shot! I need to be with him!"

Linskey nodded. "Lemme call it in." He trudged over to his little cave and picked up a phone handset.

Holliday caught a glimpse of Mason, crouched outside the car. He turned around—the back seat was empty. *Didn't even notice him getting out.*

Delgado grabbed Holliday's sleeve. "What on earth is going on?"

"I haven't got a choice, Xander. That madman kidnapped Avery. He was there when Brandon got shot."

"I didn't know." Delgado's anger twisted into confusion, then he slumped against the seat back and shut his eyes. "Are you okay?"

"Oh I'm just peachy, Chris. Just *peachy.*"

Linskey reappeared. In a flash, Mason wrapped his arms around the guard's head, one over his throat, the other clasping his forehead. Linskey's arms windmilled for a few seconds, then slowed, then stopped. Mason slowly rested him down on the floor. He'd put the guard to sleep in seconds.

Holliday grabbed Delgado's arm. "Do you recognize him?"

Delgado took a fresh look then shrugged. "I don't, but he's kinda distinctive. Those scars look painful. And that tattoo? You think he's a marine?"

Mason was over by the barrier, bending down to grab Linskey's pistol, stuffing it in his chinos as he stood. Sure had the posture of a marine. He reached over to the guard's station and the gate opened, then he waved them through.

Holliday put the car back in drive and rolled through the barrier, stopping the other side.

The back door thumped shut and the gun kissed Holliday's neck. "Go."

He pulled off and drove out up to street level.

To the left, a squadron of FBI SUVs hurtled toward them, lights flashing, sirens wailing.

CHAPTER TWENTY-SIX

Carter

Elisha slowed to a halt outside the Federal Building, almost invisible through the heavy rain, the other Suburbans pulling in behind them. The street traffic was light, just a car zooming off to get through a gap behind a bus.

Carter hopped onto the soaked pavement before the car fully stopped. He could barely hear anything above the blaring sirens, so he reached in to hit the button on the dash and cut most of the noise. He made his way up the steps.

A big black guy in uniform stood by the entrance, enough stripes on his arm to be their guy, the security chief. His badge read Richardson. "You Carter?"

With a nod, he showed his shield. "You got Holliday?"

Richardson glanced at Elisha as she joined them. "Not yet." His left eye twitched. "Come with me." He led inside, their feet squeaking off the mirrorlike marble. "My guys are searching the entire building. Room by room. We've followed his security credentials through the building. We're hunting him down now."

"I need to see the footage of him arriving."

"Them." Richardson stopped in the building's foyer, a domed-ceilinged room with multiple exits. A security desk sat over by the elevators, multiple signs still set up for the morning's congressional hearing. Something twinkled and sparked in his eyes. "The senator wasn't alone."

Carter tried to unkink it. The captor was still here, and he was with Holliday. Why? Why come inside here of all places? He just left it coiled up. "Okay, show me the breadcrumb trail Holliday took through the building."

Richardson led them down a long corridor. An open door showed a guard searching a maintenance closet. Next door, a pair of photocopiers. Richardson checked his tablet again and pointed to a door at the end. "He went in here last."

Carter got out his handgun and aimed at the door. He gave Elisha the nod.

She stepped on the other side of the door, her own pistol locked and loaded.

Carter turned to Richardson. "Open it quick and get out of the way."

"Reminds me of my cop days." Richardson swiped a security badge through the reader and nudged the door with a foot.

Carter kept his gun trained on the door, listening hard.

Silence, other than just Richardson's gut rumbling.

Carter stepped forward, covered by Elisha, and looked around the room.

Small, filled with as many desks as would fit. Piles of boxes covered the walls, halfway up the high windows. The heating was on a deep roast, enough to make anyone sweat.

And empty.

Carter holstered his pistol and let himself breathe. "Whose office is this?"

Richardson jangled the keys on his belt. "A load of desk jockeys working that congressional hearing."

Carter couldn't figure out why someone would abduct a senator's children to get at a congressional hearing's back room. He squeezed past Richardson as his radio crackled. "This is *definitely* the last place he swiped into?"

Richardson frowned at his tablet. "Ah, man." He frantically tapped at the screen. "It's click-button exits all the way back. You don't need to swipe."

"So the breadcrumb trail ends here?"

"Got it."

Carter scanned the room again and drew a blank. "Can you get me the security feeds on your tablet?"

Richardson shook his head. "Need to come back to the office for that."

Carter followed Richardson across the foyer again, thinking it all through. And getting nowhere.

"Penny for them." Elisha was walking in step with him.

"Trying to figure out what Holliday's playing at. And I just keep coming up blank. All we know is he's escaped from the hospital, then helped the kidnapper get in this building, then led him to that room."

"We know he's met up with him."

"True." Carter looked around the foyer. "Why, though? I'm stuck. We need to know what the captor's trying to achieve." He focused on Elisha. "Can you work your magic and get me an update?"

"You're such a charmer." She walked off.

Carter followed Richardson's trail, trying to tease out any more kinks from the puzzle, but he couldn't get anything new.

The small security office was filled with screens and black-boxed equipment in racks. Richardson sat at the desk, using a jockey wheel to wind through footage like a DJ scratching a record.

Carter perched on a chair next to him. "Have you got anything?"

"Nothing after the alarm." Richardson grimaced. "But I've got the senator entering."

On one of the bigger screens, Holliday marched across the foyer, up to the security desk, where he showed his credentials to the guard. A man stood next to Holliday, tall, but a few inches shorter than the senator. Must be the kidnapper, but he didn't match the appearance they'd recorded from that beat cop. Stubble on his head and clean shave, contrasting with a beard and long hair. Had that look of a marine, though. All tense muscle and precise analysis of his surroundings. A few seconds of chat, and it looked like Holliday signed him in.

"Pause it." Carter leaned forward. "Focus on that guy."

Richardson shuttled back the video feed, settling on Holliday's companion as he turned toward the camera.

Nondescript features, at least on the low-grade image quality. Preppy clothes, though the grayscale footage meant the polo could be anything from ice-blue to Day-Glo pink. If it was the same guy, he had changed his appearance, meaning he was keeping track of the investigation.

"Here's the security log from out front." Richardson showed Carter a clipboard, a landscape-oriented grid half-filled with handwritten names, companies, times, and signatures. "As far as I can tell, that dude's name is John Mason."

"Probably an alias, but you never know."

Richardson's radio crackled, and he stepped outside. "Better take this."

Carter pulled out his cell and searched for John Mason. Hundreds of results in the Seattle metropolitan area. Thousands in Washington state. Add in Oregon, Montana, Idaho, and British Columbia… He put his phone away. Felt like a long shot, would take millions of man hours, all based on an assumption.

Elisha came back. "Got you an update, but basically there isn't one. Sorry."

Carter nodded at the monitor. "Think that's enough to run through facial recognition?"

"Maybe. Tyler's got some image-enhancement algorithms that might help."

"Do it." Carter focused on the face, doubting any computer wizardry could resolve those blurry pixels into a child abductor's face.

Footsteps rattled over the marble toward them. Richardson, holding up his radio. "One of my guys is unconscious in the garage!"

Carter trailed behind Richardson as they raced through the upper garage floor. A whole team of security guards stood around the barrier, a couple of them helping up a colleague.

"Outta the way!" Richardson hauled his guys apart.

Carter squirmed through to the middle of the mêlée.

A guard blinked hard, dizzy on his feet, supported by two colleagues. No obvious signs of injury. His badge read H. Linskey. "I'm okay. I'm okay!"

Carter tried to get eye contact, but Linskey looked like one of those guys who felt shame at being attacked, instead of anger. "What happened?"

"Guy grabbed me." Linskey wrapped his hands around his own throat. "Then he put me in a sleeper hold. That's the last thing I remember until I blacked out."

"Did you see him?"

"Got me from behind. Didn't see his face."

"Before that, what happened?"

Linskey blinked hard a few times. "A Lexus pulled up." He gestured to the barrier, frowning. "Senator Holliday was driving. He was with Congressman Delgado."

Carter felt another knot tighten around the puzzle. "You're sure?"

"Holliday said his kid was in the hospital and he needed to get there. I said I couldn't let him out, but the dude was insistent. I went to check and… Last thing I remember, man." Linskey patted his holster. "Shit, he took my gun!"

Carter shut his eyes. Everything flashed with pain and rage. He pushed it all back down, trying to keep focus. He took Richardson aside. "I asked for a full lockdown. How has this happened?"

"You heard the dude. Like to see you try fighting off a sleeper hold."

Carter got out his cell and dialed Elisha. "Can you pull the footage of the attack?"

"Sure." Her hand muffled the mic. "Tyler's getting it now." She gasped. "Holy shit, the guy was brutal. Just took him down. Ten seconds and he was asleep. Precise, like he's been trained. Looks military to me."

Carter nodded slowly. "Figures."

"Max, the good news is we've got a better shot than when they entered. Got a full-frontal of his face. Tyler's running it through facial recognition now. This might be our big break."

"Good." Carter thought it through. A bruised security guard taken out non-lethally. Holliday playing along, no doubt trying to get his daughter back. And they took Delgado with them. "Elisha, get a trace on Delgado's phone and a BOLO on his plates."

CHAPTER TWENTY-SEVEN

Mason

I'm in the back seat as Holliday drives us along I90 over the Murrow bridge, rain peppering the lake surface like machine-gun fire. Another look out back and we're still clear—no sirens, no flashing lights.

I allow myself a deep breath. We're in the clear, for now. So close, though. Way too close.

I put the gun against Holliday's neck, though he really doesn't need any more threat. Just a reminder. "Where are you driving to?"

"I…" He breaks off with a sigh. Flying blind.

I thought he'd be stronger than this, but he's dangerously close to snapping.

The file box is on the floor next to me, stuffed behind the seats. Nowhere near a smoking gun, yet, but it's the start of our process, proof that we're on the right track. Proof that vermin like Olson and his GrayBox empire treat us all like cattle. They're the key. Whoever did this, they're inside GrayBox.

Having a senator and a congressman to use as pawns makes it way easier to get answers.

"Will you let her go now?"

I press the gun against the back of Holliday's skull. "This file isn't enough."

"Come on. They'll hang me out to dry for this." Holliday's eyes are wild. "I helped you get in there, then helped you break out. Just let her go!"

"Senator, this isn't over until I say it is, okay?"

"What happened at that school?"

I keep quiet. Try not to show anything to him. Guy like that, he'll look to exploit anything.

"It's Olson, isn't it?"

I look around at Delgado and shake my head. "Who?"

"Richard Olson. This is about GrayBox. You're working for him, aren't you?" His head slumps forward. "I asked Olson about it on the stand this morning, but that douchebag pleaded the fifth, didn't he?"

"How well do you know him?"

Delgado twists around to look at me. "Have to say, it's mighty suspicious that Senator Holliday here is looking for information on some exercise when his friend Olson takes the stand to deny his company's involvement." He clearly figures playing himself off against Holliday is the best tactic.

And he's not wrong. I switch the gun to Holliday, digging into his skin. "Are you friends with Olson?"

"No!"

"Come on, Senator. Don't lie."

Holliday lets go of the wheel. The car swerves, but he quickly regains control. "We're members of the same country club, that's it. Play a round of golf every month."

"Back there, you said he just donated to your campaigns, Senator. Now you're golfing buddies?"

"He's given to Xander too."

I switch the gun back to Delgado's head and pull him back into the leather seat with my free hand. "That true?"

"I'm investigating him!"

"Cut the crap."

"He gave my campaign a hundred grand."

"And what did he want for that?"

"I swear, he's asked for nothing."

"Yet…" Holliday rubs his throat, keeping his eyes on the road. "Olson likes to stack up favors. He asked me to pressure Governor Duvall to approve their new HQ in Redmond. That's it."

Like a pair of schoolkids, arguing over whose dad is the best. Distracting me with their noise and bullshit.

"What have you found out about the incident at that school?"

Delgado clenches his jaw. "Tell me you're not working for Olson."

"You really want to test me right now? With a gun pointing at your head?"

Delgado looks me right in the eye. "Tell me you're not working for him."

I put the blunt point of the letter opener against his Adam's apple. "In case you're thinking that I won't shoot you in this car, this will do a lot of damage. Understood?"

"Absolutely." His voice is twisted by the blade and the fear.

Holliday drives on. The freeway hits Mercer Island, farther away from downtown Seattle, but is it any closer to where we need to go?

"I am not working for him. And I want to speak to him." I pull back the knife but keep the gun against Delgado's head. "Which of you two is going to speak to Richard Olson about the exercise?"

Holliday looks over at Delgado, pleading for ideas, for knowledge, for leads. He gets nothing. So he holds out his hand. "Xander, just call him."

"What? I'm not doing that. Who do you think—"

"Stop!" I press the gun against Delgado's temple. Much as I like them playing off against each other, keeping them on their toes, it's not helping me get what I want. "You really don't want to push me here."

Delgado unlocks his cell and hits the screen a couple times.

Holliday looks over again, taking his eyes off the road for a few seconds, looking back and correcting our course.

A dial tone bursts from the dash speakers, the center display reading:

MR. JOHN MASON, PERSONAL ASSISTANT

So Delgado does know him.

Maybe Holliday's been right all along and Delgado's the one I should've taken.

Stop thinking like that, jackass. You've been over this. Delgado's divorced, no kids. No leverage points. Soon as I turn my back, he'll run.

This is the right plan. Keep it going.

"Good afternoon, how can I help you?" Olson's PA has a sparkly voice, but with enough steel to suggest you shouldn't try anything.

Delgado shuts his eyes. "I need to speak to Mr. Olson."

"One second, Xander."

Shows you everything that's wrong with our great country in three words. A member of Congress, a representative of the people of his ward, speaks so frequently with the CEO of a defense contractor that his PA recognizes his voice. Even uses his first name. Someone who's supposed to be investigating Olson's company.

"Xander!" Olson sounds like he's smiling. "You calling to apologize for this morning?"

Holliday motions for Delgado to speak, but he clams up. So Holliday clears his throat. "Richard, it's Chris."

"My, my, I *am* honored. Chris, I was thinking of you on Sunday as I shot three under at Inglewood."

"This isn't about golf."

"I heard about your kids, Chris. I'm so, so sorry. Forgive me. Force of habit." Olson doesn't sound bothered or sympathetic.

"I need your help, Richard."

Olson pauses. Then laughs again. "How much do you need?"

"I don't want money." A bead of sweat drips down Holliday's cheek. "I need to know about Tang Elementary."

"You punk." Olson's sigh huffs out of the speaker. "Meet me at the usual spot, ten minutes. I won't wait long." And he's gone.

I make eye contact with Holliday in the rearview. "You have a usual spot?"

Holliday looks over at Delgado then takes the exit ramp. "Why didn't you speak to him?"

"This is your mess, Chris." Delgado glances at me, at the gun pressed against Holliday's brain stem. "So what's the deal with this meeting spot?"

"Don't be an asshole." Holliday hasn't got a clear tell, but he's hiding something. "You know what it's like, Xander. You take campaign money from a guy, he asks favors. You don't want to show up at his office or his home, in case anyone spots you and puts two and two together." Onto another freeway, expensive homes sprawling on the left in amongst the trees. In the distance, you can make out the Redmond tech campuses, with Microsoft and GrayBox competing for supremacy.

I press the gun harder against Holliday's neck. "You said the only dealing you had with Olson was about his HQ?"

"It's the truth." Holliday shakes his head, but he can't brush the gun off. It sticks to him like the truth. "That's what we met about. Duvall was pushing back against it, made me beg. Knew exactly what he was doing. And Olson wasn't happy. Asshole."

Delgado sneers at him. "The price you pay for taking dirty money, Chris."

Holliday glares at him. "And it's not dirty when *you* take it?"

Delgado twists around to look at me, still trying to score points. "I've no—"

"Why's Olson in your contacts? Why does his PA recognize your voice?"

"Because of this investigation. I tried the nice way first, tried talking to Richard like a human being. But he didn't play ball. I had to get the FBI to raid his office."

"And yet he still answers the phone for you." Holliday takes a turning for a nature reserve. The road switches back around under the freeway, then we head away from civilization. Nobody around, not even some soccer moms walking their pooches before their little darlings come home from their private schools. Place seems familiar, like I came here in a past life.

Holliday pulls in at a tiny parking lot off to the right. Half-logs separate four empty spaces of bare mud and patchy grass. He takes the farthest one, leaving the engine running. "Well, here we are."

"Stay here, Chris." I open the door and put a foot on the wet mud. "I'll be in the woods, listening in, okay?" I switch the gun to point at Delgado. "This will be aimed right at your skull." I show the cell phone. "And one call on this and Avery dies."

CHAPTER TWENTY-EIGHT

Holliday

Holliday gripped the wheel tight, his rearview angled back down the lane, so he could watch for an approaching Mercedes.

Delgado looked over, his eyes burning. "Chris, you can't think you've got any right to be angry at what's going on here."

Holliday slumped back in his seat. "He has my daughter, Xander. Brandon might *die*."

"This is because of what you've been cooking up with Olson, isn't it?"

"There's nothing, I swear." Holliday tried to make eye contact, tried to make him believe it. "Answer me this—has my name come up in your investigation?"

"I couldn't tell you if it had."

"Come on, Xander. Our *lives* are at risk here. If you've got anything on me, I need to know."

"Why?"

"Because…" Holliday waved at the woods, in Mason's general direction. "If there's some bullshit you have on me and he doesn't like the sound of it, then he can—"

"There's nothing." Delgado sighed. "As far as that investigation goes, you're clean. Happy?"

"Hard to be happy in this situation." Holliday felt a rumble through the seat. He checked the rearview—sure enough, a white

Merc trundled down the lane toward them, belching out diesel like the world wasn't ending. It pulled up, leaving a space gap between.

Holliday grabbed Delgado's arm. "Play it cool, here. Okay?"

"I'm doing this for your daughter and your wife, Chris. Not you." Delgado got out and wrapped Olson in a friendly hug.

How deep does their friendship go?

Holliday got out of the car into the thin rain and circled around the back. He offered his hand and got a shake, the same clammy one as at the Fed Building that morning. "Richard."

But Olson wrapped him in a bearhug, patting him down for guns and a wire. "What's going on, Chris?" he whispered in his ear. "Delgado putting you up to this?"

Holliday broke free. "No, Richard. I'm desperate here." He glanced into the woods and caught a flash, the thin sunlight bouncing off Mason's gun. "Whoever took my kids still has Avery."

Olson brushed down his suit. "And what does this have to do with me or my company?"

"The guy who has her wants me to find out stuff about an exercise at Tang Elementary School, October second last year." Holliday nodded at Delgado. "Xander's shown me the files, so I know everything he does."

Olson stood there, quaking, like a giant bear ready to lash out with a roar.

"Richard, I need your help." Even Holliday could hear the fear in his voice.

Olson started opening the door. "Chris, this is the last time we're ever going to speak."

Holliday grabbed his arm, stopped him getting in the car. "Richard, this guy has Avery. He's going to kill her." A tear slid down his cheek. "You know what happened to my boy."

"This guy shot him?"

Holliday looked into the woods again, instinctively. He couldn't see any sign of Mason. "Yes."

"Chris, what have you gotten yourself into?"

"I just need your help."

Olson raised his eyebrows at Delgado. "What are you doing here?"

"I'm helping Chris find his kid. That's it."

"Pretty sure that's the FBI's job." Olson narrowed his eyes. "Sure the two of you aren't here to dish dirt on me?"

"Not the time or the place, Richard. I'm helping a friend."

Olson stared hard at Delgado. *He doesn't believe any of this.* "Okay, I'll bite." He shut the door and leaned back against his car, arms folded. "What do you want to know?"

"Just what happened at that school. That's all. Then we'll be on our way."

"Okay, officially, there was an exercise. US Army ran it, we supported. Went according to plan. That's the story I'd give in court."

"But?"

"But, after Delgado hauled me over the coals this morning, I thought no smoke without fire, huh?" A furious sigh. "So I dug deep. The files Xander here got his hands on weren't the complete story."

Delgado swallowed hard. "You were supposed to give us *everything*."

"Don't you worry your pretty little head, Xander. I found some interesting stuff, but there's nothing on the books, like I say. If you know where to look, there are payments. And I found out who originated them, and I hauled them over burning-hot coals."

"Who?"

"Chris, if this is really important to you, to finding your daughter, then you need to speak to Harry Youngblood. My former head of strategic operations. You know him very well."

"Former?"

"On gardening leave as of two o'clock today." Olson knocked on the driver door. "And he won't be coming back." He opened his car door and got in. Seconds later, his driver was roaring back up the country lane.

Holliday scanned the trees, searching for movement or a flash of light, getting nothing.

Does it mean Mason's on to something? Olson finds some dirty payments at his company. Do they relate to that operation?

Delgado tugged at Holliday's sleeve. "Let's get out of here."

"No."

"Come on, man. He's gone. We can—"

A revolver clicked behind Holliday, metal pressed into his neck. "Stay right there."

CHAPTER TWENTY-NINE

Mason

I step around them, keeping the gun trained on Holliday. The air tastes clean here. Just the sound of the distant freeway and a bubbling river. No voices, no calls. "Get over by the car."

Like a good dog, Holliday bounds around the front of the car and joins the congressman. I heard every word Olson said, but something's spooked Holliday.

Which part, though?

Was it just Olson's presence? Face-to-face with the big man, the campaign financier. Or were there secrets neither was letting on about with Delgado listening in?

Or was it Harry Youngblood? The name doesn't mean anything to me. Sounds like a Native American. But it sounds like he's a GrayBox exec, or at least was. And it sounds like he's up to his neck in this. Whatever they planned, whatever they did, sure seems like he was behind it.

"Who's going to tell me about Harry Youngblood?"

They stand there, looking at each other, daring the other one to spill.

"One of you. Now."

Delgado looks around. "Shouldn't we do this in the car?"

"No. We're doing it here in the rain. Who is Harry Youngblood?"

Holliday's eyes give away the fact that he doesn't know. He'd make a shitty poker player. A tightening around his jaw, like when Tom Cruise tries to show emotion in every movie. Probably where he got it from, thinking that's what real men do.

Then Delgado's cell phone rings.

I snatch it off him and toss it deep into the woods.

Rookie mistake. I need to get out of here. They'll be on to us, tracking his cell.

Two of them doubles the risk, at least.

But something hits me from behind, cracks into my skull. I sink to my knees, the muddy rain splashing up my legs. A boot in my back and I stumble forward, landing face down in it. And the gun skids away from me.

Holliday stands over me, wielding a tree branch like a club. "Now!"

Delgado's frozen, eyes wide. Then he gets the gun.

I try rolling over, but Holliday smashes the club into my hip, spearing me and sending me flat on the ground again.

"Give me it!" Holliday reaches out a hand for the revolver, and Delgado tosses it to him. He catches it and points it right at me. "Okay, you're going to take me to my daughter."

I get up to my knees and raise my hands. "Okay." Then nice and slowly, I stand up, the rain already starting to wash the mud off. "Just keep it calm, Chris, and it'll all be okay."

"How is it okay?" He's in a rage, stomping across to me, aiming the gun at my head. "My boy's in the hospital!"

I wait, breathing slow, keeping my focus. "We'll take you to her, okay?" The gun barrel is three inches from my head, ready to fire. I only get one shot at this. I look to my right. "What's that?"

It works. I kick into gear, grab the barrel and push it away, clenching my fist at the same time. Then I lash out and crack him in the cheek. I bring my other hand around and grab the gun off him, stepping back. Tables turned again. "I warned you about doing that, Senator."

His eyes are wild with panic and confusion. "Oh shit, oh shit, oh shit."

I reach into my pocket and get out my cell. "That's it. You've really done it now." I type in the number.

"Wait!" Delgado has his hands raised. "I know Harry. He's a good guy. Worked at GrayBox for a few."

"Is he in your files?"

"All over them. Every page. Signs everything off. Whatever happened at that school, Harry Youngblood knew about it." Delgado inspects his cuff links, acting like he's not at gunpoint. "The FBI interrogated him as part of our document-gathering exercise." He raises his eyebrows like he expects a pat on the head. "They let him go without charge."

"You think he's clean?"

"Hard to tell. But, I will say this. The very next day, he's on my doorstep. Said he's fighting for his career, trying to find out what I know. Olson wasn't happy with him. Wants to know what I'm likely to spring on Olson at the congressional hearing. Of course, this is months back. We searched the files, didn't find any smoking guns." His gaze settles on the handgun, still pointing at Holliday. "But I embarrassed his boss in public, made Olson look like he doesn't know what's going on at his own company. Sounds like Harry lost the fight today."

I switch the gun to point at Delgado now. "What do you think he's hidden from Olson?"

"Could be anything. Cash, bribes, fraud. Anything." Delgado shrugs. "But Olson's hung Youngblood out to dry here. He doesn't want any backlash against GrayBox, so he's containing it, blaming it all on Harry. He runs strategic operations, meaning that he was in overall charge of the exercise there. Meaning his head was on the block for what went down that day. Gardening leave means Olson's already chopped the guy's head off on that block."

I try to think it through, but there's no decision to make here. "Can you get me to Youngblood?"

Delgado nods, hands still raised. "I can."

So I shift the gun back to Holliday. "Okay, Senator. Thanks for all your help, but you've stopped being useful."

CHAPTER THIRTY

Layla

Here I am, sitting in the knock-off La-Z-Boy I should've sent to Goodwill a long time ago, when he left. But I couldn't part with it. I swear I can still smell him on it. Maybe it's just his aftershave and shampoo.

The small TV set plays the cable news, the anchor covering what they're calling "Sen. Holliday's Kids". "We're hearing reports that the Henry M. Jackson Federal Building in downtown Seattle is on lockdown in what sources describe as a matter relating to the abduction of Senator Christopher Holliday's children. Remember, the whereabouts of the senator are at this moment unknown. More on this breaking story after these messages." It cuts to yet another ad break, that actor from that show talking to the camera like he's suffered a workplace injury and should've got life insurance.

My heart's racing now. I check my cell, but I've got no missed calls from Mason. Signal is still an empty chat with Bob Smith, the same with Bob and Mason. Always delete the history. Always. I send them both a message:

What's going on at Fed Building?

I watch for a read notification as the ads play, but nothing happens. Mason and Bob Smith are both offline. So I flick it up a channel just as they cut back in from their ads.

Their anchor is a woman with blonde hair and a red blazer, her shoulder pads like something from the eighties. "It's believed that Senator Christopher Holliday was inside the Henry M. Jackson Federal Building, resulting in the building being placed on lockdown. Federal agents and local law enforcement refuse to comment, but eyewitnesses told our reporters on the ground that—"

"MOM?"

Her voice chills me, coming from the back, from the room that's been silent too long.

"MOMMY?"

I rush through and ease the door open.

Avery is lying on the bed, can barely open her eyes. But they're open and staring right at me. "Mommy?"

"It's okay, sweetie. Your mom had to rush out, so I'm helping you. Okay?"

"Okay." She shuts her eyes. So trusting at that age. Too trusting. "Who are you?"

"I'm Luisa, honey." I perch on the edge of the bed and stroke her back. "Me and your mom used to work together. We go way back."

"'Kay." She shifts in the bed, facing away from me. "I don't feel so good."

"Do you need something for your tummy?"

"It's my head."

"I've got something for that." I slip out back into the hallway, then into the bathroom. Mason's left the syringe out for me next to the faucet, locked and loaded. Ready. I hold it up to the light.

He's clearly on to something. They wouldn't lock the building down if he wasn't. We're so close to getting our answers, and all I need to do is keep Avery under lock and key.

Like that's all it is. Injecting an innocent child with a drug that'll knock her out. What have I become?

I take a deep breath and step back into the hallway.

The glass around the door mists like there's someone there. Moving around.

No, no, no.

A knock on the door, loud and insistent.

What do I do here?

I grab my cell and call Mason, but he doesn't pick up.

Another knock, louder, closer together.

What do I do? Inject Avery now? But they could see me from the road.

Actually, what would Mason do? Play it cool. Act like nothing weird's going on here.

Okay.

I put the syringe in the medicine cabinet. "Coming!" I walk over and open the door, keeping it on the latch.

A cop stands there in his uniform, thumbs tucked into his vest.

An FBI agent too, dark suit, shades, navy windbreaker. He steps forward, as close as he can get without coming inside, and holds up a photo of Avery. "Have you seen this girl, ma'am?"

CHAPTER THIRTY-ONE

Holliday

Birds tweeted nearby and a river flowed in the distance, full of Seattle rain, almost drowning out the freeway drone. Almost drowning out Holliday's frantic heartbeat. He focused on the gun in Mason's hand. Searing pain in his wrists from when Mason disarmed him. Happened in a flash. "Please, no!"

Delgado stood between them, his face twisted in panic.

"You've served your usefulness. Thanks." Mason pulled out a pair of handcuffs, the bracelets open. Must have taken them from the guard when he got the gun. "But I don't want them finding you until this is all over."

And it hit Holliday like a bullet.

I've given my life and career for this madman. Brandon's dying because of him. Just so that vermin could push me out of the way and take Delgado instead.

"He's talking bullshit. I know Youngblood better than Xander. I can—"

"No." Mason held out the cuffs. "Put these on. Now."

Holliday hung his head low. "Please, just let Avery go."

"You're not following me, Senator. She'll be freed, but only once this is over."

Something like relief hit Holliday, the tightness in his chest slipping away. But the tightness gripped again, around his heart like a vise.

Mason waved the pistol into the woods. "Now, I can't have you calling the cops or the feds until this is all over. We're going to find you a tree, a sturdy one, and I'm going to cuff you to it."

"You can't trust Xander." Holliday kept his focus on Mason, avoiding even registering Delgado as a person, let alone as a rival. "He's got no skin in this game. He'll double-cross you as soon as you turn your back. You've got my daughter. You know you can trust me. And I swear I can take you to Harry Youngblood."

Mason took a few seconds, a twitch in his eyes betraying the mental process going on there. The pros and cons, the mathematics of trust. "Dude has a point, Xander. How can I trust you'll not let me down?"

Delgado wiped at the sweat on his forehead mingling with the rain. His eyebrows were like sponges, soaking it up, only to burst free when he brushed them.

"Do you know him well enough to get in his home?"

Delgado nodded. "I think so."

Holliday threw his arms in the air. "I'm the one with something at stake here."

"And I'm in charge here. My rules." Mason held the gun to Holliday's head. "Am I clear?" He waited for Holliday's nod, then shifted it to Delgado. "Get walking."

Delgado stepped back, hands up. "You can't trust him."

"Don't listen—"

"Chris!" Mason pointed the gun back at Holliday. "Keep your mouth shut or this is all over now. Okay? Here, in this parking lot." Then he nodded at Delgado. "Why can't I trust him?"

Delgado didn't have anything concrete. *A desperate man, clinging on to whatever he could leverage.* "I can get you whatever you want."

"I'm sick of this." Mason stood between them, shifting the gun between Delgado and Holliday. "One of you two is coming with me, the other is staying here."

If I time it right, when the gun moves from me toward Delgado, I can jump at Mason and take him out. He might shoot Delgado, but if I get the gun I can force Mason to take me to Avery.

Mason switched the gun back to Holliday. He was holding a burner phone in his free hand, that old Nokia thing. The Batphone signal to whoever was holding Avery.

"Listen to me, Mason." Holliday reached out his hand, hoping neither of them noticed how badly it was shaking. "I know Harry. You've got my daughter."

"You can't trust him." Delgado inched closer. "He's in bed with these guys. He's involved in this."

"Mason, give me the phone. I'll call him right now."

Delgado's eyes bulged. "You don't have his number."

"I know it by heart."

Mason tossed the cell over. "Well, why didn't you say?"

Holliday dialed the number from memory, hoping it was right. Not many numbers he could do that with these days. Not with his smartphone in a hospital trash can. He put it to his ear. It rang and rang and—

"Put it on speaker, please."

Holliday hit the button and the ringtone filled the wet air.

CHAPTER THIRTY-TWO

Carter

Carter scanned either side of the freeway, searching for anything that could lead them to Delgado's location. Just trees blocking rows and rows of condos. He gripped the cell again. "Peterson, have you refined the location yet?"

"Getting there, sir." Tyler clicked his tongue a few times, loud down the line. "Take your next left."

Carter pointed toward a wilderness of trees and distant water.

Elisha complied, cutting in front of a Greyhound bus. "He's sure? Because this looks like it doesn't go anywhere."

"Are you—"

"Positive, sir." Tyler did some more tongue-clicking. "There's a parking lot for hikers a mile down that road. The cell towers triangulate to near that point. I suggest you start there."

That mile wasn't going to take long—Elisha was hurtling along the road like she was in hot pursuit, not chasing down a last-known cell location.

Carter spotted the parking space first, four spaces on the left, with a red Volvo sedan parked in the rightmost spot. "Here!"

The brakes squealed as Elisha pulled in.

Carter got out first. He raced over to the Volvo and peered inside. Dog crate in the trunk, but no sign of anybody.

Elisha joined him, looking around, frowning. "So?"

"This is our only lead." Carter looked around, wiping damp hair out of his eyes. "I've been waiting for him to slip up. Kidnapping Delgado and leaving his cell phone on is the mistake. Let's make it fatal."

"They're not here, Max."

Carter felt it deep in his gut, that ache that meant they'd lost him again. "We need to—"

His cell blared out. Unknown caller. His heart skipped a beat. That could be the abductor, those seeds he planted now blooming. Letting Avery go. Or goading him. He put it to his ear. "Carter."

"Son, I really—"

Bill.

Carter checked the display again. A new number, Seattle area code. "Have you bought a burner?" He stepped away from Elisha, hiding behind a minivan.

"I got this new SIM card whatchamacallit thingamabob." He'd gone the full Dick Van Dyke in Mary Poppins. Carter had no idea how many shots of bourbon it took to get there. No, he knew full well. And it was measured in quarts, not shots. "The only way I can get hold of my son. How could you block me, Max?"

"If you're after a why, rather than just instructions on how to…" Carter sighed. "You should ask yourself why I might want to block you. Might give you an insight into your failings as a father."

All that came was a gasp. "Son, I really need your help."

"Bill, even if I wanted to help, I'm in the middle of a major operation."

"Son, I'm desperate." And drunk as a skunk.

"Wasn't Mom desperate?" Carter hung up and stared at the cell display. What was the record for number of contacts blocked in a day?

Elisha raised her eyebrows. "Max, you okay?"

Carter pocketed his cell. "I'm good."

A woman came running out of the woods, panic in her eyes.

Carter stopped her. "FBI!" He held out his shield for her.

She pointed behind her, struggling for breath. "There's a man!" She gulped in air as four dogs bounded up to her. "Handcuffed to a tree!"

Three hundred and seven steps into the woods, in fact. Arms around his back, head slumped, on his knees, suit pants muddied, white shirt damp and see-through, tie and jacket gone.

Xander Delgado looked up, eyes bulging. "Mmf!" Something red was stuffed in his mouth. "Mmf!"

Carter jogged over. "We'll get you down." He rubbed at his arm, trying to calm him, then opened his mouth and pulled at the red fabric. A folded-up necktie. He dropped it on the dirt. "I'm FBI, sir. Are you hurt?"

"I'm fine." Delgado shook his head, anger leaching out of every pore. "Holliday! This is his fault!"

Carter maneuvered behind him and tried to unlock the cuffs. Nothing. Delgado had gouged away a chunk of bark. "Elisha, call Richardson and get Linskey's keys here."

"On it." She jogged off through the mud.

"We're going to get you out of here." Carter crouched in front of Delgado. "What happened?"

"Holliday. I caught that douchebag in my office, rooting through my files. With this buddy of his, John Mason. Looking for some information in my files."

"They were investigating *you*?"

Delgado lashed out, but the rattling cuffs held him fast. "Get me out of here!"

Carter held up his hands. "I understand that you've undergone a traumatic event, sir, but I need you to remain calm, okay? Now, do you have any idea where they've gone?"

CHAPTER THIRTY-THREE

Holliday

Mason was in the passenger seat now, the pistol on his lap. "I chose to bring you. Don't make me regret it."

Holliday gripped the wheel tight, like it was Mason's throat. "I'm not going to pull anything, believe me."

Mason glared at Holliday. "I know you served your country. You were a medic, but I know what you're capable of." He picked up the pistol and inspected it. "I served too. They told us it was all about the greater good. Protecting our way of life, all that jazz." He flipped the revolver open and checked the bullets. "But I also know how the guys in charge see people like me. On any mission, they know how many civilian deaths are acceptable. They know how many of their own men they can lose. Every American death in any of our wars, it can always be turned into political capital by people like you."

"Is that what this is about—you're an anti-war campaigner?"

Mason thought about it for a few seconds, his eyes losing focus. Then he snapped the chamber back and held up the gun. "Just don't make me regret my choice."

"I won't." Holliday pulled up outside the gated community. A long wall ran along the perimeter, rough stones cemented together, with flat slates lying on top. Very European. Harry Youngblood's house was anything but, just about visible through the gate. *The sort of McMansion that sprouted all over Seattle in the boom.* "What do you want me to get from him?"

"You're not going in alone. We're going in together."

"You heard him, right? He told me to come alone."

"I heard him and I'm choosing to ignore it."

No point arguing with him. "What evidence do you need?"

Mason stared into space. "I just need to know what happened that day. Every single detail. Who it was for. Why. What they did with them. And I need concrete proof." He stared at Holliday. "Now, get us in there. I'm sure you'll figure out how."

Holliday rolled down the driver window and reached for the intercom button, pulse pounding his bones as he waited for a response. Any response.

The intercom crackled and a screen blinked into life. Harry Youngblood stared out, his cheeks red. Artfully messy hair, tie loosened. He took a drink of scotch from a tumbler, ice cubes rattling.

A buzzer sounded and the gate started rattling open.

Holliday pulled through the gate and drove toward the house. He got out first.

Mason caught up with him by the time he got to the door. "Remember, play it straight." He stuffed the pistol in the back of his pants and tugged Delgado's suit jacket down. Still a visible bulge, if you knew where to look.

The house door opened and Harry Youngblood leaned against the jamb, clutching that whiskey tumbler. Looked like he'd topped it off. Youngblood was freakishly tall, way over six and a half feet. He swirled his glass around, the ice cubes tinkling. "Told you to come alone, Senator."

Holliday caught a nervous twitch from Mason. "This is John." He stepped closer to the door. "He's my new assistant. Ex-SEAL. He can be trusted."

"Chris, this discussion is between you and— WOAH!"

Mason pointed the gun at Youngblood's head. "Get inside, jackass."

Hands up, Youngblood backed inside the house, stepping slowly through the hallway. Framed stills from violent movies lined the gray walls. "What's going on, Chris?"

"I'm in charge here, okay?" Mason kept the gun on Youngblood. "Don't screw with me and you'll stay alive."

"Okay." Youngblood pushed through double doors into a colossal living room. Must've filled most of the floor. Place was a bachelor's dream, just missing the signed guitars on the walls. Six double windows, three on each facing wall. The left side of the room continued Youngblood's violent movie fetishism, at least twenty Peckinpah stills sandwiched between huge film noir posters, not far off billboard-sized. In the middle was the mother of all TV sets, at least a hundred inches, the curved screen filled with some desert warfare video game. On the opposite side, a bucket chair like something the captain in a sci-fi movie would sit in, all hinges and levers. He led over to a long dining table, big enough to seat twenty, next to a galley kitchen that looked like it'd never been used. He pulled out a bench and dropped his glass, the whiskey spraying over the flagstones. Harsh fumes wafted up.

Mason grabbed him by the throat. "We're here for information, simple as that. You give me what I want, you'll live. Screw around, and I'll kill you. Capiche?"

Youngblood nodded slowly, like having a violent assassin break into his home was a regular occurrence. "What do you want to know?"

Mason sat opposite, holding the gun in one hand, careful and calm. "You ran a military exercise on October second at Tang Elementary."

"I don't know what you're talking about."

"Harry." Holliday cut in before Mason could threaten him. "Olson fired you, right?"

"Didn't even get a chance to defend myself." Youngblood reached over for a refill. "Kangaroo court, man. All because that prick Xander Delgado had some juice on me. Fired me like that." He clicked his fingers, his frat ring catching the light. "Said my employment contract is very clear on the matter."

"What did you do?"

Youngblood looked like he didn't care. He'd just lost his job and he didn't have anything else to lose. Except his house and all the junk he'd collected.

Holliday tried to plead with his eyes. "Harry, this guy has my daughter. The only way she'll live is if I get the truth. I'd beg, but his gun saves me the effort. You're going to tell us about this exercise."

"What's there to tell?" Youngblood nudged an empty glass away like he was conceding a checkmate. "We helped the army evacuate a school and some nearby businesses."

"You didn't get fired for that."

"You don't think that's what I've been mulling over since Olson pulled me into his office? Delgado grilled him over that operation in front of a baying audience. Richard hates to be publicly shamed. I just paid the price for his humbling."

"Bullshit." Mason put the gun to Youngblood's forehead. "What you're covering up is the fact that a boy died during that exercise."

His son?

And it hit Holliday like a bullet to the chest. He stared at Mason, at his wide-eyed sneer, at the calmness and the control slipping away with each heartbeat, at his nostrils and lips twitching.

"What was his name?"

Mason looked at Holliday, his steely glare a distant memory. Tears welled in his eyes, and he swallowed hard. "What?"

"The boy who died was your son, right? What was his name?"

"Jacob." His breathing came harder, louder. "His name was Jacob, and this animal killed him."

"This isn't on me."

"Of course it is. You're involved. You did this to my son!"

"I swear I didn't." Youngblood couldn't make eye contact with him, his face set hard. "You shouldn't trust Holliday. He's corrupt. He's in the pocket of—"

"Shut up!" Mason pressed the gun into Youngblood's flesh. "Tell me what happened to my son!"

"I wasn't there!"

"But you ran it, right? That kid died because of you."

"Some kid was taken, that's all I know. All I want to know."

"Olson said you were in charge."

"He's wrong. Franklin Vance ran it. Whole thing was his baby. And if Frank Vance comes to me with a gig, I know not to ask too many questions. Just take the money and keep quiet."

"What gig?"

"If I tell you, will you let me go?"

"I'll consider it."

"Frank had a side operation. I don't know what it was, or who it was for, but the money was good. Very good. Like I said, I run a 'don't ask, don't tell' policy with Frank. If you want to know more, you need to speak to Vance yourself."

"No." Mason put the gun at Youngblood's belly. "I will shoot you. Don't doubt that. Every last detail. Now."

Youngblood looked at him for a few long seconds then pointed across the room. "It's on my computer."

Mason grabbed a handful of Youngblood's hair and stuck the gun under his chin. "Show me." He hauled him up and pushed him over to the living room, then sat him in front of the screen.

Mason stepped around to the other side of the desk and trained the gun on Youngblood.

On the giant screen, in front of a desktop photo of desert violence, a small window showed the view outside. A black Suburban sat there, idling. The window rolled down slowly, and Special Agent Max Carter peered out, looking pissed.

CHAPTER THIRTY-FOUR

Carter

Carter gave the tall gate a shove, but it wouldn't budge. "He's in there." He pointed at the Lexus then looked at Elisha. "Call it in."

"On it." She swung around and pointed at the two agents emptying out of another Suburban, got them to head around the back.

Carter put his cell to his ear, each ring another second that could allow the scumbag to get away.

SAC Nguyen sounded out of breath, her footsteps echoing in a tight space. "Max, I'm kind of busy."

"We've got him, Karen. We're at Harry Youngblood's home, and Holliday is inside with the abductor. I need approval to enter the building."

"Max, how many have you got with you?"

"Four."

"Including you?"

"Karen, I need to get inside."

"Max, the SWAT units are at these demonstrations. Stand down until I can get more agents over. I've scrambled them and—"

"I can't do that." Carter killed the call. He raced over to the Suburban and popped the trunk. Right in the middle was the Enforcer battering ram. He lugged it over to the gate and pressed it against the wood. "Step back." He pulled the handle.

The gate toppled in, landing on a brick driveway. An orange Audi sports car sat on pebbles, glistening in the rain.

Carter held up a hand while he collected the Enforcer, then he took lead, making sure the team of three knew he was fighting alongside them. A hulking porch protruded from the front of a three-story home, the sort of place where the architect just kept on adding features until it was a complete mess. He dashed over to the front door and thumped the wood. "FBI!"

No answer.

He stepped back. "Go!"

Their two colleagues stood on either side of the door, guns drawn and ready.

Carter prepped the Enforcer and repeated his entry maneuver on the house door. He was first through, pistol drawn, adrenalin powering through him, the over-warm air cutting across his face as he took it slow across the hallway's bleached-gray wood flooring. Black-and-white movie shots on the walls, Pulp Fiction and a seventies Clint Eastwood, opposite some ultraviolent Korean films. Halfway along, he held up a clenched fist and got the team to stop. Sounded like people speaking through a door.

But something in their tone didn't feel right.

The two agents took up positions on either side of double doors, waiting.

Carter gave them a nod, but held up a hand. He nudged the door and peered in. A wide living area, stuffed with sports memorabilia, artworks, and upmarket furniture. He listened hard.

Over by a computer, a man held a handgun against another man's head. The seated man looked like Harry Youngblood's headshot from the report, his giant frame tucked as close to the floor as he could manage.

The standing man was tall, muscular like a marine. No hood this time, just a suit jacket. "Let's start with what happened to Jacob." Same accent as the man he'd spoken to on the phone.

Youngblood shut his eyes. "That kid."

What are they talking about?

Crouching, Carter eased his way into the room, crawling to hide behind couches, one of three in front of what looked like the side of a building—some stenciled artwork on a pile of cinder blocks. An original Banksy. Youngblood had just torn down a wall and transported it.

The abductor pulled his gun away from Youngblood's head, keeping his aim, but at a distance. "So you do know about it, then?"

"There's a report in here." Youngblood waved a hand at the machine. "I can email you it."

Mason looked torn. "Print out the evidence. Whatever you've got. Just print it."

Youngblood clicked the mouse, and a laser printer started up somewhere in the room, zapping through some sheets.

Carter rounded the sofa and darted over to a dining table, keeping low, using another couch to block him.

Holliday stood by the computer desk, hands in pockets. He clocked Carter and his eyes bulged. Carter put a finger to his lips, narrowed his eyes to reinforce the message.

Youngblood walked across the room and snatched a document off the printer. He took a few seconds to flick through it, then walked back over and dumped it on the desktop. "Here. We done?"

"Thank you." Mason started reading, letting Carter shift closer, inch by inch. Maybe twenty feet away? He narrowed the gap to fifteen, then ten.

Mason pistol-whipped Youngblood, knocking him to the floor. "You killed him, didn't you?"

Holliday darted over, but the gun pointing in his face stopped him dead.

Mason put the gun against Youngblood's forehead. "You killed him!"

Holliday looked genuinely surprised. And he seemed to have forgotten all about Carter, especially when Mason trained the gun on him. "Come on…"

Youngblood kicked out and cracked Mason in the knee. He pushed into a shoulder charge, crashing Mason into the giant TV screen, sending both of them tumbling over.

Carter couldn't see them. He raced over.

A gunshot burst around the room, stinging his ears.

Youngblood lay on the floor, mouth hanging open, a giant hole in his chest. A thin spray of blood spattered the floor behind him, lumps of bone like islands.

Carter aimed his gun at Mason. "Stay right where you are!"

Mason stood over the body, his face hidden from the overhead lights. "It was an accident, I swear!"

Carter walked over to the body and crouched low, keeping his gun trained on Mason as he reached for Youngblood's neck. He searched for a pulse, holding it until he felt a weak throb through his fingers. He looked down at Youngblood, crimson bubbling in his mouth.

Glass smashed somewhere.

A pair of French doors sat between granite kitchen units. The left-side curtain flapped in the wind.

No sign of Mason. Or Holliday.

A hard choice—stay with Youngblood or go after Mason.

One man's life versus a child's safety.

No choice to make.

"Elisha, stay with him!" Carter raced over to the doors. The glass was smashed, looked like a wolf's mouth, all sharp and gnarled. Both doors were locked. He stepped through onto a back patio.

The yard ran downhill toward a high wall, same as out front but twice the height. Holliday was on top, reaching an arm down. Mason climbed up toward him.

Carter fired into the air then aimed at Mason, low, going for his left thigh, enough to send him falling to the ground.

The wall's bricks puffed inches to the left.

Missed.

Holliday glanced around, eyes wide.

Carter adjusted his aim and squeezed the trigger. A shout, then the climbing man fell to the ground. The wall splattered where he'd been.

Missed again.

Holliday disappeared over the top.

Carter ran, still clutching his gun as he thundered downhill.

A gunshot blasted out, echoing around the yard.

Carter hit the deck, going prone. Another shot. He looked up, scanning the wall. No movement.

He pushed himself up and raced down the hill, stopping at the foot of the wall.

Where he expected one, there was no body.

They got away.

And Carter knew he had to save Youngblood's life.

CHAPTER THIRTY-FIVE

Mason

I sprint behind Holliday, through the mud and the discarded branches, our feet splashing as we go. My arm's on fire. I look down at it. Delgado's jacket is burst open and soaking, blood pouring down my arm. Not the first time I've been shot, but it—

The pain only hits when you realize. A searing rush of agony, burning up my arm to my shoulder, into my neck and up into my brain. I wobble and almost hit a tree. I push it to the back of my mind.

The feds can't follow my blood trail with all the rain, can they? Shit, I don't know.

Where is Holliday?

I stop and listen. Just rain hitting the trees. Nothing from behind yet, but they're seconds away at best.

Something rattles.

Through the trees, Holliday stands in front of a chain-link fence. He rattles it again.

"Shit." I catch up with him and grab hold of it, but there's no getting through this. Tall, maybe twenty feet with coiled barbwire at the top, like they're protecting a prison.

Holliday looks at the fence, inspecting it closely like he can just pass through it or something.

I'm more concerned about the noises coming from behind us now. Multiple footsteps, multiple people. All FBI.

It isn't going to end like this. It can't.

I walk along the fence, grabbing the metal and shaking. There. A few feet along, there's a hole, no doubt some kids cutting a way to get in to escape the pressures of school and parents, just taking time out to smoke a joint and have fun.

I nod for Holliday to go first. He isn't going to try to get away from me. He knows the stakes, knows they just got even higher. I follow him through and stitch the fence back together, not as carefully as I'd like, but it'll do. Another flash of pain burns my arm, but I ignore it and set off through more woods, thicker now, and planted purposefully, in a grid pattern.

Then we burst out onto a street.

Holliday's ahead of me, swinging around, taking in the houses like he's looking for refuge.

Wrong move.

A VW camper van sits outside an apartment building. Old school. Easy to steal. I make my way for it, checking left and right as I take it slow, my breath misting in the rain.

No cars on the road, yet, but the shouting from behind is getting louder and closer. The FBI are almost here.

I try the passenger door, and it's unlocked. BINGO. I shuffle along the bench until I'm behind the wheel, then reach down.

Shit.

They've upgraded it. Brand-new engine, brand-new tamper-proof ignition.

Through the woods, flashlights scan along the fence, looking for a way through, close to the hole we came through.

Almost on us. Shit, shit, shit.

Holliday flips down my sun visor like he expects my stupidity. Nothing. Then the visor on his side. Keys flop into his lap.

A stroke of luck. Finally.

"Here." He tosses them to me.

I catch them and stick the key in. The engine growls. A *serious* upgrade.

"You didn't—" Holliday's eyes bulge. "You're bleeding!"

"You drive." I shift along the bench seat, letting him climb over me.

Holliday sticks it in gear and shoots off, tearing through the neighborhood, putting distance between us and the feds. He puts his seatbelt on and pretty soon we're spitting distance from the freeway.

"Did anyone see us?"

"Don't think so." Holliday's looking behind, keeping his eyes peeled. He turns onto the freeway and heads south, away from Redmond and Youngblood's mansion.

My arm is throbbing now. "You saved me."

Holliday is still checking out back. "What?"

"Back there, climbing the wall. You warned me and I dropped down. The brick exploded. You saved me. I caught a round in the arm, but it would've been worse."

"Don't think I'm doing it for you or your cause."

I don't even need to point a gun at this guy. Layla's a *genius*.

"You've got your information." Holliday slumps back on the seat. "When do I get Avery back?"

"This isn't over yet. Not by a long shot."

"Come on. You got your answers. You don't need me anymore. Let her go."

CHAPTER THIRTY-SIX

Carter

Carter stood on top of the wall, staring into the frigid woods, branches dripping with rainwater. No signs of movement other than his own agents getting deeper and deeper in. Not even any obvious footprints to track in among all the mud.

He'd let Mason go. The kidnapper was here and he let him go, a split-second decision over Youngblood's life.

And Holliday was definitely with him. Probably helped him escape.

He let himself down slowly and hopped onto the pristine lawn, the late-afternoon sun burning off the rain with the tang of ozone.

Elisha joined him, but her expression betrayed how good the news was. "Two units heading around the far side of the woods. Seattle PD are sending half their cops over, but…" She bit her lip, like she always did when she had bad news.

"Ten agents combing the area, and nothing?" Carter forced himself to look at her, letting out a deep breath. "And Youngblood's dead. I couldn't save him." He thumbed behind them at the house. "This Mason guy has escalated from child abduction to murder. We've got a dead man and we lost our suspect by inches. *I* lost him."

"Max, you've seen him now. You've confirmed our hypothesis. Our guy has Avery and is using her as leverage against Holliday."

Carter made his way back up to the house, forcing an agent to sidestep clear.

"Max, Avery isn't with them. So he must have an accomplice."

"Avery could be dead. Could be locked up somewhere. Could be walking the streets, or lost in the woods somewhere. Any of them fit." Carter settled down on a patio chair, didn't care about the rain soaking his pants. "We're still no closer to knowing why he's doing this." He looked around, searching for hope amid the deflated agents, then replaying Holliday standing on the top, the kidnapper climbing up to him. "When I aimed my gun, Holliday shouted something. Next thing I know, the guy drops down. Then there's a gunshot. Holliday saved the man who's kidnapped his children. Could be because Avery's life is at risk, but Holliday's lied to us, and he ran away from the hospital."

"Max, you'd do anything you could to save Kirsty, wouldn't you?"

Carter could only nod. She was right. Again. "We need to let the field office manage the crime scene." He took in the scene again. All those agents and cops, here because they'd let someone slip off, let a senator help the man who'd abducted his daughter. "But we still have to find Holliday."

What were they looking for?

Mason, that's what Delgado said his name was. John Mason.

If Mason was just going to murder Harry Youngblood, why bring Holliday? What does he add?

But maybe Delgado was the key.

CHAPTER THIRTY-SEVEN

Mason

I take a look at him as we pass a slow-moving Ford. "You're right, I don't need you. I should just kill you now, dump you by the side of the road."

"Like you killed Harry Youngblood?"

I haven't had a chance to even think about it. The first death I've been involved in since Basra. He was going for my gun. He was going to kill me. It was an accident, not that any court would believe me. Nothing more, nothing less.

Did Youngblood deserve it? Does it matter?

Rage flashes across my face, down my spine.

He deserved it. Boy, did he deserve it.

He keeps looking at my arm, shaking his head. "Take me to her!"

I take a few seconds to think it all through, what I've gained, what I've lost, which assumptions are blown apart.

Was Harry Youngblood just a front man, taking cash from disreputable sources and funneling it through GrayBox to his own accounts? Or was he smack-dab in the middle, in charge of everything?

If he was, then he's paid for what he did.

But he said it was Franklin Vance who ran it. But these guys lie worse than politicians. Everything they did was to line their own pockets. All the lies they told, all the truths they hid.

So, did Vance kill my boy?

Only one way to find out.

"We need to meet this Franklin Vance. You do know him, right?"

Holliday clenches his jaw again.

"Chris, I know when you're lying, so don't even think about it, okay?" I lean back and check the back for anything to fix up my wound. There's a cable lying there, a long beige ethernet. Useful for torture, so I grab it. There's a towel on the floor. It'll have to do. I shrug off the sodden jacket and roll up my sleeve to check my arm. Looks way worse than it is. Just a flesh wound, a bullet grazing my arm as I fell. Still hurts worse than if it'd caused internal bleeding or got trapped inside. I tear the towel in half in one long cut, and wrap one half around my arm, getting it nice and tight. I hold it there, let it soak up the blood, let it thicken and coagulate, then I'll be good.

I rifle through the glovebox for some Tylenol or something. Just Vicodin. Shit, I can't take that while I'm in this situation, can't afford to lose any focus or control. I pocket the pills and sit back, trying to control the pain mentally. Just block it out. "What did Harry mean about you being corrupt, Senator?"

Holliday laughs, his jaw clenching like crazy. "Nothing. He's playing you."

"Come on." I grimace as pain sears my upper arm. "I know you're lying. You got inside his McMansion pretty easily. You've got something on him. Tell me what."

"There's nothing, I swear."

"Sounds like bullshit to me."

"What would you know? You've kept this from me all along. If you'd told me it was your son—"

I lose it. Hard. I grab his throat and push him back against the headrest, squeezing and pointing the gun at his side. "You tell me now, or so help me—"

"Okay, okay." His words are gurgles, so I let go. He grits his teeth, rubs at his neck, and looks a lot more genuine now. "A few years back, Harry tried buying me. The shit he pulls with GrayBox is bad enough, but he's always looking for other opportunities. Off-the-books deals."

"You mean behind Olson's back?"

"And then some. Old army buddy of mine works in the CIA now. Told me a thing or two about Youngblood over a couple beers. GrayBox were involved in some disappearances during the Bush administration. Operations on US soil, working for the CIA."

Have to admit it, he's snared my interest. "Who did they take?"

"Wouldn't say. Just some persons of interest, you know how it is. Plausible deniability and all that jazz." Holliday flips the bird at a black Audi roaring past, too close to us. "Anyway. I confronted him at a fundraiser, told him I knew, that I'd get an investigation into it. He thought he could shut me up with money. I explained that it's blackmail."

"Did you take the bribe?"

"I refused his money, but he still thought he could buy me. He gave a couple hundred grand to a PAC in my name."

"PAC?"

"Political Action Committee. When you're in my world, you forget how most people don't know the terms. They act independently of you, but support your campaign through advertising mainly. You don't get elected without them."

"So why didn't you report him?"

"Because I needed the money. My campaign was floundering. The things I say, it pisses off the powers that be." Holliday stopped. "They don't fund me as much as they should, but I still won the primary. People like me and my image. But I still needed their money, so I sat on the info, waiting for a time it'd become useful. Didn't think it'd be to save my daughter's life."

"You seem to be in tight with these GrayBox punks. Every one that crops up, you've got their number memorized."

Holliday punches the steering wheel. "I'm a politician. You don't make an omelette without breaking eggs."

Blood drips down my forearm. Shit. I take the first wrapping off and toss the rag into the back. Takes longer to tie the second one. The blood flow is slowing, if nothing else, but still hurts like a bastard. Maybe I should take that Vicodin. "Tell me about Franklin Vance."

"You don't need to worry about how we handle him."

There's got to be a reason that our old friend Bob Smith put us on to Holliday in the first place.

As Holliday drives, I put the battery in the smartphone and power it up. The screen flashes, and I open "Signal".

No new messages, but Bob Smith is online. So I type out a message:

> Spoke to Youngblood.

Interesting. He works at GB?

> Did.
> Fired this morning.
> Fired again this afternoon.

He's dead?

> Deserved it too. He authorized the mission.
> Took money for it.

OK. What did he say?

> Franklin Vance ran the operation.
> Know him?

Ex-CIA.
Bad dude.
Did Youngblood mention CIA?

> Didn't ask.
> Didn't have time.
> He went for my gun. Him or me.
> He lost.

And that's the truth. My finger slipped as we went over. I should've got more out of him.

Bob Smith goes quiet again. Makes me feel like a stupid kid. If he wanted me to ask Youngblood some specific questions, he should've told me.

The road hurtles by, Holliday keeps looking at me, my arm keeps throbbing. All I can think about is the Vicodin bottle in my pocket.

> FBI turned up.
> Escaped by skin of our teeth.

OK.

> Holliday says Youngblood runs ops for CIA.
> That sound right?

I wait for a few seconds, but he's quiet again. I hate it.

OK. Been digging. GrayBox running a CIA op makes sense. Long history of it. Back to Bush/ Cheney/Rumsfeld. Black sites. Bad stuff.

So Holliday's story checks out. I type again, having to correct my spelling that even the autocorrect has no hope of fixing.

> Would Holliday know Vance?

Figures.
Both members of the Great Glen Country Club.
Teed off together a few times.
With Olson and Youngblood.

> Thanks.
> I'll keep you posted.

I pull out the battery and the cell dies. I put it away and reach for the burner, but my finger touches the Vicodin. I should toss it, stop the temptation.

Holliday looks over at me, frowning. "Who are you messaging?"

I hold up the gun. "Just drive." I hit dial and put the burner to my ear, listening to it ringing.

"What's up?" Layla sounds breathless.

"I'm on to something. Someone's paid part of the price for it, but there are more fish to bait. I'll call you in an hour. You know what to do if you don't hear from me."

"Good luck."

I end the call and sit back, watching the road hurtling toward us, the cars and lines blurring.

Then I see Harry Youngblood dying in front of my eyes, the revolver jerking in my hand, the sound deafening me.

I jerk awake, sucking in deep breaths.

It's way too late for me. I'm already one of them.

CHAPTER THIRTY-EIGHT

Carter

"Karen, it's Max. I'm looking for Xander Delgado. Call me back." Carter killed the call on the dash and took a left up the hill, letting a bike courier pass in the bike lane. Almost immediately, his cell rang. He answered it. "Carter."

"Agent Carter, this Sergeant Josh Anderson SPD. I'm calling in relation to a stolen VW camper van."

"You've found them?"

"No, sir. My guys suspect the men you let go from that murder site have taken it. Just had to listen to a very irate man recount how he spent ten years restoring and upgrading it, only for them to steal it."

Carter sat there, the turn signal ticking. The Seattle Field Office towered above him, just another tall downtown building. "Should be easy to find, though?"

"You'd think."

"Okay, I'll get one of my agents to pick this up. Expect a call from Tyler Peterson, okay?"

"Sure thing." And Anderson was gone.

Carter pulled up by the garage entrance. "Everything we know about this guy is he's smart. He'll dump the vehicle at the first opportunity." No time to wait for the security guard to wake up. "Park this for me." He left the Suburban in neutral on the curb and got out. A quick jog back down the hill and he was at the corner, a line of buses waiting for the lights to change.

A car door opened. "Son!" Bill Carter stumbled out of the car, sprawling across the hood. "You need to help me!"

Carter stood there. "This isn't the time, Bill. For anything."

"There's never time for your old man. I'm sick of it. You need to let me in to your life now!"

"No, you don't get to do this. Least of all now." Carter grabbed him by the collar. "Right now, I'm heading the search for a missing child. You might know something about that." He narrowed his eyes. "Might remind you of something."

"Son, I—"

"No, Bill. You're drunk and I'm way too busy." Carter flagged down a passing cab and opened the back door. "Keys." He took his father's car keys and pushed him in the cab. "Come get them from the front desk tomorrow." He pointed over the road at the field office. "When you're sober." He slammed the door.

The driver looked out of his window. "Where am I taking him?"

Carter unrolled a fifty from his billfold. "Take him home." He passed one of Bill's old business cards. "Here's the address."

The driver held up the note. "Redmond's only twenty bucks."

"That's to cover him making a mess. Keep it if he doesn't." Carter stepped back and watched the taxi set off into traffic. It zipped off at the next junction, disappearing in the direction of Redmond.

What a complete and utter mess. And perfect timing.

"Thought you'd be inside?" Elisha appeared, tossing him the keys. "Uh-uh. I know that face. What's going on?"

He couldn't look her in the eye. "It's fine."

"No, it's not. You've got something going down, haven't you? Max, it's the last thing we need in a case like this. Spill. Now."

Carter knew she was right.

But how could he talk to her about this? About all the garbage in his head? The stuff that stopped him sleeping at night, that put him on edge every second he was apart from Emma and Kirsty, when he couldn't protect them?

He knew he had to at least try.

"Okay, so I was born in London. When I was six, my father, Bill, got offered a high-paying job in Seattle at Boeing." Carter swallowed down the bitterest memory. "Thing is, Mom didn't want to up sticks and move to the USA. She was settled. So they divorced, and she got custody of me. Bill moved to Seattle, and all that time, he missed his son. Boy did he miss me, thousands of miles away, growing up without him. All because he'd chosen this over his family." He looked at Elisha now. "And you want to know why I do this job? Because I was abducted myself."

Her eyes bulged. "What?"

"One night when I was eight, Bill met me outside my school." Carter blinked away the memory of Bill trying the same trick with Kirsty that morning. Felt like months ago now. "Got in a car, took us to this private airport, and onto a private jet someone he knew had a share of. Something like that. Flew us both here, to his new home in Seattle."

Elisha reached across to rub his arm, her forehead creasing with empathy. "I had no idea, Max."

Carter sucked in a deep breath. "Mom couldn't handle the stress and became depressed. Like, really badly depressed. She got this strong medication and… She died in a fatal traffic accident. Thirty-two years ago." His tears flowed, no pouring rain to lose them to. "The hardest part was it wasn't all her fault. Those antidepressants… This was the eighties, it's not like now. You were on that stuff, you were a zombie. She veered into the wrong lane, hit a car, killed herself, killed the other driver."

"Max, you should've told me."

"I thought I was over it, but you never get over it, do you?"

"And let me guess—you blame yourself?" She held his gaze until he looked away. "It was an accident, Max. This isn't on you."

"Maybe, but Bill… That selfish prick pushed her down that path. And I'll always blame myself because I'm the catalyst for it all. When we were waiting for the plane, I remember thinking, clear as day, I should be with Mom. Then I wouldn't have been over here, and she'd still be alive, and that selfish…" The tears stung his eyes. "Of course, Bill spoiled me. And after Mom died, he doubled it, used his wealth to distract me from her death, from reality. I was that kid, you know, the one who always had the latest game consoles, the latest sneakers, the latest CDs. Vacations at Disneyland, no expense spared. But Bill…" The anger welled in the pit of his stomach. "He was always so busy with work. I was raised by a series of nannies. During college, I hit rock bottom. The pressure got to me. And that's when I met Emma. But I was broken and kept lashing out at her. She was strong and got me the therapy I needed. At the time, I needed it. I mean, I could still be playing video games in Bill's basement to this day. But I'm not. I got my degree, got my masters. And I got my sanity back. After college, I had to renounce my British citizenship so I could join the FBI. The only way. I mean, I've been back over there but it's not my home, not after what Bill did."

"Max, that's…" She exhaled slowly.

"I specialize in child abductions because I know what it's like. Every case we get, every stolen kid, that's me standing in that private airfield. Lost, alone, afraid. Everyone is different, I know, but they're also the same in so many ways. And that's why I don't have anything to do with him, Elisha. He killed my mom."

"He's still your dad, Max."

"And I've got a restraining order against him. He just wouldn't listen, kept showing up drunk at our home. And he keeps calling me so I have to block him. I should call it in. This morning, when I dropped off Kirsty at daycare so I could get some paperwork done, Bill was there. Knew she'd be there."

"And you think he was going to take her?"

"I don't doubt it. He keeps asking for my help, but Bill has a ploy for every situation."

"But he's also desperate, like you say. If he needs your help, maybe that's the only way he can ask for it?"

"He doesn't deserve my help."

"What does Em say about it?"

"Nothing you're not just now." Carter locked eyes with her again. "Feels like I need more therapy…"

"You know what you're like, Max. When you're not in control, you lose focus. I suggest you see what he wants, then you'll be back in control. At the moment, you're just reacting to him. What you do best is getting on the front foot."

Elisha's phone chimed. She took a look and got up. "Better take this." She walked off to answer it.

But he knew she was right. Probably. But how could he do that without letting that viper squirm back into their lives?

"Come on." Carter opened the door and walked up to security.

"Afternoon, sir." The security guard sat at his station, armed with a clipboard. "You can just—"

"Is Xander Delgado in the building?"

"Let me just check, sir." The guard started flicking through the clipboard pages. "You watch the game last night?"

"I didn't have the time." Carter tightened his fingers around the marble desk. A pair of agents walked past, giving him cursory nods. He let out a sigh. "Any good?"

"Best I've seen all season." The guard beamed at him, then slid the clipboard over. "Mr. Delgado is with SAC Nguyen on the fifth floor."

Carter was already halfway to the elevators.

*

Carter walked down the corridor past the interrogation rooms and stopped outside the door for Room B. Voices inside, low. One male, one female. He opened it.

Inside, SAC Nguyen sat opposite Delgado. Very cozy, all smiles. Like the congressman hadn't been handcuffed to a tree less than an hour ago. Dressed in a fresh suit, though missing his trademark red tie.

Nguyen raised a hand and joined him in the corridor, her stare glassy and diffuse. "I heard what happened. This doesn't reflect well on you, Special Agent."

"Ma'am, we did what we had to. *I* did what we had to. We almost—"

"A man is dead because of you, because you entered a property without adequate backup. And you let them go." Her voice was even, barely rising above a whisper.

"He would've died if we hadn't been there."

"But you were there. I don't think that's a good look."

"We gained some intel." Carter knew he was clutching at straws. "This Mason guy got him to print out a report. And he mentioned a name—Jacob."

"And that's important, how?"

Carter didn't have an answer, just a question. "I need to speak to Delgado. He's—"

"Another piece of baloney." Nguyen pointed into the room, her voice raising. "You left him handcuffed to a tree!"

"I took a priority call. We had intel on Mason and Holliday's whereab—"

"Mason?"

"That's what he signed in as at the Fed Building. It's as useful as anything I've got to call him."

"So why are you here? You should be—"

"I want to speak to Delgado."

Her snort was the only answer he was likely to get.

"Listen, Karen, he got away from us. This isn't the time for recriminations, okay? I'll hold my hands up to my failings. But I've been in the same room as this guy. I'm building up a picture. I need to know what Delgado does about him."

She looked down the corridor, shaking her head. "Two minutes."

"Thanks." Carter took the vacant seat across from Delgado. "Congressman, I hope you're recovering. I'm sorry I—"

"Takes a lot more than that to frighten me." Delgado narrowed his eyes, clearly wondering what Carter had on him. Typical politician. Well, today's his lucky day. "But thanks for finding me. And leaving me there was fine. I totally understand."

Carter grimaced. "After we left you, we visited Mr. Youngblood's home. Unfortunately, he... died."

Delgado stopped trying to score an angle, clearing his throat instead. "Murder?"

"I was there and I didn't see clearly. I think it was an accident, but I'm not ruling it out."

"You think this John Mason guy did it?"

"It's my working hypothesis. Congressman, you spent a few minutes with them. Is that his name?"

"Well. Holliday introduced him as that, said he was his new assistant." Delgado stared at him, shaking his head. "I don't buy that now. Didn't really at the time."

"Did you get the impression that he's using Avery as leverage?"

"As far as I can tell, that's exactly what's happening." Delgado tilted his head to the side. "Least that's what they portrayed."

"What do you mean by that?"

Delgado stared at Nguyen. "Am I being interrogated here?"

Nguyen stood in the doorway. "Xander, this is just intelligence gathering."

"Well, I'm not helping that worm."

Carter grabbed Delgado by the arms. He could feel Nguyen's glare burning into his neck, but she didn't stop him. "Listen to me. Whatever beef you've got with Senator Holliday, I couldn't care less. But that man he was with—John Mason, if that's even his name—he abducted Avery and her brother. He killed Harry Youngblood. If not for Holliday, then do it for his daughter, do it for his wife."

"You're a piece of work, you know that?" Delgado adjusted his suit cuffs, like he was expecting a spare FBI one to feature diamond-encrusted links. He settled back, arms folded across his chest. "I caught Holliday and this Mason fella in our office searching for a military exercise on October second, at a school in Seattle. Looked to me like they were after some dirt on GrayBox."

"The military contractor?"

"They supported this exercise." Delgado ran his tongue over his movie-star teeth. "I gave them what I could, but the place went on lockdown. Then this Mason guy stuck a knife to my throat, made me and Chris get him out of the Fed Building."

"Which you did."

"My life was at risk!" Delgado got up and started pacing around the room.

Nguyen raised her eyebrows at Carter, but didn't say anything.

Carter tried to process it. Nothing came out right. Mason abducted Holliday's kids to use him to find information on a school. Why Holliday, though? And what happened there? "Any idea what they were looking for?"

"Well, alarm bells started ringing when they asked. I knew the date. I knew the school." Delgado flashed a grin. "As part of the congressional hearing, the FBI raided GrayBox about a month ago. Took a load of documentation, but nothing mentioned Tang Elementary."

It meant nothing to Carter.

"Trouble is, absence of evidence isn't evidence of absence, but they were involved and there should've been reports and records. We never found any. I was going to ask Richard Olson this morning, but you saw how well that went."

"You think GrayBox is covering up something that happened there?"

"I don't doubt it for a second." Delgado rested against the seat back. "At first I thought this Mason guy was working for Olson or GrayBox, but why do all that just to find information about your own company? Holliday has a back channel to Richard Olson. Old golfing buddies. Holliday was a perfect conduit. And that madman got Holliday to call Olson. Even came to meet us near where you found me. It was their regular meeting place, by the sounds of it."

"What did Olson tell you?"

"Denied all knowledge. Told them to speak to Harry Young-blood. Olson said he fired his ass over something." Delgado snarled as he looked around. "Then those douchebags dumped me."

"Did Olson recognize Mason?"

"Mason hid. Never gave Olson the chance to see him, but I assume he listened in. Holliday asked Olson about the operation. Like I told you, Olson put Holliday on to Harry Youngblood."

"Sounds like I need to speak to Richard Olson."

Delgado laughed. "Good luck getting him to talk."

CHAPTER THIRTY-NINE

Holliday

Holliday drove along the freeway, tapping his thumbs against the wheel.

Mason held up a smartphone and checked the screen. Again, fifth time in twenty seconds. Huffing and sighing, like he was waiting for something that wasn't coming. He took out the battery and pocketed it.

"Who are you texting?"

"Never you mind." Mason stared at the bottle of Vicodin. Kept doing it. He was on his second strip of towel now and, while he had stopped dripping blood on the VW's upholstery, he was weakened and struggling.

Holliday grabbed the wheel tighter, didn't know how to use it to his advantage.

I could drive off the road, or cut across into oncoming traffic.
And then what?
Killing Mason isn't the same as saving Avery. The risk's too great.

"Do you want me to arrange a meeting with Vance?"

Mason looked over, eyes narrow. "How?"

"I can call him. I know his number. Like I said, he's a buddy."

"Senator, the people you're tight with…" Mason pointed at a gas station on the left, advertising a diner with the best burgers in Washington state. "In there."

Holliday complied, coming to a stop by the front door. The van's fan sucked in the burnt meat smell.

Mason held up his cell. "What's the number?"

"If I take you to him, you let Avery go. Deal?"

Mason stared off at the passing traffic, then back at Holliday. "Let's see."

"No. I take you, you let her go. End of story."

"I'm in charge here."

"I've got the card you need. Good luck getting anywhere near Vance without my help."

"I can't promise what I can't deliver, Senator. You take me to Vance and we see what happens."

"I'll kill you. When I get Avery back, I'll take great care murdering you. It'll be hours, days, maybe weeks of excruciating agony."

"You think that's a smart thing to say?"

"I don't care. If you were as good as your word, you should've released Avery by now. You've got whatever answers you need. So let her go."

"And let you torture me? Good one."

"Please."

"Okay, here's the deal. You take me to Vance, and I'll let her go. You even so much as think about torturing me again and I swear, it's all over for you. You think you've got a card, but you don't. I'll get Vance by any means. Your choice if you don't want to help. But helping is the only way you'll get her back."

"I swear you'll burn in hell for this." Holliday gave him Vance's number.

Mason typed it in to his burner and set it dialing, the speaker distorted and quiet. He tapped the side and the volume slid up in steps, but the distortion didn't lessen.

"*Who* is this?" Sure sounded like Vance, his cigar-ravaged vocal cords dragging his voice deep, emphasizing words to cover that stutter.

"It's Chris Holliday, Frank. We need to meet. Our worst fears are coming to pass."

A long pause. Could just about make out Vance rasping his mustache. Always did that when he was thinking stuff through, like which iron to approach the green with, or which cable tie to use on a prisoner. "Like that, huh?" More rasping. "Meet me at the country club. I'll be waiting."

"Frank, that's not—"

Click.

Mason put the gun to Holliday's temple. "Chris, you better not be playing me."

Holliday shook his head as much as he could without hitting the gun. "Vance knows it's a safe place, out in the open. Nobody can pull anything there. He's paranoid, always needs to be in control."

"What did you mean by 'worst fears'?"

Holliday looked over at Mason. "Nothing. I was keeping it vague."

"Chris, you need to be honest, okay?" Mason pushed the gun into Holliday's side. "It spooked Vance. Makes me think it's a code. Makes me think of Youngblood saying I shouldn't trust you."

"Listen to me. Youngblood told us Vance arranged the CIA op. Vance's worst fear is someone at GrayBox finding out they've been operating on US soil and trying to pay off politicians." Holliday laughed. "No, getting caught paying off politicians."

Mason looked like he was buying it. "You better not be playing me here."

"You've got my daughter."

"Where is this country club?"

"It's not far, but—"

"Drive."

*

Holliday pulled into the main parking lot. The place was crawling with golfers. Mostly older guys in the brightest colors, stopping and chatting. Resting on their bags or sitting in their carts.

No sign of Vance's Cadillac.

Holliday pulled off toward the overflow lot, taking it slow.

Mason's head kept twitching around, like a quarterback looking for the right play, trying to spot the slightest hole in the defense.

Holliday found a spot in the shade, wedged between the tennis courts and the pool complex, both looking empty. Thick bushes lined the parking spaces. Two golfers walked away from a sedan, not noticing them. He killed the ignition and leaned back in the seat, out of sight. "The deals happen out on the golf course. And I'm not stupid. I've got material on each of them. Youngblood, Vance, Olson. Insurance policies."

Mason glowered at Holliday. "You sicken me." He pushed the gun into Holliday's side, hard enough to hurt. "Act normally when Vance arrives." He pulled the gun away then pocketed it. "Now get out and wait, be a good boy."

Holliday hopped down from the van and leaned against the side, arms folded.

Mason disappeared into the bushes in front of the tennis court. Couldn't even see him from here.

I could get back behind the wheel and drive the van into him. Maybe wouldn't kill him, probably just break some bones. But I could make him tell me where Avery is.

A car crunched over the gravel toward Holliday. A black Cadillac, Vance's bushy mustache visible above the wheel.

Holliday set off toward him, but something in the van caught his eyes. The smartphone Mason used to contact his accomplice was sitting by the handbrake.

If I can give it to the feds, maybe they can find Avery...

CHAPTER FORTY

Mason

I'm on my knees, sharp foliage scratching my cheeks. My arm's on fire. Half a towel stuffed in a gunshot wound isn't cutting it. I really need to go to the hospital or get a field medic to—

Holliday is a trained medic. Two tours of Iraq on the frontline. But there's no way I can trust him to operate on me.

I tighten it, but it doesn't staunch the flow much, just slows the constant dripping.

Holliday stands by the van, frowning at a Cadillac parked a few spaces down. What is he doing?

Then it hits me—I've left the smartphone behind. He just needs to slot the battery in place and he's got us. If he gets that to the feds, they can trace Layla and Avery, and this is all over.

And he knows it. Keeps looking at it, weighing the decision.

But Holliday walks across the parking lot and gets in the Cadillac.

I let out a slow breath. Almost lost control there.

But at least I know that it is Vance in the Caddy.

I crawl off, spider-style, hands and feet on the mud, until I'm right beside the van. I ease the door open and get the smartphone and the battery, then button them in the jacket pocket. The door shuts with a sound, but nobody's listening. I crawl over to Vance's car.

They're talking, and Vance has a seriously deep voice. Sounded like it on the phone, but it's rattling through the car's body like a radio up too loud. Getting louder too, like he's getting pissed at Holliday.

Another peek through the foliage.

Vance sparks a match and sucks on a cigar.

Time to move. More spider-crawling and I'm by the back door, driver side.

They're still talking, Vance doing most of it, that deep bass growl getting louder, pausing only to suck on his cigar.

I ease the door open, so slowly it doesn't make a sound, and hold it there. Secondhand smoke hits my nostrils, in danger of sending me back to some dark places. The bitter, rubbery tang can spark off memories like nothing else.

I take a second to get a proper look at Vance. Big guy. Muscles straining at his golf shirt. Crew cut like it was still the eighties, the sort of mustache you don't even see in gay bars these days. Distracted from looking in his sideview mirror by shouting at Holliday: "Chris, I'm *not* just going to—"

I kneel on the back seat and stick the gun against Vance's head. "Take it slow, Frank."

"What the h-h-*hell?*" Vance is trying to keep it cool, like he's had a gun at his neck hundreds of times in his life. But he can't cover his stutter any longer. "Chris, you lying c-c-c-cocksucker."

"I've got no choice, Frank." Holliday has hands up. "He's got my daughter. I'm sorry."

"Cocksucking motherfu—"

I pistol-whip him, cracking the revolver off his cheek, hard enough to send a message—shut up. "I'm in charge here, Frank." I sit in the middle of the back so I can better see his face, pointing the gun at his head, the sights focusing on his left ear. "You mind if I call you Frank?"

"Of course I *mind*, you—" Another crack to the cheek and he rocks forward.

"You know, for a guy with that kind of mustache, you sure say cocksucker a lot." I pat the seat next to me. "You entertained a lot of young twinks in here, huh?"

Vance narrows his eyes at me, but keeps quiet. Lucky guess, but I've got him where I want him. And he knows it.

"I'll let you go, Frank, but you have to tell me one thing. What happened on October second."

"Nothing happened. I was in the Bahamas, getting my cock sucked by—"

"No you weren't." I stuff the document in front of his face. The page Harry Youngblood printed. Soaked with rain, splattered with blood. My blood, mixing with Harry's. "October second, you were in Seattle. Tang Elementary. Nice little place down by the lake. What were you doing there?"

Vance takes a puff on his cigar. "I'm not telling you—"

I wrap the ethernet cable around his throat. The cigar drops onto the walnut dash and rolls toward the window. "Don't think I'm one of your twinks, big bear." I tighten my grip and pull him back in his seat. His arms flail around, trying to claw at me, but I've got him good. He's not moving anywhere.

Holliday just sits watching. Attaboy.

I loosen the grip, let Vance catch his breath. Then yank him back against the seat, even tighter than before. "I will kill you if I don't get what I want."

He's frantically nodding, even makes a gurgling sound that's positive enough to sound like agreement.

"Let's start over, Frank." I slacken off the cable but don't let go. "October second. Tang Elementary. A child died there. Name was Jacob."

Vance rubs at his throat. "Little fat kid, r-r-right?"

"Jacob Wickstrom."

Vance looks around.

I tap him with the gun again. "And you killed him."

"You motherf—"

So I pull the cord tight around his throat again. "What happened, Frank?" I let it slacken off. "The truth, now."

Vance gasps, his tongue lolling. "It's easier if I show you."

"How?"

"I wore a camera that day." Vance grasps at the cable, but he can't get any purchase. "It's on my computer back home."

Something like excitement tingles at the base of my spine, mixing with sheer terror.

I let one end of the cord go and pull it back, letting him go for now. "Drive."

CHAPTER FORTY-ONE

Carter

GrayBox's headquarters sprawled out in the night sky, a mile-long two-story lizard with a thick middle and limbs hanging off every couple hundred feet.

Carter got out first, stepped onto the pavement, and led through the crammed parking lot. "My grandfather was a Redmond boy. Used to tell me when this was all logging country. Look at it now. The new Silicon Valley."

Elisha frowned at him. "Poppa Carter was a logger?"

"No, Poppa Carter is from London, England."

"Seriously?" She laughed. "That explains a lot."

GrayBox drones filed out of the front door, even on a Saturday. Mostly men in their twenties, all with that pale-skinned look you got from staring at a computer screen all day, every day.

Carter splashed through a puddle and got out his cell, answered right away. "Peterson? You got me an update on that Vee-dub?"

"Sir, SAC Nguyen asked me to go to her office. What should I tell her?"

"The truth, Peterson. We're not hiding anything. I just need to know what's happened."

A gust of wind whipped Elisha's hair.

"Okay, sir. I've got a last-known location for the van. Turned off the freeway in Bellevue, then disappeared."

"Disappeared how?"

"My assumption is it hasn't reappeared. Whether it's gone underground or the plates have changed or it just hasn't passed a camera."

"Good work. Keep looking for me, okay?"

"It's looking like a dead end."

"That's what I expected." Carter grimaced. "But keep looking, okay? Remember, you're my MVP here. Don't stop until you find it."

"Sir." Tyler seemed to put a bit of enthusiasm in it.

"How's the facial recognition going?"

"Slowly. I've been sidelined with this."

"That's your number one priority now, okay?" Carter ended the call and set off through the teeming rain toward the office building.

Richard Olson's office was at the back of the complex. One wall was floor-to-ceiling windows with a view across to the famous Microsoft campus a half mile away. Baseball memorabilia filled another wall, signed balls and bats and muddy shirts. War mementoes covered the third, guns and photos and a dummy in desert camouflage, the chest overflowing with medals. Looked like a general. Probably Olson's old uniform.

Olson stood behind a desk in front of the fourth wall, wearing a thin VR helmet, a fraction of the size and weight of the one Carter bought for Kirsty's birthday. He swiveled around, toting a plastic gun, then crouched low. "Don't mind me."

"You can see us, then?"

"And hear you too. A window pops up when someone comes in the room." A large monitor sat on the desk, showing Olson's point of view as he got shot at in a desert city by masked terrorists. "You're FBI, right? Special Agent Max Carter and Agent Elisha Thompson."

Spooky. Carter took a seat, gesturing for Elisha to do the same. "Need to ask you a few questions, sir."

"Should I have my lawyer here?"

"Depends on the answers you give."

"Cute. Very cute." Olson walked slowly, like he was inching along a corridor. "Take that!" The CEO swept his plastic gun around like it was real. "This is how I blow off steam. That hearing this morning sure raised my blood pressure." He ducked low, pointing the gun high. "This is immense. We're looking at acquiring the company." He was back up, pacing slowly, his head scanning around. "Started as a training tool for the military, but the tech's so advanced now that you can get this working on a five-hundred-dollar laptop. I want to get in before Microsoft or Valve. We could make a few bucks selling this to losers in their moms' basements."

"That what Harry Youngblood was playing at home?"

"What?" Olson tore off his helmet and chucked it on the desk. He blinked hard a few times, adjusting to natural light again. "He shouldn't have it at home."

"You know he was murdered, right?"

Olson let out a deep sigh, full of bitter regret. "You know, when security called up, Special Agent, I checked out your name and credentials. Kind of odd that the lead of the child abduction team is coming in here, asking about a murder, don't you think?"

"Very insightful." Carter nodded slowly. "Mr. Youngblood's death came up as part of our investigation into the abduction of Senator Christopher Holliday's children."

"I saw that on the news." Olson swung his chair around to look out the window, across his empire. "His son's dead, right?"

"He's in the ER, sir, fighting for his life. His daughter's still missing." Carter left a long pause, trying to goad him.

Olson wasn't giving anything up easily though.

"Why did you fire Mr. Youngblood?"

Olson collapsed into his leather chair and pressed a button on his PC. The screen went blank, but the fan kept whirring. "Harry was a buddy. We served together in Desert Storm, way back when."

"You were a general, huh?"

"Three-star." Olson looked out of his window. "Afterwards, we went our separate ways. I built GrayBox. Harry started doing private security work for the competition. Got married, had a couple of gorgeous kids, but then divorced." He grimaced. "Guy fell apart. Quit his job, ended up staying in his mom's basement. Can you believe it? Guy like that, reduced to living like some loser?"

"So you took him on?"

"Least I could do. I was setting up a strategic deployment division, and Harry's good people. Solid. Dependable. Loyal." Olson rubbed his neck. "Or so I thought. And with so many connections. Within a year, I put him in charge of the division. We support the US military, mostly overseas."

"Mostly?"

"About ninety percent. The home-soil stuff is usually security work. Either way, Harry's job is to identify areas where our expertise would be appreciated and then help roll it out. Grease the palms, make the deals. Before you get all het up, we're doing a service for our nation, plugging gaps our military can't fill. We're protecting this great nation of ours."

"So why was Xander Delgado looking into your company?"

"That congressional investigation is horseshit." Olson settled back in his chair. "Delgado put you up to this?"

"No, sir."

"Shoulda seen it. Delgado was up on stage, grandstanding, tearing me a new one, just to make himself look good." Olson sniffed, then leaned forward, his elbows clunking on the table. "Listen to me, my company supports our nation's soldiers in foreign theaters. We're heroes. Someone like Xander Delgado wants to drag our good name through the mud, just to help his own career, help him get re-elected. Thinks he can be president one day."

"But Delgado was more interested in a home-soil operation, right?"

Olson held Carter's gaze, the steely glare of a CEO, then picked up the VR rifle and used it to scope Carter. "You sure this shouldn't be on the record?"

"My objective is finding Senator Holliday's daughter. You're close, right?"

"Wouldn't say *close*. I play golf with Christopher once a month. Good guy, but not a friend."

"Must get a lot of time to talk on the golf course, right? Do some deals?"

"We're members of the same country club, that's it. Governor Duvall's invited us to play Inglewood a week Saturday. That's it."

"Did you meet Senator Holliday this afternoon?"

"Huh." Olson picked up the VR headset and slammed it off the desk with a loud thud. A crack ran down the plastic case.

"Breaking things isn't going to help."

Olson shot him a glare. "Okay, so what if I did?" He ran a finger along the visor's edge. "That slimeball Delgado was there too. Pair of punks, asking for help from me. But they were snooping, weren't they?"

"The man who took Avery and Brandon Holliday also abducted Congressman Delgado—that 'punk' as you put it. Left him handcuffed to a tree, stuffed his necktie in his mouth."

"Well I'd wish the honorable representative a speedy recovery, but after hanging me out to dry this morning, he doesn't deserve any sympathy."

"This abductor was there, you know? Must've been watching you."

"You need to try a lot harder to frighten me."

"Must've been an interesting phone call to get you to meet on the weekend."

"There are no weekends in this job, son. You see how busy the parking lot is? We're running four separate overseas engagements just now, three hot places, one freezing cold." Olson laughed. "Okay, so I met them. They talked about some cockamamie exercise they thought GrayBox was involved in. Some school in Seattle. Looked very much like Delgado was using Holliday to get at me."

"And you put them on to Harry Youngblood, right?"

"Right."

"Why?"

"The reason I sent them to Harry is because that's his wheelhouse, not mine." Olson rocked forward on his chair and rested his arms on his desk. "I've been involved in too much strategic decision-making, like this piece of garbage." He picked up the visor and tossed it in the trash. "This morning, at the congressional hearing, Delgado asked me some questions about this horseshit operation. All we did was loan some operatives to support the US troops helping secure our citizens in the event of an attack."

"Tang Elementary, right?"

"Why do you have to ask, if you already know all the answers?"

Carter caught Elisha's eyes narrowing. She looked his way but broke off eye contact as soon as she made it. He parked it for later and focused on Olson. "What was Delgado so interested in?"

"Always trying to make himself look better than he is." Olson let out a sigh. "But it got me thinking, you know? When I got back here after the hearing, I started digging. I found some documents that… Well, they showed that Harry was up to something, but not quite detailing what it was." He picked up the VR rifle from the desk and inspected it like he was out in the field and it was a real gun. "Every morning, I have press clippings delivered, anything that mentions my company. Usually it's fluff. Community outreach, investor analyst speculation, but sometimes my press guy delves the depths of the internet, looking for anything salacious."

"He ever find anything?"

"Every single day. It's almost always nothing. But sometimes there's a bit of meat in amongst all the noise." Olson reached into another drawer and got out a printed page, covered in scribbles. "He found this on some conspiracy page, some horseshit written

by a real libertarian goon who's read a bit too much Ayn Rand."
He chuckled. "People say that describes me, but I believe in society
and opportunity for the common man to better himself." He
passed the page to Carter. "Have a look."

At the top, there was a short digest of the article, followed by the
original text. The sort of website other parts of the FBI waste a lot
of time investigating and finding nothing, either in the damning
gossip they post or the people posting it.

This article focused on an alleged cover-up at Tang Elementary,
mentioned GrayBox by name. Said a child was taken and never
heard of again.

"This nibbled away at me, you know?" Olson reached for the
page again. "Ate away at the fiber of my being. People say I'm a
sociopath, but I swear… This then spread like wildfire to places
like 4chan and Reddit. Anywhere people talk about military stuff,
they were talking about how GrayBox—*my company*—abducted
a child from a school in Seattle."

"Is it true?"

"I didn't believe it. *Couldn't* believe it—not GrayBox, not my
company. No way. But no smoke without fire, you know?" Olson
pulled out another document, many pages thicker. "Turns out
Harry Youngblood ran a little side-exercise, off the books. Hadn't
run it past me. Left us wide open, let that punk Delgado haul
my company through the mud. I dug deeper and I found some
payments, all made to offshore tax havens. I'll never get at them,
doubt even you could. But I found a document relating to the
payments." He stuffed the VR rifle in the trash too, the plastic
cracking. "Harry refused to explain it, so I fired his ass."

"You're not worried about him talking?"

"It's a moot point now." Olson shook his head, slowly, lips
pursed. "Harry had NDAs coming out of his ass. His grandkids
couldn't even speak about anything he told them from his time
here." He walked over to the window, taking his time, then leaned

back against the glass, arms folded. "I'll tell you this because I want to help find Holliday's kid. Offshore money means one of two things. First, the money is Russian, Israeli, or Saudi. I handle all those myself, personally. Harry doesn't have any dealings."

"What's the other explanation?"

"That'll be business from a certain government organization."

Carter glanced at Elisha. This wasn't going how he expected it. "You mean the CIA?"

"I didn't confirm that, okay?" Olson leaned back against the glass again, like he wanted it to suck him out. "There's a guy works for Harry, name of Franklin Vance. Brings in a lot of work from that quarter. All paid from accounts in the Caymans, Bermuda, British Virgin Islands, you name it. Tax havens. Places where you can't trace the flow, can't discover the identity of the accounts. Whatever Holliday and Delgado were looking for, whatever Harry was running off-books, the trail would lead straight to Frank Vance's door."

CHAPTER FORTY-TWO

Mason

Vance opens his apartment door but stops on the threshold. "You don't need to point that gun at me. I *know* you're armed."

"Cut the shit." I press the gun against his spine. "We're here for the evidence. If it's good enough, I'll let you go."

"And if it's not?"

"Just show me it."

Vance steps into the apartment. It's a small space, minimal like a white-collar worker's Tokyo pad. Hardly any personal effects, just a base model TV and a small Bluetooth speaker. Vance strikes me as the kind of guy who'd have a packed bag in the trunk of his car, ready to disappear at the first sign of the heat.

"You guys sure do like to live alone."

"Best way, believe me." Vance sits at his coffee table and opens a sleeping laptop, a ruggedized model like you'd see in service. All padding and hard edges, several inches thicker than the latest slimline Apple or Microsoft models.

Holliday stands by the window, looking shell-shocked. At least he's stopped going on about me letting Avery go. Him whining would be too much to take just now.

I sit next to Vance and press the gun into his side. "Just take it nice and slow, okay?"

"Think I don't hear you?" Vance enters his password and logs in to a custom desktop, some bespoke GrayBox Linux build. "This is my work machine. The video footage automatically backs up to here in real time." He switches to a directory structure and navigates through the files. "Here's the operational report." He clicks on a few, and a printer fires off, hidden in a piece of furniture. Pages and pages of documents spew out, lightning quick. Within seconds, they're spilling onto the floor. Guy has some high-end laser printer rigged up so he can get everything he needs and fast.

I stick the gun deeper into his side. "You brought us here to show us what happened."

"We were *told* to take a kid and pass him on, that was it."

My mouth's gone dry again. "Let's start with what the kid's name was, okay?"

"I don't know."

I push the gun into a rib, reminding him of what I can do with it. "Come on, Frank. You can do better than that. It was Jacob, wasn't it?"

"No. It was something Muslim." He points across at the heap of papers. "It's on the prints, I swear." He rubs a hand across the mustache. "Just let me get the papers and I'll show you."

I take another look around the place. Nowhere to hide anything, let alone a gun. The kitchen's in the other direction, and no sign of any sharp knives or heavy pans. "Go."

Vance walks over and picks up the prints. He hands me the first document. "This was required to action the wire transfer between my Caymans account and GrayBox."

"How much did *you* take?"

"A good chunk. It's still in the Caymans, waiting for a rainy day." Vance hands me the rest of the pages. Must be hundreds of them. "The rest is the mission log."

As I scan through, my shoulders deflate. The abduction of Faraj al-Yasin, in black Times New Roman. Signed and counter-signed by Harry Youngblood, like these guys are realtors selling a house.

I feel numb.

Vance rubs his mustache. "The hassle I had to go to for some little kid."

I punch Vance in the balls, hard, my follow-through aiming for the next state. He goes down and I follow up with a kick to the gut. He lies on the carpet, whimpering.

I crouch down and put the gun underneath his left eyeball. "Where is he?"

"Don't know." Vance takes a halting breath. "We took him, drugged him, and passed him to some guy in a van. Don't know what happened after that. I swear."

I fold the pages and stuff them inside Delgado's jacket pocket, the other side from the blood. "Does Olson know about this?"

"He doesn't know anything." Vance gets to his feet and laughs, despite all the pain. "Guy's so out of touch with what's going on at his company. The reason he fired Harry is because he realized how much control he'd lost."

"He didn't fire you, though?"

"I'm not technically employed." Vance reaches over to the printer and passes me another set of documents. "He had this."

I snatch it out of his hands. "You just gave me the mission report."

"This is the official one. The one GrayBox gave to the army. No mention of the abduction, just supporting the military. This is what Olson knows. He doesn't know the truth. Happy to take the dough, but he doesn't ask questions of me or Harry."

"You mentioned a camera."

"Right." Vance picks up his laptop and enters an address into a web browser and clicks.

The screen fills with footage of soldiers running down a corridor, point of view like in a video game, but too low down, like a child was recording it. I can barely watch as they burst into a changing room and grab Faraj. The sound distorts and I can barely make anything out over the shouting. Arms reach out and someone sticks a bag over Faraj's head. His sports coach looks on.

And then Jacob bursts into the shot, fists clenched, punching at the soldiers, shouting to let his friend go. Vance's arms reach out and pick up Jacob. He's breathing hard, too hard, too fast. Then he stops and his face turns purple.

It happened so quickly. Way too quickly.

He's on the floor and Vance is giving him CPR, punching his heart and trying to get him to breathe, the camera shaking as he gives mouth-to-mouth.

All I hear is, "He's gone, Frank."

Jacob's dead face fills the screen.

My son.

My beautiful, brave son. Dying while he tried to save his friend. His only friend.

I can only stare at the screen.

One of the soldiers takes the coach aside. The guy is freaking out. Jacob lies on the floor, dead.

Then the camera-wearer jogs back out into the school corridor, catching up on the other operative carrying the sleeping Faraj away.

"Where did you take him?"

"Like I told you, some dude in a van. That's all I know. All I want to know."

I stand up tall and pace away from him, over to the window. I've got *my* answers, what happened to my boy. The brutal, disgusting end to his short, short life.

But is it what I wanted? Is it enough?

I point the gun back at Vance. "You killed him."

"I didn't."

"Looked that way to me."

Vance rubs his fingers through his mustache. He doesn't believe what happened either. "That fat kid was freaking out because we took the Muslim. Started hyperventilating. I grabbed him, tried to calm him down. I tried bringing him back to life, but I... couldn't. He just... stopped breathing." The words sound hollow and empty compared to the video. "I tried to save him. You've got to believe me. The kid had a weak heart. Just died in my arms. He would've died at some point. Could've been soccer practice. Could've been running for the school bus."

"He died because you took his friend!"

Holliday is standing behind Vance, leaning on the sofa back, watching the screen, frowning at me. "Was that your son?"

I don't answer him.

"If that's your son, well I'm sorry." Vance shakes his head, no sign of the stutter. He's back in control now, or at least thinks he is. "But this isn't on me."

"He died in your arms, you murdering piece of shit." I point the revolver at him, cock the hammer, ready to fire, to enact Jacob's revenge on this bastard. I take a deep halting breath. "One last chance. Where is Faraj?"

"I don't know and that's the truth, you cocksucker. It was out of our hands the moment we passed him over."

"The CIA have him?"

"That's who Harry said we were working for. Don't know what happened after that. I swear. Youngblood must know."

So Bob Smith was right, then. But only partially so. "Frank, he said you brought in the mission."

"That sleazeball." Vance clenches his fists. Looks ready to lash out. "The next time I see him I'll—"

"There won't be a next time."

"He's dead?" Vance smooths down his mustache. Getting really annoying now. Maybe I should shave it off before I kill him.

These pricks, all chasing the dime, then the next one and the one after that. All just a game. But these are people's lives, the lives of their loved ones. Kidnapping and killing and—

Shit, I *am* the same as them.

No.

I'm never the same as them. I'm stopping these bastards doing this, I'm taking revenge on them for what they've done.

I move over, keeping the revolver trained on Vance. "On your knees."

He looks at me, then pleads with Holliday, like he can save him. "Come on—"

I pistol-whip the back of his head and push him forward with my boot.

He tumbles onto the coffee table, his hands hauling the table over the perfect parquet floor as he goes down. He lands on his hands and knees, at least.

I put the revolver against his head. Franklin Vance, my son's killer. Does he deserve this? After what he did?

Of course he does.

So I shoot him through the head.

And again.

CHAPTER FORTY-THREE

Holliday

Holliday stumbled back and collapsed into an armchair, the only one in the room.

Frank Vance's dead eyes stared at him, stared *through* him. Two bullet holes in his forehead. The corpse slumped forward and collapsed onto the couch.

Holliday gripped the arms, trying to hold himself upright, stop himself following Vance down.

I brought Mason here, and I could only watch as he shot him. This is my fault.

Mason stood there, eyes closed, still holding the gun in the position it settled in. No more edgy twitching. He looked almost at peace, his justice served.

Did Vance deserve to die for killing Mason's son?

Maybe, but was it for Mason to decide? Whatever Vance deserved, he deserved a court deciding it. Mason didn't seem the sort to agree with the rule of law.

Holliday pushed up to standing. Took him a couple of attempts. Felt like he could fall over at any moment. "Can you let Avery go now?"

Mason glanced at him, frowned, then went over to Vance's dead body. He reached under his chin and held it for a few seconds before nodding. Didn't seem like an answer to Holliday's question, more that Vance was dead. He pointed the gun at Holliday. Then fell back in the armchair.

Mason walked over, raising the gun and resting it against Holliday's forehead. But he just stared at Holliday, sucking air in through his nostrils, eyes narrowing, Adam's apple bobbing up and down. A grunt, then he lowered the gun and walked off, fumbling in his pocket for something. He put his smartphone to his ear, making brief eye contact with Holliday before looking away. "It's me." He walked over to the window. "I've got answers. I know what happened to Jacob." He paused, like he was listening. "The CIA took Faraj."

Holliday tried to stand again, but his legs wouldn't let him.

Mason glanced back at Holliday. "No, keep Avery where she is. I'll think about what to do next." He ended the call and rested against the windowsill, typing on his cell, jaw clenched. Seemed like a long message.

Mason has two conspirators. Someone has Avery, but there's someone else pulling his strings. His wife? Someone else?

Can I use Mason as leverage? Swap him for Avery?

Or do I grab his cell phone, take it to the feds, and get them to track the calls?

Holliday looked around the apartment, searching for anything he could use to distract Mason, anything to use as a weapon if it came down to it.

Mason put the gun against Holliday's forehead. The barrel was still warm from shooting Vance. He just held it there.

Holliday tried to replay all the times Mason had used the gun he stole from the guard at the Federal Building. He shot Youngblood, accidentally or on purpose, right in front of that fed. Then he shot the glass to escape. Once in the air when they left Youngblood's home, to distract that FBI agent. Then he shot Vance, twice.

He doesn't want to kill me. And only five bullets. One left, still enough to kill me.

Mason stood so close that Holliday could smell his sweat. *Kick his ankles, kick his knees, kick his balls, overpower him. Kill him, destroy his body, tear his limbs apart.*

"You've got your answers." Holliday stared into Mason's dead eyes. "Please, you don't need anything else from me. Give me back my daughter. Let me go."

Something thumped down on the street. Loud.

Mason ran over to the window and peered out. "Shit."

CHAPTER FORTY-FOUR

Carter

Elisha pulled off the freeway, siren wailing, and passed two Priuses. She shot Carter a dark look. "What do you mean?"

"When I mentioned the name of that school, you freaked out." Carter grabbed the door handle like his life depended on it. The way she was driving, it felt like it did. "What's the story?"

"It's probably nothing." Elisha powered along the straight road, then slalomed around the corner.

Four Seattle PD cruisers surrounded a low-slung block of upmarket condos. Wide and low, two stories tall. Six uniformed cops crouched behind their vehicles, using them as shields.

Elisha screeched to a halt, the cabin filling with the stink of burning rubber.

Carter got out first, drawing his gun and crouching as he made his way to the nearest officer. "Have shots been fired?"

"Not since we got here. Not that I've heard, anyway." Officer S. West shook his head, but kept his focus on the apartments. "Had a report of two shots in apartment 3312 at eighteen twenty hundred hours." He waved over at the building, pointing at a window lit up in the evening sky. "Lopez and Ginty went inside a couple minutes ago. No word since."

The apartment complex door hung open. Two cops inside, at risk, in danger. And Vance inside. Was Mason here too?

"Okay, stay here." Carter squeezed through the gap between the cars and scooted over to the apartment block, keeping low. No movement inside the apartment. He pressed himself flat against the wall beside the door and sneaked a look. The carpeted interior was empty. He stopped outside the staircase door and waited for Elisha to join him. Got a nod from her, then he crouched low and pushed in at waist height, Elisha following at standing. Nobody.

He took a deep breath and took the stairs one at a time, careful to dampen the sound, keep it as quiet as possible. Up to the second floor, and he paused, his free hand held out to stop Elisha. No threatening sounds, just a low rumble of someone's TV turned up too loud, the sort of person who thinks it's okay to run a subwoofer in an apartment block.

He started climbing again, nice and slow. Up to the third floor, marked 3300—. He looked down the corridor, spotting 3310, 3311. Up ahead, the door to 3312hung open.

Carter stepped over, gun drawn, and stood outside the door, waiting for Elisha to join him. He chanced a peek inside.

Two uniformed officers stood on either side of a couch. They stepped aside and showed a body, two bullet holes in his forehead.

Franklin Vance. Another dead end.

And no sign of his killers.

CHAPTER FORTY-FIVE

Mason

Holliday is behind the wheel of Vance's Cadillac, easing it along the freeway. If you looked in the car right now, you'd see two regular guys hanging out. Just not talking to each other. Maybe they're at ease in each other's company.

But I can see the cogs grinding behind his eyes. Every turn we take, every approaching car, he sees them as opportunities to take control. Hit it right, and the odds are in his favor.

A Nissan crumpling the passenger side, injuring me, him reaching for the gun, killing me before the car even stops spinning.

But me dying doesn't equal him getting hold of Avery. And that's what makes him stop. All that stops him from doing that.

"Take a right here." I press the gun into Holliday's side, my arm burning, sweat coursing down my back, sticking to the leather seat.

As he turns, the asshole keeps looking in the rearview, no doubt hoping the feds are following us.

Another look and the road behind is empty.

But still Senator Holliday hopes. Craven, pathetic, lost, like a small child. Like a small, scared child. Weak, frightened. Not brave like Jacob had been. His last action on this Earth trying to save his friend from—

Vance.

That filthy degenerate.

Jacob died trying to save his friend from that vermin.

That cockroach.

That *human being*. That twisted, evil, barbaric human being.

Someone who knew better, someone who knew precisely what he was doing, but who ignored it and abducted a child for money.

After what I've done today, I'm no saint, but at least I can say I've done it for the right reasons, if such a thing exists. I'm trying to find answers, trying to unravel what these monsters did to my boy.

The gun feels heavy. Someone else's weapon, someone else's bullets. But my revenge.

Vance died far too quick a death for what he did. I should've stretched it out, tortured him. One thing I've learned over the last year is there's no heaven or hell, just the here and now. Vance isn't being tortured by Satan for eternity, or even waiting in limbo. He's gone. Dead. He can't cause any more harm to anyone. Besides, there's nowhere near enough time left in the universe to make him suffer enough for killing my boy.

Or for taking Faraj.

"Where now?" Holliday looks over at me, more determined than before.

I check the road ahead. Try to speak, but it catches in my throat. Feels like I'm going to cry. "Next left. Then pull over."

He does, leaving the engine idling. "Killing and torturing for some documents and a video. Was it worth it?"

I swallow down the bitter taste of freedom after a year stuck inside this mental prison, looking for answers. "Of course it was. Two evil men have paid for their crimes. No court would ever convict them. Their lawyers and the corrupt politicians they're in hock with would never let it get anywhere near that. But I've stopped them doing this again. And they *would* do it again, believe me. Again and again and again and again."

Holliday looks at me, like he's sizing me up, waiting to ask, but he doesn't, just sits there.

"People like Harry Youngblood and Frank Vance, people like you as well. In your eyes, the rest of us stopped being people a long time ago. We became cannon fodder, ends to your means. Doesn't matter who dies, does it? Collateral damage, or any number of euphemisms. But you're all just small boys comparing dick sizes in a locker room. It's all just a game to you."

"I went to public school."

I don't speak. Just watch the long straight road for feds. They'll be out in force now, looking for a man who has murdered twice.

Layla's answers died with Harry Youngblood. I was going to take him alive, leave Holliday there, get Layla to let Avery go, but the stupid bastard got himself killed. Made me cross a line.

But he's dead now. I won't be able to make him feel the pain Layla or I have felt over the last year. And we'll never get to the bottom of what happened, never find her son. Harry Youngblood will never truly suffer for the impact his greed has had on innocent people like me or Layla.

Holliday makes puppy-dog eyes at me. He knows he's no use to me, thinks I'm going to kill him now.

I've been using Holliday as a chess piece, pushing him around the board, bending him to my will. What do I do with him now?

His son's in the hospital, could even be dead. He's suffered the trauma of knowing his kids have been abducted and, even worse, that there's something he can do to save them.

But he's also witnessed two murders, one accidental, the other very deliberate. And I kidnapped his kids. He'll bring in the feds, help them find Avery and Layla.

"Stay quiet." I get out the burner and hit dial.

Layla answers immediately, sounds out of breath. "What's happened?"

"It's over, Layla. I've got our answers."

She doesn't say anything for a few seconds. "What." A statement, not a question.

"You want to do this—"

"Tell me what happened to my son!"

So I do.

Cars whiz past us, pulled up just off the side of the freeway.

Layla's breath comes slow, almost a whisper down the line. "Thank you."

"I wish it was different. I wish it was better news."

Even though I can't see her, I can tell she's processing it in that way she does, staring into space, frowning. "If the CIA have him, then it means he's, I don't know, somewhere. Right? Means he's still out there. I need to find him."

"I want to help."

"You're a wanted man. You need to go. Leave, now."

Through all of this, I haven't thought much about what to do next. I never expected to get any closure.

"Where can I go?"

"We talked about this. You need to escape. You've got a new identity, you could move to Alaska or Europe. Somewhere where they won't ask too many questions. Somewhere you can recover and become someone new."

It sounds good. Too good.

"You're right." Now *my* breathing is fast. "One last thing. What do we do with him?" I look at Holliday, eyes shut, like he's meditating.

"What do you want to do?"

"I don't know."

"You want to give him his daughter back?"

Avery hasn't done anything wrong. She's suffered and she doesn't deserve any more. "Seems like the right thing to do."

"I'll see you back here." And she's gone.

"Are you going to take me to Avery?"

I didn't expect it, but the prospect of Holliday being reunited with his daughter hits me in a part of my brain I'd closed off. Raw emotion, something like hope or joy, maybe. Or just something other than death and hate and destruction.

I put the gun away. "Come on, let's get your daughter back."

CHAPTER FORTY-SIX

Carter

Carter leaned back against the wall and let out a deep breath as the Seattle police uniformed officers started taping off the vicinity.

He knew that John Mason had gotten to Vance, just like he'd gotten to Harry Youngblood. But where was he? Always one step ahead of them, first murdering Harry Youngblood, now Frank Vance. And he still had Avery. The only good news Carter could see was that Holliday playing along meant that she was still alive.

Something to hold on to.

Unless he only thought she was.

A black Suburban pulled up, and Nguyen got out of the back, hugging her suit jacket over her shoulders like a rain cap. "Well, Max. Another body."

He just nodded at her.

"You have any idea why this guy's taking out GrayBox employees?"

A shake of the head was all he had to give.

"Why is he doing this, Max?"

Carter definitely didn't have that answer yet. He stepped away from the wall and joined her. "Holliday's working with him. Either coerced or…"

"What have you got on Vance?"

"Franklin Leonard Vance." Carter held up his laptop. "Unmarried. Military service record, Third Armored during Desert Storm, then redeployed to First Armored after they retired it."

"That's not a whole hill of beans, is it?"

"They've been asking questions about a military exercise at a school. Olson reckoned there's something shady there, but whatever it is died with Frank Vance and Harry Youngblood."

Nguyen looked up at the house for a good few seconds. "Okay, Max." She smoothed down her pants. "You've done good here, but this isn't finding Avery Holliday. And I'm tired of listening to your belly rumble. There's a Tex-Mex place around the corner."

Carter bit into his burrito. He hated Mexican food—too much fat and starch, even with the vegetables—but he ate it anyway. He was so hungry, he almost liked the taste. He bit into some lumpy chicken that wasn't so nice.

The tiny cantina was busy with customers sinking bottles of Corona as they bit into their silver-foiled wraps. Two of them were arguing about whether a third had paid for their guacamole.

The real world and all its trivialities.

Nguyen took a bite of her burrito. "So."

"So." Carter washed down his burrito with some coffee and tried to think things through. Everything was like sludge in his head. "What do we have?"

"Nothing. We must've just missed them."

"Keeps happening."

"Means we're getting closer, Max."

"Or it means our luck's running out." He picked up his burrito and bit into it.

"Max?" Elisha charged toward him through the doors of the cantina. "Tyler's got something." She sat next to him and flipped open the sleeping laptop. "He's run the facial recognition on the footage from the Federal Building. He's identified the kidnapper."

Carter snatched the laptop from her.

Mason John Wickstrom. Long red hair, bushy beard. A dead ringer for the man who'd killed Harry Youngblood.

The animal they'd been chasing.

Underneath was a redacted excerpt from his military record.

Ex-Navy SEAL with a photo of him a few pounds and a lot of hair lighter, much closer to the man he'd seen in Youngblood's home.

And they had an address.

CHAPTER FORTY-SEVEN

Mason

I point to the right. "This exit."

Holliday takes the turn and heads through the intersection. He accelerates down the street, takes us past Layla's house.

"Right here."

He follows the turns, taking us around the long block, the diversion I've used so many times. Shit, what if they know I do and they're—

Too late for that. Too late for anything. If they're after me, they've got me. And I don't really care. It's over. I'm a dead man walking.

He stops at the end and waits. "Which way?"

"Right again."

He sets off into traffic, following the curving road back to the freeway intersection. "We've been here before."

"Good observation, Senator." I can't even put any menace into my voice. It just sounds flat. "Pull up here." I wave at a space by the mailbox halfway along the stretch. He parks and I let the seatbelt go. "Stay here, okay? Remember that I'm still armed and we've got Avery."

"I've seen you murder two people."

"Don't even begin to tell me they didn't deserve it."

"I knew it." It's like a thought slipped out by accident.

"What, you knew that I didn't think they'd face a fair trial? That some high-price lawyers would get them off?"

Holliday barely lifts his shoulder, but it's still a shrug. "Just bring me my daughter." Spoken like a man used to getting his way.

I fix him with a hard stare. "This is where we're storing her, okay? Nobody lives there. Don't think you can return and find us sitting around the fire. We'll be long gone."

He nods, eyes moistening. "Just get her."

I get out onto the street, soaked, but the rain's off for a brief respite. I cross the road, keeping an eye on Holliday as I reach into my pocket for the key.

That bastard is watching me, like I didn't expect that. The threat should be enough—it has been so far.

I unlock the front door and take my time, listening hard. It's dark and quiet. Too quiet. Layla should have the lights on. Avery should be awake now, my magic potion long since run out. She should be watching some Disney shit, keeping her distracted from the reality.

Trying to hide my fear, I open the door to the bedroom. Empty. Layla has even made the bed.

I set off through the house, into the bathroom, the bedroom, the kitchen, the living room.

All empty.

There's a note hanging from the mailbox on the inside of the door: SORRY.

CHAPTER FORTY-EIGHT

Carter

Elisha turned into a low-rent neighborhood, a long row of single-story buildings, chain-link fences around each. Some had been lavished with love and attention, with fresh paint and hanging baskets.

Mason Wickstrom's house sure had, even had an extension out back, painted wooden boards that matched the rest of the home.

Another two FBI SUVs were parked a few spaces down, two agents in each.

"Not exactly inconspicuous, huh?" Elisha drove past the house and pulled up in front.

"Hopefully whoever's inside thinks they're Jehovah's Witnesses or something." Carter got out, walked over to the first Suburban, and got in back, as Elisha got in the second. He tugged on his FBI windbreaker. "Give me an update."

The male agent behind the wheel swiveled around. "Sir, we've had no entry or exit since arrival. We've got a TacOps unit on the back street, guarding the rear. Again, no entry or exit there."

Carter needed to do it properly this time. Keep Nguyen off his back. "Good work." He took another look at the house. "Do we know if there's anyone inside?"

The TacOps agent handed Carter a device, like the pair of binocs Buck Rodgers would wear. "Have a look."

Carter peered through the eyepiece. The green screen seemed to follow his eyes as he scanned the low-rise building. A figure glowed in reds, oranges, and yellows, sitting in the middle of the home. "Just one?"

"Confirmed."

Carter exhaled slowly. So Avery wasn't inside. But they might know where she was.

Then something caught in his throat. Or she'd died, long enough ago that her body was cold.

He passed the binocs back, his hand shaking slightly. "You're the experts—what do you suggest?"

"Covert entry." The driver narrowed his eyes. "Surprise the occupant. Take them down, then question them. Our priority is to secure the accomplice and identify the location of Avery Holliday, right?"

"Agreed." Carter opened the back door and put his foot on the curb.

"Sir." The driver was raising his eyebrows. "I know you like to lead from the front, but it's best if you leave this to the professionals. Don't want any more blood on your hands."

Carter wanted to punch the guy. He held up his hands instead. "Come on, then. Show us how it's done." He joined Elisha on the sidewalk, getting out his Glock handgun.

The four TacOps agents were all about the same height, telltale bulges in their suit jackets visible through their windbreakers.

Elisha unholstered her pistol and checked it. "You know the drill. Usual formation."

Four tight nods, like they'd spent weeks practicing their timing. Then they broke off toward the house. Two stayed at the end of the path with Elisha. Carter followed the other two at a distance, jumping over the chain-link fence into the front yard, a patch of mud. Then he crouched low and crept around the side of the house, following the path of the two TacOps agents. The side gate hung open, and he stepped through. The back yard was overlooked on all sides. Two homes at the back, a block of low-rent apartments to the left, and a clone house on the right. The yard was overgrown, just some faded kids' toys hiding in the long grass. A set of swings that looked like they hadn't even been looked at in years.

The two agents went into a flanking position, pistols drawn, one on each side of the back porch.

Carter inspected the windows as he stepped over to the door. No signs of movement inside. The agent who'd been in the passenger seat put a device up to the door lock and pressed the screen of a smartphone.

The door clicked open.

Carter went first, taking care to keep the door quiet, waiting to pass it to the first TacOps agent. He stepped into a grubby kitchen, and let the agents scan the room.

"Clear."

Carter waited by the door to a hallway, letting the TacOps agents go first. No dead bodies yet. But no live ones.

"Hands on your head!"

Carter raced through the house.

A woman cowered on a wheelchair, her shaking hands held aloft. The two flanking agents trained their guns on her. She looked late thirties, but frail and drawn, her skin pale, her blonde hair thin. She put her hands behind her neck, panic in her eyes.

Not what Carter had expected, sure, but maybe she was still capable of collaborating with Mason. Maybe she knew where he was keeping a small girl hostage. He crouched in front of her, gripping the arms of the wheelchair. "Who are you?"

"Grace. Grace Wickstrom."

Wickstrom's wife.

Carter looked around the room. No sign of any dead bodies. "Where is Avery?"

"Who?" The fear in her eyes betrayed a complete lack of knowledge.

"Where's Mason?"

"He's not here. Hasn't been all day."

"When did you—"

"Last night. He fixed dinner for me, then left." She looked away, her face full of shame, like not being able to cook for her husband was the worst she had to contend with. "Mason's staying with a buddy. We had a fight, and he's not responding to my texts or calls."

The two agents appeared in the narrow hallway, shaking their heads. "She's not here, sir."

So where is she?

CHAPTER FORTY-NINE

Holliday

Holliday sat in the Cadillac's passenger seat, eyes trained on the house Mason had entered.

Ten minutes now. Doesn't take that long to retrieve a girl. Unless…
Unless something's happened to her. Or him.
I'll never get her back.

A green Range Rover circled the block again, a young couple in the middle of a thundering argument.

I've got to do something.

Holliday got out of the Cadillac and carefully pushed the door shut. He looked around, but there was no sign of anybody, let alone anyone homing in on them. He followed Mason's path across the road and crouched by the low fence. The house sat in a dust yard, a chain-link fence securing it from the street. No features of note, just two windows facing the road, both with thick curtains, and a wooden door, hanging open.

Holliday got up and crept over to the doorway. He stopped by the door and listened. Somebody inside, pacing around, shouting. Got to be Mason.

He opened the door wide enough to peer inside.

Mason tore through the apartment into the kitchen, oblivious to Holliday watching him. Thumping came from another room.

He hasn't noticed me.

Mason walked back into the hallway.

Holliday pushed himself flat against the front wall. He spotted the Range Rover just down the road, but the occupants were still locked in their deep argument.

"Jackass!"

Mason cursing himself isn't good.

Holliday peeked back inside, his heart hammering away. Sweat drenched his forehead.

Mason had his cell phone pressed to his ear, keeping his focus on a room on the right. "Layla. Call me. Where are you? Have you still got her?"

Layla? His accomplice?

And he doesn't have my daughter?!

The things he's made me do and he doesn't even have her?

Mason ended the call and entered the room, leaving Holliday's field of vision.

Think.

He doesn't have her. But he knows who has her.

Holliday crept forward, stepping over the threshold.

Something banged in the room, loud like a weight had fallen on the floor.

Holliday chanced a peek in. Mason was going through a closet, throwing stuff around.

Holliday shot past the bedroom floor, then stopped, listening hard. Just swearing and shoving clothes along in the closet, the hangers squealing off the rail. He started walking again and kicked something, a crumpled-up sheet of paper. He reached down for it.

SORRY.

Holliday stepped over to the kitchen. Spartan, just a stove and a small countertop cooler. Curled-up wallpaper, battered and bruised cabinet doors, the countertop cracked and scored. Aluminum pans hung from a shelf made of metal rods screwed into the wall. *Aluminum wouldn't hit hard enough and it'd take too long to get a rod down without being heard.*

Holliday opened the top drawer. No knives, certainly nothing sharp enough.

"Shit." Mason was back in the hallway, staring at his cell phone in disbelief, raised eyebrows twisting together in a deep frown, looking back into the bedroom like Avery would magic herself out of thin air.

Holliday jerked to the side, out of Mason's line of sight. He scanned the room again. Hiding behind the aluminum pots was a cast-iron griddle, the surface rough and charred like burnt meat. He chanced another look.

Mason was still staring into the room. He put the cell to his ear and entered the bedroom.

Holliday stepped over to the pans and parted them to get at the griddle. He took it—felt weighty enough.

Two of the pots clanked together.

Holliday froze, listening hard.

Mason's voice came from the bedroom: "Layla, it's Mason. Where are you?"

Holliday stepped through to the hallway, hiding the griddle behind his back, barely breathing. A floorboard creaked as he passed over to the bedroom doorway.

Mason was standing by the closet, head bowed, phone to his ear, facing away. "Layla, call me. Now." He stabbed a finger off the screen, then just stood there, thinking hard.

Holliday lashed out with the pan and cracked it off the back of Mason's skull.

CHAPTER FIFTY

Carter

Carter leaned against the window, looking out onto the street. Outside, Elisha was coordinating the quartet of agents as they fanned out, knocking on doors. No sign they were being watched. No sign that Mason Wickstrom was anywhere near his home. Meaning he hadn't fled here.

So where was he?

And where was Avery?

He turned back to face the room—a small kitchen area, spartan, the furniture jaded. The walls needed painting, and the shaker kitchen could do with some new doors. Probably the least of her worries. The place smelled of strong coffee, a pot hissing on the counter. The dark liquid inside was more opaque than coffee should be—looked like the sort where one cup at ten in the morning would keep you up all night.

Grace Wickstrom sipped from a glass of water, her hand shaking.

"Your husband didn't come home?"

"Weren't you listening?" Grace slammed the glass on the small table. "Staying with a buddy. So he said."

Carter poured himself a cup of coffee and another for Grace. "That a common occurrence?"

"It's become more common." She pounded her hand off the wheels. "Since this happened." She scowled at Carter. "What's he done? Why are you looking for Mason?"

"Your husband abducted two children."

Her hand covered her mouth, her wedding band slipping over her knuckle. "The senator's kids?" She leaned forward, head in her hands.

Looked genuine, like this was all news to her and she wasn't involved. No acting, just the truth.

Carter left her with her shock, let it play out in her head, all the possibilities, all the probabilities. Might dislodge something useful.

She shut her eyes. "You know about Jake, right?"

"Jake?"

She looked up, frowning at him, then wheeled over to an open fire, the red bricks charred black. The coals and embers glowed, heating the room, but the ventilation wasn't doing its job—the air tasted of bitter wood smoke. A row of framed photographs ran along the mantelpiece. Grace was in most of them, smiling and about thirty pounds heavier, a weight that suited her. Her husband was in fewer than a quarter, obviously the photographer in the rest. A boy grew from a baby to a chubby kid, maybe ten, maybe thirteen, hard to tell. "This was Jacob. Our son." She handed Carter the most recent photo of Jake, a shot of him and his dad fishing. "Jake died at school."

Carter inspected it. The boy had his father's red hair, but a heft neither of his parents seemed to have. More burgers and fries than linebacker strength. Kid didn't look too happy either. Welcome to modern America.

But his father did. In every shot, Mason Wickstrom grinned at the camera, like he had everything in the world. Shaved head, smooth face. Muscular physique.

If the boy was dead, then he'd lost it all. Was that enough to do what he did?

But why Holliday?

"His heart stopped when he was warming up for soccer." Grace looked over, her red eyes probing, then took the photo back. "The autopsy said it was some congenital defect that we didn't know about, that we couldn't know about, that we shouldn't blame ourselves for." She took the photo back and stroked it. Her body jerked as she started crying. "He could've died at any time, they said, but it happened last year. It's all a blur. I was at work, got a call and my world fell apart. They said my boy was dead. I raced over to the school and he was being taken out in a body bag. My boy, my Jacob. Dead. He was *nine*. How does that happen?"

Carter stroked her back. Made her flinch.

She twisted her head around in a sideways figure eight, like it was all she could do to stop herself breaking down, from descending into the abyss. She fiddled with her wedding band, spinning it around her bony finger. "I couldn't cope with what happened. Threw myself onto the freeway. Missed the front of the bus and landed on the top. Bounced. And broke my back." She punched her useless legs.

Carter had to step away, shutting his eyes.

Grace had tried and failed.

His own mother hadn't just tried to kill herself, but had taken two lives. Hers and someone else's.

Grace hadn't, instead returning here to an emotionally broken husband, her body as smashed as his mind. Returning to only the memories of a happy life.

He pictured her standing over the freeway, resting on the bridge, watching and waiting. Her broken heart still beating. Ready to time her fall to kill herself.

The bus driver wouldn't forget.

Nobody thinks of the others in that situation.

Carter dragged himself back to the present and tried to piece it together. They were getting somewhere, some kernel of a motive forming.

A son dying could make anyone do anything.

But why Holliday? It still didn't add up.

Carter wiped his cheeks and eyes, then turned to face her. He flashed her a sympathetic smile. "Mrs. Wickstrom, did your husband ever talk about Christopher Holliday?"

Grace frowned at him. "You really think he's taken those kids?"

"We know he has, I'm afraid."

She slumped back in her chair and swallowed hard. "Mason got let go from his job six months ago. He worked security at a tech firm, but they sold up to some company down in Silicon Valley. Paid off most of the staff, took the good ones with them. My husband was good at his job, but it was security, so they didn't need him. He blamed the government for not protecting their jobs."

"Including Holliday?"

"Everyone. The president, the governor, both senators. He wrote to them, but they just sent back form letters, if they even bothered to read them in the first place."

That didn't feel like a strong motive. Especially not with the questions he'd been asking.

"I really need to speak to your husband, Mrs. Wickstrom. Any idea who this buddy is?"

She looked up, but didn't say anything, just spun the ring on her finger.

"Is he having an affair?"

"No." Grace shut her eyes and snorted. "Maybe. Maybe not."

"What is that supposed to mean?"

"Mason's..." She gasped and kneaded her forehead. "Mason found this hard. And with my, um, accident, on top of Jake, well..." She slumped back in the chair again. "My husband tried dealing with what happened in his own way, which meant he didn't accept it. He didn't believe the autopsy, didn't believe that our boy had a heart attack. Or didn't accept that it was during *soccer*."

"What did he think happened?"

"I don't know. When he lost his job, Mason got a chunk of cash, enough for a couple years' living. I told him to get another job, that we should save it." Grace rolled back to the table pressed against the wall, still set for three places. At some point, a family would've eaten there. Now it was empty, her son dead, her husband a child abductor and murderer. "But he sat here, every single day, searching on his laptop. From the moment he helped me up, till I went to bed again."

"What was he looking for?"

"Jacob died the same day this military exercise went down."

Carter took a sip of coffee, savoring the bitter tang. Tried to focus on that to keep his mind from racing ahead. And he failed.

A dead son, and a military conspiracy. Delgado said they were looking for information on an exercise at a school.

"When was this?"

"October second." Grace looked at him, her eyes locking on to his through the mist of tears. "Mason thought Jake's death was somehow connected to a military exercise. He found stuff on the internet about military conspiracies. YouTube, Reddit, you name it. He searched and searched for his truth." She reached up to the counter and took her coffee, cradling it on her lap. "I thought it'd help, but he just kept getting deeper and deeper. I told him to stop. But he couldn't. By that point it was an obsession. It had taken over his life."

"Did he find anything concrete to back it up?"

"Not that he told me."

"Did Mason speak to anyone else about his suspicions?"

"The school, of course. Tang Elementary. I mean, the principal denied it. But Mason thought someone had paid to shut them up."

"What about any of the kids' parents, anything like that?"

"Not to my knowledge. He thought the school told them to keep quiet, but..." She locked eyes with Carter, her glare steely. "My husband isn't a well man. Not like me. I mean, mentally."

"Did he ever share anything with you that might make you think he was onto something, that the school was indeed covering it up?"

Grace frowned. "I don't know." She took a drink of her coffee, grimacing at the taste. "Mason kept asking me to explain how Jake died the same day his friend went missing. Faraj. Lovely boy. Jacob's best friend. He disappeared that night after school. They never found him again."

Carter could now see the logic Mason Wickstrom had followed. One mighty coincidence. "Did he find any evidence?"

"Not that I know of."

But a missing kid meant a Child Abduction Rapid Deployment case.

Meant that Carter had another lever to pull.

CHAPTER FIFTY-ONE

Mason

I can barely open my eyes. The room's dark, just outlines of shapes. Dulled light coming from a window, thick curtains blocking it. I'm propped up against something and my head is getting worse, throbbing hard now. Feels like someone's opened up the back of my skull. I reach up to touch it but my hands are tied together.

I try to pull my wrists apart, but there's no give. Can't even get my fingers around. Feels plastic, like cable ties. The bonds on my wrists glow bright yellow in the gloom. Twisted nylon rope, the modern stuff, coated plastic. Shit, I need a sharp knife to get out of that. My eyes are adjusting to the light. I can see shapes, maybe a desk with a chair. I twist around and it's maybe a bed that I'm propped up against. But nothing I recognize.

Something creaks, then the door opens and light crawls across the brown carpet toward me. "You're awake?" Holliday stands in the doorway, arms folded, lit up from behind. But I can still see his politician smile, his teeth glowing in the half-light. "You won't be able to move, Mason. If I know one thing, it's how to tie a knot."

"Good old boy scout, huh?" I try to move my head, but it feels like my scalp's on fire. "What did you do?"

"I hit you with a griddle." Holliday squats in front of me. A cast-iron frying pan is face down on the floor at his feet. "You turned your back on me, Mason. Bad move." And it's his turn to put the gun in my face. Point-blank range, pressing against my teeth. I can taste the steel, dull like the pain in my arm. The way he's holding the gun, the one I took from the guard, he's obviously used a weapon before, and not just on a firing range. He's trained, he knows how to shoot. Or he's a very good actor. Can't take my chances. "Just so we're clear, I'm in charge here from now on. Okay?" He tears the towel off the wound on my arm and pokes at it with a wooden spoon, handle end first.

A trail of fire burns up to my skull, making me gasp.

"Where is Avery?"

I clench my jaw, tight. Keeping quiet, but I know what's going to happen.

Sure enough, he sticks the spoon back in my wound.

The weirdest sound comes out of my mouth, like a hushed squeal. I focus on it as everything tightens around the pain.

He lets go, but the agony stays with me, blood thudding in my ears. "Come on, Mason. Enough of this. Where's my daughter?"

"I don't know."

"Why did you bring me here?"

"I was working with someone. She was supposed to wait here and look after your daughter. She's gone."

"Where has she taken Avery?"

"I don't know."

He pushes the spoon in, deeper this time.

I try to swallow down my gasp, but it hisses out like a deflating balloon. I bite my teeth together, trying to be strong, trying to hide any signs of weakness. There's no way out. He's got my ankles tied together.

Maybe if I overpower him, I can get to the kitchen. Find a knife, slice through the bonds.

Maybe.

Turning my back on him like that... Should've cuffed him to the wheel, but I used my cuffs on Delgado when I didn't have to.

I deserve everything I get.

He pushes the spoon into my wound. "Who has her? Layla, right?"

No choice but to give it to him straight. Play it slow, calm, and wait for an opening. "How did you know that?"

"You said her name when you were calling her." It doesn't buy me any time, just a whole new world of pain. "Who is she?"

I can't stop myself from panting as he pulls the spoon away.

"Her son went missing during the exercise. Kid called Faraj. The official line was he disappeared, but they never found the body. She thinks they kidnapped him. Layla found me, we knew each other from play dates. We were looking for the same answers." I swallow hard. "Faraj going missing and my boy dying on the same day as this military exercise? Far too much of a coincidence. So we started digging. Together."

"And you think that justifies abducting my kids?" Anger flares in his eyes. He's going to kill me. I can tell. "Because your son died, you think you can endanger mine?" He digs the spoon into my wound like he's stirring a pot of soup.

The searing pain makes me black out.

Holliday slaps me, brings me back around. "You think you can do that to me? To my family?" He's gasping, out of breath, out of control. "That was your son in the video, right? The one who died? Heart-attack boy."

"You sick fu—"

The revolver cracks off my jaw, pushing me back against the bed. I taste blood, thick and bitter. And he pistol-whips me again, hard metal hitting my cheek this time. My head jerks back and hits the bed. Another wave of pain floods through me, from the back of my skull.

I black out again.

Another slap brings me back.

I try opening my mouth. Feels like his pistol-whipping cracked the bone. Probably the least I deserve.

"I don't know how to find her." I make eye contact with him, or as close as I can when I see three of him and he's lit from behind. "And that's the truth."

"Why me?" Holliday grabs my shirt with his free hand and pulls me close.

I could head-butt him, if I wasn't too woozy.

"Why did you target me?"

"We thought you'd know the answers."

"Me?" He rocks back on his heels. "Why would I know?"

"You sponsored a bill through the Senate." I give him a shrug. "It's one of those things where you're following the logic as they tell you, but as soon as you leave, you can't remember any of it."

He hits me again with the gun. Different cheek. Sorer, harder, but I don't black out this time. The pain builds and vibrates then gives enough ground that I can breathe again.

"I don't give a rat's ass about your stories." His hand grips my throat, squeezing my windpipe. "You've put my family through hell based on an assumption. I'm going to kill you."

CHAPTER FIFTY-TWO

Carter

Carter yawned. The coffee hadn't kicked in yet and boy did he need it. He clutched his cell tight. "Karen, I need everything I can on it. Everything."

"Max, I don't want you dredging up old cases. The family are at peace with what happened to their son."

"And they never found his body, Karen. Makes me think there's something in the connection."

"Max, you sound like you're wearing a tinfoil hat. You're sure of this?"

"Mason Wickstrom is. Isn't that enough to at least explore it?"

"I'm dealing with all kinds of fallout here. Two dead bodies now, and you're getting further and further from finding Avery. It's probably time you thought about standing down, let Lori take over."

Carter stabbed the End Call button and pocketed his cell.

Elisha's frown released almost as soon as it formed. "She playing ball?"

"Told me to stand down."

"And are you?"

"I hung up on her." Carter stretched out in the car. "Childish, I know, but I can't give up on this." He looked out of the window just as the rain started up again. Thin strands, giving way to stair rods. "We should visit the school and ask about the boy."

"On a Saturday?"

"Fine. We find the principal's home address. Visit, dig into it."

"You think there's something in this conspiracy stuff?"

"Olson mentioned possible CIA involvement. Hard not to fall down that rabbit hole."

"Did Karen give you anything on it?"

"Shut me down. Respect the families, blah, blah, blah. She doesn't get it, Elisha. It's just statistics to her."

"Karen Nguyen ran that case. You were on leave. Maybe she just doesn't like being audited. You were in Hawaii, right?"

"Right. You worked that case, didn't you?"

She nodded.

"Go through it from the start. Okay? Everything you remember."

"Max…"

"I'm serious. Fresh pair of eyes, a year's distance. Sometimes that's enough."

"You'll be the death of me." Elisha ran a hand through her hair, let it fall back into exactly the same position. "Kid went missing on his way back from school. Never heard from again. We went through standard procedure, yada, yada, yada. Karen had it pegged as a parental abduction. The boy's father."

"What did you have to back that up?"

"First, we got several witness statements of an Arabic man seen near the school around the time of abduction, matching the description of the boy's father. Second, we got an Interpol message saying the kid was in Syria, safe as you can be over there."

"Read it out."

"You don't believe me?"

"I believe you, Elisha. It's everyone else I have a problem with."

"You can be such a dick sometimes…" She logged into her laptop. "The Interpol message said that Faraj was alive, quite well, and had no intentions of returning to the USA. Happy living with his father."

"You believe it?"

She laughed. "I must be getting like you, Max, because I don't believe anyone these days."

"Best way to be."

"Take your word for it."

"You ever find the father?"

"There's a warrant out, but he's believed to be in Syria. He's on a watchlist, so if he comes back in the country, he'll be spoken to at customs."

"If he comes back, he'll use a fake passport. Nobody's that dumb, are they?"

Elisha hammered the laptop's keys, her forehead creased in concentration. "Either way, no extradition treaty and we have no jurisdiction in that part of the country, unless we topple the Assad regime, which I don't see happening any time soon. And SAC Nguyen put it in the unsolved bucket."

Carter played it through, trying to get inside her head. He could buy keeping it open so the father got spoken to, but there were plenty other ways to achieve that. No, there was something strange going on. Something he couldn't quite put his finger on.

Oh yeah, those three letters.

CIA.

Carter twisted around to look straight at Elisha. "Mason Wickstrom thinks his son died during the military exercise."

"Jacob." Elisha swallowed hard, like she'd personally been at fault. "Kid died of a heart attack warming up for soccer, Max. There's nothing to suggest his son's death is connected to what happened to Faraj. The exercise was early afternoon, and Faraj went missing after school. Besides, he was on the roll call from the evacuation, and we've got eyewitness reports supporting it."

"Who from?"

Elisha tapped at her laptop. "The principal. The sports coach."

"Anyone else?"

"Max, are you auditing *my* work now?"

"I just want the truth."

"*Max.*" Elisha slammed her door, then ran a hand through her hair again. "Stop being a prick. You know how hard these cases are. You think we didn't do our jobs just because you were in Hawaii?" She held his gaze, long and hard until he looked away. "This was the hardest case I ever caught."

Carter nodded slowly. He'd been to that dark place a few times himself, but always kept coming back to the light. Those kids needed people looking for them. Luck of the draw meant one or two would stay missing. "Can I check the paperwork?"

Elisha laughed. "Be my guest." She handed him her computer, logged into the case file. "A roll call was taken before the exercise, then after when the kids returned to the school."

Carter checked through the file structure. Everything in the right place. He found the scans, twenty-seven pages of roll call. He opened the first one, crystal-sharp on her screen, like the original was right in front of him.

Right at the bottom of the page, two signature boxes.

One for a teacher, signed N. Anthony Smith.

The military signature was Franklin K. Vance.

Carter let out a groan loud enough that Elisha tutted. "This guy." He tapped the screen. "Olson told us he does a lot of work for the CIA."

Elisha rubbed at her face. "You don't seriously think the *CIA* took Faraj?"

"Maybe. Or maybe it's enough that Mason Wickstrom thought they did." Carter played it through, slowly. Wickstrom's belief that the school covered something up started to look a whole lot more sane. "If the CIA took the kid and someone covered it up, who stands to benefit?"

"GrayBox."

"Right." Carter sat there, silent, focusing on it.

Jacob Wickstrom died warming up for soccer. Congenital heart defect, undiagnosed. Happens all the time in college sports, even in the NFL, the NBA, the MLS.

Faraj al-Yasin went missing somewhere between school and his home. Elisha was right—it looked like parental abduction, taken to a country that might as well have been Mars.

Carter knew that feeling. He blanked it out, trying to extricate himself from the case.

That Interpol message smoothed off the jagged edges. Easy if the message was from Canada or somewhere in Europe. From Syria? Who knows how legit it was.

"What did the mother think happened?"

"She had no idea." Elisha let out a deep sigh. "She reported Faraj missing when he didn't come home from school that night. Other than that Interpol message, we never had any leads on the father." She bit her lip, hard, like it could break the skin. "He left Layla two years earlier. Just walked out. No forwarding address. No calls. No birthday cards for Faraj. Layla was the breadwinner and she stayed strong for her son. Faraj needed his mother and she had to work hard to pay for their home, to put him through school."

"What do you have on the father?"

"Born Kenny Hassan. His parents were Egyptian. Standard immigrant folks, working a horrible job to pay for a better life for their kids. And they gave Kenny that life. Software engineer at one of the big tech firms. Amazon, I think. Could've been Microsoft, I'd need to check. Maybe Valve. But he hated it, so he quit and became a yoga instructor. Next thing, Kenny Hassan has changed his name to Quraish al-Yasin. Made his wife change her name too."

"He was radicalized by yoga?"

"I mean, he was certainly radicalized. We checked his message history, but he was smart, knew how to cover his tracks. Two years ago, he just upped and left. I followed the route through his transactions. One-way flight to Turkey before we cracked down on that sort of thing. Got surveillance footage from the airport, definitely him getting on. And from there, it's just a short trip to the Syrian border. You can guess the rest."

Carter nodded. "ISIS."

It fit the official story.

And it was so close to home. Father abducting a son against a mother's wishes.

But it also fit another narrative.

If Kenny Hassan, an American citizen, fled the US to fight for ISIS in the Syria desert, then it made some sense for the CIA to want him.

And Olson figured the CIA paid Vance and Youngblood to abduct the boy. Would they abduct his son? Interrogate a kid, find out if he knew where his father was. The darkest of all black ops. Looked like it'd been covered over.

And if Faraj's father hadn't taken him, and the CIA had, did they still have the boy?

It sent a shiver up Carter's spine. He stared at the laptop screen again. "Okay, let's speak to this coach first. See if the boy was definitely at school that day before we hare off elsewhere."

CHAPTER FIFTY-THREE

Carter

Tony Smith lived in a one-bed condo in Highline, a good commute from Tang Elementary. The apartment building was three stories of beige-painted wood, a carport cutting into the first floor and the developer's profits. Cars hurtled past on the street outside, not far from I509. Jaunty disco music blared out of an apartment above.

Elisha hit the buzzer and leaned back against the wall, arms folded.

Carter looked around. Hard to figure out which apartment it matched up with in the crazy layout.

A weary sigh rasped out of the intercom. "What?" Male voice, high-pitched.

Elisha leaned in close. "Looking for a Tony Smith."

Another sigh. "That deadbeat moved out months back." Texan accent. Long way from home. "Dude moved out in a big hurry, headed back to Minnesota. No forwarding address."

"You know him?"

"Who are you?"

"FBI."

And he was gone.

Elisha's turn to let out a sigh.

Carter tried to swallow down the butterflies in his gut. "This guy oversaw a soccer practice where a kid dies. Then another of his kids goes missing. And now he's gone?"

"As much as I don't like coincidences, what if this is unrelated?" Elisha grimaced, like even she didn't believe what she was saying.

"This guy's son dies and then he's digging into the worst parts of the internet, looking for the truth, but conspiracies are much easier to find. The hard part is finding proof. Sometimes a grieving father just needs time to grieve."

A door opened under the carport. A three-hundred-pound monster stood there, sporting a rolled-up Mariners baseball cap, his distended belly poking out the bottom of a Houston Texans tee. "Can I see your ID, ma'am?"

Elisha showed her shield, waiting for him to paw it. "What's your name, sir?"

"Douglas." Took his time inspecting her badge.

"That a first name or a last name?"

"Take your pick."

"Like that, huh?" Elisha held his gaze, then glanced at Carter. He gave her a shrug. It didn't really matter.

She focused on Douglas again. "Any idea where we can find Mr. Smith?"

"Nope." Douglas pulled off his hat and twisted the brim. His hair underneath was surprisingly long, all twisted into a topknot. "Jerkwad didn't leave a forwarding address or nothing." He tossed a package to Carter. A bunch of mail, all bound up. "Would you look at all that mail. Still comes every day."

"You own this place?"

"I'm the concierge."

Last place you'd expect a concierge. Maintenance man, sure.

Carter smiled at him. "When did Mr. Smith move out?"

"December fifteenth. Remember it like it was yesterday."

Carter checked the mail pile. "This seems a bit light for almost a year."

Douglas snorted then spat on the ground. "Dude came back and cleared out his apartment in July, just after Independence Day. He'd paid the rent in advance, so..." He shrugged.

"You speak to him?"

"Nah." Douglas pointed at the other end of the carport. "I was out washing my truck and there was an Econoline parked over there, in the space allocated to another apartment. The tenant, Krist, he came back, and man that dude was *pissed*. Got me to have a word with Tony, you know? So I went up. Guess what? The deadbeat didn't answer. An hour later, the Econoline was gone and the place was empty. Key was under my door."

"Thanks, sir." Carter walked off, getting out his cell and dialing Tyler's number. "Peterson, we're at Tony Smith's apartment now. He hasn't been sighted in months. Have you got anything on his whereabouts?"

"Sir, SAC Nguyen gave me strict instructions not to speak to you."

"Did she? Well, just pretend I'm Elisha, okay?"

"Right. Well, there's nada. Tried all variations of his name. Smith with an I and a Y. Anthony, Antonio, you name it. Getting a lot of hits, sure, but no sports coaches. Not even a teacher."

"Can you contact the Minneapolis Field Office and get some agents out looking for him? It's possible he might've returned home. Call me if you get any kickback from them. And check his bank records, cell phone, yada, yada."

"Sure thing, sir."

"Okay, Peterson. Thanks." Carter killed the call and leaned back against his SUV. "I don't like this. You know, I could almost buy Jacob dying and Faraj disappearing on the same day."

Elisha flicked up her eyebrows. "But?"

Carter waved a hand at the condo block. "Add in Jacob's sports coach going missing, the only witness to his death? I'm starting to think Mason Wickstrom might be onto something."

"Maybe. Maybe not. Doesn't bring you any closer to finding Avery, though."

"No, no it doesn't." Carter tried to run through the options. Time was running out, every second that passed was one where they didn't have Avery.

"So, Max, why is Nguyen telling Tyler to not speak to you?"

"Beats me." Carter started flicking through the mail. Mostly generic junk, the lifeblood of capitalism. "You said there were two witnesses who said Faraj was at the school. The coach and the principal, right?"

CHAPTER FIFTY-FOUR

Carter

Carter got out of the SUV just as the rain started again. Heavy, like cannonballs coming out of the sky. His phone blared out. Tyler. He answered the call, facing away from Elisha. "Agent Peterson, what have you got for me?"

"Better be quick, SAC Nguyen's here."

"I'm listening."

"Sir, I've gotten a hold of Tony Smith's credit card and banking details. Balances all look okay to me. Only thing is, his address changed to a place in Minneapolis. Looks like his folks' place."

Slowly clicking into place.

"So I spoke to the Minneapolis Field Office like you asked, and they just matched the MisPer info his parents raised to a John Doe found in Duluth, place north of Minneapolis. Suicide, sir." Tyler was typing in the background. "Overdose of prescription fentanyl. The agent said it was how Prince died."

"Anything suspicious about it?"

"Said it looks genuine. Guy probably feels guilty over what happened here, a kid dying in his care like that. The horror must've been too much."

"If you can look at the records for me, it'd take a weight off my shoulders."

"Sure thing, sir. Oh, and the cell phone records? Still waiting on that. A few extra steps to jump through. But we'll get there."

"Okay, thanks. Keep me posted." Carter killed the call and frowned at Elisha. "Suicide. Found his body in Duluth."

"So he cleared out his Seattle apartment only to then kill himself in Duluth?" She shook her head. "I've seen stranger things, but not many."

"You're catching me up." Carter headed for the address they had for the school principal. A mid-range Victorian, best house in a bad street. A light shone in a room to the right where a man sat behind a desk, thumping at the keys on an antique typewriter. His movie-star blond hair didn't suit his face, wrinkled and wizened. He looked over when Carter pressed the doorbell.

Seconds later, the door opened. The man looked up at them and folded his arms across his chest. "Can I help you?" A real East Coast accent, somewhere between Brooklyn and Boston.

"FBI." Elisha showed her credentials. "Looking for a David Quiroga."

"That's me." He didn't offer a hand, though. "I remember you. What's happened?"

"We need a word, sir. Can we come in?"

"Sure." Quiroga opened the front door wide and shuffled down a long hallway, into the room with the typewriter. A home office, filled with wooden furniture, some potted plants up high, their leaves drooping to the floor like jungle vines. He sat behind the desk and slammed a laptop lid. Not that there was anywhere for Carter or Elisha to sit. "So, what do you want?"

Elisha leaned against the counter. "We're with the Child Abduction Rapid Deployment team, and we're searching for a girl who was kidnapped this morning."

"Oh man. The senator's kid. I saw that on the news." Quiroga frowned at her. "Why do you want to speak to me?"

"Our lead suspect is very interested in a military exercise that happened at your school on October second."

"Day from hell, man." Quiroga arched an eyebrow. "I taught for twelve years, then been principal for seven, and in all that time, I've never seen kids so excited. Real-life soldiers running all over the place, taking them from their classes, getting them out to safety. The amount of paperwork I had, and the grief from the parents? Man…"

"Anything unusual happen?"

"That exercise passed without incident. Slick. I received a commendation from the governor. Shook his hand, you know?"

Carter held his gaze for a few seconds, trying to figure out if he was lying or just nervous at two federal agents showing up at his door. He held out his service smartphone. "Do you recognize this man?"

Quiroga took one look then leaned back in his chair with a sigh. "Mason Wickstrom, right? His son was a student at the school."

"I understand Mr. Wickstrom's son died that day?"

"Heart failure during soccer practice. Saddest thing I ever had to deal with."

"Same day as the military exercise?"

"Before. I shoulda cancelled it, but if the commies are rolling tanks towards you, you don't get to cancel that, do you?"

"We've tried speaking to the sports coach who was running the soccer practice."

"Ah, good luck with that." Quiroga frowned. "Tony took sick leave. The guilt, you know? Left town. I haven't heard from him since."

The story was checking out. Kind of.

"You ever speak to Mr. Wickstrom about what he believes happened?"

A bead of sweat ran down Quiroga's forehead. The room was bitterly cold. He frowned at Carter. His eyes bulged. "Oh my god! Did he kidnap those kids?"

"I can't comment on that, sir."

"Listen to me, I don't know what you think you know, but Mason Wickstrom's mind has been poisoned by conspiracies and what happened to his poor, dear wife." He snorted. "I attended his boy's funeral, offered my sympathies, which he and his wife seemed to accept, but..." Another snort. "He came in not too long after and... Something had changed in him. He kept asking about what happened. I told him the truth. Jacob died while he was warming up for soccer."

"Did he believe you?"

"A guy like that, it's not about believing you, know what I'm saying? They've got their opinions, which they think are as strong as my facts." Quiroga wiped a second bead of sweat away. "The problem is that Mr. Wickstrom has put two and two together and got, I don't know, fifty-seven billion. I mean, he connected his boy's death with Faraj disappearing."

"Faraj al-Yasin?"

"You know any other kids with that name? Good kid. Quiet, but real smart." Quiroga shook his head. "You feds looked into it, said they thought he ran away. Parental abduction. The boy's own father now living somewhere in the Middle East. What a world, man. What a world."

"Mr. Wickstrom thought those two events happening so close together was suspicious, right?"

"Listen to me." Quiroga was on his feet now, squaring up like he was going to fight both of them. "I lost two boys that day. I only ever lost one kid in all my time, then two in one day. You know how hard that was to take? I had FBI agents all over my school, cops crawling all over my stuff. In my home, at my parents' home back in Maine. Thought I was involved or something. Week from hell, man. Week from hell. Kid was at school all day, then afterwards, he just vanished and I don't know what happened."

Carter held his gaze. What was he covering up? Anything? Everything? Nothing?

His phone rang again. Tyler's number. "Back in a second." He stepped out of the room. "Peterson, what's up?"

"Sir, I've got the autopsy report for Tony Smith. Weirdest thing. He died on June twenty-ninth."

Carter gasped. "A week before his apartment was cleared out."

"Right." Tyler sighed down the line. "And I've got the cell phone records. Mostly calling for pizzas, occasional chat with a buddy back in Seattle. Only thing is, the day before Smith died, he exchanged a bunch of calls and texts with a David Quiroga."

Carter swallowed. He looked back in the home office. Quiroga was shuffling through a file cabinet, facing away from the door.

It didn't fit together in any nice way. Coupled with the timing, it made Quiroga look like he'd covered up what happened, or at least been involved.

"Dig deep into Quiroga for me, Tyler. Okay?"

"Sure thi—"

Carter put his cell away and stepped back into the room.

Quiroga was riffling through some paperwork. "I'm sure it's here, somewhere."

Elisha frowned at Carter.

Carter held up his hand to silence her, then raised his gun to point at Quiroga. "Need you to come down to the FBI Field Office, sir, to answer a few questions."

Quiroga stopped what he was doing and let out a deep sigh. "What about?"

"I think you know."

Quiroga nodded slowly, then turned around, holding a revolver in his left hand.

"Drop it." Carter stepped closer, training his pistol on Quiroga's center mass. "I said, drop it!"

"This isn't my fault." In a flash, Quiroga put the gun to his own head and fired.

CHAPTER FIFTY-FIVE

Holliday

Holliday let go of Mason's throat and stood up tall again.

So tempting to just squeeze and squeeze until he died, until this was all over.

But it wouldn't be. It'd never be over. Not if I crossed the line and became one of them.

And not while they still have Avery.

"Give me a reason why I shouldn't just kill you."

Mason stared up at Holliday, looking pathetic, like a kitten pleading to be fed. The light was low in the bedroom, but Holliday could still see the cuts on Mason's face, the bruises starting to form. He didn't speak, didn't have a defense.

"You abducted my son and my daughter." Holliday had Mason's gun now, casually waving it at him. As he had assumed, there was only one bullet left. He'd have to make it count. "What happened to Brandon, that's on you. I should kill you. Right here, right now."

"Let me pay it back to you." Mason was more like a worm now, crawling in his own filth. Blood dripped from both cheeks, caking his neck. The flesh wound on his arm was open to the air. "I can help you find her. Take me with you. I can help."

"The only place you should go is a hospital. But you don't deserve that." Holliday trained the revolver on Mason. "How do I find her?"

"You won't be able to."

"I'm not giving up that easily." Holliday stepped over and pressed the gun into Mason's gut. "Tell me or I will shoot you. Leave you to die here."

"You'll never find her."

Holliday fought to keep his hand steady. "You'll be dead, though. That'll be enough for me."

Mason stared at him, then looked across the room. "There's a burner taped to the toilet cistern. It's got her number on it."

"Thank you." Holliday stood up tall and walked over to the bathroom. Halfway there, he spotted a picture, a woman posing with her son. Kid looked Arabic, but she… She could've been from anywhere hot. Tanned, almost-black hair. Pretty. "Is this her?"

Mason nodded slowly.

Holliday carried it over to the toilet and lifted the lid. The cistern was filled up. A Ziploc taped to the side, an old Nokia inside. He walked back over, pressing the gun to the side of Mason's head. "Time's up."

CHAPTER FIFTY-SIX

Carter

"Going to need you to give a statement, sir." The Seattle Field Office agent stank of cheap cigarettes and strong breath mints. His wool overcoat was frayed at the seams, just like his face. His chubby skin was scored at all the joints, but worst around his neck. "When would be a good time?"

"Tomorrow." Carter stared at the body of David Quiroga, what remained of his head obscured by another detective crouching low. "I'm running a child abduction case, and that's got to be my priority."

The cop pointed his silver pen at the corpse. "This connected?"

"Unfortunately."

"Guy chose to take his own life like that instead of answer a few tough questions. Sucks, huh?"

"It does." Carter passed his card. "Give me a call."

"Sure thing. Might leave it until Monday."

With a nod, Carter stepped outside into the cooling air and let the agents work in peace.

Not that there was much to do. A case as open-and-shut as they came. A guy shooting himself in front of two FBI agents. Guilt implicit.

Elisha was waiting by their Suburban, staring into space. She clocked his approach. "Max." All she said, all she could say.

"You okay?"

"I'm fine." Elisha didn't look like it.

"We were never in any danger."

"Sure about that? Guy with a gun?"

"He shot himself, Elisha. Trying to cover it up. And how are you doing? I mean, really."

"This isn't my first rodeo, Max. We still need to find Avery Holliday." She paused and held up her cell. "Tyler's running Quiroga's finances just now. Anything we should be looking for?"

"No, but get him to look extra close, okay? This guy killed himself rather than answer our questions. There's something, alright, and I want to find it."

"Roger." She put the cell to her ear but dropped it. "Shit." She bent down to pick it up. Looked like she was struggling to get up.

"Are you sure you're—"

"I'm *fine*." She stared hard at him, her piercing blue eyes penetrating his skull, like she could see down to the neurons and read their arcane patterns. "Why did that happen?"

Carter couldn't figure out why. Kept asking himself that, but kept coming up short. He could only shrug.

"Why kill himself like that, Max?" Elisha folded her arms, shivering. "We were asking questions, that's all. They weren't particularly hard, were they?"

"No, but they were questions he couldn't answer."

"He didn't run, he didn't hide. He chose to end it all in the most brutal way possible. Why?"

"Because he was scared."

She just stared at the parking lot's damp asphalt.

He knew he needed to conjure up the answers, to progress the case, to find Avery. But how? He let out a breath. Start again. "Assuming Mason Wickstrom's theories are correct, then David Quiroga and Tony Smith helped cover up what really happened here."

"You really think GrayBox operatives abducted that Faraj kid?"

"Starting to look that way, Elisha. Franklin Vance was here, signed the roll call with Tony Smith. Next thing we know, the kid doesn't turn up at home. Not sure I buy the whole disappearance story anymore."

Elisha looked around the school again, over to the sports hall. "You really think they took him from here?"

"Either way, Mason Wickstrom believes that theory enough to abduct Holliday's kids, forced him to investigate what happened here. His son's death. Faraj's disappearance. And I'm all out of ideas."

"I'm not." She locked eyes with him again. "I want to speak to Faraj's mother again."

CHAPTER FIFTY-SEVEN

Holliday

Holliday shut the front door behind him and let himself breathe again. He took in the street. Nobody around, the neighborhood quiet. The Cadillac was still over on the other side of the road, a fifty-thousand-dollar car on a street where the homes weren't worth that. He got out the key, smeared with Mason's blood, wiped it, and set off toward the car, checking the photo he'd taken from the house.

Layla. Pretty, if you liked that kind of thing. Intense, and seriously annoyed with whoever photographed her. Maybe Mason, maybe someone else.

Holliday reached into his pocket for the revolver, the one Mason had taken from the guard. One bullet left. Have to make it count. No time for missing, no second chances here. He got out the cell phone and powered it up. The Nokia logo flashed up, and it seemed to take forever to load.

A car pulled up over the other side of the road and sat there, the engine idling.

Holliday hid behind a van, peering out to get another look. He couldn't see much.

The engine died and a man got out, looking around nervously. Not Layla, but he looked across the road toward her apartment. Then up and down the road. Almost spotted Holliday by the van.

He pressed himself flat against it and waited. A car door opened and, seconds later, it shut again.

Holliday checked the cell again. Showed the time and date now. He hit the menu button and found the contacts. Just one, marked "SAFE." He hit it, the cell started dialing, and he chanced another look over the road.

The man was pulling something out of the trunk. A golf bag. He dumped it on the ground with a sigh.

"Hello?" The female voice in Holliday's ear sounded like she'd died. So cold, her voice level.

"It's Mason." Holliday pushed away from the van and walked down the street, keeping an eye on the golfer. "We need to meet."

"Who is this?"

Holliday stopped, eyes wide, mouth hanging open. "I've got Mason, Layla."

"So?"

Something bit into Holliday's ankle and he fell forward, landing hard on the asphalt, cracking his cheek off the curb. Someone kicked him in the side. Another pair of hands tugged a hood over his head. He was lifted clean off the ground and pushed into the van.

He felt a jab in his neck. "No!"

Everything went black.

CHAPTER FIFTY-EIGHT

Carter

Carter knocked on the door and took in the neighborhood while he waited. A long row of single-bed homes, the road at the far end curving around to meet the freeway. What a place to live.

"You know, I'm hoping she's involved." Elisha sucked in a deep breath as she looked through a window. "Hoping she's his accomplice, that she's guarding Avery." She seemed to shiver. "Everything else… He could've killed her, could have her locked up alone, could've sold her to—"

"Elisha, focus on the here and now. Okay? We've no reason to think this boy's mother is involved."

But they both lost something that day. They both wanted answers. It made sense to Carter too. Still—keep focused.

He knocked again, the feeling deep in his gut that they'd never see the girl again. "FBI!"

Elisha thumped the door.

No response, again.

She stepped back and waved a hand at the nearby agent holding the battering ram. "Get us inside."

He stepped into place.

Carter drew his pistol.

A loud crack and the door tumbled off its hinges onto the floor.

Carter stepped inside first. "FBI!"

A dark hallway, three of the doors shut.

Carter walked over to the open door.

Someone lay on the bed. A man, on his front, trussed up like a turkey, hands and feet bound together. Salmon-pink polo, gray slacks. Not moving. Blood caked the back of his shaved head, tiny dots of red stubble poking out of the follicles. Gashes taken out of both cheeks.

Looked close enough to Mason Wickstrom's old service photo.

Carter charged over and put a finger to his neck, checking for a pulse. He got one. He scanned the bonds, looking for a way through. Thick yellow nylon rope. Impossible to snap with your hands. "Get me a knife!"

"Mmmf!" Wickstrom was trying to say something.

Carter opened Wickstrom's jaw. Something red in his mouth, looked like cotton. He pulled it out. A towel, soaked with blood.

"Holliday!" Wickstrom was gulping in breath like he'd just surfaced from the deep. "Holliday!"

Elisha appeared in the doorway with a pair of scissors. "No knives. Hope these will do."

Carter took the scissors off her and started snipping at the bonds. "Where is Holliday? Does he have Avery?"

Wickstrom spat blood on the bed. "You tell me."

CHAPTER FIFTY-NINE

Mason

The FBI agent saws at the ties around my feet with a pair of scissors, taking long hacks at them. The amount of grunting he's doing, it's not going as well or as quickly as he'd like.

All I can do is lie on the bed, belly down, trussed up like a free-range chicken at a farmers' market. Facing up to the crimes I committed. Every slice into the bonds cuts through my bones, like he's sawing my leg off. Everything hurts now, not just my wrist or my head or the gunshot wound in my arm. The back of my head, it's like—

I jerk awake again. The pain is just too much.

It's over.

Despite the agony, I wouldn't change anything, wouldn't trade safety for the knowledge of what happened to my boy.

I found my answers, but Layla didn't get hers. She took Avery, but where? Hung me out to dry. And I still don't know why. Maybe she figured it was best to get out of here, maybe she's using her fake passport right now.

I'd done most of the running, and she'd left me when she got the answer she needed. Not the one she wanted.

Shit, maybe she's in custody, maybe the FBI have her.

They found me here, after all. Have they got her?

Letting Holliday get the upper hand like that, turning my back on a snake like him... A desperate, poisonous snake. He realized I'd lost Avery, snuck in here and took me out.

I'm such a jackass.

The agent breaks through the ties and frees my legs. I can relax now, a tiny amount. He grabs my left wrist and carefully rests the scissors against the bonds. "Need you to sit up, sir." He hauls me up and props me against the wall. "My name is Special Agent Max Carter of the FBI. You're going away for a very long time. Child abduction, murder, you name it. Mason Wickstrom, you have the right to remain silent."

His words wash over me. I don't even look at him. Part of my brain, the one still wired with all that training, tells me to wait. Four other agents in the room, standing around. Take him out, then get away. Normally I'd like my odds, but I'm sore and tired, and my skull's cracked…

"… one will be appointed for you." Then he's back to sawing away at the yellow twine. He's going much slower than with my legs, taking his time, making sure he doesn't cut me. "You're going to help me find Avery Holliday. Whatever you've done to reconcile yourself with kidnapping small children, whatever you've gained out of it, a mother is missing her daughter. Okay?"

He's slipped—he doesn't know about Layla. Meaning he doesn't have her.

So, do I play along? Help him find Avery? Or do I protect Layla?

I kidnapped two innocent children to use as leverage against Holliday. We were going to return them when we had our answers.

Holliday was right here with me. I was going to give her back.

But he's right. I need to help him find Avery, return her to her mother. Problem is, I don't know if Layla still has Avery.

Where has she gone?

The burner I gave Holliday was the only lead I had. I forgot about it in the rage, only remembering when Holliday got me. But I told her they took her son, and she thinks Holliday's involved in this.

An eye for an eye, a tooth for a tooth.

No.

No, no, no.

She couldn't.

Not Layla.

I swallow hard, but it's hours since I last drank anything. My lips are dry, my mouth like a Basra backstreet. I make eye contact with him. His head is perfectly still despite the sawing motion. And I realize that I've no idea how I can help.

Carter breaks through the twine and beckons over an EMT. "Can you check that wound, please?"

The guy does as he's told, resting on his knees behind me, the bedsprings crunching. His gloved fingers work my scalp, making it burn with pain.

"How long before I can get him in an interrogation room?"

"He needs to go to the hospital." The EMT stops his probing. "He needs an X-ray. This looks like a fractured skull to me. Possibly even brain damage."

"So, how long?"

"You're talking days."

"I don't have days." Carter stands there, thinking about it. Then he gives the EMT a nod. "Give me five minutes while you get the ambulance ready. Okay?"

The EMT thinks as hard as Carter did, but does as he's told, leaving me alone with the agent.

Carter pulls over the desk chair and sits, crossing his legs. Very casual, like two buddies hanging loose on a back stoop, sipping ice-cold beers. "Once you're out of the ER, I'm going to charge you. Then you'll be taken to a maximum-security prison while you await trial." He turns to look at me and I can see years of pent-up anger and rage simmering away. This guy does this shit for a living, hunting down people like me. Day in, day out. Soon enough, he'll snap. I hope it's not today.

"What do you want?"

"Don't think you'll ever be free again, Mr. Wickstrom. I know enough of your military record to make sure that I'll have a very strong guard outside your hospital room. Child abduction is four years. I know, right? Should be life. But you're facing two counts, and most judges will make you serve that sequentially. But then you murdered Harry Youngblood and Franklin Vance. Normally, that'd be twenty to life, each. But in this state? Two murders counts as a spree killing, so you'll face the death penalty. They're trying to get rid of it, as you probably know, but they haven't. Better hope the governor likes you. Abducting a senator's kids? Probably pushes the odds against you."

I slump back against the wall. Can't say anything. This is the price I have to pay for what I've learned.

"Right now, Mason, my highest priority is finding Avery Holliday. I hope there's some semblance of a human being left inside your head, enough to help me find a small girl and return her to her parents."

It's like he expects me to say something.

"Now. If you cooperate, we can make it life in prison. Commute the death penalty."

Maybe he's right. Holliday's wife doesn't deserve this, just like Avery and Brandon didn't. One kid in the ER, another missing. I could do some final good, reuniting the girl with her mother.

Baby tears tickle my nostrils, not quite formed, but stinging anyway. "I want to help, but I honestly don't know where she is."

Carter processes it, slowly, looking deep in my eyes. "Did Holliday get her back?"

"No." I let out a breath, a wave of pain across the back of my skull making everything clench. "We got back here and she was gone."

"Could Avery have left on her own?"

"No. My—" I break off. "We were keeping Avery here. She was supposed to be an insurance policy."

"Your accomplice was looking after her, right?"

"Right."

"Layla al-Yasin, yes?"

So, he knows.

Do I give her up? Or do I let her go, let her live her life while I pay for both of our sins. I did the damage, so I should pay for what I've done. But should she?

He leans forward, resting on the chair's front two legs. "It is Layla al-Yasin, right?"

He already knows, doesn't need me to confirm it. "I've no idea where she's taken Avery." I rest my head against the wall, but the pain flares all over my body, jerking me forward. "I came back here with Holliday, left him outside. I swear I was going to give Avery back to Holliday, then leave the state. Disappear. But I came in here, and she was gone. Next thing I know, Holliday attacked me." I rub at the fissure on the back of my head. "He hit me with a frying pan, then tied me up. Started torturing me, interrogating me, asking where Avery is. But I don't know. I don't know where Layla went or why."

"You lost touch with her." Carter gets up and starts pacing around the room. "Is there anything you can think of that might help us track down Holliday?"

"I just can't think of anything."

He stands up tall, fists in his pants pockets. "Was Holliday helping you?"

"He was. And you know why. Helped me get my answers, helped me connect the dots. If it wasn't for him, we wouldn't have found the men responsible for my son's death."

"Harry Youngblood?"

Hearing his name hits me hard. "It was an accident."

"Like Brandon was an accident?"

"That cop shot him. You were there. You saw it. Youngblood jumped me, I had a loaded gun on him. It went off and I had no choice. And I was going to return the boy. I brought him with me to show Holliday that we meant business, but also that he'd get his kids back if he just played along. Then... what happened, happened and..." I can't look at him anymore. "You ever felt such bad guilt that the only thing you can do is block it out of your mind?"

"I haven't, no." Carter sniffs. "But Frank Vance's death looked very deliberate to me. You executed him."

"You tell me he didn't deserve it." I let him see the pain and hurt, let it control my face, my muscles, let all of it out. "He deserved it. Vance and Youngblood both deserved it. Both of them. My son died because of their greed. Vance killed my *son*. That day, Jacob died trying to save his friend. Frank Vance held him, shook him, and my boy's heart gave out. He murdered my son!"

The emotion hits me like it's been shot with a hundred rounds from an AR15. Everything I've been blocking out. All the pain, not even crying at Jake's funeral. All the rage, all the anger, all the shock. A wave of grief rolls over me, pulling me under. I shut my eyes, but all I can see is Jacob in his coffin, Grace's hand tight around mine, her nails biting into my flesh.

"I just need to find Avery and reunite her with her parents, like you—"

"Vance showed us the money trail from some shell company in the Caymans or somewhere. The CIA paid them to take Faraj."

"The CIA?" Carter lets out a slow breath, like he's been down this mental avenue already. "Have you got any evidence?"

"I did. Vance gave us a document showing the payment from the CIA. I left it in his car, a black Cadillac. Should be outside, but maybe Holliday took it."

Carter clicks his fingers and one of his agents leaves the room. "That's a start. Now, let's focus on Avery's whereabouts, huh?"

I want to help, I just can't think how.

And then I see it.

On the floor behind the door, resting against the wall. Layla's laptop, the cheap thing she got from Walmart. Wiped, some Linux thing installed on top. Ultra-secure.

I suck in a deep breath, and something rattles in my lungs. "Bob Smith." I manage another breath. "It's not his real name, I don't think anyway. It's the username of some guy Layla found online. Don't ask where, because I don't know. That's her area of expertise. She worked at Microsoft and Amazon, knows her shit." I spit blood on the bed. "She set up a chat with him for the three of us on Signal."

"Signal is that app that journalists use to protect their sources, right?"

"That's one use for it, yeah. Layla says it's just like WhatsApp but not owned by Facebook. It's completely secure, end-to-end something or other, so nobody can even see who you're talking to."

"End-to-end encryption. And it breaks if you've got access to either end of the pipe."

"Right."

"So how are you—"

"Listen, I've got an idea." I suck in a breath, tasting blood. "There's a group chat, the three of us, but I've been chatting to Bob Smith solo on there. I think Layla speaks to him too." I nod over at the laptop. "Pass me that."

Carter thinks it through for a few seconds, but a female agent comes into the room. "No sign of a Cadillac, Max."

"So Holliday's taken it." I look at him, pleading. "Pass me the laptop. I might be able to get in. I can help you find Avery."

He snaps on rubber gloves and picks it up. "This is against protocol..." He sets it on his lap and taps the keyboard. "You know her password?"

"No."

"So how did you think you could help?" Carter reaches into his pocket for something. Looks like a thumb drive. He sticks it in the side of the machine and drums his fingers on the lid. "Okay. I'm in."

So much for her ultra-secure Linux build. "Can you see Signal?"

"It's already open. There are two message threads here." Carter swings the laptop around. "This the one you want?"

I was right. There's a string of messages between Bob Smith and LayLadyLay. Layla. Discussing the operation in detail, worrying that I'm not up to it. Then her most recent message...

Shit.

> Mason called
> It's over for him, but I don't have answers
> My boy's still out there!
> Mason wants to let her go
> What do you think?

> NO
> I have plans for her
> I need you to meet me

Are you sure?

> Positive
> It's OK
> I'll help you find Faraj

> Get out of there now
> I'll get someone to secure Holliday and Mason
> Wait for a silver Audi
> Do not speak to Mason or Holliday
> Okay?

OK

Good
Wait for my instruction

Then fifteen minutes later:

They've arrived. Silver Audi A3.

I can see it
Bye

Carter is off, talking into his cell on speaker. "Tyler, need you to run a check on a cell number." He read it out, slowly. "It's for a 'Bob Smith,' but I doubt that's his name."

Keyboard sounds click out of the speaker, all shrill and tinny. "Okay, sir, it's a burner."

Carter shakes his head, snorting hard. "Another one?"

"Cell was switched off long ago. Dead end, sir."

"Okay, Tyler, need you to get in here and— Shit!" Carter kneels in front of the laptop, his mouth hanging open. He looks around at me. "Are you doing this?"

"Doing what?"

He's got his cell out, pointing it at the screen. "Someone's deleting Layla's messages."

"It's her. She's doing it. It's our protocol to make sure you—"

"Enough." Carter's on his feet, the phone against his head now. "Tyler, get me a trace on her cell."

CHAPTER SIXTY

Holliday

Holliday jerked awake. He couldn't see anything. Someone pulled him up to standing. He breathed hard, but fabric stuck to his lips.

How long was I out for?

He tried to piece it all together. Could only draw a blank. Leaving the house, standing behind a van, gun in his hand.

Then nothing.

Wait, someone put a hood over his head. Who?

Stiff fingers gripped his shoulders and pushed him forward. He stumbled to his knees. The fingers dug into his ribs, hauling him up to standing, then nudged him forward, keeping him upright. His heavy footsteps sounded like they were on wooden boards, echoing like he was in a big room, maybe even a hall. The hand gripped his arm and pushed him faster.

He almost tripped again, but he stayed upright. "Where are you taking me?"

"Shut up." A Boston accent. "I will hurt you unless you keep your trap shut."

"I can pay you. Whatever they're paying you, I'll double it."

"I said I was going to hurt you if you didn't shut up."

Something jabbed into Holliday's side. Blunt and applied with force. He stumbled and tripped again. His knees cracked off the wood. His hands caught the brunt of it, stopping him from falling flat on his face. The varnished floor was maybe a basketball court.

Then his hood was tugged back into his face, bunching up around his mouth and cutting off his breathing. Then it released and bright lights flooded his eyes, stinging. Behind the lights, it looked like a school gymnasium. White plastic lines marked out a basketball court, just like he'd thought. Rows of bleachers led up to a scoreboard, but the time was blanked out.

The rest of the room was in darkness. Seemed like the spotlight pointed at him got even brighter.

Hands grabbed his suit jacket and pulled him up to standing. A man mountain, standing so close to Holliday he could taste his Paco Rabanne Ultraviolet aftershave, his face crisscrossed with scars, slicing through a trimmed goatee. His tailored suit was standard-issue black, meaning security goon.

"Who are you?"

"He's nobody." A door opened at the far end of the hall and a woman walked over, slowly, her footsteps almost silent. She stopped just beyond the edge of the light, tapping her foot. "You've been a bad boy, Senator." Her voice echoed around the hall. Familiar, but Holliday couldn't place it.

"Have you got Avery?"

"All in good time." She stepped forward, but the lights still blocked her face, just outlined her shoulder. "I like people to pay for what they've done, Senator. And you've been a very, very bad boy, haven't you?"

"Have you got Avery? Because if you haven't—"

"I know what you've done, Senator."

"Listen to me, I need to—"

"Oh, I have her. Don't you worry about that."

Holliday jumped for her. The scar-faced muscle pulled him back and wrapped a bulky arm around his throat. "You! You're the reason my boy's in the hospital!"

"No, Senator. The reason he's fighting for his life is all because of you." Her foot kept tapping the floor like she was counting time in a jazz band. "Do you know where you are?"

"What? No." Holliday's breath came in short gasps. "Give me my daughter, now!"

"Senator, this is the gymnasium at Tang Elementary." Holliday could make out the outline of her hand waving around the room. "On October second last year, a boy died and another was abducted."

"What? That's got nothing to do with me!"

"Don't play that game, Senator, it's unbecoming." She took a step forward, still shrouded by the light. "The reason your son is in the hospital is because you covered up what happened here."

"That's a lie." Holliday felt his shoulders slump. "This has nothing to do with me!"

"Now, *that* is a lie. What happened here has everything to do with you. I know you helped people get away with it. These people bribed the school principal and killed the sports coach. Maybe you didn't do it yourself, but you were certainly involved. Franklin Vance or Harry Youngblood, one of the two, they paid you, didn't they? Gave money to a PAC supporting your election campaign." The woman slid a paper file across the basketball court. "And that money went from the PAC to a Caymans account owned by you, didn't it? You took all that *filthy lucre*, right down to the last cent."

"Let my daughter go!"

"Of course, I'd ask Vance or Youngblood, but they're both dead, aren't they?"

"That lunatic, Mason—he killed them. Youngblood was an accident, sure, but Vance… He shot him in cold blood."

"They deserved it, Senator. Just like you deserve what's going to happen to you."

Holliday looked away, reaching for a way out but coming up short. Everything was closed off. Except… "Listen, there's a file in a Cadillac near where you abducted me. It proves everything, proves my innocence."

"You're guilty, Senator. Caught red-handed."

"You have to believe me. I swear I was not involved in—"

"You took the money."

Holliday didn't have a response, just let out a moan.

"No questions asked, Senator. You helped Youngblood and Vance cover up what they did." A gun emerged from the gloom, catching the harsh light from behind as it pointed straight at Holliday's head. "You brought the mission to Harry Youngblood in the first place, didn't you?"

"No, it was the other way around!"

"So you *were* involved?"

"No!" Holliday gasped. Breathed hard. "No, it's… I…"

"You make me sick." The gun pressed against Holliday's teeth. "What I've pieced together is that some guy you know in the CIA came to you, had a real tasty gig for you, one they needed absolute discretion for, just needed to acquire a target for them. And you couldn't resist. You wanted to be front and center of everything, so you told him you knew some people who could do it, could help cover it up. In exchange for this, Harry Youngblood slipped you some dough for the privilege. Just doing an old buddy a solid, that's all. No harm, no foul."

"Listen to me." Holliday's voice sounded thin and too deep. "They told me the target of this military operation had sensitive information, something the country needed to prevent a terror attack on domestic soil."

"Just one of those golf-course discussions, wasn't it? Right?" The woman laughed. Then it cut dead. "The target of the operation was *nine years old*, Senator. They kidnapped him from his school and they tortured him, made him give up information. And he was never heard of again. But you know that, don't you? Because that intel ended up on your desk, under the name Operation Honey Bear. You approved the mission, didn't you?"

"That's not my purview."

"You're on the Defense Committee, Senator. Makes you favorite for a cabinet position in 2020, assuming the presidential election goes the way you think it will. You sick, sick bastard. The target of that operation was the boy's father. Quraish al-Yasin. Because of what you did, that boy was tortured into giving up his father's cell number. They traced it to a compound in Syria."

Holliday jerked his head back, pulling away from the gun. He couldn't deny it. Felt like the walls were closing in. "I don't want to know what happens behind the curtain. It's how I sleep at night."

"You animal. You know what happened to that boy?"

"Why don't you enlighten me?"

"Once I knew the CIA had him, it was easy. I got some people to track what happened to Faraj. They took him to a black site, one of those that people don't come back from. I thought you were just lining your pockets, but you're involved with these punks, aren't you?" The man pulled the gun back then pointed it at Holliday's cheek. "You helped organize a mission where a small boy was abducted from this sports hall, where he was tortured for information, and then you ordered the death of his father. How much did you get for that?"

"You have no idea what you're talking about." Holliday lurched forward, but he was held back again. "Just give me my daughter."

"You have no power here, Senator. Nothing to bargain with. Not even your life. You know that, don't you?"

"Just give me Avery. Please."

"The problem was you were sloppy. Or unfortunate. One of the two. Because when your friends were abducting a child, another one died. In this building. Call it collateral damage, call it what you like, but it was a mess. And you needed to cover your tracks.

But you didn't, certainly nowhere near as well as you thought." The gun dropped low. "You know, I found a man and a woman, not married or a couple, but they'd both lost their sons that day. They were angry, full of righteous fury and venom. One of their kids died the same day another went missing. Sure, people can buy that. But the same day and place as a military exercise? That many coincidences aren't easy to cover up. So I told them about you, Senator, not the details, no, just that you could help them find out what happened here that day. That's why they took your kids."

"You were that woman, weren't you? Brandon's dying because of you."

"You helped them in their search, didn't you? Had no choice, they had your kids. But the information you found, well, that proved what happened here last year."

"So what? The ends justify the means. I was protecting our great nation. National security trumps everything. You of all people should know that."

The woman stepped closer and jabbed a finger at Holliday. "You're a senator. You should be hunting down corruption in our great nation, not adding to it, not lining your pockets. Not helping the CIA to kidnap and torture *children*."

Holliday swallowed hard. He stared at the gun for what felt like the millionth time that day. A Glock 26, small and stubby, designed for concealed carry, but expensive. "I can live with my decision. It was the right choice."

"You can tell that to her." She shifted back behind the light and returned, carrying a sleeping girl. Black hair, dressed like Megan.

He jerked forward. "Avery!"

"Shhh, she's asleep." The woman was still out of sight. She rested a hand on Avery's cheek, her ring catching the light. "Go on, Senator. Tell your daughter what you just told me."

"Let her go!"

The woman was still shrouded by the lights.

"I won't mention any of this, just let her go!" His voice hissed out.

The woman stepped forward, holding Avery so close to Holliday, just inches away. He could see her now, her thin face twisted by rage and fury. The woman in the photo he'd taken. "My name is Layla al-Yasin. My son, Faraj, was taken from here and I never heard from him again. All thanks to you."

Holliday couldn't look her in the eye. He felt the iron grip on his shoulders again. "Just let her go."

"Listen to me." Layla held Avery up high. Holliday could see her chest moving. She was still alive. "My son is dead because of you! You and your games! Your greed and arrogance! You killed my husband! You destroy people's lives! Real people!"

"And you kidnapped my kids, you animal. My son's in the ER because of you! This isn't on me!"

"This is on you!" Layla pressed a knife against Avery's throat.

Holliday lurched forward, but the goon still held him. "No!"

"Why should I spare her life?" Layla pressed the steel tight to Avery's skin. "Why shouldn't I just kill her? My boy is dead because of you."

She's going to kill my daughter!

"I'm sorry for your loss, truly I am." Holliday tried to move but couldn't. "But this wasn't my fault. You've got the wrong guy."

"You started this. They kidnapped my son. They tortured him. They got information out of him, found where my husband was. You ordered a child's death! How can you live with yourself?" Layla shifted the knife to Holliday's cheek.

"You didn't see the intel reports. He killed honest Americans in cold blood. He was a terrorist."

"My son wasn't. My son was *nine years old*. And he's dead because of you."

"Please, this isn't my doing. Let Avery go. *Please*."

Layla eased Avery up onto her hip and stared at her. "If I'm never going to see Faraj again, then it's only fair that you never see Avery again."

"No!"

"Goodbye." Layla dropped the knife to the floor and walked off, carrying Avery with her.

"Come back!" Holliday tried to move, but the goon stopped him. "Come back here!"

Almost hidden in the gloom, Layla took one last look at him, then slipped out through the door.

"No!" Holliday's scream echoed around the hall.

CHAPTER SIXTY-ONE

Carter

Tang Elementary was turn-of-the-millennium new, a stark-white building lit up in the evening sky, the square roof hanging low in one corner like it had melted. Hard to figure out whether it was designed that way, or was just in dire need of repair. The schoolyard was quiet, all the kids back home on the weekend, but there were lights on inside the gym.

Carter hopped out of the SUV and raced toward the sports hall, his cell to his ear. "Tyler, have you got an update on the APB?"

"Negative, sir. Layla al-Yasin is still at large."

"Call me the second that changes."

"Sir. Her cell's still reporting that location."

"Thanks again." Carter ended the call and slowed his pace as he entered the building. He raised his hands to halt the agents trailing them into the sports hall.

Inside, the room was mostly dark, just a spotlight at the far end, focused on a man slumped underneath a basketball hoop.

Carter ran toward him.

It was Senator Holliday, in floods of tears, his chest racking with each fresh wave. He looked up and raised his arms, but he was handcuffed to the stanchion, like a prisoner in a transport. "Avery was here!"

A cell phone sat at his feet, powered on and the screen glowing.

Carter tried to grab the cuffs, but Holliday was shaking his arms too much. "Where is she?"

"That bitch has Avery! She took her!" Another shake of the cuffs. "And she was right here. Avery! Right here! This crazy bitch, saying I'm responsible for her son's death. She has my baby girl!" Holliday's crazed eyes scanned the room as he rattled the cuffs. "She's got my daughter!"

"What was her name?"

"Something Muslim. Layla, but the last name sounded like Klingon to me."

Mason's accomplice, then.

"Do you have any idea where she might've taken her?"

"I've never seen the woman before in my life."

"Okay." Carter waved a pair of agents over. "Cut him out of there."

Carter rushed out of the sports hall into the parking lot. The soccer field was used every weekend, armies of kids and parents descending to watch an impenetrable game. Kirsty'd played here a few times. Carter even started to get into the flow of it the last time. He couldn't spot his Suburban among the ten or so other identical models. Someone joked a while back how the FBI bought so many that Chevrolet couldn't get enough of them on the sales lot to sell to Joe Public.

But he did spot a black Cadillac. Mason Wickstrom told him that was Vance's car. Holliday drove it here. Or someone drove him here in it.

Carter tried the door and, wonder of wonders, it opened. Pristine interior, like the owner suffered from OCD. Or just never left any personal effects in there, no food packaging in case it left a DNA trace. He opened the glovebox and found a cleaning kit, spray and cloth. No doubt to wipe down after every trip.

But the sterility made the document folder in the rear footwell stand out all the more.

Carter reached down for it, his knee digging into the leather seat, and started flicking through it. Seemed to be a wire transfer from the Caymans to a GrayBox suspense account.

Just like Mason Wickstrom had said.

Two dead GrayBox employees meant only one thing. Richard Olson must've known what was going on here.

Carter got out and powered across the parking lot, scanning for his vehicle. There, with the ding on the hood.

Another Suburban pulled up, splashing through puddles. Karen Nguyen got out, shoving the door shut with some force. "Max!" She blocked him off, grabbing his shoulders. "What are you doing?"

"We've got Holliday. Barely a scratch on him. Elisha's taking him back to the field office for debriefing."

"And Avery?"

Carter shook his head, then held up the document. "I need to speak to Richard Olson."

"What? Why?"

Carter took a step back, pulling free of her clutches, then handed her the file.

"Max, I told you to stand down." She was sifting through the document. "Lori's running this operation, not you."

"So where is she?" Carter waved a hand at the sports hall, now swarming with suits. "Because I tracked Holliday here, almost caught the person who has Avery. And whatever's going on here involves Olson's company. Two of his guys died at the hands of Mason Wickstrom. Now I find that, linking an offshore account to Olson. I need to speak to him."

Nguyen stared hard at him, exhaling slowly. "Okay." She pointed a finger in his face. "But I'm coming with you."

*

"You can't go in there!" Olson's PA blocked the office door like she was guarding the entrance to Fort Knox. "He's in a meeting!"

"Ma'am, I'll ask you once." Carter took a step closer to the door. "Get out of my way."

She looked behind her, then bit her lip. "Okay."

"A wise choice." Carter pushed past her, leading Nguyen through the office door.

Olson sat behind his massive desk, sipping whiskey from a crystal glass. "Back so soon?"

Carter took one of the chairs and glanced at the figure in the other chair.

James Rickards. A slimeball lawyer, the kind who didn't want his clients ever getting inside a courthouse. His curly black hair was pulled over in a side-parting, held down by a ton of gel and hairspray. Regulation black business suit, pink shirt, lavender tie. "Maxwell."

"It's just Max." Carter took out a notebook and clicked his pen. "Need to ask you a few questions, Mr. Olson. Kinda convenient that your lawyer just happens to be here."

"We're just having a drink." Olson raised his glass, but didn't offer any to Carter. "Now, what brings you back, huh? Thought you'd have found Avery Holliday by now."

"Do you know where she is?"

"You hear this, Jimmy?" Olson laughed hard.

"Your lawyer being here saves us a lot of dicking around."

Olson shook his head. "Me and Jimmy here have been shooting the shit." A fresh VR headset rested on his desk. Olson picked it up and took a look at it. "Finally got some contracts through for this hunk of junk."

Rickards nodded. "That's correct."

Carter focused on him. "Thought you were a criminal defense attorney."

"Oh, Mr. Carter." Rickards curled his lip. "Just because you've only seen your dog hunt doesn't mean it can't raise pups or guard your home. Criminal defense is but one string to my bow. Mergers and acquisitions is actually my specialty."

Carter felt Nguyen's glare burn into his neck. He tossed the document on the desk. "Need you to explain why money's passing from Caymans accounts to GrayBox."

Rickards rolled his eyes but didn't join in laughing. "I presume you have better evidence in support of this serious allegation against my client?"

Nguyen stayed standing by the window, the spotlights catching her hair. "Richard, we're duty-bound to investigate any allegation involving child abduction."

"And this relates to child abduction, how?"

"Mr. Olson, I'm going to ask you straight here." Carter got up and walked over to the display of baseball memorabilia. "The man who took Senator Holliday's children did so to obtain information about a military operation in Seattle. His son died during that operation and another boy went missing."

Olson put the headset in his desk drawer. "Who do you think I am? You think I paid someone to take his kids to chase around getting information?"

"Their strategy worked." Carter pressed his finger into the document. "This proves a connection to GrayBox. I'm not accusing you of doing the actual abduction, but I think you know what happened that day."

"Give me a break."

"Layla al-Yasin." He left him a space, but Olson's poker face was good. "It was her son who went missing during the military exercise your operatives were involved in. The exercise you received dirty CIA money for."

Olson took a few seconds to think it through, then smiled at Nguyen. "Can you give us the room?"

She gave Carter a long hard look, her cheek twitching. Then she tilted her head to the side and left.

Olson watched her go, eyes narrow, then he held out a hand. "I need your cell, Mr. Carter."

"Why?"

"Never know who's listening to an FBI agent's cell phone."

Carter held it out, but didn't give him it. "Why did you ask her to leave?"

"Because now it's just you, me, and my lawyer." Olson tried to reach for the phone. "So, are you going to give me it?"

"Fine." Carter passed him the cell.

"Good boy." Olson turned it off, then put it in a drawer. "Now I know that none of this is on the record."

"I will get you in an interrogation room if there's anything I deem pertinent to the well-being of Avery Holliday."

Olson sat back in his chair, arms folded. "You can leave, then."

Carter took his seat again. "Fine. This is off the record."

"I built this company up from *nothing* to becoming a Fortune 500 business. I'm proud of what I've achieved. I've made the world a much safer place."

"You needed Karen to leave for that?"

Olson settled back with a sigh. "Listen to me. We had a good chat earlier, you and me. I think I can trust you. Your heart's in the right place. You should know that Senator Holliday isn't as innocent as he makes out."

"Go on."

"After you left this afternoon, I was pissed that the FBI were looking at my company. So I did some more digging. Remember that missing document? Well, I found it." Olson opened a drawer and took out a hefty wad of paper. He held it there, then rested it on the desk. "And so did you, but only part of the story. The second-last thing I want to find is evidence of money transferring from a CIA shell company to Frank Vance's offshore accounts through my company. The last thing I want is the FBI knowing about it too."

Carter stared at the document. This wasn't finding Avery Holliday, but it was something.

"I'm a smart guy, Mr. Carter. I run a keylogger on all my exec's machines. Amazing little bit of tech that logs every single keystroke they make. Means I had Frank Vance's passwords. Means I have access to this account in the Caymans, saw the money coming in from a known CIA shell company in Bermuda. Means I found a cool half-mill payment to one David Quiroga. And Vance somehow had a record of all of Mr. Quiroga's *substantial* gambling debts, totaling just shy of half a mill."

"So Vance paid him off?"

"Sure enough. Also, he paid two mill to Holliday's PAC."

"That isn't under Holliday's control."

"Maybe not, but somehow Harry Youngblood has a login to the account, and I traced that payment—all two million bucks went to Holliday's own account in Bermuda. The accounts list it as a service charge, but Holliday pocketed blood money from two corrupt operatives."

"That evidence going to stand up in court?"

Olson looked over at Rickards. "Jimmy?"

"This has all been independently audited. Our firm can provide concrete proof of these transactions."

"Proof that Harry Youngblood, Frank Vance, and Chris Holliday made them?"

"Accounts like these, that handle transactions of a certain size and nature…" Rickards flattened down his hair. "They require a higher level of security and biometric identification than your cell phone banking app would. That these men made these transactions is indisputable. Of course, I trust your own experts will validate that for you, so don't just take my word for it."

Carter gave a nod. Don't commit to anything yet.

Olson opened the document and flicked through to a point. "The name Tony Smith mean anything to you?"

Carter nodded again, still keeping quiet. Let them spill what they want to and see what sticks.

"The sports coach at that school, there when Faraj was taken, and when Jacob died. Body found in Duluth, right?"

Carter grimaced, feeling a tightness in his gut. "How did you know that?"

"I have my sources." Olson tapped his nose, then swiveled the document around on the desk. "Turns out Frank Vance was in Duluth that day. Two days later he cleared out Tony Smith's apartment. Very charitable of him, huh?"

"Very."

The lawyer handed Carter a folder. "This is the evidence my client has to back up Senator Holliday's involvement in the matter. You should, of course, repeat some of the searches yourself to validate the evidence trail. The security credentials to access Mr. Vance's accounts are in here." He licked his lips. "And there is, of course, a message trail between Youngblood, Vance, and Holliday regarding the payments for covering up activities."

"Messages? I thought this would be done on the golf course."

"They needed to process the transactions, hence a last-minute discussion of account numbers and amounts between the parties. Access credentials to the accounts are in there. Again, biometric security provides proof that the messages were between those individuals."

Carter sifted through the folder. Senator Holliday's involvement in the abduction of Faraj al-Yasin. Conspiring with two dead men to break federal law for the CIA. Enough to bury a man. He rested the document on the edge of the desk. "One last time, Mr. Olson, do you know where Avery Holliday is?"

"I wish I did. That kid's poor mother…" He shook his head slowly, like he cared about what Megan Holliday was going through.

So there it was. Everything Olson had, all of his evidence against the three men he believed had acted against his company.

It was all there. The facts, the evidence, the motive. But it didn't quite add up, did it?

The why was there. Why Faraj had been taken, and who by. But it stopped there, the story ending too soon. Like a financial transaction, you needed a party and a counterparty. Someone who gained, someone who lost. This was only one side of the coin—Olson's truth.

Mason and Layla had taken two children. Mason had killed two people. And yet he barely featured in this. Mason and Layla were everything.

Carter leaned forward, resting on his elbows. "You know when hacker kids on the internet strip someone of their anonymity they call it doxxing, right?"

A frown twitched on Olson's forehead. "Okay?"

"Something to do with documents, I think. Anyway, I suspect that's what happened here, right? You told me this afternoon about how you found some people sullying the good name of your company. Just some keyboard commandos, saying GrayBox was involved in some military operation at a school. But that got to you, Richard, didn't it? Stung you. So you doxed them. Found their real identities, their real names and addresses. Layla al-Yasin and Mason Wickstrom. And everything clicked into place for you. They'd lost their sons. Both of them, the same day. So you used them to look into what happened. Gives you plausible deniability, right?"

Olson just grimaced.

"Come on. You helped Layla. Got your goons to bring Holliday to the sports hall. Let Layla tease him with his daughter and torture him for what he'd done to her son, but more importantly to your company."

"We're done here." Olson waved at the door and beckoned Nguyen back in.

She entered, pouting.

Olson gave her a smile now. "I can only apologize for my company's involvement in this sorry mess. I gather that Harry Youngblood and Franklin Vance are sadly dead, so you're unable to prosecute either of them. I've given Special Agent Carter here evidence against Senator Holliday, covering his involvement in a clandestine operation that I had no knowledge of. I will ensure all employees of my company fully support the investigation." He held out Carter's cell phone.

Carter got to his feet and took his phone back. "I will get you for this." He followed Nguyen out into the hallway, heading to the elevators, knowing that he'd lost.

Olson had played off two desperate people, tormented Holliday's kids, all just to protect the name of his company.

But he'd also found evidence of a cover-up, of corruption at a high level.

Did it balance out?

Carter didn't know, so he said nothing, just waited for the elevator. He handed the document to Nguyen. "That's enough to—"

"The walls have ears, Max." She raised her eyebrows. "Wait until we're outside."

Carter got in the driver's side of the SUV and looked over at Olson's office. He could pick him out in the window, playing with his fresh VR visor. Rickards stood next to him, staring down at them, his lips moving.

They'd won.

By their covert means, they'd cleaned up GrayBox and removed their bad apples, with neither taking any blame.

"I want to take him down." Carter gripped the steering wheel. "Olson's responsible for this. He goaded Mason Wickstrom and Layla al-Yasin, fed them information. Okay, so they kidnapped the kids, and they're responsible for Brandon's shooting, and the deaths of Harry Youngblood and Frank Vance. But Olson pulled their strings. It's all on him."

"Whatever you think, we have less than no chance of charging Olson with anything."

"Come on, Karen."

"I know how this gets to you, Max. Whenever there's a case that you don't solve, it eats at you. You've chosen to specialize in a particularly harrowing crime. Every time some kid goes missing, you're the one who shoulders the responsibility." Nguyen flared her nostrils. "Mason Wickstrom is going to burn for what he's done. Chris Holliday, if he's done what that document says he has, then he's in deep, deep trouble. Richard Olson hasn't done anything other than let some bad people commit some barbarism on his company's time."

"You didn't hear what Olson said to me."

"And I don't need to." She held up the document. "We're going to investigate his company. That'll accelerate Delgado's investigation. Richard Olson will suffer, believe me."

"Karen, he's…" Carter leaned back in his seat, bumping against the headrest. "That's not enough."

"Max, Avery's still out there. Still missing. That's your focus. Okay?"

Carter looked over at her. "It's time I spoke to Holliday."

CHAPTER SIXTY-TWO

Holliday

The door opened and that FBI agent marched in like he was the boss. Carter. He sat opposite Holliday and pulled out a paper file, spreading the documents across the table in front of him. "Senator."

Holliday gasped. "You have her?"

"I'm afraid not, but I need to ask you a few questions about—"

"My daughter is still missing and you're in here, acting like I had something to do with it?"

Carter leaned back, his suit jacket splaying behind him, nodding slowly. "Senator, please don't play that card. My primary focus is still on finding your daughter. But it's not that simple, is it?"

"What are you talking about?" Holliday held his gaze, but Carter wasn't giving anything away. "Listen to me. I know the FBI director."

"So you told me just before you eloped from the hospital."

"Want me to call him and have a nice chat about you?"

"See, if it was me and my kid was missing, I wouldn't be so concerned about covering my ass."

"Excuse me?"

"I'd be doing everything I could to find her. You're not."

"This is ridiculous! You can't just sit there and accuse me of this bullshit. You need to find my daughter!"

"Senator, as part of the investigation into the abduction of your children, we found some troubling evidence. Evidence that you covered up a covert operation, then—"

"You're lying!" Holliday banged a fist off the table, sending a wave of pain up his arm. "Whatever you think I've done, it's… These people have my daughter and you're sitting here feeding me this bullshit!"

Carter kept his gaze then pushed a page across the table. "Senator, GrayBox carried out a covert operation under the guise of a military exercise. Problem was, someone's kid died during it, so they had to cover it up." He handed him another page. "You helped, didn't you?"

"This is all Richard Olson! Everything, all that you've found, it all leads back to him! He put Mason up to this, fed him lies. It's all him! That son of a bitch is framing me to deflect attention from his company!"

"And you've got evidence of his involvement?"

Holliday threw the pages back at Carter. "Someone abducted me, knocked me out, and took me to where you found me. Avery was there. My daughter. And that woman had her."

"Senator, I visited Richard Olson and he—"

Holliday thumped the table, his fury building. "You should have him in chains, you hear me? That bitch has—"

"Seriously?"

"What, do you expect me to call her a princess? She has my *daughter*."

"I've checked it out. We've accessed Franklin Vance's offshore bank records and found a deposit of four million, half of which stayed there and half of which went to your PAC."

"This is a lie!"

"We then traced that money to a company you own, a service business in Bermuda. That's wire fraud. Care to enlighten us as to what those services were for, Senator?"

"This is a pack of lies."

"You're involved in a conspiracy to cover up an illegal military operation for the CIA on American soil that resulted in three deaths so far." Carter passed him another page. "Harry Youngblood and Frank Vance you know about. You were there for both of them. David Quiroga, the school principal, he shot himself. He took his own life rather than answer my questions. You paid him, right?"

"No!"

"This is Tony Smith." Carter passed another page over the table. "He was the sports coach, in charge when Faraj al-Yasin was taken during the exercise. When Jacob Wickstrom died. Of course, you paid him off, but he felt so much guilt. Called Mr. Quiroga, so Vance visited him in Duluth. Made his death look like suicide."

"This is such utter horseshit. You should be looking for my daughter! I want that bitch in chains!"

"You're going to prison, Senator." Carter patted a paper file. "You'll be forced to resign your seat in the next few hours."

"I'll do no such thing."

"Your superiors in your party have a different viewpoint. We'll let them have a word with you when their flight gets in."

Holliday couldn't breathe.

It's all falling down because some schoolkid had a heart attack.

Vance said it was all going to be okay, that it was all going to be fine.

The door jerked open and Carter's boss walked in. Nguyen, or something. "Senator, there's someone here to see you."

Megan stood in the doorway, brushing tears from her eyes. She couldn't even look at him.

Holliday stared at her, trying to make eye contact. "Everything is going to be okay, honey."

"What?" Megan lurched into the room. Nguyen tried to hold her back, tried to stop her from attacking him. But she failed, Megan's nails scratching his bruised cheek. "You animal!" Carter grabbed her in a bear hug. "You subhuman piece of trash!"

"This isn't my fault!"

"You're an *animal!* A lowdown stinking animal!"

"What are you—"

"Brandon *died*, Chris." Tears streaked mascara down her face. She'd given up struggling. "He died an hour ago."

Holliday slumped back in his seat, toppling it back. He didn't go over. *I should've murdered Wickstrom when I had the chance.*

"This is on you, Chris!" Megan pulled off her wedding and engagement rings and threw them at him. "Our son died because of you, Chris. All the games you've played, all the stunts you've pulled over the years. You! Nobody else! You!"

Spit hit his face.

"Come on." Nguyen grabbed Megan by the shoulder and took her away.

Holliday crumpled forward, leaning against the desk.

My daughter is missing.

My son dead.

I'm going to have to quit my seat.

What else is left for me?

CHAPTER SIXTY-THREE

Carter

Two huge police officers were stationed outside Wickstrom's room, both built like football stadiums.

Carter let them inspect his shield. "How's he been?"

The older of the two just shrugged. "What's that word, Marv?"

"Catatonic?"

"Right. Catatonic."

"That a medical opinion?"

"Nah, dude's just sat there." He laughed. "Like when Marv's staring at his phone on duty, know what I mean?"

Marv looked like he wanted to kill his buddy. "The doc's cleared him for interview. Minor concussion, but nothing's broken."

"Thanks." Carter entered the room and took in the view across the lake. For a man who'd abducted two kids, murdered two men, and blackmailed a senator, Wickstrom had a prime view overlooking Lake Washington and the university's Husky Stadium, the sports field still glowing under the bright floodlights hours after the game. "Pay a lot of money for that vista if this was a hotel."

Wickstrom focused on his hands, like they were to blame for his predicament. "I'm not looking at it."

"Mason, this is your last chance to tell us where Avery is."

"You didn't find her?"

"No. I found Senator Holliday." Carter took the seat next to the bed, sat there with his legs crossed. "And, because of your little hunt, what you found, what you learned, it's ruined his career."

"What?"

"He's just resigned his seat." Carter showed him the news story on his cell: SEN. HOLLIDAY QUITS: "I'M GOING TO FIND MY DAUGHTER."

Carter pocketed the cell. "Not that he'll get much of a chance. We've charged him with corruption and a whole host of other lesser charges. He's going to spend a good chunk of time in prison."

"Not enough, though." Wickstrom snarled. "Guys like that don't suffer from the justice system like the rest of us. He'll be under house arrest or something. Minimum-security at worst. Then when he gets out, a few photo ops outside a church, handing out soup to the homeless, and he'll be running for governor. People love a redemption story." He focused on Carter for the first time since he entered the room. "Frank Vance showed me the video footage from the mission. Jacob died in his arms. I didn't know his heart was defective. I couldn't know. But the stress, that's what killed him—soldiers grabbing his friend. Holliday, Vance, Youngblood. One of them, maybe all of them, they made it look like my son died warming up. Took the GrayBox operation completely out of the picture. Faked the documentation to make it look like Faraj went missing after school. But I saw them take him. That video. You have to get it."

"We're doing what we can. Our security penetration only goes so far. GrayBox laptops use some pretty advanced tech."

"We got our answers, though. I had a hole in my gut because of what those assholes did to us. They killed my son. Might as well have shot him themselves. I don't regret a thing."

"Mason, Brandon died."

"Shit." Wickstrom ran a hand down his face. Rubbed at his forehead. Now that he saw the cost of his answers, maybe he did regret something after all. "I never meant for that to happen. The kid's mother, she doesn't deserve this. And that poor cop, the one who—"

"Calhoun. He's not doing too well. Hard to take shooting a child."

"That's on me, then." Wickstrom let out a sigh. "I accept the blame. I own it."

"We know you're working with Layla al-Yasin. We know she has Avery." Carter left a pause. "Where has she taken her, Mason?"

Wickstrom just lay back on his bed, his thumbs dancing.

"I've seen so many cases. Few like this, though. In those, where the abductors are trying to get something, they have a plan for afterwards. New IDs, new passports. Some likely destinations, places without extradition treaties back here."

Wickstrom let out a world-weary sigh. "We hadn't thought too much about it. We talked about going to Alaska, but that's about it."

"You expect me to believe that?"

"That was her job. Looking after the kids, monitoring the news, organizing the getaway. I've been tailing Megan and her kids for two months, day and night. That was my job." Another sigh. "She could be on a flight right now. Could be in the building next door. I don't know."

"With Avery?"

Wickstrom shut his eyes. "She wasn't supposed to take her."

"Do you know her new identity?"

"No. Like I said, that was Layla's job. She bought the fake passports off the dark web. I don't even know how to get on, let alone buy stuff with bitcoin or whatever. They were in her house, taped to the inside of a drawer. Mine was John Mason, close enough that if someone saw me in the street it wouldn't seem weird." Wickstrom looked at Carter again, his eyes damp. "She didn't tell me the name on her passport. Said it was Mexican. A Muslim woman finds it tough enough in Seattle. We'd talked about going to Alaska, Montana, or Wyoming. It's all white-bread country. They don't like Muslims there. They don't much like Mexicans, either, but at least there were some, you know?"

"Were you sleeping with her?"

"Always comes down to that shit with you, doesn't it?" Wickstrom shook his head. "I haven't slept with anyone since my boy died. Not even my wife." He sighed. "Not that she wanted to."

"And what do you want, Mason? Do you want to see Grace?"

Wickstrom raised a shoulder, as close to a "Yes" as Carter was going to get.

"Tell us where Layla has taken Avery, and you can see her. Otherwise, you can wait until you're in jail."

"I genuinely have no idea." Wickstrom sat forward on the bed and winced, his hand going to the bandages on his head. "Please, let me see my wife."

"That view across the lake—that's probably the last thing you'll see of the outside world, save for the prison transport. You've got your answers, sure, but that's the cost."

"The part I hadn't planned, the one thing I didn't consider, was what this would do to Grace. They were her answers as much as mine or Layla's. I planned to write to her when we got away. Tell her the truth, let her know what went down that day to our boy. Reassure her that the men who did it were all suffering. Then let her get on with her life, without me. Shutting off my feelings for so long means I shut myself off from her. She was going through the same torment as me. She tried to deal with it. Maybe if I hadn't been so obsessed, maybe I could've helped and stopped her trying to take her own life. I can still remember the call. Standing in a waiting room at a hospital just like this. So lucky I still had health insurance. But so numb. I couldn't help my wife, hadn't helped her."

"And it didn't shock you out of your search, did it? Just made you more obsessed. Made you want to hurt them more."

"Those bastards have paid for taking my son, but they took my wife too. And me. I died that day. So did Grace. We just didn't know." Mason ran a hand over the bandage on his head. "Try walking a mile in my shoes."

Carter sat up, resting his elbows on his knees, squinting in the darkness. "Mason, tell me about Layla."

He made eye contact again, like he was letting Carter know he was for real, that this was the truth. "I've got my answers. I've got justice over who killed my son."

"Tell me about her, Mason. Help me find Avery, Mason."

He flinched, like he hated the way Carter kept using his name. But he kept his mouth shut.

"Mason, you need to talk to me. You're up against some very serious charges here. You don't want to add another child's death to that, do you?"

He reached over to hit him, but Carter saw it way too early and grabbed his hands. Mason tried to fight him off, but he was weak like a day-old kitten. The painkillers sapped all his remaining strength.

"You think what happened to you justified taking the law into your own hands, Mason?"

"I don't regret a thing." Mason gulped, trying to stop the flood of tears. He lay there, shaking his head, looking like he was trying to stop himself from crying. Trying to crawl back into his cave again, where he didn't feel anything, where he was numb.

But it was hitting him. The pain of losing his son, of what happened to Grace, all of it. Everything.

And kidnapping kids. Killing. Realizing he was a monster.

Carter saw it all in those eyes.

"Start with Layla's husband."

"Kenny. Layla says he was a good guy. Worked in tech but hated his job, just wanted out, and something made him connect with his Muslim heritage. I don't know what. She didn't know either. Doubt he did. Got in with some bad dudes at the mosque."

"Terrorists?"

"Not sure which faction, but they radicalized him. I know Islam is supposed to be a peaceful religion and all that, but any religion can be used by evil people to control the lost." Mason blinked away tears. "Layla was worried about him, then one morning he just upped and left. She didn't know where he went. Kicked up some shit with the guys at the mosque. They told her he flew over to Turkey and walked to Syria. The pilgrimage of the righteous, or some horseshit like that. Fighting the righteous fight, or whatever these nutjobs preach."

"Did she ever hear from him again?"

"She didn't."

"But her son did?"

"She suspected so. Didn't know how. Scoured his room for a cell phone or laptop, but nothing. And she was pissed. Kenny had left her son without a father. Then she didn't even have a son. Your guys, the FBI, the agents investigating, thought his father had taken him."

"But she didn't buy it?"

"No." Mason shook his head, grunting like he'd just made the pain ten times worse. He reached up to give himself another shot of morphine. "One morning, some army officer turned up. Told her that her husband died in an attack on an ISIS compound in Syria. Didn't even have enough remains to bury."

"This was after Faraj went missing?"

"Right. I mean, she thought maybe he did come back, maybe he picked up Faraj, maybe he took him back to Syria, but... It didn't add up. So Layla tried to find out what really happened to her son. She spoke to the school principal, who confirmed the official story. Then she found me. Her son going missing the same day Jacob died..."

Carter nodded, but didn't say anything.

"Next time we met, Layla said she'd been on this website, found a story about Operation Opal Lance. Lasted a month, but it said a military exercise happened at Tang Elementary on October second. The day Faraj disappeared. The day Jacob died. Felt like too much of a coincidence."

"What did you do?"

"We tried speaking to the soccer coach, but he was out of state. The principal said the dude was out sick, back home in the Midwest somewhere. Losing two kids was too much for him to bear. Layla tried to find him, but it was a dead end."

"Did you speak to anyone official?"

"Layla spoke to Governor Duvall, but he brushed her off. She contacted Senator Holliday's office, same deal. Congressman Delgado met her, to his credit, but we got nothing. So Layla got talking to this guy on some website called Bob Smith. She set up a group chat, and I talked to him as much as she did. Bob Smith knew a lot of stuff about it."

"You ever meet him?"

"No."

"Did Layla?"

"Can't say for sure. You've got her laptop. You should be able to find out. He told us Holliday was the best person to use. We could take his kids, leverage them. Told us Holliday could access the information we needed."

"So Bob Smith put you onto Holliday in the first place?"

"Right."

"So you decided to kidnap his children and get him to give you the answers?"

"You've no idea how desperate we felt. I'd lost my son... Layla lost her husband as well... And it all just stank of corruption and greed and..."

"You get any idea who Bob Smith was?"

"Is he involved in this?"

"Maybe."

"No, I don't. Who is it?"

"What happened to your son, to Layla's son, it looks very much like Holliday was behind it or at least involved. He took a chunk of cash to arrange the mission to abduct Faraj. He seems to be complicit in covering up your son's death." Carter snorted. "What did Bob Smith tell you?"

"Told us how Holliday proposed the operation as a bill in the Senate. It was supposed to be a Pacific States version of Operation Jade Helm from back in 2015. That was held in Texas, California, and Nevada, maybe a couple other states. He said there's too much risk of the Pacific Northwest being overrun. The whole area was completely unprepared for an invasion. Russia, China, North Korea, even from outer space."

"Did Bob Smith ever mention Operation Honey Bear?"

"No?"

"Did Layla?"

"What is it?"

"It was the operation that killed Layla's husband, among many others. They kidnapped Faraj, and it seems that they got his father's location."

"Those bastards."

"Mason, I need you to help me find Avery Holliday. Her mother doesn't deserve this grief."

"Her father does." Mason stared hard at Carter. "I've got my answers. Frank Vance killed Jacob, and he paid for what he did. Same with Harry Youngblood. I got closure, but Layla didn't. Hasn't. The truth about her son is still out there. Nobody knows what happened to Faraj. Nobody cares but her and me." He ran a hand over his face. "And if what you're telling me is true, that Holliday covered up what happened, that he ordered the strike on Kenny? Then that's why I'm at peace with Layla having Holliday's daughter. Nobody will find her. Nobody will find Avery Holliday. An eye for an eye."

CHAPTER SIXTY-FOUR

Two weeks later

Monday, December 16, 2019

Holliday

Holliday couldn't stay sitting, instead walking around the small interrogation room. Hard floors, lime-green walls. No recording equipment, just a desk for lawyers to consult with their clients.

Today it wasn't a lawyer seeing Holliday.

"Please, Megan." Holliday shut his eyes, trying to stop the tears. "I'm trying to find Avery."

"In here?" Megan scowled at him. She'd dressed down, jeans and blouse, no makeup, hair in a loose ponytail. She looked exhausted, even worse than he felt. "You think you can do anything in here?"

"I know who has her."

"And what did the FBI say to that, huh?"

"They…"

"Either you haven't told them, or they didn't believe you. I know which one my money's on."

"Megan, I can get her back."

"So do it. Don't just sit there saying you can do this or that. *Do* something. Bring her back to me."

"My lawyer, I got his PI to dig into R—" He coughed. "Into the people who have her. He found something."

"So go to the FBI."

"I've already told them about him. They didn't believe me."

"What do you expect me to do? I've been all over this city putting posters up. Every second I spend driving out here to see you is a second I'm not actively looking for my daughter."

"Megan, I'm begging you. Just listen to me. We can use this to—"

"Chris, have a look at yourself. Our son's dead, our daughter's been missing for over two weeks now. You've lost your seat in the Senate. We're losing the house, our whole life. It's over, Chris. I need to get my head straight and I need to find Avery. If I don't, then I..." She let out a slow breath. "I'll start again somewhere else." She burst into tears, raw emotion overcoming the precise control she normally had. She pushed back and stormed over to the door, then thumped hard. "I've got to organize Brandon's funeral, Chris. He's going in the ground Tuesday. Our son, Chris. Brandon. My baby boy."

"I'll kill myself."

She looked over, mouth hanging open and trembling. Then she snarled at him. "Do it, Chris. I don't care anymore. I just need to get my daughter back, and you're no use to me."

The door opened.

"Megan, I will do it."

She took one last look at him, then walked through the door.

CHAPTER SIXTY-FIVE

Carter

Carter sat and waited. A wide row of interview tables, split by glass windows, handsets connecting the sides.

To his right, a couple argued over the phone, but he could only hear her side of it when she raised her voice. Trouble with their kids at school. A cycle of violence repeating itself in the next generation. While he couldn't hear the other side, he knew the words:

"When I get out of here…"

"I'll get my brother to sort them out…"

Never taking responsibility for their actions, never owning up to anything. It wouldn't likely be a federal crime, but it was always the same story:

I didn't do it.

Yeah, right.

And still Carter sat there, staring through the glass at the empty table where Holliday should be. Some mysterious message about his daughter's disappearance, some get-out-of-jail-free card.

Choosing to meet Mason Wickstrom without the cops, against his direct order.

Helping Mason at the Fed Building. Helping him take Delgado, leading him to Olson, to Youngblood. Not stopping him from murdering Youngblood.

Saving his daughter's kidnapper from being shot.

Helping him kill Vance. Then braining him and running off to meet…

Who?

He still didn't know. He swore it was Richard Olson, but proving it was a dead end.

Holliday had gone off the reservation so many times. Maybe others would make that decision, desperate to keep their kids alive. Either way, it all added up to a desperate man with something to hide. Desperate because his kids were taken, only increasing as his son fought for his life in the ER.

What was he hiding?

What was worth risking everything for?

It wasn't just his daughter, it was something else. Was he ready to tell Carter, spill his guts, in the hope of clemency? Two weeks in a cell, losing his career, his wife, his son, was that what it took?

"Sir?" A tap on the shoulder.

Carter looked around at the guard. "What's up?"

"It's about Senator Holliday…"

Another interview room, the private place to discuss matters with his attorney, away from the prying eyes and ears of the authorities. Holliday lay slumped forward, blood pooling on the table like Seattle rain. He clutched a red-smeared razor blade, having had just enough energy left to move it away from his throat when he died.

"Do you want to see the wound?"

Carter sucked in a deep breath. "No thanks." He wanted to see inside Holliday's head, to walk around the secrets hidden inside those brain cells now losing electricity and dispersing through the ether. Maybe Holliday had a soul. Probably not. "Has Mrs. Holliday been informed?"

"She's already here, sir." The guard gestured outside. "She was in the process of leaving when this happened."

"That didn't answer my question. Has she been informed?"

The guard just swallowed, all the answer he was giving.

"Let me see her." Carter took one last look at Holliday's body, his eyes still open, still half-accusing that he hadn't found Avery. But hiding some secret shame. Maybe it was all true, and the documents weren't lies. Maybe Holliday had ordered those deaths, approved the missions, helped cover up the screw up. Or at least didn't stop those who did.

He went into the corridor—cool, but the air stale.

Megan was in an identical room across the corridor, legs crossed, arms folded, a sour look on her face. She took one look at Carter, then rolled her eyes. "I knew you'd be involved in this somehow."

At least she was sitting down.

Carter joined her and waited for the door to shut. "I'm afraid there's been an incident."

"What do you mean?"

"Your husband has taken his life."

Megan's icy expression melted for a brief moment. She looked up at the ceiling, swallowing hard, then back down at Carter, drilling into his skull. "And life goes on."

"That's a bit cold, Mrs. Holliday."

"Please don't call me that." Another deep swallow. "My Avery is still missing, and that man is the reason. Everything else is secondary to finding her."

"We're still searching, Megan. Every day, we get fresh reports."

She didn't say anything. Didn't respond. "Now I've got to bury two bodies." The grief hit her hard, just like that, tears flooding her cheeks. She let down her hair, let it splay across her face, hiding from him.

"I can only offer my deepest sympathies for what you're going through."

She tucked her hair into a loose ponytail, moist eyes blazing. "No, you can find my daughter and bring whoever did this to justice."

"We've got Mason Wick—"

"Not him. Her. The woman who has my girl."

"We're doing—"

"You're doing absolutely *nothing*." She pushed up to standing and slammed a fist on the table. "Outside our house, two weeks ago, you promised me you'd do everything you can to find our children."

"And I am."

"But you're getting nowhere. I've lost my son. Now I've lost my husband. And Avery… God knows what's happened to her. Where she is."

"This isn't easy."

Megan waved at the door, fresh tears streaming down her face. "Go, please."

Carter could only nod as he got up and walked over to the door. One last look at her, head in hands, rocking.

CHAPTER SIXTY-SIX

One week later

Monday, December 23, 2019

Layla

I sit and wait, focusing on the glass partition, the phone next to it cracked and broken. Scarred by years of waiting, years of meetings. Prisoners coming and going, not trusted to be in the same physical space as their partners and lovers and friends without being listened to and watched. They even take that away from them.

And then he appears on the other side of the glass, his beard grown back, but his hair's freshly shaved. Mason slumps in the chair and grabs the other phone, tugging at the collar of his orange jumpsuit. He's lost muscle mass and that fire in his eyes. They've broken him.

I pick up the phone on this side. "Hey."

"Hey, Layla." His voice is sharp and hissy, but quiet like all the life's drained from it.

"Layla's dead." I lean forward, clutching the phone in my hand. "It's Luisa."

A smile flickers on his lips. "I'm glad you came."

"You know why I'm here, don't you?"

"I heard the news." Mason curls a few hairs in his beard around his fingers. It's nowhere near as long as before. "I don't regret what we did." And he looks like he means it. A flicker of a smile on his lips, warmth in his eyes. Then something catches in his throat and he coughs. "Except for Brandon. He didn't deserve to die."

I can only nod. Almost brings the hollow feeling into my gut. "Are you okay?"

"Just taking it day by day."

"How are you going to plead?"

"Guilty." He shrugs a shoulder. "I don't want to waste public money." He looks away, smoothing down his eyebrow. "I'll probably get the death penalty. They offered me a deal if I told them where Avery was."

I look around. The guards are chatting amongst themselves, but they're watching us, eight eyes all focused on me, all looking for me. I shouldn't have come here. So stupid.

But, they're looking for Layla al-Yasin, not Luisa Hernandez.

Layla wore pants and baggy sweaters, trying to make people focus on her brain.

Luisa wears short skirts and low-cut tops. If they're looking at me, their focus is on my body, not my face. And my haircut hides most of it anyway, makes them think of screwing that body, not recognizing that face.

"Relax. I said that I can't help them. Told them I'll never hear from Layla again."

I look back and give him a smile. "I'm sure she'd thank you, if she could."

He leans forward and locks eyes with me. "No regrets. Okay?"

"But Brandon…"

"We did what we did. Forget what happened, okay? I got my answers about Jacob. Took my revenge. Have you…?"

"That's next. Once I get away again, I'll find who did this to my son." A sigh escapes my lips. "I'm angriest with Kenny. If he hadn't done what he did, none of this would've happened. But I need to find who killed my son."

"He could still be alive."

"Don't." The tears might ruin my mascara. "Don't, Mason."

"I want you to live a full life."

"It won't be easy."

Mason leans forward, his forehead almost touching the glass. "Do you know who Bob Smith was?"

I shrug. That's all I can give him. Is he pushing for some information? Something he can use?

"I'm sitting in here, all day, just thinking. The reason I abducted Holliday's kids is that Bob Smith suspected Holliday was responsible for what happened during the raid. We confirmed it, and we got justice. It's Richard Olson, isn't it?"

"Be strong, Mason." I get up, leaving the handset dangling, and give the nearest guard a coquettish smile.

One last look at Mason, and he's crying.

I wish I could cry.

The car stops outside the church, dark clouds emptying the rain over Seattle. A few weeks away from it in the Southern California sunshine and you forget all about it. Then you come back and it's like you never left. I rest my knee on the passenger seat and lean around to the back. "You be good now, okay? I'll be back soon."

The little girl looks up at me and smiles, her dark roots showing through the blonde. "Okay."

With a wink, I get out of the car, don't say anything to the driver, don't even look at him. The car drives off and I pull my coat up and hurry inside the church.

I sashay to the front, my black nylons brushing my legs, my heels clicking.

Megan Holliday is near the front, accompanied by family and friends, there for her, not her husband. The church is pretty empty—a disgraced senator's funeral hardly the hottest ticket in town. Guess she's discovered who her real friends are. She gets up and looks around, like she expects Avery to just waltz back into her life.

Every day will be like that, looking for her daughter. She's aged in the short time I've been away, but her jaw is set. She's not going to grieve, not for *him*.

And I confirm it. Christopher Holliday is lying in the coffin at the front. Dressed in a navy suit, white shirt, red tie. Presidential. Eyes closed, definitely dead.

I thought he'd be the sort of man to blow his brains out, but he got a cut-throat razor from someone in his four-star prison, the downtown Marriott. Different rules for the powerful.

Still, they've done a good job on his neck, can barely spot the wide cut.

"How did you know my husband?" Megan's next to me, looking me up and down, seeing Luisa, not Layla. Focusing on the black skirt and the blouse, the auburn hair, the glasses. Whatever she sees, it's not Layla.

"I knew him in DC."

"Oh?"

"We did some stuff together."

Anger flashes in her eyes. Another nail in the coffin lid. "I see." She stiffens. She's refusing to grieve for a man who let everyone down. And I don't blame her, I've been there, worn those shoes. "Well, thank you for attending, anyway."

"You have my deepest sympathies, Mrs. Holliday."

"It's Robinson. Megan Robinson. My husband's name died with him."

"I'm sorry I missed Brandon's funeral."

She shuts her eyes. "It was much better attended than this."

I walk away. It's done. Over.

An eye for an eye.

A tooth for a tooth.

And he's sitting there. Dark shades, dark suit, black tie. Takes a look at me, but doesn't see the face plastered everywhere, the face from the FBI's ten most wanted list.

I walk past him and take a pew on the aisle near the back, sitting back, the wood cracking behind me.

The pastor calls the funeral to order. "Dearly beloved..." His words rattle around the church, and I slip off out the door.

CHAPTER SIXTY-SEVEN

Carter

Part of Carter expected a bigger turnout. One of the mourners couldn't face any more, getting up and leaving before the service began. She looked familiar. Maybe one of the support staff working in Holliday's office they'd interviewed. Maybe a DC escort sad to see her sugar daddy in the ground. All bets were off when it came to Holliday.

Carter couldn't follow the words, kept getting pulled back to the last funeral he attended, what was left of his mother lying in the casket.

His cell rumbled in his pocket. He was far enough back to let him chance a look at it.

Emma calling.

His heart thudded as he shot out of the church, answering before he'd even left. "What's up?"

"Bill's at the house!"

Carter pulled up next to the Toyota parked diagonally across two parking spaces. Got out with the engine still running.

Bill was over by the door, lurching around, swaying. "I know you're in there!"

Carter rushed over and grabbed Bill, tugging at his coat. He stank of liquor, seeping out of his pores. "Get outta here!"

Bill swung around to stare at his son, eyes rolling in his head. "You!" He stepped forward, but slipped on flagstones and stumbled forward, then went headlong across the grass. And stayed there.

"Get up."

Bill was still as the grave.

Carter stepped onto the lawn and nudged him with his foot. Then again. And again. He'd gone too far this time.

But the old goat rolled over.

"What are you doing here, Bill?"

He tried to sit up. Had to brace himself on the grass. "I've tried calling you."

"I have nothing to say to you." Carter grabbed his coat and pulled him up. "You're shitfaced. You can't drive in this state!"

"Why don't you answer the phone?"

"Because it's you who's calling me." Carter got in close to taste the age of the scotch on his breath. "You know, I was going to speak to you, try to build bridges. Let bygones be bygones. But you don't deserve anything from me, you worm."

"Son, I need your help."

"After what you did to Mom, you can burn in hell for all I care."

Bill looked away. "I'm dying."

It stabbed Carter in the heart, like a six-inch knife. Even with all the rage, buried deep and packed in ice, those words still hurt. Assuming they were true. Assuming this wasn't another power game.

"I know you're thinking, 'Well, good, he'll meet Satan soon enough,' but I just wanted to make amends, son, for what I've done."

"You can't come here and terrorize my wife and child. You can't do that."

"Son, I'm desperate."

"Get out of here." Carter pointed away from the house. "I'll call the cops. You'll be locked up. And so help me, I won't get you out."

Bill got up to standing and set off, looking back at his son for a long moment, then trudged off toward his car. Even he saw sense and walked past, idling up the street.

"Has he gone?" Emma was standing on the front stoop, still dressed for work. Salon-perfect hair despite a probably hellish day. "What was he after?"

Carter joined her on the steps, taking her hand in his and staring deep into her green eyes. "Are you okay?"

"I'm fine. A bit shaken, but it takes a lot more than Bill Carter to rattle me." She clenched his hand tight. "Kirsty's in her room, completely unaware of this."

"Good. You shouldn't have to put up with this."

"Neither should you, Max. It's both of our problem."

Carter felt a flutter in his stomach. He swallowed it down. He pecked her on the cheek and set off toward his Suburban. "I'm going to put a stop to this."

"Don't do anything rash, Max."

"Em, I'm not that kind of guy."

Carter stomped through the field office, passing the cubicles and the stares, loosening off his black tie as he reached Elisha's desk. She had her headphones on, locked in to watching some surveillance footage.

He craned his neck around Nguyen's door, but the room was empty. He went to his own office instead of bothering Elisha or Tyler. He picked up the desk phone and hit 1, letting the machine call Nguyen. Just ringing and ringing. The window looked across to Bainbridge Island. Now that the clouds had cleared, it was a beautiful winter's day, the sun low, but blue skies all the way.

It hit voicemail and he hung up.

What was he doing here? Going to the boss, getting her to fight his battles, apply pressure to her contacts in the chief of police's office. Why couldn't he handle Bill himself?

Because he didn't know where he'd stop.

Carter rolled his black tie and dumped it in a desk drawer, ready for the next funeral. There was always a next time. He clipped on his service tie and took a seat, hands stuffed in his pockets.

Didn't know what to do with himself. Check his emails? Go through the Holliday case report again? Update the Amber Alert for Avery with some slight tweak that might trigger a memory in someone? What, though?

He picked up the phone and called Nguyen again. Same result as last time.

A knock on the door frame. Elisha was standing there, forehead creased. "You okay?"

"Had better."

She took a seat in front of his desk, the frail winter sunlight catching her hair. "You want to talk about it?"

"Not really." Carter settled into his desk chair and toyed with talking to her about it. "Got any fresh leads on Avery's whereabouts?"

"Wish I did."

"Figured." Carter shut his eyes, tight. "Think she's even still alive?"

"Who knows? Better to hope, right?" She reached into her pants pocket for her ringing cell, then got up. "Better take this." She left the room at pace. "Thompson."

Another knock on the door. The mailman, head low, earphones dangling down to his left pants pocket. Always with that same grin. What Carter wouldn't give to swap for his carefree existence. The guy tossed a document on Carter's desk and shuffled off again, bap-bap-bapping along to his tunes.

Carter glanced at the envelope, then back out of the window at the ferry swimming through the water like a turtle. Slow and steady. Always on time, no matter what the weather. And it endured all sorts of storms.

Wasn't that Holliday's law firm?

He picked up the envelope and tore it open. A hefty document, at least fifty pages. The cover letter was from Holliday's attorney:

> As per my client's wishes, this document was to be delivered in the event of his interment.
>
> Note that my firm can provide no further information at this time.

Carter turned the page. A photocopy of a handwritten letter on legal paper, signed "Chris".

> Agent Carter,
>
> You probably know by now that I've done what I planned to do. Maybe you came to my funeral. Maybe not. Either way, I did what I had to do.
>
> See, my life is over.
>
> Hard as that is to write, the much harder part was accepting the truth. I've done things I'm not proud of, and the law of unintended consequences is a bitch. If I'd known that approving that operation would lead us where we are, there's no way I'd have done that. I'd have spoken up, stopped it there and then.
>
> But I didn't. I've paid for my mistakes with my career and my marriage. I gather Megan's speaking to a divorce attorney, so that's just a formality. My son is dead. My daughter is still missing. And I know I'm to blame. I accept it all. But I don't want her to suffer, and I don't want Megan to either.
>
> But enough about me.
>
> Please find Avery for me.
>
> PLEASE.

I've done all I can, but nobody will believe me. So I'm sending this to you so you can take it on trust and find my daughter.

I know the FBI are powerful, but sometimes you need something else. I paid my attorney's PI to dig into Olson. Like I told you, he has Avery. He's working with Layla al-Yasin.

Bob Smith was behind Layla and Mason's operation. That name should mean something to you. He fed them information about Operation Opal Lance and the perpetrators, the shadowy men who did that to their kids. To Faraj and to Jacob. Harry Youngblood and Frank Vance.

Layla and Mason weren't hard to find. Their anger fueled them, made them search out the weirdest military conspiracy websites. Made them post about how their sons died during Opal Lance. Then Bob Smith got in touch with them on the site's private message system. Layla replied. He gave her a number, told her to contact him on Signal. And they did.

And the PI found proof that Bob Smith is none other than Richard Olson.

Carter sifted through the rest of the document, detailed transactional reports, financial and telecommunications. Details he knew by heart. That's as far as his team had got in unpicking the trail. They'd subpoenaed the server, and whoever Bob Smith was, they used a military-grade VPN, killed their trail.

But Holliday's PI had the last message on the website: "Sen Holliday is behind it all."

A betting man would stick a few bucks on Richard Olson, but a federal agent needed hard proof. Carter read on.

My death is going to bring her back. I know it. She's punishing me for what I did. If I'm right, and I know I am, she'll bring Avery back to Megan.

Watch out for me.

I hope I'm not wrong.

Carter set the document down. A madman's dying confession, stapled to pages and pages of data, information that led Holliday down this logical path, making him take that leap into the unknown. No hard evidence.

But it backed up what they knew—Bob Smith had messaged both Layla and Mason, together and apart. Fed them information, led them toward Holliday. Led them to abducting his children and where they were now, with Holliday killing himself because he believed.

Many men had done the same, for a cause or otherwise. He was convinced his death would liberate his daughter.

What were they overlooking?

He turned the page and saw one last line:

The PI is going to be tailing Olson for me. One last throw of the dice. If he finds something, he'll get in touch with you.

Thanks,

Chris

Carter woke up his computer and took three tries to unlock the thing. Into his emails and there, right there was a message from Raeburn Logan, subject: "Holliday photos". He clicked it.

He might be smart online, but offline? Sloppy.

The email was inlaid with timestamped photos. First Olson leaving GrayBox in his limo, then arriving at a private airfield, where a woman and child got into his car. Carter double-clicked and opened the image to get a better look.

Could be anyone, but that could also be Layla and Avery.

Meaning Holliday was right, meaning Layla had come back with Avery. Would she give the child back to her grieving mother? Would she flee again?

The next shot was the car outside the prison, then waiting outside the funeral.

Carter let out a deep breath. She was there? In the same room as him?

That's the last I've got. Time ran out, sorry.

Tx,

Rae

Carter got up and left his office, racing over to Elisha's desk. "Where's Layla's laptop?"

Elisha looked up with a yawn. "All those messages are gone, Max. Remotely deleted, remember?"

Carter perched on the edge of her desk, the partition just giving him a view of Tyler's half ear as he listened in. "But we've still got it running, haven't we?"

"Tyler has it." Elisha stood up and leaned over to the partition board filled with Garfield and Dilbert cartoons. "You got—"

"Still here." Tyler held up the laptop, the power cable dangling, the power box clunking off his desktop. "Still unlocked. I don't dare let it sleep." He checked the screen and frowned. "Wait. There are new messages." He looked up at them. "She said, 'Landed'."

Carter jogged around to Tyler's desk. Holliday's gambit was paying off. On the screen, there was a reply from Bob Smith:

On my way.

But they had her cell—it had been at Holliday's feet.

Carter hit the trackpad, double-clicking on Layla's contact information. A cell number with an LA area code. Carter pulled his coat on. "Tyler, trace that!"

CHAPTER SIXTY-EIGHT

Layla

The car parks outside the house, the FOR SALE sign glowing in the streetlights, already on despite the day still having an hour to go.

I try to imagine what it was like that day, when Mason abducted those children from right there on the front stoop. When he knocked Megan out and left her with a note she ignored. My idea to leave her, so if any cops stopped Mason, he had less explaining to do. But in truth, it made it much easier for me. I was just looking after a kid, not a mother as well.

But Mason was right. No regrets.

Holliday, that prick, shouldn't have messed with our families. Shouldn't have taken my son. Shouldn't have killed my husband.

Lights on inside, but most of the guests have left.

"Luisa?"

I look around at the back seat and smile at Avery. "Hey, baby girl. You okay?"

She's yawning. "Where are we?"

I smile at Avery. "It's time to go home."

"To Mommy and Daddy?"

"To Mommy." I bite my lip, cracking the lipstick. "Now, remember what we say? This is our little secret."

"Okay, Luisa."

"Attagirl."

It doesn't matter if she tells them, I just need to keep her quiet for a few hours.

I get out onto the street and open the back door. She's gotten good at unbuckling the seatbelt. Almost too good. I help her out, and take her hand.

The street's quiet, so I lead her across the road and up the path, her little hand warm in mine. I crouch down to kiss her on the top of her head. "I've got to go now, princess. Okay?"

"Okay." Tears roll down her rosy cheeks. "I want to see you again, Luisa."

"I know, baby girl, but this is our little secret. I'll try and see you again, but I can't promise anything, okay?"

"Okay." She huffs, stamping with a foot. Still crying and it breaks my heart.

"Now, remember. You stay here, okay?" I wait for her to nod then knock on the door. "Goodbye, Avery." I walk back to the road and get in the car. "Wait." I look back at the house.

The door opens and Megan appears, frowning. She sees Avery on the doorstep and screams with relief and joy.

"Go."

Richard Olson drives off, slow enough so we won't be heard, fast enough to put some distance between us and the house. "You okay?"

"The debt's now paid in full. A son and a husband dead. I have no business with her or her daughter." I wipe a tear away. "I don't want anyone else to go through what I did. Unless they've done something really bad."

"You know, I could really use someone like you." Olson reaches into the door and picks up a packet. "That's another fake ID and a new passport. Lana Diaz can go wherever she wants."

I open the envelope and take out the documents. Wads of cash in there too, thousands and thousands of dollars, the same in euros. "I didn't do this for money."

"No, but you deserve to be compensated for your loss. In time, you'll find that Holliday killing himself isn't going to be enough. And you really helped me, rooting out all that corruption in my company. Every day is a living hell right now, but I'm doing the right thing."

He thinks money solves every problem, doesn't he? I'll let him have this one.

"So. Where to, Lana?"

I don't know where. Some leads, some people to chase down. Or I can do what Mason said and get on with my life. What's left of it.

"Take me to the airport."

CHAPTER SIXTY-NINE

Carter

Carter hit the floor, siren blaring, pushing past a slow Greyhound bus, leading the convoy of black Suburbans filled with agents. "Where is it heading now?"

Elisha was in the passenger seat, talking quietly to Tyler, then she looked back at him. "It's stopped at Bear Creek private airstrip."

"That's where he collected her from, right?" Carter tightened his grip on the wheel and weaved around the traffic. "She's going to get away!"

"Tyler, get that airstrip shut down ASAP."

"On it."

Then the dashboard screamed out, Carter's cell ringing. Unknown caller. He swerved around a car and answered. "Hello?"

"Are you related to a William Carter?" A woman's voice, young and with a Latina accent. Wherever she was, it was busy, sirens whooping around her.

"I'm his son. Max. What happened?"

"My name is Jocelyn. I'm an EMT. You're listed as his next of kin."

"Where's Bill? What's happened?"

"He's been in a car accident."

The last thing Carter needed. "Is he okay?"

"He'll survive, but—"

"I can't deal with this right now." He hit the red button and killed the call.

Bill in a car accident. And Carter, the heartless bastard, couldn't be there for him. It wasn't even a choice.

In the passenger seat, Elisha held her cell tighter, her face screwed up as she focused on her call. "Oh my god."

Carter chanced another look at Elisha. "What?"

Her mouth was hanging open. "Avery's been returned."

Carter thought it through as he plowed down the road, weaving along the path of the creek.

Holliday's risky gamble was paying off—news of his death had triggered events. His PI had caught them on camera, connected the dots. Would it be enough to pin this on Olson? That smug face, laughing at them. Thinking he was above them all, pushing pieces around a chessboard.

If anyone was responsible for this—over and above Holliday—it was Olson. And he needed to pay.

Time for Carter to extend Holliday's gamble.

"I've got an idea." He reached over to the central display and punched in the number, then hit dial.

It rang once before she answered. Didn't speak, though. Didn't acknowledge them. Just the sound of her breathing.

"Layla, thank you for returning Avery."

A pause, then a harsh sigh. "How do you know that was me?"

"I know who you are, Layla." Carter turned right—he could see the airstrip now, the narrow runway lit up, a plane taxiing over. "I know what drives you, Layla. You're not a bad person. Avery's back with her mother. I want to help you find your son."

Another pause, one she wasn't going to fill.

"Layla, I've got approval to offer you immunity from prosecution if you help me prove Richard Olson is Bob Smith."

Elisha glared at him.

But Layla was gone. His gamble failed.

Carter pulled off the freeway into the airstrip's parking lot. A small, low building, just one way in and out. A stretch limo sat on the curb, the exhaust chucking out fumes into the twilight. Carter boxed it in, another two Suburbans joining the pattern. He got out, cracking his pistol as he stepped over to the limo.

The back door opened and Richard Olson stepped out, hands up, a smug grin on his face. "This is an illegal stop and search."

"Where is she?"

Olson swung around just as a deafening roar erupted. A Learjet lurched up into the blue sky, powering away from them. "There she goes."

Carter looked over at Elisha. Tyler hadn't been fast enough. He grabbed hold of Olson by the throat. "Where is she going?"

"Flight plan is for Panama." Olson held his gaze. "But plans change, right?"

Meaning somewhere with no extradition treaty to the USA.

Olson shook Carter off, and his grin widened. "Good luck in getting her back."

"Was all this worth Holliday's life? Brandon's life? All for your company?"

"You'd never understand."

Carter's cell rumbled in his pocket. A text, unknown number:

> My insurance policy is in my Dropbox account. File name BS.docx, find it and it'll give you all you need on Bob Smith. Layla

Olson opened the limo door and tried to sit down.

Carter grabbed his arm and pulled him away, pushing that smug face against the hood. "You're going away for a long time."

"Right." Olson laughed. "I'll have your badge by midnight."

Holding him there, Carter got out his cell and called Tyler. "Peterson, can you search Layla's laptop for a file called BS.docx? Should be in her Dropbox account."

"Just a— Got it." Tyler laughed. "Oh, this is good."

"What is it?"

"It starts with messages between LayLadyLay and Bob Smith, plus with someone called BabyDaddy100. There's a link too." Tyler paused. "It's a cell phone video. It's dark. Holy shit. It's Holliday in a basketball court? And there's Richard Olson by this big light."

Bingo.

"Thanks, Tyler." Carter ended the call and leaned in to whisper in Olson's ear: "I know you're Bob Smith."

"Do you? Confident you'll prove it?"

"Extremely." Carter pushed him away toward Elisha. "Read him his rights."

She led him away to another Suburban. "You have the right to remain silent. Anything you say can be used against you in court." She ducked his head and pushed him into the back seat.

Leaving Carter standing at a private airport, an adult remembering his own trauma as an eight-year-old.

Holliday and Olson were just like Bill Carter, the same stupid arrogance, the same desire to stop at nothing to meet their selfish goals.

And the old goat was in the hospital somewhere. Desperate.

Maybe Elisha was right. Maybe Carter should speak to him, bury the hatchet.

CHAPTER SEVENTY

Carter

Carter charged through the hospital, clutching his cell to his ear, listening to it ringing.

Answered, finally. Emma, out of breath, locker room laughter, the hiss of a shower. "Max?"

"Em." Carter pushed through another door, into a long corridor in the ER. "Where are you?"

"I'm at racquetball. What's up? Are you okay?"

"It's Bill... Look, can you get Kirsty from daycare?"

"Sure. Is he okay?"

"I don't know. He was in an accident."

"My god. Are you okay?"

He gave her a pained laugh, all he could manage. Despite everything Bill had put him through, he was still flesh and blood. "Let's just see about that. Love you, bye." He killed the call and pushed through one last door into the ward.

The nurse's station was overstaffed, three of them hovering around. All he got from a hulking brute of a guy was a nod.

"Here to see Bill Carter. Might be under William."

"Got it. And you are?"

"Max Carter, his... His son."

The nurse clicked his fingers. "Dr. Frear? Here's the Carter son."

A slim red-haired woman in green scrubs sashayed over, clutching a tablet computer like it held the secrets to the galaxy. "You're his son?"

"For my sins. What happened?"

"Come with me." She led him through to a private ward, tugging a curtain back behind them. "Mr. Carter appears to have gotten drunk then crashed his car into a wall."

"Right." Carter struggled to breathe. Couldn't even think. "Was anyone else involved?"

"I don't believe so. His blood alcohol level is three times the legal limit."

A low amount for him.

"He likes to drink. Was it deliberate?"

"I can't tell that. He's coming around, so if you could…?" She nodded at a door, her lips pursed tight.

"Okay." Carter followed her in.

Bill lay in the bed, propped up. Battered and bruised, his face cut to ribbons, both eyes black and puffed up. His barrel chest couldn't fit under the sheet. With tremendous effort, he opened his left eye and shut it again.

Carter perched on the edge of the bed. "What were you thinking?"

"I kept calling you, son. I need to see you."

"And your needs trump everyone else's?" Carter took the chair next to the bed, gripping his thighs so he wouldn't do anything stupid, like strangle him. "Always thinking about yourself."

"I wasn't. It's… Every year, on the anniversary of your mother's death, I… I fall to pieces. Most of the time, I can handle it."

"That was in July."

"This has been going on for months." Bill groaned. "Normally, I hang around outside your house and watch you. I know you don't want me in your life, but I see how you've turned out and think I did the right thing."

Carter had to laugh. "You *seriously* think that?"

"Okay, so maybe it's more that I didn't ruin your life. But it's how I cope with the choices I've made."

"You mean kidnapping me? Bringing me to this country illegally, knowing your lawyers could outspend Mom's? Making her so wrecked that she killed herself."

"You've got to understand, son. Your mother wasn't this saint you've got in your head, okay?"

Carter got up.

"Max, you were a kid when… You only saw one side of her. She could be manipulative and—"

"I'm outta here."

"I deserve that. I deserve a lot more for what I did."

Carter couldn't leave, no matter how much he wanted to. "Bill, you got loaded and smashed your car into a wall. Were you trying to kill yourself?"

Bill looked away, then spoke quietly: "If I admit that, the insurance won't cover this."

Carter walked off.

"Son, wait!"

Carter couldn't help but stop. The voice of your father and all that. He didn't show him anything, just faced away.

"I've been struggling with the guilt over your mother's death. For years, son. Every year I've thought about ending it all. I haven't—I'm not that strong. But I'm not well, son. Not anymore. My health insurance ran out and won't pay for any more chemo."

Carter gritted his teeth, clenched his fists. The number of times he'd prayed for a long, lingering death for the man who ruined his mother's life.

And now that it was here? It tasted sour. Like Mason Wickstrom's truth.

"It's early stage, son, but it's taking up all of my savings. I've had to sell my house."

Ill, old, and broke.

In complete contrast with the healthy, affluent young dad who abducted his son all those years ago.

The worst man alive, barely clinging to his life. Trying to end it. Here he was, reaching out, trying to apologize, but only when it was too late.

Carter didn't know if he could bring himself to help. If he could let Bill get away with what he had done.

Who was he trying to kid?

He walked back over to the bed. "What do you need?"

A LETTER FROM ED

First, thanks for reading *Tell Me Lies*. If you enjoyed it, and want to keep up to date with all my latest releases, just sign up at the following link. Your email address will never be shared, and you can unsubscribe at any time.

www.bookouture.com/ed-james

Aside from the terrifying subject matter, this novel was the most enjoyable for me to write. I've written countless British police procedurals from a single point of view, and I needed to try something new, to develop new muscles and to experience a new location. I hope you enjoyed meeting Max Carter and his team as much as I did. They'll be back soon enough.

While the military operations in *Tell Me Lies* were fictional, they were based on real events in the USA. Operation Jade Helm 15 in the southwestern states carried as many conspiracy theories as column inches in the news, and the Pacific Northwest seemed like the perfect place to hide a clandestine operation on American soil. I also don't want to diminish in any way the sacrifices of the heroes and heroines who protect their country, with Max and Tyler among their number before they became federal agents.

The FBI CARD unit sadly has to exist, but they provide a great service in the most trying of times. I wanted to thank the FBI for reading and commenting on the novel for procedural accuracy.

And I hope you loved it. If you did, I'd be grateful if you'd be able to write a review. I read every one—good, bad, and ugly—and I love hearing what you think. It can also help new readers discover my books.

Finally, I'd love to hear from you. However you want—Twitter, Instagram, Goodreads, or an email through my website. And if you want to subscribe to the mailing list for my British police procedural series (Cullen, Hunter, Fenchurch, Dodds), you can do so at the following link: *http://bit.ly/EJMail*

Thanks,
Ed James

 @EdJamesAuthor

@edJamesauthor

6552489.Ed_James

www.edjamesauthor.com

ACKNOWLEDGEMENTS

First, thanks to Allan Guthrie for being my perfect agent, for tolerating my impatience during the submission process, for getting two book deals for me out of it, and for persuading me the book really didn't need those parallel universes after all. Ahem.

Thanks to Helen Jenner at Bookouture for buying these books and giving me the opportunity to expand creatively and commercially. I've loved working with you on this book, particularly the aggressive editing (as requested!) and helping define, develop, and name Max Carter. I'm really excited to see where we take him next!

Also, thanks to the rest of the team at Bookouture. I write this early in the process, so I don't know who to thank yet, but I'm genuine in appreciating all your hard work to get my book out there in the hands of readers.

Thanks to my author friends in the crime-writing community. To Susi Holliday, AKA SJI Holliday, for a character name and a great friendship. To Katerina Diamond for her advice and mediocre friendship. To Mason Cross for letting me use his pen name for a character this time, rather than a pub. To Howard Linskey for letting me use his name, which I now know is Irish, not Polish. And to all the other writers in the crime scene who've helped and supported me but I haven't mentioned here, I raise my glass to you!

And finally, to Kitty for putting up with me and my nonsense on a daily basis. You're the best and you know it.